Beginnings

Beginnings

L.T. Smith

P.D. Publishing, Inc.
Clayton, North Carolina

Copyright © 2007 by L.T. Smith

All rights reserved. No part of this publication may be reproduced, transmitted in any form or by any means, electronic or mechanical, including photocopy, recording, or any information storage and retrieval system, without permission in writing from the publisher. The characters herein are fictional and any resemblance to a real person, living or dead, is purely coincidental.

ISBN-13: 978-1-933720-33-3
ISBN-10: 1-933720-33-6

9 8 7 6 5 4 3 2 1

Cover design by Stephanie Solomon-Lopez
Edited by: Day Petersen/Medora MacDougall

Published by:

P.D. Publishing, Inc.
P.O. Box 70
Clayton, NC 27528

http://www.pdpublishing.com

Acknowledgements

This is my opportunity to thank so many people. So many. But, unfortunately, I have only a limited amount of space.

So, here goes...

First and foremost, I would like to thank Linda and Barb for believing in my writing enough to give me a crack at a second offering. After the daze of *Hearts and Flowers Border*, they agreed to take on *Beginnings*. I, for one, could not believe my good fortune. I mean, how many people get the opportunity to work with women as special and dedicated as these two? Not many. I believe all of the authors signed with PD Publishing are extremely fortunate. Not only because of the care and attention given to us as writers, but the way Linda and Barb embrace us as people too. Thank you. You are both worth your weight in chocolate. The good stuff.

Next on my list is Stephanie Solomon-Lopez. Wow. Your design for this cover is fantastic, and I believe you may have the ability to read minds. Another wonderful piece. Thank you.

As for my editors...you two are stars. Absolutely, positively, and ultimately two wonderful gifted women. You have polished and polished this work until she has actually turned into something I am proud to be a party to. So, here is a huge thank you to Day Petersen and Medora MacDougall.

Finally, but not lastly, I would like to thank the people who gave me the inspiration to write *Beginnings* in the first place. I could say it was you the reader, but...I have Alison to thank. You told me I could do it and to always keep the faith. Thank you. Also, Dec and Heike — you should be proud of your beta reader skills. I know I am.

Dedicated to sisters...
To *my* sister in particular.
Ju? What *did* possess you?

And...
Hope

Chapter One

I could tell you what has happened, but for you to understand, I need to take you back...right back. To 1974, actually. When people talk about the Seventies, they will fill your head with free love, drugs, and rock and roll. Actually, that sounds pretty good, especially the free love part.

But what I'm going to tell you is initially from the eyes of a six-year-old — me. I know you're thinking that you want to put this down, but bear with me. We all like to peek into someone else's life, however boring it may be to the person living it.

So. Let's find our setting. Are you sitting comfortably?

Then I'll begin.

1974

Summer — 1974. Hot, sticky, and filled with promise. Days filled with nothing but what my imagination could conjure up, and that could be pretty frightening. Streets were packed with children on school holidays, playing 'tiggy-it' and kerby and avoiding cars as they raced to retrieve an errant ball. For those of you who haven't a clue what I'm talking about, 'tiggy it' is a game in which you run around trying to avoid 'it', and if unsuccessful you then become 'it' yourself, after having a clammy hand thwack you on the back and 'Tig! You're it!' screamed at you. Kerby is played with a ball and a kerb. Very creative. Space hoppers were the new black — a must for any up and coming kid on the street.

I was six years old. It was in Levenshulme, once an affluent part of Manchester but now filled with students and ethnic minorities. Old radios blasted *Shang a Lang* and *Puppy Love* into the street. Mothers bawled at kids climbing the fence to the railway tracks where they would flatten pennies, completely oblivious to the fact that they could be flattened, too.

I loved my childhood, loved it in a fucked up way. We were poor, dirt poor. I came from a family of five brothers and two sisters, all older than me, and all avoided me like the plague. Except Jo. She was sixteen months older than me and my idol. Her role on this earth was to be my surrogate mother, and to this day she still holds that place. We were like Siamese twins, but without the shared organs. Even our farts smelt the same. Uncanny or what? Jo still brags that hers don't smell. They always did, but I tried to ignore it and closed my mouth sharpish. She and I looked completely different, but relatives still confused us, and my mother had to resort to colour coding to differentiate. Of course we mixed and matched outfits, just to be little bleeders, and Jo hid her pink-rimmed National Health glasses at family gatherings as the final straw. Kids. Gotta love 'em.

Having told you this much, I might as well introduce the other spawn in my family. Five brothers...urgh! Every girl's nightmare, and if you met them you would understand why. Patrick, aka Sniffer (which characterises his approach to the opposite sex), is the eldest son. Simon, who is fondly known as Ebenezer (need I say more?), is the second eldest. Brian was the third, and in the words of my mum, 'such a bloody liar'. After Brian's birth, the doctors advised my mother to use birth control in the future.

No such luck. Aiden popped out, much to the disdain of my mother, who initially disowned him. Pity she didn't stick to her guns. But then came the crowning glory: Queen Angie, Queenie, Dammer, Screamer. 'Who is this bundle of fun?' I hear you ask. She's my big sister, sometimes wonderful, sometimes a psycho — which I found out the hard way. Playing chief babysitter and tyrant, she was a git to all of us while my mum was working at the nightclub. Over the years our relationship has grown stronger, though, probably because now I can protect myself.

The last brother finally came; what a prize! Alan. Our Adge. Skid mark. Yup...Skid mark, on account of the very fancy designs in his underpants. David Hockney, watch out: abstract (f)art.

Then it was Jo's turn, short for Joanne, the last but one. She had a myriad of names...but Bulber and Mazda were the main two. Reason being — her head was uncannily shaped like a light bulb, and it made it look like her body was constantly having brilliant ideas.

Now me, I had a fine selection of nicknames. So many in fact I had trouble remembering my real name, which didn't add to my appearing intelligent. Primarily I was known as Bergans (left for five hours outside the butcher's of the same name and not missed until tea was being dished out) and Chunky (generic name with the rest of the family). I introduced myself as Chunky. Other names sneaked in — Henry the Eighth. No — I wasn't a fat polygamist with syphilis...or a beard; it was just the way I used to eat. You know, like it was the first morsel that had passed my lips in ages.

But wait. I think I need to go back just a little bit further to complete the picture of the darling child I was. I'll totally understand if you don't want to read any more, but please believe me — it does get better.

I was born (very David Copperfield-ish — not the magician, but the sponging whining fucker Dickens wrote of), in the Year of Our Lord, Nineteen Hundred and Sixty Eight. To say I was a beautiful baby...would be a lie. I was very long and very ugly, with a bald head and eyes like a lemur. Of course I developed into a fat toddler but still with very large eyes, which, fortunately, enabled me to see in the dark when the electricity company cut us off.

I was the last of the bunch. One look at me and my mother finally cried, 'No more!' Years later she admitted that if the umbilical cord had not been attached, she would have sworn I wasn't hers. Angie loves to recall the day that they brought me home from the hospital. Her job was chief guard, standing at the front door like a bouncer, barring entrance to the neighbours: 'As not to frighten the womenfolk and kids.' This tale is told at every opportunity, usually between bouts of hysterical laughter and finger pointing in my direction — where I would sit...glowing pink. She loves to retell it, as, like the Ancient Mariner, she feels 'cursed' to regale others with it over and over again. She even takes on the features of the decrepit old seaman — drooling accompanying the overexcitement and spitting.

My mother used to bounce me and Jo down the road in a dilapidated pram, trying to avoid well-wishers in her path. Jo, who was cuddly, beautiful, and always had a ready smile, removed people's attention from my owl-like eyes, but on the occasions she wasn't present, the focus of the admiration went on the pram. I didn't care, as long as they left me alone to chew through the plastic mattress at the base. It was bliss on raw gums — cool, yet satisfying.

I wasn't the bravest of children. I was even scared of a rabbit once. Yes. You read that right — a rabbit. You may think that rabbits can't hurt you, but they can, as I will prove.

There was a woman who lived up the road from us. Weird bugger. Smelt of bleach and cigarettes. Well...she was a creative soul and a bit of an animal lover — and I mean 'bit'. In her back garden she had erected a majestic centrepiece consisting of soil, broken bricks, and bottles. It was beautiful...in a soily, brokeny bottle and brick kind of way — almost modern art...and very underrated by the rest of the community.

The hutch itself sat pride of place, resembling an Anderson shelter sawn in half and lovingly decorated with chicken wire. I can remember it as if it was yesterday...it was class. My sister, Angie, led me up to the monument that proved women should never be given free rein with a drill. (This was the Seventies and I can be Politically Incorrect — just this once). All it took was the aid of climbing gear and (in the words of the host of the children's show Blue Peter), 'a responsible adult'.

The ascent began.

Never in my young life had I been so scared. Thoughts flitted through my mind about what terrible monster would be imprisoned in a fortress like that. So, being an idiot, I started to back off, caught my heel in a broken Dandelion and Burdock bottle, fell backwards onto an artistically smashed house brick that was coyly peeping from the middle of the mound...and gashed my head open.

Have you ever noticed that children initially cry with no sound? Their mouths stretched to capacity, eyes dry, but not a sound to be heard. Then suddenly a low whine is discernible, culminating into the loudest, most annoying howl audible to mankind (heaven knows how dogs cope), and the waterworks go into overdrive. Of course, my wailing started. Many of the elderly residents thought the Germans were invading, as they had been secretly and quietly preparing for it for years.

I raced away, vowing silently I would never trust another Blue Peter presenter again, with my hands rising in slow motion up to the cut on my head, needing my mum like I'd never needed her before. All this amidst the initial laughter of the neighbours. Bastards. Concern came later, especially when my family came 'round to sort out the 'caged monster' and the smelly weird fucker who would allow a child to climb her monument unarmed.

As I said before, Levenshulme was very multicultural — especially with those of Asian descent. There was an Indian kid who lived down the road, who Jo and I were friends with. One day, his father gave us an onion bahji. We had never seen one of these strange things before. So...Jo and I played catch with it for a while and then bounced it home. How were we to know that this was a special culinary offering from one culture to another? Just think how offended we would have been if we had given them a Holland's Steak and Kidney pudding and they had played cricket with it. But we were kids... How were we to know?

Anyway...Jo's best friend, Tina Brace, lived in the road opposite ours. Tina's nickname was the 'Rooter', as most of her playing time was spent rooting through my mum's drawers and the kitchen cupboards. We used to slag her off, but she did come in handy. If we couldn't find anything, Tina always knew where it was and would direct us to it. 'Oh, I noticed that when I was going to the toilet. It's in the lads' bedroom...in the cupboard in the far left corner...second drawer down, right up the back.' She was to be one of many strange friends who would come and go over the years.

I was unfortunate in that I had to share a bedroom with Angie, Jo, and the whole Osmond family, especially Donny. Donny Osmond was Angie's idol. Whatever pop tune rattled forth from between that enormous set of teeth was like the national anthem for my sister. The whole family had to stand to attention (in absolute silence) for the King of the teenybopper world. When I woke up frightened in the night and couldn't sleep (being a 'whinging little git' as Angie called me), she would try to calm me down with the words, 'Donny's laughing at you.'

Right enough, he was. Wherever I looked...he grinned back. Even when I opened the drawers, he was flirting with me through the mound of my underwear. God, I hated him...smarmy bugger — and the rest of his family! I hated *Puppy Love* and bloody *Paper Roses*. I hoped he would get distemper and someone would pour petrol over Marie's roses...ending with a delicate kiss with a lighted match. This whole Osmond thing should have mentally scarred me, but it just made me stronger...so thankfully, when Jo's Cliff Richard obsession kicked in, I was prepared.

Before I go on to tell you what happened to me when I was six, I need to tell you how I became the distrustful person I am today. Nothing spectacular, but let's just say a lesson learned, okay? You can be the judge.

Would you be tempted by a free glass of lemonade? Especially if all you usually got was Corporation pop (water), except for when your mum was flush and you got the fruity drink, Vimto? I was tempted by the offer of lemonade. Very.

It was an ordinary evening, atypically quiet, and it all boiled down to my sister Jo. She asked me if I would like a drink of the aforementioned lemonade. Of course I did! What sugar-craving child wouldn't? As free gifts usually do, the lemonade came with a catch. I had to carry her on my back, on all fours like a donkey, for half an hour. I should have guessed that Jo did not have any lemonade — she did not have any money to buy lemonade — but I trusted her. She *was* my surrogate mum, after all.

On the floor I went — not even four years old and scrabbling around on all fours, building up my thirst. I asked intermittently when I was going to receive my well-earned refreshment, only to be told, 'Soon. Soon.' Now, looking back, the crooning tone of her voice should have told me something was not right. The innocence of youth, eh?

Eventually, through sheer exhaustion, I rebelled and demanded that I should be paid in full for my services. Jo paid in full...by God, she paid in full. My payment of lemonade came as pee — donated by her, over my back. I can still hear the laughter in her voice as she shrilled, 'Enjoy your lemonade, you deserve it!' All I can say is it's a good job that she never promised me chocolate. To this day, she still can't tell me why she did it, just mumbles something about being possessed.

The story doesn't end there, I'm afraid. My brother Patrick's latest victim, sorry...girlfriend, was staying with us at the time, and every time a police car went past she wanted to play *Let's Hide Under the Bed*. Once again — children are so gullible. Nowadays I would be at the bedroom window screaming 'She's here...in here...under the bed!' Unfortunately, she had to share the room with me, Jo, Angie, and the Osmonds — all of us in a dilapidated double bed, but when she walked into a puddle of pee, I thought the shit was going to hit the fan. Obviously it was my fault...and she classed me as a disgusting degenerate (my face said 'huh?') and promptly stormed off to sleep with my brother. Many years later I realised this was her golden opportunity to get between the sheets with Sniffer, and I wasn't really a freak of nature — still not sure about Jo, though.

I know...I'm going off the point.

Oh...all right then...

Summer — 1974. Hot, sticky, and filled with promise. Days filled with nothing but what my imagination could conjure up — and that could be pretty frightening. Streets were packed with children on school holidays, playing tiggy-it and kerby and avoiding cars as they raced to retrieve an errant ball. Space hoppers were the new black.

I was six years old. It was Levenshulme. And that's where I first spotted Ashley Richards...or Ash, as she liked to be called...

Chapter Two

Ashley Richards. Even today, when I say her name my whole body smiles. I can still remember it vividly...the day she fell into my arms...fell into my life. Yes. Fell.

In our front garden there was a huge tree in the corner...huge. I used to love climbing up as high as I could to get away from the brood, and even at six years old I could get pretty high. My mum, to this day, doesn't know I used to climb it. I used to sit above her when she would be bellowing out into the streets the litany of names of my siblings, all in rank order, announcing that, 'Your bloody tea's on the table!'

Amazing what power you can possess by being just a little higher than everyone else. I felt on top of the world. Every teatime it was the same. Until one Sunday, that is.

I had climbed one branch higher than usual and was perched there, gloating. Mum had been and gone, and I had watched my brothers and sisters trundle in the front door one by one, ready for tea. I had just climbed down when I heard a distinct rustling of leaves coming from overhead.

It was, or so it seemed, a split second later when something landed on me. It was big. It was heavy. It was wriggling like crazy on top of my battered and bruised body. It was Ash (as I later found out).

Blue eyes wide with shock and panic — and pain...if my aching backside and stomach were any gauge. Instinctively, my arms wrapped around her, and our squirming bodies meshed into each other. Black hair tumbled forward, and part of it went inside my mouth, an obvious distraction when I was trying to scream.

The more we tried to separate, the more entangled we became. A voice from above me hollered, 'Stop!' and like the good girl I was — I did. I lay there completely rigid as the blue-eyed girl systematically pulled herself free, allowing my scrawny arms to flop lifelessly to my sides.

'Are you okay?' Her concern was evident. The tears I had felt welling up in my throat — you know the ones we try to swallow but become like footballs — miraculously disappeared. Silently I nodded my head, looking at the now towering girl looming above me. I wasn't okay, but damned if I was going to admit it to her.

She held her hand down towards me to help me up, and for a split second I considered the idea of refusing, but the pains shooting up the cheeks of my arse told me to stop being a martyr and accept. So I did.

Her hands were cool in comparison to my clammy, dirty ones, and with one deft movement I was on my feet. I don't think I even had the chance to bend my legs. I staggered forward only to be captured by her once again, my head hitting her in the chest. Jesus...she was so tall. The feeling I had whilst lying on the ground came back — she still towered above me!

'Sorry about that.' Her eyes flicked to the tree. 'I kind of lost my footing somewhere along the line.' I just stared at her, gobsmacked. I wanted to demand why she had been there in the first place, but nothing would come out. I must have appeared simple...and I think for those few minutes I was. 'Are you sure you're okay?' A quick nod was all I could muster. Her face took on a concerned look...and my arse was still throbbing to the tune of the birds singing.

After about a minute of staring at me, she stuck her hand in my direction. 'Ashley Richards. Erm...or Ash. I just moved down the Avenue about two weeks ago.'

I was just about to answer — my mouth had formed around a word and was ready to let it slip through my gormless lips when, 'Bloody hell, Lou. Your tea's on the table. In!' Mum. And she was pissed off. Big style.

I turned back to Ashley and flashed her a smile. 'Got to go. See ya around, yeah?' Her face broke out into an enormous grin, and she nodded, her hand still outstretched. Impulsively, I grabbed her hand and pumped up and down like I had seen my mum doing to people she had just met. Those cool fingers clutched at mine for a brief moment before my mum's increasing ire got in the way.

'Inside now, lady. You can speak to your friend tomorrow.'

Another smile lit up my face. A friend. Yup. I liked the sound of that.

Before I had a chance to say anything else, she was gone. And I turned back and wobbled indoors, the cheeks of my arse screaming, but the smile on my face said, 'Stuff it. I have a new friend.'

Sunday night was always nit inspection night. My mum was like a woman possessed when it came to our six-legged friends who liked to party in her kids' hair. So Sunday night was known as *The Treatment* night.

Every Sunday was the same. Bath. Clean pyjamas. And a thorough grooming, ready for school the next day. Just because we had broken up for school holidays didn't stop the de-lousing regimen. Unfortunately. And let me tell you, if you have never had the 'pleasure' of Derbac...well...you've been lucky. At least it didn't set in your hair like Suleo.

Anyway, Mum would line us up in order of age and douse the lice with the most foul-smelling lotion ever invented. Even today I prefer dog farts. It wasn't just the lotion, it was the combing. I think the person who invented the comb must have done so with the help of a microscope and evil intentions. My hair tangled easily, and it was agony having something so fine scraped through. The effect was tearstained cheeks, red rimmed eyes, and Christopher Lee hair. The lot of us were like a band of extras in a Hammer House Production.

Over time this regimen dwindled down to just Alan, Jo, and me, as the others had grown and adamantly refused. And they used to sit...smugly...in the front room, while the 'infested trio' would have to stay in the dining room and were only allowed to go in the best room if we stayed away from everyone — especially out of line of draughts from the windows, which would waft the smell around the room. God help us if we sat on the furniture. We could have been hired out on safaris — elephants would have been stunned at twenty paces.

This Sunday was no different. The agony...the screaming...the pleading for mercy. And that was just my brother. He was such a boy sometimes. It was funny...in retrospect, obviously. Especially watching my mum crack the little critters between her nails when she had caught them in the comb. Word of warning — never struggle with your mother when she is de-lousing you. There is only ever one winner, and it sure isn't you. And...and this is a big-gie...always be ready to run in case her cig sets your head on fire. No. That's a lie. She always made sure it never went near enough to actually catch alight, properly balancing it on top of the gas fire.

But Alan...Alan was a mard-arse — always was and most certainly still is. It still makes me smile to remember him in the throes of a rain dance, wailing to the gods, informing everyone and everything he hated them...with all his heart. He was always the main attraction on Sundays. We probably could have charged admittance, but we were used to it. Every week the same. Then the doorknocker went. The insurance man had dropped by for Mum's contribution...and we didn't even have time to hide behind the furniture. Not that we could have gotten away with it, as Alan was in the throes of his jungle fever. Only now I realise my mum was embarrassed by the smell and the noise. No one else actually paid any attention to what was going on. In a household our size, it was very unusual to have quiet time.

All the time the insurance man was there, Alan danced. Every question the man asked, my mum had to ask to be repeated because of Alan's rantings. Jo and I just sat on the floor, quietly doing Christopher Lee impressions, but inside laughing our arses off. Alan was a knob head — still is.

I still believe this episode scarred my brother, mainly because he had the lotion on longer than the thirty minutes. I don't know — all that medication soaking through his scalp, breathing in all those fumes whilst screaming *must* have taken its toll. Definitely the reason why he has never intellectually advanced. Or maybe it's because he was always a wanker. Who knows?

After the insurance man had gone and Alan had been thoroughly dealt with, Jo and I were sent to bed under the watchful eyes of Donny et al. Fucking Osmonds.

It was only after Mum had gone back down to give Alan another pasting to stop his crying (go figure) that Jo asked me where I had gotten my bruises from. Her eyes held concern...and I knew she must have been worrying about this since bath time, as the bruise started at the base of my spine and curved itself around one cheek. There is no way she wouldn't have noticed it...although Angie hadn't. She was too busy trying to get us sorted so she could get up to the park with her mates.

Donny was smiling at me as I turned to Jo. 'I was standing under the tree—'

'What have I told you about climbing that tree? I'll tell Mum if you go up it again.'

'I didn't fall out of it. Ash did.'

'How on earth can ash cause a bruise like that?' I started laughing. 'It's not funny, Lou. You'll end up killing yourself, or worse.' Nope. I didn't get it either: killing yourself or *worse*? Never mind.

'Not ash! Ash!' She looked at me like I was an idiot. 'Ashley...Ashley Richards from down the Avenue?' Still a vacant look. 'Moved in a couple of weeks ago.' Realisation dawned, and I could see it replace the blank expression from earlier. It was short lived.

'What do you mean Ash fell out of the tree?'

I loved my sister, but sometimes she was too overprotective. It was a full twenty minutes later before she was satisfied I had not been ambushed.

As I snuggled into bed, the big dilapidated double I shared with both Jo and Angie, I smiled to myself. I'd got a friend. Then I silently wished Donny goodnight.

I couldn't wait to see what the next day would bring.

It wasn't long before we were firm friends, although Ash was Jo's age. As for Jo...well...she wasn't too pleased my affections for her had been split. But being her, she took it on the chin and allowed me some semblance of freedom.

Days were spent in childish adventure. Ash was so much fun, although she barely said a word to anybody else. Mum nicknamed her my shadow, as she was always standing quietly behind me whenever she was in the company of any of my family.

Now, my family were friendly, don't get me wrong. They were just...big. There were loads of us. The only person Ash hadn't met was my dad. And come to think of it, I hadn't seen him myself for quite a while. He was a long distance lorry driver and spent a lot of time on the road. The time not on the road was spent in the pub.

I remember when I was about four, my mum had got me up in the middle of the night, or so it seemed, to introduce me to him. Years later I realised they had been in the middle of an argument. To put it mildly, my father was a tosser. He didn't give two shits about his family; all he cared about was himself and the pub. I can still remember him sitting there in the front room, sunglasses on (at night time), listening to Dean Martin's *Everybody Loves Somebody Sometime*, and singing really badly.

Mum had ushered both Jo and me into the room, and it was like the rabbit incident all over again. A feeling of trepidation flooded through me, just like it had when I was climbing up the mound. My heart was hammering in my chest, and I had a sense of foreboding. Who was this man who sat in the chair singing whilst wearing sunglasses? Even to this day I read people's eyes. I don't trust people if I can't see their eyes. I learned that the hard way.

It was only because Jo seemed to know him that I let down my guard. I wish I hadn't bothered.

Enough about him for now... You'll hear more about that tosser later.

Ash. Every time I thought of her, I wanted to skip. She was a lot taller than me, probably because she was nearly eight (well...seven and three-quarters — eight in October), but she appeared bigger. Black hair cascaded down her back; her face was slightly tanned from all the outdoor activities we shared. But the most striking thing about her was her eyes. Blue, a light blue, a twinkling blue that captured the sun's rays and made them dance.

It wasn't long before she became the centre of my world. Everything I did, I wanted her to be a part of it. Everything I saw, I wanted her to see. We were inseparable. It was fantastic.

Jo backed off from me and spent more time with Tina, telling me I was always welcome to hang about with her anytime. I don't know why, she didn't really take to Ash...but at the time I didn't give it much thought.

Summer days were spent in play...in adventure. Things I had done a thousand times on my own seemed to take on a different meaning when I did them with Ash. She even showed me how to climb that damned tree properly. Although I still had the memory of her plunging down from quite a height, I trusted her. Completely.

I fit quite nicely into her family, too. She had two brothers, Stephen and Anthony — one older, one younger. Her dad used to torment her, saying it was an Ashley sandwich. I could tell she was their pride and joy.

It was strange to watch her family together. Her parents were so interested in what they all were doing, taking time to chat with them, ask how their day had been. Her mother was a full-time mum, always there for them. Her father was a policeman, and he made my brothers nervous — and especially Sniffer's girlfriend.

It made me reflect, in my childish way, about my own parents. I loved my mum so much. She tried as hard as she could to provide for us, considering my dad was AWOL most of the time. Now I'm an adult, I fully realise what she had to go through — eight children and barely two pennies to rub together. No wonder she had to work at a nightclub to earn enough to clothe and feed us. A man can't support both the pub and his family, and my father preferred to support the local brewery.

Ash's family semi-adopted me. I spent most of my free time there, reading her books — especially loving it when she read to me. This treat sometimes followed us up the tree where we would sit, hidden from view, and she would read to me. I had to be careful I didn't relax too much and fall backwards...again.

Ash, her two brothers, and me used to perform ABBA's *Waterloo* in her bedroom. I don't think Stephen and Anthony really wanted to be Benny and Bjorn, but they didn't have a say in the matter. Ash could be quite forceful when the mood took her.

We practised for days trying to get the moves right, turning our heads at just the right moment. I still haven't got the hang of coordination, but that's beside the point.

When we thought we had perfected it, we put the single on the small box record player and performed our masterpiece for her parents. I followed her every move...as usual...and shrilled out, 'My my...At Wa-ter-loo Na-po-le-on did sur-render...yeh yeh...' The applause from her parents was deafening...nearly as bad as our singing. I felt on top of the world. Again. I should have sung the Carpenters.

One of my favourite memories was the day we went to Concroft Park. It was the day I realised Ash was everything I would ever want or need in my life.

It was quite a walk from our house, and we were toting carrier bags full of sandwiches and pop to consume on our day out. Inside the bags were also two books, Ash's jumper, an old blanket, and a ball. It was looking to be a good day; it was.

The very first thing we did was feed the ducks. We stood there, side by side, looking for all the world like a pair of ragamuffins, not speaking in our task but fully content just...to just...be. I think we gave them nearly all our sandwiches, but we didn't care.

Swings, slides, roundabouts, and reading. In that order. Then, we did it all again, but this time we had a game of catch before we lay back on the grass and just read.

I didn't know how long I had been asleep when I suddenly felt the splodge of rain hit my skin like an ice cube. And again...and again...until it was constant. I felt Ash looming above me, her shadow blocking my view, her body sheltering me from the downpour.

'Lou...come on, Lou. We need to go.' Her voice seemed echoey, distant. The chill from the rain made me shiver. I was wearing only a t-shirt and shorts and I was freezing. I could see Ash shaking with cold, too. Her hand was trembling as it reached down to me, rivulets of water running down the bare flesh.

'We need to get back.' I grabbed her hand, and with one deft movement she pulled me to my feet. 'Here.' A jumper was shoved in my direction. My eyes looked into blue, which were clouded with worry. 'Put it on...you'll catch your death...'

'But—'

'But nothing. Put it on...no arguments.' I watched her as I pulled the jumper over my head, missing the sight of her as the thick red material fell over my eyes. The jumper was barely on my skin before she grabbed my hand and began to pull me along.

Rain lashed against us as we struggled against the downpour. There was no point looking for shelter, as the rain looked as if it would be with us for quite a while.

Ash had the blanket and books (the ball long forgotten) shoved under her arm, her other arm occupied with pulling me along, my short legs struggling to keep up. We had gone a little way before she pulled me under the bus shelter just outside the park.

'We can't get the bus, Ash, we haven't any money.'

'Shhuuusssshh. We're not getting the bus. Here, hold these.' She thrust the books into my hands and started fluffing out the blanket. Her face was filled with concentration as she struggled with the chequered cloth, her black hair sticking to the side of her face. I was freezing, and by the looks of her shaking body, so was Ash.

'Come here.' Her voice was quiet, barely a whisper, but I went without question. 'I'm going to try and stop us getting completely soaked.' I looked up at her, forever in awe of my older friend. She made me feel so protected. I knew she would take care of me, whatever happened. 'I'm going to hold the blanket over us. Here...put your arm 'round my waist and hold on.'

As soon as I slipped my arm around her, which was quite an effort because of our height difference, we were off — the slick and slippery pavement beneath our feet almost a blur.

Ash was determined we wouldn't get any more wet than we already were. The books I held were becoming soggy and heavy, and my grip tightened about them with grim determination. I wanted to keep my part of the bargain.

It seemed like forever that we slogged along. The rain really slowed us down, but I didn't feel frightened or worried. The presence of Ash calmed me. The feeling of her guiding me both with her body and the top of her arm made me feel secure...and, strangely enough, happy.

When we got outside her house I fully expected her to dash in and send me on my way, but no, she insisted on seeing me to my front door, with a mumbled, 'That's what friends are for.' Secretly, I was pleased.

The front door loomed ahead of us, and I could feel her slowing down. It wasn't until we reached the gate that she stopped. 'Go on...you get in.' Impulsively, I threw my arms around her neck and planted a kiss on her cheek. I think I surprised her because she dropped the blanket to her shoulders and looked me squarely in the face. 'What was that for?' Her voice was quiet, but I heard every word as if it had been shouted.

'For taking care of me.'

'Don't be daft.' But I could see she was pleased by my words. 'Go on...get gone.' And she planted a little kiss on my forehead before she gave me a gentle shove.

I raced toward the door and hammered the knocker, turning to face Ash whilst I waited for someone to let me in.

The image of her standing there will forever be etched into my mind. Rain pummelled down on her, but she just stood there, staring right back at me. Her hair was a tangled mess of wetness, clinging to the sides of her face, her fringe dripping water into her eyes. The pale cream t-shirt was like a second skin, transparent and heavy. Rivulets of water raced down her legs and collected at the tops of her ankle socks. Splodges of dirt coated her calves and knees, but they were beginning to be washed away.

'Bloody hell, Lou! You're pissed wet through!' Mum's voice broke through my thoughts and I turned to face her. 'Get in and get those clothes off before you catch your death.'

Ash's jumper! I still had it on. I turned to speak to her, but she was on her way out the gate, the blanket covering her shoulders. 'Ash!' She stopped, and turned toward me, a question in her eyes. 'Your jumper!'

'Keep it. I'll get it later.' Her face broke into a dazzling smile, and I forgot about the rain, forgot about the jumper, forgot how cold I was. That smile lit up everything and made me feel warm inside.

'Come on, Lou...in!'

'Laters, Ash.'

'Laters.' And she was gone. Racing through puddles, water splashing up her legs, the blanket billowing out as only soaked blankets could do.

But there wasn't going to be any 'laters'. 'Laters' had to wait for another ten years. My father made sure of that.

Bastard.

After a hot bath, shared with Jo of course, it was tea and an early night. I felt so happy going to sleep, but the happiness didn't last long.

Voices woke me. Not gentle voices by any stretch of the imagination. These voices were raised in argument, words spewing forth that no child should ever hear. It was my parents. Funny thing is, even though my mum and dad didn't get along as well as other parents, they rarely argued. So, this was a surprise, to say the least.

Honestly speaking, though, surprise was the last emotion I was feeling at the time. Fear was top of the list.

'You all right, Lou?' Jo's voice filtered through the darkness, and a small hand came and landed on the top of my arm, stroking up and down.

The shouting was getting closer, the anger more evident. I could feel the tears welling up and slipping from my eyes. I began to shake, couldn't stop it. I was scared and confused. I could hear Jo trying to comfort me, but I could hear the fear in her voice also. This must be bad if she was scared.

Raised voices were right outside our door now, the words clear to everyone. We were leaving. Tonight. Mum had found out about all the affairs my father had been having and the child his girlfriend from Scotland was carrying.

Only later did I understand the full impact of these revelations. Only later did I overhear my mum telling one of her sisters of a letter she had found, addressed to her, in his work bag — a letter from a seventeen-year-old girl who was three-and-a-half months pregnant. Only later did I fully understand this man was a total wanker, although I'd always had my suspicions.

Even Donny didn't seem to be laughing now.

Light blinded me as the door flew back, and my mum came into the room with a roll of black bags.

'Come on, girls. Get yourselves up. We're going on a trip.' She tried to keep her voice cheerful, but we knew this trip wasn't to Butlins. 'Here...' She passed us a couple of bags she had torn off. 'Pack as many clothes as you can into these...Angie's too.'

'Over my dead body!' my father bellowed.

'That can be arranged.' Her voice was a growl, and even my father slunk back, knowing that she would rip his head off if he so much as made a move in our direction.

Not that he would have put himself on the line like that. He was neither brave, nor did he give a damn. His kids and family meant nothing to him. He had proved that with his inability to give two shits about anyone but himself.

My body was shaking. My small hands were grabbing everything and anything, randomly shoving clothes haphazardly. Jo was crouched next to me, tears trickling down her face as she slowly placed each item carefully into the sack.

My world was falling apart...falling apart...falling apart. Each refrain mimicked the action of my hands as they silently packed the few belongings we owned into shiny black plastic. Every movement seemed to vibrate through me...panic and fear vying for dominance...until it struck me — Ash.

When could I see Ash? Could I say goodbye to her?

I didn't want to say goodbye. A noise danced in my throat...a wail waiting to be released into the silent room. I didn't want to leave Ash...she was my friend...I didn't want to leave.

Tremors shook through me, the wail winning out, the tears flowing freely now. I brought my hand to my face to smear the tears across my cheeks, my nose bunging up, breathing becoming difficult.

'Come on, sweetheart. It'll be all right.' Mum was crouching next to me, trying to get me to calm down, her loving hands on my shoulders, quickly rubbing the knotted muscles. 'We'll still be together.'

Instead of calming me, this thought just made me cry even harder. Loving hands slipped underneath my armpits, and I felt myself being lifted into the familiar scent of my mum. 'Shush there, sweetheart, I've got you.'

It was ages before she let me go. She rocked me back and forth, stroking up and down my spine. Jo stood silently next to us both, her hand tangling through my hair.

That's just like my sister. She must have been feeling just as scared as me, but she still rose above it and worried about me first. That is why I love her as much as I do.

An hour later we were in the back of a black cab. Mum, Angie, Alan, Jo, and me...five bin bags and not much else. We looked a sorry sight. The rest of the lads decided to stay with their father — their father, as he was no longer mine...and I doubt he ever was...although biologically I could never escape that fact.

I can still remember the taxi driver reversing into Ash's road, and my eyes staring up at the dark window of her room. I wanted to wake her up...tell her that whatever happened, she was still my friend and I loved her.

As the taxi pulled away, I felt a part of me staying there in Levenshulme. I just hoped that Ash would find it and know I didn't want to go...didn't want to leave her. I had to take some comfort from the knowledge that no matter how long it took...I would find her again.

That was a promise.

Chapter Three

1984 — Ten years later

Loads of things had happened in those ten years. Too many to go into any detail, but the main thing was, I never had the opportunity to see Ash again, never had the chance to say goodbye. It was strange, but it was only years later that I realised we hadn't actually moved very far away from where I grew up. Definitely in walking distance. When you're a kid, everywhere seems like a million miles away, but on the map Levenshulme was actually next to North Reddish. Three miles max. However those three miles separated me from my life with Ash and my new life without her.

Every time it rained, I thought about her. I know...weird. Even to this day, as soon as it rains heavily, I still have the image of her standing there, drenched to the skin, hair and body soaking wet, smiling at me even though she was freezing cold.

I still have those books from that day. They look like concertinas, all bevelled and ruined. The pages barely separate, and they look tired and old. I keep them wrapped up in a bright red jumper. Her bright red jumper. They were the only things I had of hers, and there was no way I would part with them.

Ever.

After my mum left my dad, I found out she had actually been seeing someone else. It was funny in a way, because I had met him on more than one occasion. He worked with my mum at the nightclub. He was the head chef, so I had never thought it was weird when my mum had taken me and Jo around to his flat to meet him.

To tell the truth, I thought he was wonderful. He always had time to chat, always took an interest in what we were doing, and in retrospect I realised he thought the absolute world of my mum. It was good for the soul to see her so happy. Years had been wasted with a man who had told her nobody else would ever give her a second look, but now she was with a man who thought the sun rose and set because she was on the earth.

Those ten years were not easy, by any stretch of the imagination. My dad took great joy in divorcing my mum on the grounds of adultery. All his philandering meant nothing to him, and he expressly emphasized in his statement that he would never forgive her for leaving him…'for another man at that'. He failed to acknowledge his own shortcomings — the affairs, the lies, the fact he got a girl who was a year older than his daughter pregnant, believing it was his right to do all these things.

My brothers were on his side, following steadily in his footsteps as womanisers and drunks. All except Alan, and as soon as he was old enough, he was off to join the gang. I told you he was an idiot, didn't I?

Angie married a man who looked like Brains from Thunderbirds, although most of the time he reminded me more of Joe 90. Four of my brothers got married, and then three of them got divorced. They were definitely like their father. Actually, Aiden was remarried...and wifey number two was getting sick and tired of his absences...and I don't mean the times he spent in nick, either. I doubt they will ever learn.

At sixteen I left school and started college to do my A levels, and that is when I saw her again. Ash. My Ash. In the flesh. Bigger, taller, darker, and absolutely, positively the most gorgeous creature on the planet.

I hadn't been enrolled very long and was still trying to find my way around Stockport College when I saw her. Don't get me wrong here. I didn't look at her and say to myself 'Oh look! That's Ash.' It was more embarrassing than that. A lot more.

As 'newbies' we were constantly the butt of everybody's jokes. When we asked for directions, we were sent the opposite way; we were told stories about teachers to make us wary of the staff. They took the piss out of us constantly, but that was to be expected. All in all, it worked out fine. Until the incident.

I still cringe about it to this day, but I realise if it hadn't happened I would never have met Ash again.

I had been at college for two weeks and had made a few friends who insisted I go along to the karaoke night at the student union. As you well know, I couldn't hold a note (still can't), but I agreed, on the understanding I would not be getting up there and making a fool of myself.

Big mistake. I should have stayed home and washed my hair...watched telly...read a book. Even studied. But no. Karaoke night it was.

My friends were there, all cramped around a table with some older students, laughing and fitting in well. I bought a Coke from the bar and joined them. They seemed like a nice bunch, although slightly pissed already and it was only eight o'clock.

As the night wore on, more people were getting up the nerve to sing. Not me. I just sat there and sipped my drink, laughed in all the right places, and chatted — mainly with Mandy, a girl who was in my A level Sociology course and at whose house I would be staying over that night.

I felt quite relaxed. I think it had something to do with what Ray, an older Art student, kept slipping in my drink. He thought he was being sly about it, but he was too pissed to realise he was being obvious.

Then came the joints. I had never even smoked a cigarette, never mind a joint, but hey — it was college, and everyone else was doing it. Another...big...mistake.

I swear, I only had a couple of drags...honestly, Your Honour...just the two. But it felt like I had smoked ten. And that's how I found myself on the stage, in the student union, singing *Waterloo*. Fuck. And then... Double fuck.

The lights in the place were blinding. The smoke in the air was making my throat dry up even more than it was already, but for some strange reason I didn't care. I was waving my arm above my head and croaking out the jumbled words to Abba's winning song. I was killing it...slaughtering the poor song... hanging it up and slitting its metaphorical throat.

About a third of the way through, I felt someone come up behind me on the stage and begin to sing with me. I was overjoyed, and not a little zealous, to thank this person for becoming part of my act. I turned and stumbled into something warm and tall. I knew it was female because my face was pressed into some very impressive breasts. A laugh escaped as I stumbled back and looked up into...pale...blue...eyes.

I froze. The eyes had me.

The rabbit incident happened all over again, but this time it wasn't a case of meeting a man I didn't identify as my father. Or worrying about seeing something I wasn't familiar with. The vision standing in front of me was something I definitely recognised, even though it had been years. Therefore, I don't know why I stepped away, maybe it was to focus my attention on the whole package and not just those blue eyes gazing intently into my own.

This was the biggest mistake of them all. I know...drinking alcohol as a minor, smoking pot, murdering an Abba song — they were mistakes, kind of. But stepping back...stepping backwards on a tiny stage and not paying attention...that's the show stealer.

I landed squarely on top of a table full of empty cups, surrounded by amorous young men, ready for a woman to drop into their lives. Plastic glasses flew in all directions, my arse hitting the edge with enough velocity to tip the table forward and enable me to slide gracefully to the ground.

The music stopped. The room was silent for what seemed like an age, and then the laughter began. Raucous laughter that ricocheted off the walls and pounded in my befuddled ears. The room began to spin — not a good sign, especially because my stomach began to spin with it.

A concerned face hovered in front of me, and I struggled to control my wandering eyeballs, which were moving about the sockets of their own volition. They landed on blue eyes, twinkling blue eyes that captured me in a tractor beam gaze. I was transfixed. My body ceased to squirm, my eyeballs decided to behave and focus on this vision in front of me.

'Lou?' That voice — so familiar, yet so different. 'It is you, isn't it?' I couldn't answer. I was struck mute by the situation, the alcohol, the pot, and her eyes. 'Louise Turner? It's you, isn't it?' Her hand came out and stroked my cheek, my eyes fluttering closed.

'Ash.' The word parted my lips in a gesture of hope. I couldn't believe it was her...couldn't believe after all these years she would just pop into my world again.

'Yup...in the flesh.' I opened one eye to focus on her, taking in her classic beauty. My reaction to this vision was one I bet many of you have experienced at one time or another.

I threw up. All over her. In a bar full of people. And then I threw up again.

I told you it was embarrassing, didn't I?

Chapter Four

Grey dawn peeked through the window and nearly blinded me. My eyes felt like red hot coals in snow. Not good. The taste in my mouth was indescribable, as all the flavours that had spewed forth the previous night came back to haunt me. And I mean spewed.

The bed I was in was big...and not my own. And even in my state, I knew I wasn't alone. Shit. What had I done last night?

I tried to think...but my brain was AWOL...and the empty space where it should have been sitting was occupied by a full-out drum section.

Mandy's. I was at Mandy's. It must be Mandy's bed I was curled up in, and that must be Mandy who was spooning up the back of me with her arm draped over my belly.

Just a minute...spooning the back of me? With her arm around my middle?

A quick look under the covers told me I was undressed...a t-shirt that obviously wasn't one of my own was covering my top half, but the bottom half was...naked. Shit...again. What had I done last night?

Tentatively I turned around, fully expecting to see Mandy's ruffled brown hair on the pillow behind me.

I was wrong...oh, so wrong. The sight that greeted me was like a blast from the past. Long black hair cascaded over the pillow, a finely chiselled face angelic in sleep, the nose straight and perfect. Older, yet still faultless.

Ashley Richards.

My eyes shot open at this revelation. I was half-naked in bed with Ashley Richards. Ash. My Ash. *The* Ash I hadn't seen for over ten years. And there I was, hung over, with the taste of dead kittens lingering in my mouth. Shit...big time.

To say I was embarrassed would be redundant, as images of me puking over her the previous night came gallivanting back into my mind. Not sick on her once...but twice! How was I going to explain that one? I wanted to get up, dress, and run. My wild eyes scanned the room, looking for my jeans and top from the previous night. They weren't anywhere. Fuck.

The idea of going home with just the t-shirt on actually became an option at one point. But could I really do with all the stares on the bus? Well...

'Morning, Lou.'

Too late! I took too long! I was caught. Oh crap. I resigned myself to the situation, albeit unwillingly, and said the only thing that popped into my mind.

'Can I borrow a toothbrush?' Sweet, eh? I hadn't seen her for ten years, and all I could manage to do was throw up all over her and then ask to borrow a toothbrush.

Her face broke into an all-out grin, white teeth shining in the morning's growing light. She threw her arms above her head, and I felt the loss of the contact immediately. She stretched, making a little mewling noise as she did so. 'Sure. I'll just show you where the bathroom is and get you a toothbrush.' That smile again. 'I bet your mouth tastes like crap, doesn't it?'

Could I go any redder? Nope. Not unless you dipped my head in ketchup.

'Come on, then...I'll show you.' With that, she leapt out of bed, exposing miles of naked legs.

Did I say I couldn't go any redder? I lied.

I spent ages in the bathroom. Ash had told me to grab a shower if I wanted one, and by one quick sniff of my skin, I decided she hadn't offered out of politeness.

The water was like a gift from the gods — cool on my overheated skin. The throbbing of the brass band in my head was calming to a dull roar. Minty toothpaste tried its very best to replace the lingering tastes in my mouth...and eventually I calmed down enough to feel a little more confident about speaking to people.

I had been in the bathroom for a good forty minutes before I realised I was at Ash's house. That is, I knew I was at Ash's house, what I meant to say was *Ash's* house — from when we were kids. I couldn't believe it. After all these years she was still in the same place where I had left her. I also couldn't believe I hadn't noticed where I was before that.

Blame the hangover.

A sense of sadness washed over me. Why hadn't I written to her? I had missed her so much in those ten years; I could have dropped her a note to tell her what had happened. I honestly can't tell you why I didn't. I felt so stupid...so shallow. The only excuse I could think of was that I had been only six at the time, and by the time I could have written to her, tried to find her or made some effort to try to contact her again, too much time had passed. I wasn't even sure she'd remember me.

What must Ash think of me? What must she have thought when I just disappeared off the face of the earth one night and never even contacted her...especially when she lived at the same fucking address she always had?

The sadness flopped into my gut, stopping the churnings of misspent youth and weighing heavily on my conscience. I sat on the toilet seat, my head in my hands, trying to find some semblance of reason in my fucked up mind.

Then it dawned on me, like a lightning bolt from the subconscious: why hadn't she tried to find me? Unreasonable, I know, but anything to pass the buck.

I leaned back against the cool wood of the toilet seat and sucked in a breath. What was the point of going over past events? It wouldn't change anything, would it?

At least I had the opportunity to see her again...like I always promised myself but was too bloody lazy to do anything about. A grin split my face. I was there, in Ashley Richards' house, and she was just down the hallway from me. I had the opportunity to have her back in my life once again. A bigger smile lighted my face.

'Lou? Are you okay in there?' Her voice was like nectar to my ears. I felt like I had been transported back ten years. 'I've made you a coffee.'

'I'll be right there!' Then I quickly rubbed the towel through my long hair again, threw on the dressing gown she had given me, and opened the door to my future.

Ash. My Ash. Back in my life again. What a day! What a bloody fantastic day!

Hangover forgotten, I nearly skipped down the hallway to my old friend's bedroom.

Over coffee, Ash told me about her life up to then. She was studying Law, Psychology, Social Sciences and Maths at A level, as she wanted to join the police force like her father. Well, she had the height for it; she must have been getting on for six foot if the length of her legs was anything to go by. They went on for miles.

I don't know what possessed me that morning, but I had difficulty tearing my eyes from the long expanse of flesh sticking out from the bottom of her sleeping shorts. Weird. I had never before had the inclination to eye up another female's legs. But they were really long...and I mean really long. Probably because mine are really short.

Time with her seemed to fly by, and we chatted about college courses with ease, but at the back of my mind I really wanted to tell her why I hadn't contacted her, why I hadn't had the chance to say goodbye. The problem was, I didn't want to broach it...it was still painful for many reasons. Luckily enough, I didn't have to.

'Sorry to hear about your parents splitting up.' My eyes shot up to her face, were captured in the blueness of her eyes. Concern radiated from them...and once again I felt her protectiveness, her willingness to take care of me...just from her voice. 'It was a bit of surprise when I came 'round to get you the next day.' A small laugh escaped her, and she shook her head from side to side.

'Did you speak to anyone?' My voice sounded small, childlike.

'Your dad, actually.' She shifted in her chair, and I could sense the unease pouring from her. 'He...erm...well, let's just say he wasn't very forthcoming about giving much away.'

'What did he say?' My voice was firmer now, and I could feel the hatred I had for my father welling up inside. Bastard. He had still found an opportunity to fuck up my life. No wonder she hadn't tried to find me. I know, I know...she was only a child...but I had to blame someone; I had to try to rationalise what had happened.

Blue eyes looked at me nervously. 'It doesn't mat—'

'What did he say?' The anger in my throat was choking me; I wanted to scream out. And this made me even more angry. After all these years, he could still get to me. Every time I thought of what he had done — not just to me, but to us all...especially my mum — I couldn't seem to control my emotions.

'Look, Lou, it's in the past.' As she spoke, she leaned forward and placed her hand on my leg. The contact made me suck in my breath, and I felt the fight leave me just as quickly as it had popped up. 'Don't let him win.' Her voice was so soft, so caring, so Ash. How could I fight that?

My gaze drifted down to her hand, which was making gentle circles on my thigh, and I could feel a sensation building inside my gut. It wasn't a feeling one friend should have about another. Definitely not.

Embarrassed at the sensation, I jerked back on the chair to escape her touch. My eyes drifted to her hand...stopped...and...stared at the long tapering fingers moving serenely over my goosebumping flesh. I shook my head to break the gaze, and then my eyes travelled up to meet her face. Those blue orbs just escaped seeing my bewildered look as they slipped down to rest on the unconscious action of her hand.

Surprise, unmasked and raw, coated her face, only fleetingly, granted, but still there for the briefest of moments. Without warning, she snatched her hand away, curling the fingers into a pose of protectiveness, like she had been burned.

'Ash?' The questioning tone I used on her name drew her attention back on my face. Her eyes seemed troubled, like whirlpools. Troubled...yes, that was the word to describe her look. She seemed troubled for some reason. I don't know why. 'What is it?'

It took less than a heartbeat for her expression to change from perturbed to the face-splitting grin she always had ready. A shrug of the shoulders was followed by a hard, resounding slap on my leg. A familiar gesture between friends.

I laughed, even though she had a good slap on her, and my reddening leg was living proof. The sound seemed to break the mounting tension in the room, and it seemed to fit with the situation. Then she joined in, her eyes still a little distant at first, but gradually softening as the hilarity took hold.

It was through this sharing that her previous words of comfort came crashing back into my mind.

She was right...the past didn't matter; it could only guide us to a better future, a learning process we needed to acknowledge before we could move on.

I decided to move on. And hopefully take Ash with me.

It wasn't long after that I got my clothes back (which she had kindly washed and dried because of the splattering of vomit that speckled them) and got dressed. It felt good being in her company again, and I found I didn't actually want to go home.

But, I had to go. I had promised Jo, under duress, I would go shopping with her. I hated shopping with her; everything turned into a marathon. It was as if she was on a bet with God, and the bet was she could spot every bargain...try on anything that remotely fitted her...and piss me off in the process.

Nevertheless, I had promised. Even now, I can't contain the sigh that escapes when I think of shopping with my sister.

Ash and I exchanged addresses and phone numbers, and I distinctly remember folding the little sheet of paper very neatly and tucking it in the back pocket of my jeans. It felt like an offering.

As I was leaving, her mum appeared. She didn't look a day older than I remembered — her hair was still jet black and long, just like Ash's. They were similar in appearance except for the eyes. Her mum's were grey, whereas Ash's were blue like her dad's.

'Well, I never... It's little Lou Turner, isn't it?'

'In the flesh, Mrs. Richards.'

'Well, I never... How long has it been — ten...eleven years?' As she was saying it, she was walking over to me, peering into my face just to make sure.

I should've known what was coming next, but the years had been kind to me. Mrs. Richards had a habit of nearly crushing the life out of you when she was happy, and then, to add insult to injury, she would pinch your cheeks and wobble the flesh up and down until your mouth made a farting sound. Not a pretty sight...or noise, for that matter. And it hurt like buggery...but nevertheless...it felt good to be remembered and with such fondness, too.

'You're not running off already, are you? Stay for a cuppa.' She still had my face in a vice-like grip, and my answer came out like a wet fart. 'Soon then?' I looked at her wide eyed. How on earth had she understood my answer? 'Come for tea one night, yes?'

I nodded and then sighed with relief as she let go of her death grip on my cheeks. The blood had fled in fright, and I must have looked a vision — with my pasty, fingerprinted face surrounded by a big red blob.

'I'd love to.' As I answered, I automatically turned to face Ash, who was grinning idiotically behind my back.

'Tomorrow, then? Sunday tea?'

'I...I...well...'

'Mum, don't pressure the poor girl. She's probably got arrangements already, haven't you?'

'Well...no, not really.'

'So you'll come then?'

There was no point arguing with her, so I just nodded, which earned me a huge smile from both of the Richards women. Women.

Women. Ash was a woman. That little girl of seven and three-quarters was nearly eighteen. A woman.

Emotions flashed through me — happiness, sadness, maybe a little anger, too. I had missed the ascent from childhood to adulthood, not just with Ash, but my own as well. It is amazing how different your life becomes when one day it's all turned upside down through no fault of your own.

Ash's eyes clouded with concern at my expression, and with a beaming smile I staved off the question I knew was bound to come. Keeping my voice light, I answered, 'I'd love to.'

Sorted.

Stockport Market was heaving with people. I can't tell you how many times I lost Jo amongst the crowds. She was like a spitfire, racing around the stalls, holding up the most hideous clothes to me and mouthing, 'This will look great on you.'

Yeah...when I'm dead. Then I wouldn't be able to argue about the shit colour and the crap style. At least it was more fashionable than the creations my mum used to pick out. Jo and I could tell what she was going to pick up even before my mum spotted it. It had to be multicoloured, or just a biddy colour, and preferably with a kitten looking wide eyed on the front...ball of wool, etcetera. It makes my stomach churn just to think of it.

As I was saying, Jo was in her element — picking up shit and measuring it against herself whilst I was trying my damnedest to look alluring, propping myself up against the small wall at the side of the stall. I realise now I must have looked like a prostitute or maybe just plain simple. The beauty of youth, eh?

I was lost in thought, mainly about Ash, and didn't hear Jo's question the first time 'round.

'Oi...gormless...I'm talking to you!' My eyes shot up to meet the daggers my sister was throwing me. 'Returned from Never Never Land, have you?' I shrugged. I thought I was so cool. You know what it's like — never let your guard down in front of absolute strangers.

I went for bored, hoping she would take the hint and take me home so I could lie on my bed and think whilst blasting the neighbours with music. 'What?'

'I asked if you had a good night last night.' She looked me squarely in the eyes. It was funny, but I hadn't even mentioned bumping into Ash. I don't know why. Maybe it was because I was embarrassed about how it all happened.

'It was okay, I suppose.' I looked rather sheepish at this point, and there's one thing you can't keep from my sister. That's it...you can't keep one thing from her. She could read me like a book. The smile slipped from her face, and I knew I was on the verge of being interrogated.

'What happened?'

'Not much.'

'Really?' She laid the blouse over the rack and slowly stepped away. Shit. I knew what was coming next. 'Fancy a coffee?'

Here we go — her perfect interrogation technique was underway. She always thought I would crumble if she took me to a café and bought me a coffee.

Funny thing was...I did.

I didn't expect laughter. What I did expect was a thorough telling off, especially for smoking pot. She surprised me by laughing, loudly, and pointing her finger at me. When I told her about falling off the stage, then throwing up, she laughed even harder, spluttering words along the lines of me deserving everything I got.

It was strange to watch the total change in her when I mentioned I had met Ash again and that I had slept over at her house.

She went silent. All the laughter and finger pointing ceased. I didn't get it. One minute laughing, the next, stony silence.

'Are you going to see her again?' The question was so quiet, I had to strain to hear it.

'Well…erm…her…erm…' Why was I acting like a dickhead? Why did it bother me that Jo didn't like Ash?

'Are you, or aren't you?' Clipped words.

'Yes…erm…Ash's mum invited me for tea tomorrow.' I looked at her, my eyes wide, one eyebrow raised and my mouth slightly open. I did look slightly simple, but I think I was waiting for her to say something.

She didn't. She just got up and paid the bill. It was only when she had nearly reached the door that she turned to me, flashed me a huge grin, and said, 'Come on, lard arse, there's bargains to get.'

I shuffled under the table to collect the three carrier bags she already had me carrying and scuttled after her.

I had a grin plastered on my face, but underneath I was confused…and a little intrigued. I couldn't help but wonder again why Jo seemed to put a distance between my friendship with Ash and my relationship with her.

Maybe one day I would get to the truth.

Chapter Five

Sunday tea is always a good tea, isn't it? It's the time where you have the opportunity to go all out and make something nice. Now, personally, I love my mum's roast dinners, although my dad (yes…he's my dad) is the chef. I think it's what you get used to, really.

But Sunday tea is still a time where the family gets together and shares stories. In my family, we always told stories of the past…the funny ones…especially stories about what we did as kids. I used to love those teas…erm…still do, in fact. It's tradition — eat sandwiches and cake, drink bucket loads of tea, and laugh at each other.

Perfect.

To miss Sunday tea at our house, there had to be a good reason. Near-death experience was okay, as long as you had a doctor's certificate, but general pissing off to see your mates was a no no. It was family time — or as my sister Angie always says, and this is enough to fuck anyone off, 'quality time', sounding a lot like a Hallmark greeting card.

I wanted to go to Ash's for tea. Obviously. My parents wanted me at theirs. Obviously. Therefore, there was no competition. I was going to Ash's. Come hell or high water, I was going to her house for tea. Stuff the consequences.

Initially my mum just gave me The Look. Instead of explaining, I did what all teenagers do best — I went *'into one'*. Having a paddy…as my mum always said. I ranted and raved about never having any freedom and when were they going to realise I was an adult. Mum just shot me another look, daring me to continue.

I'd had enough. I stomped up the stairs, making sure I banged every door on the way. Twice.

After throwing myself on the bed, burying my head in the pillow, and screaming into aforementioned pillow about how unfair my life was, how everyone was out to get me, I did the thing teenagers do next best. I fell asleep.

It seemed like I had been asleep for hours, although it was more like forty-five minutes, when I awoke to a gentle shaking of my shoulder. My head was still buried in the pillow, and for a split second, I thought I had gone blind. Then, unreasonable teenage angst traded places with fear of a life in the dark, as I remembered why I was in that position in the first place. Muffled warnings about being left alone to grow old and fester in my room escaped from the confines of the pillow.

'You can go. I've explained.' Jo. But…Jo? Jo didn't like Ash. Why would she explain for me? 'Mum said you can go to Ash's, but to make sure you are back before ten.'

Ten! I didn't care I had a curfew…that would leave me plenty of time to get to know my old friend again.

I turned over, leaving the pillow slightly damp from where I had drooled. Jo sat on the edge of the bed looking at me with some concern. All the love I felt for her raced to the surface, and I threw my arms about her. 'You're a star, Jo. An absolute star!'

I could feel her smile on my shoulder as I hugged her senseless. Once again, my sister had gone out of her way to make me happy, knowing I was too awkward to do anything about the situation myself...knowing I was too much like a typical teenager to back down and talk about things reasonably.

Then a doubt crept into my mind. Why would she do that so I could see someone she obviously didn't like? Confusion masked my features until a thought poked itself into my brain.

Because she loves you, dumb ass.

Once again, I felt my face crack into a grin.

And I love her too. Wouldn't you?

Tea at Ash's house was exactly like ours. There was a huge spread laid out, and even though my stomach was in knots, I still could have eaten half of what was there.

All the family were present: Anthony, Stephen, Ash's mum and dad. Stephen had brought his girlfriend for tea, and she sat quietly in the corner of the front room watching every move he made.

It seemed like yesterday when I had last been with this family. They all greeted me like an old friend, which of course I was, and made me feel like part of the family.

Tracy, Stephen's girlfriend, just sat there taking in the scene unfolding in front of her. Her face shouted suspicion, and her lips became thinner and thinner. I was introduced as the long lost family member, and she stuck out her hand in a gesture of welcome, but the sentiment never reached her eyes.

Nobody noticed but me. Ash was too busy running around finalising the spread; her parents were poking fun at her, shouting, 'Faster, Ash! Faster!' and the lads were talking about football.

It was just me and Tracy. Unfortunately.

She looked over her shoulder to make sure nobody was watching, gripped my hand tighter, and pulled me closer to her. A harsh whisper spat out of her mouth. 'Keep your fucking hands off Stephen.'

Uh? What the hell had brought that on?

It was only halfway through tea that the penny actually dropped — well, fell, clinking and cluttering on top of the table in front of me. By all accounts, they had all been ribbing Stephen before I came 'round about how he'd had a crush on me when we were kids. He had been only nine then, and I couldn't believe his girlfriend was reacting in such a way. What a gormless mare.

I had to put up with glaring looks from her, the Child Catcher, when all I wanted to do was take her outside and slap her around for a bit. All because Stephen used to have a crush on me ten years ago. I mean — ten years! How sad is that?

But my attention was diverted as my eyes drifted over to Ash time and time again. It was so good to be back with her and her family after all these years, and for some strange reason, it didn't seem like I had been away. It was the same chitchat, the same ribbing, joking, and love bouncing back and forth to each member of the family. I felt reborn. And it felt good.

Stories were thrown around of childhood experiences...times that made us all flush with embarrassment. Ash even told the story of how I'd got my foot caught in the flared bottoms of my jeans and had somersaulted arse over tit and landed, ungraciously, in a heap in the middle of the playing field.

God...I loved those jeans. Pale blue with embroidery of cornflowers growing up each leg. Pure class.

Before I knew it, we were clearing the pots away and stacking them in the kitchen ready to wash. The whole family joined in, me included. The only one who didn't help was Tracy, which was no surprise. She just plonked herself back onto the chair and picked up the Sunday supplement from the newspaper and began flicking through the pages.

Everyone took turns giving her a look as they passed, but she didn't pay any attention, just carried on turning the pages and ignoring us all. I honestly couldn't see what Stephen saw in her. She was nothing to look at, and he was gorgeous. Tall, with raven black hair that seemed tousled in his boyish way. His eyes were a darker blue than Ash's but still intense...although they didn't catch the sunlight like hers did.

I caught myself staring. Not at Stephen...at Ash. She was so beautiful and had a body to die for, although that would rather defeat the purpose, I suppose. Every movement she made seemed effortless...almost like she was a dancer on stage, captivating her audience with her graceful way. And she was only washing up!

I stood there with the tea towel in my hand, gawping at her...mouth open...the works.

'Ah, we have a fly catcher amongst us.'

Ash's dad had decided to come and stand directly in my line of vision and make a smart arsed comment. I can vividly remember ducking my head to the side to continue to watch and then feeling embarrassed for some reason.

Funny how memories go. I can't really remember much else apart from embarrassment...the scarlet sheen my face had adopted more than compensated for the memory lapse, and the voices around me took on a definite burring quality. The next thing I recall was a pair of twinkling blue eyes looking into my own and a firm hand on my arm. Her voice swept through me — caring tones, soothing tones. I looked at her, startled back into reality, and flushed even harder. If that was possible.

'I have...' I coughed to relieve all the emotion in my voice, changing it from a high-pitched squeak to a tenor with a cold. 'I have to go...I have to get home.' Why did I lie? It was only eight o'clock, and I still had two hours before curfew.

Worst thing was...Ash knew that. She looked at me slightly puzzled, and her face dropped, just a little, but it dropped all the same. A nod, swift and sure. She turned around, her back was my only view.

'Okay. Will you be all right getting back?' She sounded different somehow, distant. 'I can get Stephen to run you home if you want. Tracy will have to lump it.'

'I'm fine...honestly. I can walk.' She turned around so quickly, my eyes spun in their sockets trying to focus.

'You'll do no such thing! Stephen! Stephen!' And she was off, racing into the front room, leaving me standing there in her kitchen like a lemon.

Thirty seconds later, she was back, her grin splitting her face. 'Sorted. Stephen says he'll take you at nine.' I looked her squarely in the eyes. She cocked her head at me, one eyebrow raised in challenge. 'And you'll still be early.' Her expression begged me to argue with her, but I was no fool. Not then anyway.

We spent the next hour in her room, sprawled on her bed, her music blasting from her record player. Every teenager's dream — loud music and idle chatter. Ash had Yazoo's *Upstairs at Eric's* playing, and we were lying on our backs, staring at the ceiling. I had listened to the album before, as it was already a couple of years old, but hadn't really paid it much attention before.

Then I heard it — the song. *The* song. Alison Moyet's pure and sensuous voice filtered through the gloom of Ash's room as *Only You* started. The words hit a nerve — especially the reminder that her love had only come back yesterday...

I felt my heart open and then...crack. A splintering, splitting noise reverberated through me...

All I ever needed was the love you gave

All I needed for another day...

'Lou? Lou? Are you alright?'

I snapped myself into consciousness, now fully aware I was sitting bolt upright, my hands balled into fists, the covers of her bed wrapped firmly within my grip. My knuckles were white and nails were jabbing into the sensitive flesh of my palms. For a reason I had no clue about.

'Are you—'

'I'm fine, Ash...honestly...just felt a little bit of cramp coming. It's gone now.' Her face was so full of concern, I felt like a git lying to her...again. What was wrong with me? I had developed a deep-rooted need to lie through my teeth.

The song finished, and the next one on the album started. I couldn't concentrate on the lyrics, as I felt slightly dazed with emotion. It was confusing, to say the least. How on earth...or should I say, *why* on earth had I reacted that way to a song? I had heard it hundreds of times before and...nothing.

Fifteen minutes later I was in Stephen's beat-up Ford Escort, Tracy in the front, glaring at me, her eyes screaming, 'Fucker!' but her face oozed anxiety at my predicament of being without either a car or a boyfriend with a car. At least I understood why she was such a troll. A fucking shallow one at that.

I left Ash with a promise to get in contact in the week, maybe have lunch if our timetables allowed it. She waved vigorously from her doorway and was still there as her brother's car turned the corner. I settled down into the back seat.

What a day. Or evening...I should say. I made a promise to myself to buy Yazoo's album. I don't know why, especially after my earlier reaction. It just seemed the right thing to do.

But being a teenager at college, money was scarce, well, more like non-existent. So I decided to get myself a Saturday job...up the coffers a little bit. It would do me good to have a bit of cash to spend on things. And the sacrifice of part of my free time seemed a small price to pay for a little bit of monetary freedom.

Bugger. I hate work...although it does fascinate me. I could, without doubt, watch it all day.

Chapter Six

The week flew by in a blur, and I hadn't seen Ash at all. This was mainly due to me avoiding all of the usual haunts and telling Mum I was too busy to take messages when Ash called...twice.

I felt bad. I don't know why...and I didn't know why I was avoiding her. I wanted to see her...really wanted to meet with her for lunch, become part of her circle of friends...get to know her again.

Another week passed, this time with no phone calls, and I was withdrawing more and more into my own little world. I still had friends, but they didn't seem to be enough. I didn't see Ash at college, but strangely enough, I saw Tracy six times. Six fucking times!

Each time was an experience, to say the least. Each time made my skin crawl as if I had scabies. A bunch of cronies sporting bad mullets and peroxide blonde fringes always flagged her. How cool is that? Lacy tops showed wife beater t-shirts underneath, and scrawny white arms reflected fluorescent lighting. In a word — trashy. If I wanted two words, they would be trailer trash.

I ignored her snide remarks as I passed, but I swore one day to paste the living crap out of her. She was trying to intimidate me, thinking I was scared of her. If she only knew the thing that scared me the most was her smile. Now that was freaky. Black kohl-pencilled eyes showed a blankness that belied reason. She appeared to have the intelligence of an amoeba...and the sexual allure. God only knew what Stephen saw in her.

But I didn't care about Tracy...oh no. It paled in comparison to how I was missing Ash. The pain I experienced as a child when I had lost her seemed to disappear when I realised how much I missed her now. And I had only seen her twice. The third time came on the Friday afternoon.

Now there's a memory. Even better than the rabbit incident...the treatment night and Alan's dancing...even the free glass of lemonade. Although the overall effect combined caused more fear, laughter, and embarrassment than the previous three memories put together.

Do you want to hear it? Tough...you've got this far...now deal.

I had just finished A level English and was making my way out of the door, chatting with Sue, another student, when I heard my name being called above the din. I couldn't mistake that rich alto voice. Ash.

I turned to see her fighting against the tide as she tried to get to me. Students shoved and mumbled as she ducked past them, her eyes never leaving mine...like a tractor beam drawing her to me. I just stood there. Transfixed. Waiting for the ear bashing she was going to give me. I did feel guilty for ignoring her phone calls and the messages to call back.

That wasn't all I was feeling. No. Not by a long shot.

Adrenaline pumped through me as I stood there waiting for her to get to me. It must have been less than a minute, but it seemed like a lifetime before she was standing in front of me, grinning, making my heart bounce around within my rib cage. I think it was in fear...or...I don't know what. It was just there, like a tennis ball rebounding and punching the inside of my chest.

'Hello, stranger.' That voice could melt butter straight from the fridge.

Hold on a minute! Melt butter straight from the fridge? Where the fuck did that come from?

I just stood there and grinned like a Cheshire cat...clearly the simple-looking, grimacing, beetroot one you don't usually come across in the illustrations for the children's book. I started to nod, my mouth opening and closing, words escaping me; the only sound was that of a fish on the line.

She just stared at me, the grin fixed on her face in genuine affection, waiting for my dumb brain to acknowledge her with a simple hello.

When it didn't come, she shifted nervously, the smile leaving her face briefly, but coming back twice as powerful. 'Where've you been? I've called a couple of times...left messages...'

Thankfully, the mute spell that had bewitched me lifted, and I spluttered out an incomprehensible excuse, which only made her grin wider as she grabbed hold of me in a bone-crushing hug.

'Oh...I've missed you, Lou. Don't ask me why...but I have.' Her breath tangled in my hair and brushed my cheek. Her arms were strong, and I felt the feeling of safety cascade through my whole body...like I always did when I was with her.

She pulled back and released me, the air of the corridor bouncing off my skin like an alien concept. I missed her closeness. Weird, I know...but I did.

'Fancy a coffee?'

I started to say no, but the look on her face melted my resolve. I couldn't remember why I was avoiding her in the first place. Come to think of it...why *was* I avoiding her?

'Love to.' I didn't want to analyse the reason for a teenager's whims. I must have had a good reason, but for the life of me I couldn't think of it. All I could think of was the enchanting look on her face, the crooked smile playing on her lips, an eyebrow lifted in question as she waited for my response.

And maybe that was the reason...

And maybe I should have said no and walked away...

And maybe I wouldn't have experienced the combination of rabbits...Derbac...and lemonade all rolled into one.

Well, 'maybes' don't build experiences...and I was on a one-way trip to Experience Land.

Unfortunately.

The canteen, or refectory as some sad git called it, was packed, and we had to scrunch up in the corner with hot chocolates in polystyrene cups. A couple of art students were sitting opposite us with the traditional dyed black hair, makeup that would make Alice Cooper blush, and pasty white skin. They were giggling and touching each other religiously...quite inappropriately for a college canteen…erm…refectory. Boys today, eh? It was a bit of an eye opener, that's for sure.

Before long, I had forgotten about why I had tried to avoid Ash and just glowed in her presence. She gabbled on about her courses and what she had been up to, whilst I barely said a word. I was content to just sit in her shadow and soak up all that was her.

It was such a wonderful feeling…intense…but wonderful. The smile on my face grew wider and wider as she entertained me about some sad bastard in her course that couldn't even make a cup of tea without adult supervision. He wanted to be a Solicitor…and couldn't even work the washing machine. I felt sorry for his future clients.

Within thirty minutes, I was laughing aloud at her antics and was finding it increasingly difficult to breathe. My chest ached with laughter…and with something else, which at that time I didn't want to put a name to. Well…maybe not as much didn't, as couldn't.

I can't tell you how long we sat engrossed in conversation, but I could distinctly feel the canteen empty. The touchy feely boys had long since gone, and then it was just me and Ash…again.

'What are you doing tonight? Are you free?' She leaned forward and looked me squarely in the face. 'Me and a few friends are thinking about going to the student union. They've got a Karaoke night on.' She watched for any signs of refusal.

But that was the last thing in my mind at that moment. I was caught by her eyes. I felt the room melt into nothing as I just sat there and stared at her eyes…transfixed by them…pulled into her by them…feeling emotions one friend shouldn't be feeling for another…again…

She didn't back away. Her body leaned halfway over the table, and she just kept on staring…waiting…and if I wasn't mistaken…

'Excuse me, ladies.'

Was that voice in my head? That rich, deep voice?

Neither Ash nor I moved…or blinked.

A cough. Then another…louder, more insistent.

Ash leaned back in her chair, her face slowly changing from the absorbed look of moments before, into a mask of slight confusion, her eyes squinting slightly as she searched my face.

'Ash?' That voice again. 'Have you forgotten our date?'

The sound of brakes screeching to a halt in my chest nearly deafened me. The room seemed to grow terribly small, and I grew huge and very exposed. Ash blinked just once and broke our gaze. Her eyes swung around to rest on the person standing next to our table.

'Ben. Hi.' My eyes followed hers and took in the tall man leaning slightly towards Ash. And like a female, I digested everything about him: the blond hair…green eyes…the solid build of his body…the tight fitting t-shirt that left nothing to the imagination. Which matched up kind of nicely with the tightness of his jeans.

But it wasn't attraction I was feeling, not by a huge stretch of the imagination. No. It was something I wasn't used to, had never experienced before that moment. It was jealousy. The anger at being interrupted — that I had felt before. But jealousy? Definitely a new sensation, and to be perfectly honest, I didn't like the way it made me feel.

I sat there and watched him lean over me and kiss Ash on the mouth...on her lips...in front of me...on the lips. The kiss was featherlike and lasted all of a split second, but I felt it...and not in a nice way.

Ben was leaning across in front of me, trying to stroke the side of Ash's face, but I saw her pull back, only slightly, but she did pull back. A smirk flitted across my lips, and I had the urge to stick out my tongue at his back. Either he didn't notice, or he was trying to ignore it.

'This is Lou...a very good friend of mine. Ben, say hello.'

He turned his head to look at me, but his eyes only rested briefly on my face as they travelled slowly down my body, rested on my breasts, then travelled back up to my face again. I felt like I had been visually undressed...almost an optical rape. Whatever did Ash see in a wanker like that?

'Well...hello there.'

What a creep. He stuck his hand in my face, and I lifted mine in greeting. I was well trained, after all. Then the slimy fucker kissed me on the knuckles. I wanted to backhand him right across the mouth. Instead I ripped my hand away from his lips and gave him a look that could pickle testicles.

Ash looked at me, and I'm sure I saw the remnants of a smile flicker across her face, but she didn't say anything.

'Feisty little creature, aren't you.' God! Could this bloke be anymore of a twat? 'I like feisty.' Yes. He could.

'Glad you two have met.' That flicker again. 'I was just asking Lou to join us tonight.' Her face turned to me in question and I was just about to refuse when I spotted a fleeting look of pleading swipe across Ash's face.

'I'd love to.'

Where on earth had that come from? I didn't want to spend my evening being leered at by this jerk. But I did want to spend the evening with Ash. And that is what it all boils down to, isn't it?

The smile she bestowed on me actually illuminated the whole room. Whatever doubts I harboured were all sent whistling into the wind.

Not the experience you were expecting, is it? No. Well, I haven't got to that part yet. Give me time.

We arranged to meet inside the student union at seven-thirty, and at seven-fifteen, I was nervously waiting outside, plucking up my courage just to go in. For the tenth time, I smoothed down my top and ran my hands along my jeans. For the tenth time I licked my lips, bringing them to shine. For the tenth time I tried to make my breathing slow down, as I imitated a cross between an asthma attack and a panic attack, with a bit of hyperventilating for good measure.

Finally, I entered the lobby, where I was greeted by the smell of pot. As it drifted up my nose, images of me sprawled on the floor after falling off the stage danced about in my head.

I felt my face burn up. Christ...it had only been two weeks ago. I hoped no one would remember.

'Look, it's Agnetha!'

Shit. I felt my face burn and smiled weakly at the group of lads seated around the stage, the same group of lads I had landed on two weeks previously. I think.

I made my way to the bar and tried to hide in the darkest corner. Hopefully my face would return to a more natural shade after I had been served my Coke by the truly inept bartender who was likely better equipped to serve chips in McDonald's...or not...as he would definitely fail the health and hygiene test.

After securing my drink and pushing drunken students off me, I scanned the room looking for Ash. It was dark and smoky, and my eyes worked hard acclimatising to the gloom, especially because the bar area was bright enough to nearly cause a tan.

I could feel her rather than see her, feel her eyes on me. Slowly I turned to look behind me. And there she was...half standing, as if she had just started to get up from her chair. Her eyes focused straight on me, and she looked dazed for some reason. Ben, the dickhead, was next to her, but when he reached to grab her hand, she pulled it sharply away from him, her eyes never leaving mine.

It felt weird. Tingles spread up my spine, and for some reason I was beginning to feel uncomfortable. So, I waved at her.

No response. I waved again. Still no response. So I began to walk over, feeling a little self-conscious by this point but pasting a smile on my face to hide the tumultuous emotions inside. I couldn't understand why my heart was roaring inside my chest so loudly I believed everyone could hear it.

Then I saw her shake her head...just a little shake...but a shake nevertheless. Her eyes lost the glassiness and began to squint a little. It was my cue to make contact, so...I waved again and did the cheesy 'Hi' thing.

This time her face broke out into a grin, and I smiled in return, the uncomfortable feeling disappearing, replaced by a feeling of excitement as I approached the table. Ben was eyeing me up and down, and I wanted to tell him to fuck off, but evidently I'm too much of a lady.

It wasn't until I actually reached the table that I realised the other people around it were Stephen and Tracy. Shit. I liked Stephen...but Tracy? Christ...could my night get any worse?

It was fun, for the most part, anyway. I enjoyed being in Ash and Stephen's company, but little could be said about the other two. Ben was an out and out wanker; I couldn't see what Ash saw in him. All he did all night was hit on girls in the bar. Funny thing was, Ash didn't seem to mind! I'd have gone bonkers.

As for Tracy...well, you know my views on her. She is what is commonly known as a 'Twattette', and spent most of the evening glaring in my direction whilst sipping a Pernod and black. How common. She didn't even realise she had red lines up the side of her face (made by the blackcurrant as she drank), making her look like either the Joker or the Count from *Sesame Street*.

Funny...nobody could be arsed telling her. She sat there like Lady Muck from Turd Hall thinking she was something she most certainly wasn't, looking for all the world like she would suddenly shout out 'One Pernod and black ahahahah...Two Pernod and blacks...' You get the message. It's a pity she didn't. And I for one most certainly wasn't going to be the one to tell her. I know. But honestly...would you?

It wasn't until the end of the night that the experience happened. Remember...the one I threatened you with earlier.

I had just gone to the phone booth to call my parents to say I would be leaving in about twenty minutes and would be on the next bus home, when it all kicked off.

I should have seen it coming, but I didn't.

I should have known she would do something, but let's put it down to the innocence of youth...or just plain stupidity.

And I should have been paying attention instead of rummaging around in my purse looking for change for the bus.

Silly me.

'Think you're so fucking clever, don't you?' Tracy snarled. 'I bet you were laughing at me all night.' She skulked out of the shadows and drew closer to me; her face was devoid of blackcurrant by now. 'I'll fucking teach you.'

Smack!

In retrospect, I should have ducked. In retrospect, I should have smacked her back...but I didn't. Do you know why? No?

I didn't smack her back because I didn't have to. Ash did. Right in her blackcurrant gobbling mouth.

Now for the embarrassing thing...

'Why the fuck did you do that? I don't need you to fight my battles!'

Ash looked stunned...more stunned than Tracy, who was on the floor nursing her face at this point. 'But I—'

'But you what? Think I can't look after myself?'

The bar had gone completely quiet, and I knew people were staring at us...at me in particular. Someone came up behind me, and I felt my whole body tense. A deep male voice spoke firmly into my ear. 'I think it is time to go, love.'

It was the bouncer. And he didn't sound pleased, and neither was I, for that matter. I was getting kicked out for doing absolutely nothing, whilst Tracy was being helped up by a member of the staff and Ash just stared at me, her face pale.

'But I didn't do anything...' My voice sounded whining, even to my ears.

'It doesn't matter, love. It's for the best.'

Ash tried to interrupt and tell them what had happened, but I rounded on her, the tone definitely one of anger.

'Look! However hard it is to believe...I've grown up, Ash. I'm not a child anymore, for Christ's sake.'

With that, I turned and marched away, but not before I heard Ash mumble something. I don't know what she meant, or even if I heard right, but it sounded like, 'I've noticed.'

It was a pity she only figured that out when I had given her a mouthful.

Chapter Seven

I spent the whole of Saturday kicking myself...and wishing I was kicking Tracy instead.

I was at work...the crappiest job this side of the Pennines. I worked as an assistant at Stockport Market, serving cooked meats. It wasn't the cooked meats that were disgusting, it was the smell of the indoor market. Fuck me. It was gross.

Imagine the smell of curdled milk mixed with the smell of a cow's stomach lining. Yep...totally disgusting. Inside the market, cheese, tripe, eggs, and cooked meats were served to people who obviously had no sense of smell. It always took me at least thirty minutes to acclimatize myself to it, and this was only my second Saturday.

I worked with six other girls and one lad who was solely in charge of the meat slicer. Very glamorous. It was a long day, nine and a half hours on our feet, and we only got half an hour for lunch, which we took in pairs.

I got on with most of the girls, but one girl, Sarah, really stood out from the crowd. Strangely enough, she had taken me under her wing, and for the two weeks I had worked there, we had taken our dinner together.

As I said before, I was pissed off, and Sarah noticed. She kept on asking if I was okay...if I wanted to talk about it. Each time I turned her down. I was just angry about things...about Tracy...about Ash. All this in between serving people whose main concern was how much sliced ham they would need for Sunday tea.

Lunchtime couldn't come quick enough, and I grabbed my sandwich and bottle of orange and made my way to the locker room to get out of my overall...which by this time stunk to high heaven of sour milk and fat.

Sarah was right behind me, and neither of us said a word as we made our way into St. Mary's churchyard, where we ate our lunch and looked over Stockport.

It was amazing how quiet it was there. We were completely on our own as we munched our lunch and stared over the hills. The rest of the market din was like a distant monotone.

'Do you want to talk about it?' Sarah's voice was low, almost non-existent. And if I hadn't been looking at her at the time, I would have missed it entirely.

'There's nothing to tell.'

Sarah looked up from her sandwich and into my eyes. She had blue eyes...a little like Ash's, but darker. I felt an ache skip across my chest and, without thinking, raised my hand to it and rubbed, all the while staring into Sarah's eyes. I can't tell you how long we just looked at each other, but it was as if I was transfixed by the blueness.

'Are you free tonight?' There was a pause before she continued. 'I was wondering if you'd fancy going to the pictures or something.'

I held her gaze, and nearly a minute went by before...'I'd love to.' My voice seemed distant, almost as distant as the sounds of the market.

A smile broke out on her face, and mine followed suit. 'We'd better get back before they send out a search party.'

I nodded, scrunched up my sandwich wrapper before finishing the last dregs of my orange, stood up, and waited for Sarah to join me.

I was still annoyed about last night. I hadn't heard from Ash, but I had a feeling tonight was going to be more interesting.

I met Sarah outside the pictures at seven PM. We were going to see *A Nightmare on Elm Street*, which was an 18. I was only sixteen (nearly seventeen, though). Sarah was okay, as she had turned eighteen in July. There wasn't a problem getting in, though, as the boy on the desk looked younger than me...and his acne...I won't go there, in case you're eating.

We made our way into the darkened cinema, the adverts blaring out Pearl and Dean's memorable tune as they flashed on and off the screen promoting a mixture of crap and shit...in that order.

I did a double take as Sarah struggled along the back row, past all of the teenagers who were already snogging before the main feature began, but I just followed behind her, whispering, 'Excuse me' and 'Sorry' as I tripped over extended legs, trying to duck at the same time. It was not as if they were actually watching the film, but I felt a little unnerved to say the least.

Finally, Sarah settled into a chair that had a couple of empty chairs on either side. She patted the seat next to her, her blue eyes glowing with the reflection of the lights from the screen. I think she knew I was going to sit in the chair that would leave an empty one between us. Don't ask me why, I just...felt...like...I should.

Before long, the film was underway. And I was not happy. Freddy Krueger frightened the shit out of me...and not just because of his exceptionally bad taste in stripy tops, either. I felt the fear of the characters grip my throat and was scared I was going to fall asleep later and see the melted-faced freak coming at me. Sarah seemed cool about all the blood and asked if I was all right on more than one occasion.

As it approached the end and nearly all of the characters had copped their lot in one way or another, I could feel the fear climbing up my throat. I had never been one for scary movies, and this was in a class of its own on the fear factor scale. Seeing the young lad trying to escape something that, to me, seemed inescapable was playing on my nerves. It took me quite a while to realise I was actually holding Sarah's hand.

The only reason I realised I was, was the way she smiled at me and raised an eyebrow when I turned to see her reaction to a particularly gruesome bit. My face must have showed confusion, and she nodded to where my hand was resting on her thigh, totally enveloped in her own.

I looked back at her and was just about to apologise and pull away, when she smiled at me, moved closer until she was firmly pressed against my side, and began to stroke the back of my hand with her thumb. I should have felt disgusted...a woman was holding my hand, and not in a way friends would usually hold each other's hands, if you know what I mean, or do I have to repeat it again?

However, I wasn't disgusted. Far from it, in fact. I felt a growing excitement build in my gut...the same excitement I felt every time I thought of Ash...and her smile...and her eyes.

Shit...I didn't know what this meant. Was I gay then? A lesbian?

But I had never...

Me? Gay? A lezza? A dyke? A queer?

Nah. I wasn't one of those...was I? I had been with lads, not...erm...like...all the way, you know...but I did fancy lads...didn't I?

'Are you all right, Lou?' Sarah's face was close to mine, and I had an urge to kiss her...on her mouth...her lips...taste her lipstick...slip my tongue... Fuck.

'Ahem...yeah...yeah...fine.' My face was incandescent. I could feel the glow racing through my body, shouting to all who were listening, 'Lou's a lezza! Lou's a lezza!'

'Why are you sitting forward like that? Sit back. Come on, enjoy it.'

What? Enjoy what? Shit! Did she know? Fuck! Was she a lezza, too?

As these thoughts trotted around my mind, going to every corner of that grey matter asking for directions, I felt Sarah's arm sneaking around my back. I also felt myself stiffen at her touch.

'Hey, Lou, it's okay...it's okay.' Her voice was soothing...sweet and soft...and I drifted back into my seat, with her arm around my shoulders and her hand in mine.

We sat that way until the end credits, which by that stage came all too soon.

Sarah had passed her test in the summer and had her own car. It wasn't anything special, just an old Mini, but at least she had transport. When she asked if I would like a lift home, doubt flooded my mind.

Did I want to get in the car...alone...with her? What if she...if I...if we...

Never mind. To cut a long story short, I got a lift. Sarah was easy to talk to, and we laughed a great deal on the way home. She was a student at Manchester Uni, and she worked two jobs as well – one on the market and one in a pub on a Thursday night. My expression must have said it all: how on earth could she work on a Thursday when she had to get up for Uni?

She explained student life at the higher level was less demanding. More focus was placed on independent learning, and students didn't have to be in class all the time.

And the added bonus was...she never mentioned the hand-holding incident or the arm around my shoulders. But, I honestly didn't know my arse from my elbow by the time we reached the top of my road. Not that I usually do, but still, I was becoming confused.

She pulled up on the side road – as my house was on a corner – and turned her ignition off. If you had been there I guarantee you would have heard my heart rate speed up and up and up. The silence in the car was making screeching noises...and was finally put in its place by the thudding in my chest...gut...and maybe even a little bit lower. The blood gushing in my ears was beginning to become a problem, especially when I had to ask Sarah to repeat what she had just said.

A sheepish smile flittered across her face, and she cast her eyes down to her lap before raising them to meet my own.

'I said...I've had a lovely night tonight...and thank you.' A smile danced along the corners of her lips, not a crooked one...but still quite charming in its own way.

'Same here.'

'Could we...would you...erm...like to do it again...erm...sometime?'

Why was she so nervous? Said me, who had an entire butterfly collection fluttering around in my gut. 'I'd love to.'

Her face broke into a grin, and she bit her lip whilst bobbing her head up and down. 'Good...good.'

I just watched her, transfixed by this woman seated next to me, watching the lights from the street lamps do wonders with her eyes...making them glisten and sparkle...although they didn't twinkle. I had only ever met one person whose eyes twinkled.

But this was not the time to be thinking about her, was it? I was sitting in a car with Sarah. Not Ash. Sarah.

I looked at her, sat there, staring ahead at the quiet road, and really digested this girl who was there with me. She was pretty...very pretty in fact. Her hair was darker in this light, but it was typically a dark brown. Her face had an angelic quality; her skin smooth and clear. Her lips, although slightly parted, still held a slight plumpness...and looked soft...and tender.

Shit. I was a lezza. Why else would I be thinking about how soft and tender her lips were? Crap. That's all I needed.

But she was so pretty...

My thoughts were interrupted by a movement...from Sarah. She had turned herself to face me, and her expression held a question. Obviously, being a wuss, I thought this was the time to make my excuses and leave. 'Well...I had best get gone. I've really enjoyed myself tonight.'

'Lou?' Her voice stopped my escape, and I turned to look at her once again. 'I've had a lovely time tonight, really lovely. In fact—'

At this point, she leaned towards me, and I leaned back on the door, willing it to open and let me out. I saw her come closer and then...pull back, her face showing the confusion I was feeling. All my senses were in overdrive. I could smell her perfume: it was intoxicating. I could hear my blood whistling through my veins, racing to parts that shall be left unmentioned. And I could see this situation getting out of hand if I didn't do something...and quick. So I did.

I leaned forward and planted my lips to hers, quite clumsily at first, and I think I took her by surprise...and that made the both of us. I could taste her lipstick in my mouth as I kissed her...and it tasted so much better than when I tasted it on myself.

When the surprise wore off, I could feel her responding to me, and I followed suit, our mouths moving against each other's in a steady rhythm. I could feel her hand stroking the side of my head, so I lifted my hand and started doing the same. Then she tangled her fingers into my hair, and I felt a groan leave my stomach and race upwards to burst out of my mouth and into hers.

She moaned back and then slipped a very inquisitive tongue into my mouth.

This was the first time I had ever kissed a woman. Ever. I had never even thought about kissing another woman. Ever. Or...had I? This wasn't the time to start questioning what I had or hadn't thought. I was kissing a woman, in the front seat of her car, parked outside my house on a Saturday night...and I was thoroughly enjoying it.

Her lips were so soft...softer than I thought they'd be...and they had looked soft. Her tongue was gently probing inside my mouth, and I couldn't help but suck it in. It was getting deeper and deeper. I was falling deeper and deeper into the kiss, the outside world was leaving me behind as I pushed myself into her and felt her do the same.

Sensations bulldozed through me. The feeling of kissing another woman was totally mind blowing, and there was a definite tingle between my legs — a pooling of want forming there and begged to be assuaged.

Why...I don't know. All I knew was I was feeling liberation from the inside out...and I felt completely under its spell. Until...

Until she moved her free hand and delicately stroked the outside of my breast. That stopped me.

I pulled back sharply and looked at her. Her hand was still in my hair...her eyes closed...lips slightly parted, emitting short pants as she waited for me to continue...and waited.

'Sarah...I...' Blue eyes slipped open and glassily focused on me, and I could see desire burning behind them. 'I...well...I...'

Her fingers left the safety of my hair, and she trailed them down my cheek and across my lips. 'Shush, Lou. It's okay. We don't have to do anything you are uncomfortable with.'

Her voice was deeper than earlier, almost smoky. I felt the stab in my groin again and gently kissed one finger, and then another...then another...then I slipped one into my mouth and sucked. The noise she made was enough to drench my underwear. A low moaning noise seeped from between those soft lips I had just tasted, and I suckled even harder. Her eyes drifted closed again, and she leaned her head back, exposing her throat.

I was definitely feeling more than confusion by this point...and it felt strangely good.

After what seemed like hours but was more like seconds, I set her finger free, and she trailed the wetness around my mouth before delicately brushing her lips across mine again. I breathed in, quite fiercely, and opened my eyes to look her in the face again. 'I'd best get in. I should have been home ages ago.'

Why did I lie? It was only ten-thirty and I wasn't expected back before eleven-thirty.

Sarah didn't say a word, just nodded acceptance and looked kind of sheepish. 'Okay then...night.' I leaned to open the door, and her hand stopped me. 'Can I see you again?'

Her voice held a quiet pleading quality that struck straight at my heart. I nodded and sat back in the seat to scrabble around in my bag, searching for a scrap of paper and something to write with. After writing my phone number down, I shot out of the car, 'round the corner, and into my front door without so much as a backward glance — and then felt like a right baggage for not even waving to the girl I had just been kissing minutes before.

I didn't even wait to see her turn the engine back on...make sure she was okay...nothing. I was like Zola Budd on speed.

Jo and my parents were seated in front of the telly, watching a really dodgy black and white horror film on BBC2 — *The Curse of the Mummy* with Boris Karloff. My only greeting was an eye flicker and a nod from my parents and the finger signal and a grin from Jo, who was sprawled with her legs up the wall and her head hanging off the chair. Perfect film-watching position.

I felt totally exposed. It was as if everyone knew I had just made out with a woman mere feet away, although they'd need good eyesight so see through nine-inch brick. This feeling of exposure punctured the excitement I had been feeling, and I could feel it draining away.

'Ash came 'round looking for you earlier.'

'What?' I wanted to swear, but I doubted my parents would appreciate it. 'When? What time?'

Jo sat up on her chair, looking twisted and very uncomfortable, and turned to face me. 'Erm...about...eight-thirty...and then again at about ten.'

'Ten! But it's only ten-forty now!' I don't know why I shouted out the time. It just felt right for some reason or another. Jo looked confused at my reaction but just shook her head and resumed sprawl position. 'What did she say?' I tried to keep my breathing under control. Ash had been there, and I had been out with Sarah...kissing Sarah, just 'round the corner...and we would have been there about ten-fifteen.

Shit. What if Ash saw us in Sarah's car?

Shit. Me making out with a woman.

Shit. What to do? What to do?

'Just asked if you were in and what time you would be back...not much else.'

'Where did you say I had gone?'

'Where you went, of course — to the flicks with that girl you work with...Sarah, is it?'

I nodded, as I was unable to speak. My throat had dried up big time, and I felt the wind leave my sails. I turned and left. Upstairs in my room, I turned on the record player and aimed the needle halfway across the vinyl. Alison Moyet's voice drifted softly around...

All I ever needed was the love you gave

All I needed for another day...

I felt depressed. All the new feelings disappeared completely, and I didn't even have the energy to beat myself up about what had happened earlier. All I could think about was I had missed Ash...twice. And that she might have seen me with another girl.

Kissing.

Crap. This was not good. What if she got the wrong idea about me? Thought I went around kissing girls?

But I do.

Not all of the time.

And? Your point is?

This was getting me nowhere. I was arguing with myself, and I didn't have any answers. My opinions were trite and contradictory, and I was getting on my own nerves.

Next thing I knew, I was standing in the front room in front of the telly. My parents were not impressed that they were missing the end of the film.

'What else did she say? Does she want me to call her?'

'For God's sake, Lou...shift!' I sidled to one side, leaving enough room for both my mum and dad to see the telly but completely blocking Jo's view. I heard her 'tutt' before she raised her eyes from the direction of the TV, rolling them for effect.

'Said something about catching you later. Give you a ring tomorrow or you ring her or something.' I think my expression said it all, and she tutted again. 'She'll ring you tomorrow morning...okay? Now shift your backside.'

A smile lit my face. Ash was going to call me tomorrow. I might even get to see her. I turned to go to bed, nearly skipping, and then it hit me: what if she had seen me? What would I say? What about Sarah?

The life of a teenager, eh? Wouldn't trade places for all the tea in China.

Chapter Eight

I lay on top of my bed staring at the ceiling, arms behind my head, my body giving the impression of being relaxed when inside I was tighter than a drum.

Thoughts flitted through my mind, and I was only given brief glimpses of what it wanted me to concentrate on...and it was starting to make me feel rather sick. Names and faces zoomed in and out...in and out...and I was becoming more perplexed by the minute.

Images of my clinch with Sarah were vying for first place with the image of Ash's gaunt look at the Students' Union on Friday night after I had shouted at her.

Ash had come looking for me...twice. Come 'round to my house...twice...looking for me, whilst I was out getting it on with another woman.

A groan escaped me...not a pleasurable groan like what had happened in the car. God, no! This one was a groan of pain...of confusion...of not being able to grasp what was happening to me. My arm came in front of my face, believing it could block out the images my overzealous brain was conjuring. Hot breath soaked through the material of my shirt and landed on my arm, as my breathing became more and more laboured the more I thought about what I had done.

I didn't like it...but I did like it...I didn't...yet...I did. I had no concept of what being a lesbian was all about, and I couldn't classify what it entailed. All I could muster were images of women who dressed like men, acted like men, and slept with other women who looked like men, dressed like men, and acted like men.

Yep. Totally naïve. I didn't realise then, lesbians didn't have to be categorised into the stereotypical interpretation most people still put on us lady lovers.

Funny thing was, Sarah didn't fit into this 'type'. She was absolutely stunning...and all woman. She dressed feminine, spoke feminine, smelled, tasted, felt feminine. God...was she feminine!

As I thought about the kisses we had shared in the front seat of her car, I felt moisture puddle once again between my legs.

A thought drifted into my head...almost like a voice from somewhere else...from someone else. It was calming, soothing, pliant, and nourishing. A thought. An idea. A concept drilled together by want and guilt. Words welded into sense by feeling and desire...an option that blanketed the reality of my confusion with a promise of experience versus fantasy.

Being with a woman was a fantasy, a dream that had been so deeply embedded within me I had failed to notice its existence. Until now...until Sarah.

With a deep breath, I came to some sort of understanding. I would try this discovery...taste it...mould it...feel it and embrace it. If it wasn't for me, it wasn't for me. But I had tried it...tried Sarah...tried this new and wonderful gift that had fluttered into my path.

Maybe I would understand it more if I held it close to me and nibbled at it, untied the wrappings with my teeth to find out what was under all the expectation.

A smile graced my lips. A genuine one this time. A smile that made me feel lighter, more in control of the situation.

Yep. Why should I worry about something that might only be a phase? It might leave as quickly as it came...so I should just go with it.

I lifted my arm from in front of my eyes and stared at the wall straight ahead of me. Cliff Richard stared back. Hundreds of smiles grinning at me as if he was in on the secret. I grinned back, stuck out my tongue, then turned onto my side to see the solitary poster of Madonna gracing the wall, her breasts on display.

I felt the smile slip down my face as the realisation crashed down on me: Jo had Cliff Richard on her walls, ceiling, dresser drawers, and stuck all over her headboard. I had one picture of a woman flashing her tits and pouting for the camera.

Fuck. This was going to be a long phase.

Sunday morning shouted 'Hello!' too bloody early, like usual. This took the form of my dad, whose philosophy in life was 'If I'm up, everybody's up.' The grating sounds of Conway Twitty's (make what you will out of the surname, I can guarantee it will be not far off what Jo and I called him) *Hello Darling* boomed around the house.

The neighbours must have really hated us. I hated us...especially at 8:46 on a Sunday morning. Before ten, I hated everyone.

I had found sleep difficult, to say the least. Every time I had drifted off, images came into my mind – some good, some very unnerving. Talk about confused. My body and my brain were finding it damn near impossible to keep up with the stirrings within. At one point I nearly woke Jo up to tell her, leaned over to her bed and everything, but the courage left me as my hand hovered over her exposed arm.

I lay there, listening to my dad ultimately kill a dire song and just thinking about what I was going to do next. The thought of being 'different' to everyone else still played on my mind, but the excitement...the taste of her mouth made my insides crawl around and simper. I knew there and then, whatever happened with Sarah, I would be happy to try.

It was not love...by any stretch of the imagination. Lust...a little bit. Inquisitiveness...most definitely. Just wanting to feel what I had felt last night...maybe a little bit more.

The grin split my face, and I stretched my arms above my head, only to make a little whimpering sound.

Amazing. Truly amazing. Conway Twitty, duetting with my dad, couldn't wake Jo, but a whimper...Bam! Her eyes flew open, and she stared at me in the way only someone who has just woken up can do.

'Get your arse out of bed, Cliffy lover.'

'Go fuck yourself...Madonna lover.'

The grin I had been sporting slipped painfully from my face. 'What do you mean by that?' The tone screamed GUILTY! I'M A LEZZA! But the volume was low...deathly low...menacingly low, and I felt myself sit up in a rigid, back sprain kind of way.

Jo seemed non-plussed, just stretched, yawning widely and loudly, whilst trying to speak and point at the solitary poster on my wall. 'Cw...iff...y...' Hand to her posters, yawn well and truly underway, 'sh...ll...apper.' The hand pointed at Madonna pouting from the wall.

My heart rate should have slowed down at the realisation Jo didn't mean anything by what she said, but it didn't. I think it was because it was closer to the truth than I was ready for...or would ever be ready for.

That thought haunted me for most of the morning. Until I saw Ash again.

The time was 2:16 PM. It was Sunday afternoon. I had just finished the washing up. Yep. I feel like being clipped. Not for long, though. It's boring.

As I was saying, it had just turned two o'clock when the doorbell went. Obviously, being a teenager, I had to be told 'three bloody times' to answer the door.

Imagine my surprise when I flung the door back, scowl firmly in place, and Ash stood there looking absolutely breathtaking. Her raven hair was tied loosely into a ponytail, her fringe wisped all over the place, blown by the wind. She stood there, one hand behind her back, one holding her bag, her whole body language screaming submission. I think that was the thing that surprised me the most; I had never seen her looking this way...almost vulnerable.

'Can we talk?'

The voice of rich velvet crept over my skin and made all the hairs on my arms stand to attention. The newly found knowledge about myself made me acknowledge what I felt every time I looked at Ash. Desire. Lust. Want. Need.

And love. I knew I could easily fall into her arms and never want to leave. She was my dream...my goal, something I wanted to aspire to again and again and again. I also knew Ash had a boyfriend, however much of a wanker he was.

Then I realised I hadn't answered her. She stood there, eyebrow raised...waiting. 'God...Ash...yes. Come in, come in. Sorry...erm...come on in.'

I actually saw her lip curl into her crooked grin, and my heart went BA BOOM! My legs felt unsteady, so I gripped the door harder and harder and harder, willing myself to be sensible. Ash stepped forward, and as she did so, she brought forward the hand that had been hidden behind her back and presented me with a bunch of carnations. BA BOOM!

'Sorry, Lou...I...shouldn't...I need...well...erm...well...I...you... Sorry about Friday.'

Jesus. The words came out like a band of juggling acrobats, and I had to blink to tidy them into some kind of order so I could process what she had said. Me being half in a daze didn't help much, especially when I tried to take the flowers. It came out as a lunge instead, and I fell forward and straight into her arms.

Sounds romantic, doesn't it? Well, it wasn't. She was at the bottom of three steep steps, whilst I had been at the top. The top of my head cracked her in the mouth with quite a force, and I heard her jaw click. The carnations were flattened between us both and apart from the cracking of her jaw, I also heard the distinct snap of the stems.

She had her arms about me in a flash, and I didn't actually touch the floor. I honestly think I could feel myself melting there...into her...into her warmth...into her smell. God, the smell of her filled my senses and made me want to curl up into her and stay there forever. I looked up into her face, which tilted down to my own, her blue eyes twinkling... Yes...twinkling.

Heaven. I was in heaven. I was being held by an angel with twinkling blue eyes and...a little bit of blood trickling from the corner of her mouth. Unconsciously, I lifted my hand to wipe it away, my eyes staring at it as if it would suddenly grow wings and fly away, and just as my fingers connected...

'Lou! Phone! Someone called Sarah!'

My eyes shot up to meet Ash's, which seemed so much closer than a moment before. I felt guilty...standing there in her arms, thinking unnatural thoughts, thoughts I doubted Ash had ever thought I would have about her. And then I was reminded about how different I actually was. The proof was waiting on the other end of the phone line. Sarah.

Shouldn't I be feeling something other than guilt right about now? Shouldn't I be racing to the phone and be giddy just about *now*?

What I was feeling wasn't giddiness or excitement...just plain old guilt...plain old confusion at my sudden traitorous emotions...my traitorous body.

I felt Ash lower me to the floor, my bare feet hitting the concrete in cold realisation. My arms loosened from around her, and I felt hers follow suit. The height difference became apparent, and I looked up at her, only to be met by a confused smile. I was captivated.

'Lou! For God sake! Phone!'

'You'd better get it.' Such a sweet voice...so soft...so...so...

'Lou!'

'Right! For God's sake, I'm coming!'

Ash's hands left my waist, and I staggered back, smacking the back of my foot on the step but barely feeling it. All I was feeling was the loss of her arms.

Then I felt embarrassment, and the blood raced to fill my cheeks. I felt heat devour my body like I had stood in a flame. 'Come in.' They were the only words I could squeeze out of my mouth.

With that, I turned and bounced (even with a throbbing ankle) up the steps, down the hall, and grabbed the phone from my dad's hand. He was not best pleased to say the least, and I heard him mumbling as he shuffled off back into the living room.

'Hello.' I had forgotten it was Sarah. Der. How could I forget something so important? I turned to face the door, and there was my reason. Ash stood there, her back leaning against the wall, her face turned towards me, eyes hooded...lips slightly parted.

I didn't hear Sarah. I couldn't. There was too much noise in my head to hear her. Blood is a very loud substance when it is whipping around inside your head. Did you know that?

'Lou? Are you there? Lou?'

Reality forced me back to the voice at the end of the line. 'Sarah...hi.'

I spoke to Sarah, but my mind, and eyes, were fully focussed on Ash. I could hear a little confusion from the other end of the line, and I did feel bad. That's the reason I agreed to see her again that night. Seven-thirty. Here.

I hung up the phone, stuck my hands in my pockets, and then smiled the weakest of smiles at Ash. Inside I felt I had just screamed, 'I'm going out with a woman tonight! On a date!'

Ash leaned forward, and it seemed as if it happened in slow motion. I was mesmerised.

'Are you free tonight?'

'Huh?'

'I said...are...you...free...tonight?' Her face held a huge smile that aimed straight at my heart, and if truth be known...a little lower. I just stood there, mouth open...fish impression firmly in place. 'Tonight. You and me...do something fun. Are you up for it?'

Fuck. Fuckity fuck fuck fuck.

I didn't say anything. I was stunned. Erm...maybe stunned was the wrong word. Gutted was more like it. Yes. I was gutted.

'I can't.' It came out as a whine. I realised I was getting good at whining, especially when I saw the smile slip from her face and knew it was because of me. The world had lost sunshine because of me. 'I'd love to...but...I've...just...'

What? Said you'd see your girlfriend tonight.

She isn't my girlfriend.

Really? That's not the impression I got when you had your tongue down her throat.

Why don't you just fuck off?

Touchy. Are you ashamed of being a lezza?

Just fuck off!

You are, aren't you? Ashamed.

Why I am having an internal monologue, which actually consists of two voices? Mine and...erm...mine. Why am I feeling the pinch of coming to terms with a growing confusion regarding my sexuality? Why am I so upset that I had just made arrangements to see Sarah when all I wanted was to do was sit in Ash's shadow?

And all the while I was deliberating, she waited. Silent. Patient. Content to wait for me to finish the sentence I had started.

'...made arrangements with a friend from work.' Friend as in *girlfriend*. 'Maybe tomorrow?' The hope in my voice was apparent, but it disintegrated as I saw Ash shake her head, and I knew what was coming next.

'Can't make tomorrow.' My heart sank even further, if that was possible. 'But Tuesday's good for me.'

Was I metaphorically skipping? Most definitely.

Sarah was on time; I was early. Call it nerves.

Ever since Ash had left, I had been replaying the events from the previous night. Sometimes it was me and Sarah...and sometimes Sarah was replaced by someone else. I don't have to tell you who that was.

She took me to a café in the heart of Manchester. It was trendy, and we were surrounded by students from the university. Conversation once again came easy, as we talked about what our futures would hold. Sarah wanted to go into social work, and I was leaning towards that field too, although I knew I would change my mind many times before settling on a career.

Before we knew it, it was ten o'clock and we were being ushered out of the door. I have to admit it...I'd had a good time. Relaxed...casual.

On our way home, I could see Sarah sneaking looks over at me. Excitement burred inside my gut at the expectation of kissing her again, although I did feel weird getting my knickers in a twist at the prospect of kissing another woman. Doubt vied for dominance. This wasn't right. Wanting to kiss someone of the same sex wasn't right. Why did I have to be different from everyone else? Why did I have to want something different from everyone else?

Apart from Sarah. A snigger held itself behind my lips and waited to be freed. Not tonight. That snigger was staying put.

Once again I had missed Sarah asking me a question. I just said the first thing that popped into my mind. 'Whatever.'

And that led to a very interesting evening. A very interesting evening indeed.

Good job I hadn't been listening, right?

The question must have been 'Would you mind going somewhere else before I drop you off?' I doubt I would have said yes if I had been listening, so in retrospect, I'm glad I have the attention span of a fruit fly.

I watched in fascination as she manoeuvred her car down the dark country lane that led to the Vale, a nature reserve that was reputedly the high spot for couples. Anticipation guided my thoughts as she pulled up underneath a tree that blocked the last vestiges of light from the night sky.

The car was strangely silent, and I am sure I heard a pin drop somewhere outside. The squeak from her leather seat made me start, and I turned to face her, barely making out her features, just her shape.

I felt her hand take mine, cool, yet slightly shaking. Her thumb brushed over the top in much the same manner as she had done the previous night at the pictures. My breath caught in my throat, and I wanted to reach forward and kiss her again.

The moisture in my mouth was beginning to form, just as it was between my legs. I must be gay...must be. I had been in situations like this with boys and all I felt was boredom...nothing in comparison to this wild, unchained feeling that decided to reveal itself to me tonight.

Her voice whispered to me in the darkness, sending messages to all parts of me that needed to hear it. Soft, smooth, alluring, enticing. The words she said were nothing spectacular, just, 'You know I really like you, Lou?' But to have a woman say them to me...phew.

My tongue poked out and wet my lips. She mimicked the action, making me want to do it all over again just to see her repeat it.

She leaned towards me, and I followed suit. This was it. The kiss I had been anticipating all afternoon, all night.

Her lips slipped onto my own as if they had always known the way. And I melted.

Slow movements at first, but they gradually began to build and build and build. Our breathing was getting heavy, panting, unrestrained. Snuffling noises matched the sloppiness and wetness of two mouths thoroughly engaged in combat. Tongues were slipping in and out...touching and caressing swollen lips. Hands began to tangle in hair, and I felt Sarah pull me into her, and I went willingly.

God, I was horny. She was horny. We were both so horny...so fucking wet. I felt her hand sneak down the side of the seat, and before I knew it, the chair was reclining, taking both of us down.

She was above me, her lips never leaving mine. Her body was hovering slightly over mine and I could feel a rhythm starting within her. Her hips were moving up and down...up and down, trying to find purchase on something.

And I should know, because I wanted the same thing. God, the ache building up within me was crazy...agony...bliss. I lifted myself up from the seat, a mammoth task in the space provided, and attempted to slip one leg between hers.

Her mouth left mine and began to kiss my face before moving down my throat, her hot tongue tracing a line down the overheated flesh. A groan left my lips, which was shortly followed by a moan from Sarah...a moan that travelled along my skin, between my breasts, down my stomach, and straight into my groin.

Hot lips suckled my neck, and I could feel Sarah's fingers fighting with the buttons of my top. Pop. Pop. Pop. Slip. Stroke. Stroke. Fuck me. The sensations rattling around were becoming overbearing. Sarah was pushing the suffocating material away to expose my bra, which by now only half covered my breasts. Wetness enveloped my nipple, bringing it to attention even more than it already was. Jesus...it was...oh, God!

Sarah's lips were in control. I felt as if my whole body was taken over by a greater being...a greater need. And I didn't care. God, no.

My breathing was laboured; my heart was working so hard I felt the vestiges of delirium take me. My fingers were in her hair, pushing her face into me...wanting her to eat me whole...eat me alive. Hips were pumping against legs...jeans chafing my need, hoping for something more...something solid.

A fleeting image of Ash's face flickered in front of me, and I felt a tinge of shame. Whatever would Ash think of me if she could see me now? Surely she would think this was wrong...this unnatural act between two women. Wouldn't she?

A pause. Only briefly, as I attempted to dispel this emotion. Sarah didn't notice and began to caress the other breast, and I pushed it into her hand in an attempt to recapture the magic of seconds before.

However hard I tried, the feeling of shame gripped me. What was I doing? This wasn't right.

My hips stopped, and I gently untangled my fingers from her hair. Sarah started to slow down as the realisation dawned that I wasn't as into it as I had been, and she lifted her face to look into my own.

Concerned eyes, darkened by the night, searched my face for some rhyme or reason. I felt my heart crack just a little when she asked, so softly, so beautifully, so tenderly, 'Lou, are you okay?' A weak smile trickled onto my face, and I nodded. 'Am I going too fast? I know...well...I think I know...this...erm...is your first time, right?'

I nodded again and found difficulty looking into her eyes, which I believed had the power to read my mind. Don't ask me why. 'God...Lou, I'm sorry...so sorry.'

With that, she lifted herself up from over me and plonked back down into the driver's seat. She stared straight ahead of her into the blackness. I lay there, sprawled backwards on the seat — my legs spread, my breasts exposed. The cool air whipped around the exposed nipple, causing the wetness to feel like ice, yet drying it off at the same time.

Slowly I sat forward, fumbled at the base of the seat to bring me back to sitting position before popping my breast back into my bra and, with unsteady fingers, buttoning up my shirt. It was totally quiet. I honestly believed I could hear the buttons pushing back through the material.

Sarah's fingers were gripping the steering wheel, and I could see her head dropping forward, her eyes scrunching up...her lips twisting into a grimace.

What if she didn't want to see me again? What if she thought I was frigid?

Panic shot through me. I know, I know...one minute I was so turned on I didn't think anything could stop me, the next — shame, then fear. In hindsight, it was probably the most natural feeling in the world for the newly discovered lesbian. Well, not even just for lesbians.

'I'm sorry, Sarah—' I didn't get the rest out.

Sarah's head shot around so quickly, I had to refocus my eyes. 'No! *I'm* sorry, Lou. God...I really like you...really like you. I've blown it, haven't I?'

Huh? 'Huh?'

Her hand came out and gripped my own, her face panicked. 'I'm sorry. I don't know what got into me. God, I went too fast, didn't I?' I tried to say she hadn't, that I wanted what she had wanted, but she didn't give me the chance.

'I promise, I won't do it again. You mean too much to me...too much. Can I have another chance? Please?'

I could hear the pleading tone in her voice. To say I was startled would be an understatement. To say I was touched would be redundant. So, I did what any right-minded girl in my position would do — I leaned over and kissed her. Hard.

An hour later saw me at home, dishevelled and smiling like a Cheshire cat. I didn't even notice that my shirt was buttoned up completely wrong and only got an inkling when I saw my mum look down at my now rumpled top.

Good job it hadn't been Jo; she wouldn't have been as forgiving. The ultimate twenty questions would have been well underway less than thirty seconds after I closed the front door. Thankfully, she was staying over at 'a friend's' house, or as I knew it...her boyfriend's. But my parents, bless them, were truly ignorant concerning their children's nocturnal meanderings.

After making them both a cup of tea (with mutterings of 'personal slave'), I feigned tiredness, trundled upstairs, performed my ablutions, and slipped under the covers.

Images of what had transpired between Sarah and me danced about my head. We hadn't progressed past the kissing and breast fondling stage, but boy...we were both panting before Sarah put the brakes on things.

I just wished she had told my libido that it wasn't getting anything more. My groin was throbbing with unrequited need, and I knew sleep would be a long time coming. Especially if I didn't find some kind of release.

I lay there in the darkness thinking of Sarah's kisses, her smile, her lips, her mouth, her tongue...on my breast, and I felt a surge of desire scoot southwards. A thin line of sweat formed on my top lip, and I licked it off, enjoying the saltiness that greeted me, enjoying the sensation.

God. I was dying. I was being consumed by a need that far outweighed anything I had ever experienced. Unconsciously, my backside pressed into the mattress, pushing my wetness into something firmer. It felt good...not exactly enough, but a start.

Inquisitive fingers slipped underneath my t-shirt and grazed the underside of my breast. Now that felt good...but still not enough.

A little more boldly, I ventured to the centre, only to be stopped by a very aroused and taut nipple standing, waiting for some company. With the tips of my nails, I flicked it from side to side, whilst quickly suppressing the gasp within my mouth. My eyes fluttered closed. That felt good...really good.

Using my index finger and thumb, I casually rolled the nipple around, causing a fluttering to concentrate in the area, causing a pooling to congregate between my legs. Hips had decided to begin a dance, as I pressed and released my hips from, and into, the mattress. I crossed my legs and gloried in the contact as I squeezed the limbs together.

Obviously, still not enough. I needed more. Definitely...something more.

Using my free hand, I brushed the outside of my shorts above the throbbing and stifled a groan. Before I knew it, my hand was inside, fingers combing through the soft downy hair before venturing lower. Much lower.

A solitary finger dipped between the folds and was greeted by a wetness. And it felt wonderful.

I pushed down even further, then pulled the lonely digit back up to nestle in the hairs again, sighing at the same time.

A second finger joined the first, and they both slipped effortlessly between the folds, straddling my clit, just adding enough pressure to make the tingles turn into sparks of light.

And back up.

And down...

And up...

The moisture was becoming thicker and more needy...or was it me becoming more needy?

I had set a rhythm up — slow pushes...slow pulls...slow pushes...slow pulls. But this was becoming increasingly difficult to keep up. The hand fingering my nipple was increasing the tempo, increasing the pressure, so therefore...harder pushes...harder pulls...quicker pushes...quicker pulls...hard quick pushes...hard, almost grasping pulls. Hips joined in, aiding the pace. The mattress was a good battleground for the fight in my hand...my increasingly wet hand...the hand that was becoming progressively more frantic with this growing desire within me...this raging desire that threatened to knock me unconscious...

But...I was loving it...loving the friction this hand, this mattress, these fingers could inflict on my unspeakable need...my growing delirium.

Nipples were forgotten as I grasped the whole breast in my hand and squeezed and rubbed. The hand down my shorts was increasing the pace, and I was panting unrestrainedly. I was clenching my legs around my hand...falling deeper and deeper into this sensation.

In my state, I imagined blue eyes in front of me...like they were part of this experience. The image only made me pump harder with both hands. My breast was loving the attention, but not as much as my wetness. God...it was *loving* it...I was loving it...loving being loved...

I was staring straight ahead, enraptured and captured by the blue gaze...the crooked smile...the twinkling blue gaze...twinkling...twinkling...twinkling...

'Fu...uh...uh...uh...ck!' It came out as a hiss as the orgasm ripped through me, leaving me shaking...leaving me wanting...leaving me craving those blue, twinkling eyes. The eyes of Ashley Richards.

Not Sarah's blue eyes...as it should have been...but Ash's.

I turned onto my side, feeling an emptiness fold over me like a blanket. I should have been ecstatic, but I wasn't, obviously. I should have felt the droplets of sleep envelop me, but I knew sleep would be a long time coming. I should have been content with what I had with Sarah. But I wasn't.

She wasn't enough for me, although I wished she was. Because the person who could ease this ache didn't think of me that way. And it was something I had to live with.

Ashley Richards. Now *she* would be enough.

Chapter Nine

Tuesday night eventually crawled around and stood languidly at my door, saying in an off-hand manner, 'Whatever.' I must have lost weight, as my appetite plummeted and everything I put in my mouth tasted like, and had the texture of, cardboard.

Sarah had called just before I had left and asked if she could see me that night. I didn't even feel bad when I told her I had made other arrangements, but when I heard the disappointed, 'Oh…right,' and then the silence, I suggested Friday. I could hear her smile down the phone.

Jo had been watching from the doorway, feigning reading the back of the newspaper, but I knew by her stance she was ear wigging. As I placed the receiver back down, her eyes popped over the top of the page, and I could see a question forming. But then…nothing.

It was just that brief look that put me on my guard. I felt exposed all of a sudden, well…all of the time, and believed everyone could see what I was up to…how different I was from everyone else. Sadness washed over me so quickly, only to disperse like a sprinkling of water on a summer's day. The urge to tell her rose to the surface, and I had to physically rein it in.

I loved my sister…still do…but I didn't know how to tell her I wasn't who she thought I was. Deep down I thought she would be fine and help me make the right decision. But there was still an area of doubt, which played with my sensibilities. What if she thought I was a freak? What if she disowned me, told me I was an abomination? I couldn't bear to think of her thinking of me that way. You could say I always tried to be what she wanted me to be…whatever that was.

For two days, I had been a bag of nerves. Don't ask me why…I couldn't tell you. Well, apart from the fact that I was infatuated with one tall, dark-haired beauty who still thought of me as her six-year-old friend. And apart from the fact that I was supposed to be involved with another woman. A woman…Jesus! A woman.

I digress.

I met Ash at Granada Bowling in Belle Vue. Quite out of the way, but definitely worth the trek on the 317 bus with all the people who were going into Manchester for the evening. I did feel a little out of place, sitting on the top deck with all the smokers, watching the world go by. But I didn't care…I was going to see Ash. And that made me smile out of the window like an idiot.

I had always…and I mean ALWAYS…been shit at bowling. I was definitely 'Miss Gutter Ball 1984'. Every well-meant lob with the excruciatingly heavy ball (with the sticky holes) ended up rolling complacently down the side and into the gutter. I did manage to scrape a 36 in the first game, which I was quite proud of. I ignored all the well-laid advice Ash told me. I think that was more out of embarrassment than thinking I knew better.

Eventually I caved. Ash, my saviour, took it upon herself to teach me how to bowl. Her first move was to change the weight of the ball I had been brandishing about from a 14 pound to a 10.

Secondly...and this is the point I liked the most...she stood behind me, manoeuvring me into position using the arrows — the feeling of her standing so close behind me her body pressing into my back and side, the smell of her filling my nostrils like an enchantment.

Whatever she said, I can't tell you. Whatever she did is a blur. All I could concentrate on was the feeling of her hands moving over my arms and back...even the view of the top of her head bewitched me as she knelt down in front of me moving my feet into position. I could see her lips moving, but I couldn't hear a word. I was deaf...and mute, by all accounts. I just nodded like the proverbial village idiot and grinned vacantly.

Ash was a good player. Of course, in comparison to me, anyone was. But to put it into some kind of real perspective, she scored 186 in her first game. And I think I put her off...trying to hold in all that laughter. Yeah...sounds about right.

Obviously, with all my free tuition, my game escalated — to a grand score of 92. To Ash's 179. I was getting better and she was *going down*, which I took great delight in ribbing her about. Mutterings of, 'I've gone up fifty-six and you've lost seven points.'

She just smiled, that crooked smile, but the rest of her face said, 'You wait, lady.'

But I was flying by this stage. Not because of the score...not by any stretch of the imagination. It was just being with her...her and me...Lou and Ash...Ash and Lou. My heart was singing. I was floating, and my blood was bubbling like a wild stream rushing down the side of a mountain.

Yep. That corny. But that's how I felt...corny. My blood was doing Julie Andrews impressions, and I was loving it. Until the third set.

I should have quit whilst I was ahead. I should have plucked off those freaky striped shoes, jumped on the 317, and gone home whilst I still had any credibility left. But no. I stayed and took it like a man...woman...teenager...whatever.

Ash was relentless in her heckling. I thought she was trying to help me, not make me fuck up more than usual. Just as I was about to throw the ball down the alley, she would cough, sneeze, mutter something obscene (which I quite liked). Generally, she was out to teach me a lesson.

After the fourth consecutive gutter ball, Ash jumped out of her seat, raced over to me, and as I was nearly fully around, threw her arms around me to deliver a bone-crushing hug. My feet lifted off the floor as she swept me in a circle, the room spinning around me, but not because of the movement.

It was the kiss on the cheek that was my undoing. A full smacker right on the left cheek, the onomatopoeic slap on the skin informed me it was slightly wet, as I had no sensation left in any part of my body...apart from the places where her body encountered mine. Skin pulsed and grew hot under hers, and once again, I was totally lost in her.

I didn't even realise I had done it, kissed her, I mean. I felt such a fool...but I couldn't help pushing my face into the nape of her neck and inhaling her scent. She smelled perfect...perfect...perfect...and I was lost in her for those brief seconds before she lowered me back to the ground. I missed the closeness of her, but she didn't let me go straight away. I looked up into her face, and a small splodge of air slipped out from my mouth.

Her eyes were slightly hooded, and the cocksure smile she had sported had vanished, to be replaced by a look of confusion...of indecision. Lips slightly parted in wonder: the fullness mesmerising. I wanted to stretch up onto my toes and just...brush my lips across them. Just the once...and I would be contented.

Just the once.

But no. Reason gripped me before I made an even bigger fool of myself than I already had, and I pulled out of the encirclement of her arms. I watched them fall limply to her sides, and she looked a little dishevelled...but beautiful. Obviously.

'Your turn.' Was that my voice? Small and distant? I felt like a ventriloquist's dummy, the mouth moving but the noise coming from another person.

She nodded but stood there for a few more seconds before she walked past me, picked up her ball, and threw it down the lane without even focusing. And she still knocked down nine pins.

And I lost...miserably...49 to her 198.

I think it was all the touching...or the thoughts of touching that made me lose my ability to focus, big time. It was worth it, though.

After the games, we sat in the café area sipping Coke in polystyrene cups with straws. What is it about drinking Coke through a straw that makes you feel like a kid? Or maybe it was sitting with Ash that made me feel like a kid. Who knows?

We chatted as if nothing had happened, although my mind kept on drifting to the feel of her arms, hands, body...the smell of her...the longing to taste her, however briefly.

What was wrong with me? Couldn't I just have her friendship?

The internal struggle was trying to choke me. I wasn't concentrating on what she was saying, and before I knew it I was agreeing to bowling lessons every Tuesday. Not that I minded seeing her every Tuesday, but...bowling? My arm was throbbing as it was. Jesus! I'd look like a one-armed weightlifter before I even hit the hundred mark.

But I would see Ash...definitely see Ash...once a week. I could feel the smile sneak up from a dark place inside me and trickle onto my face.

That was definitely worth the pain.

Stephen picked us up from outside the bowling alley. It saved me clambering on the bus by myself, as I didn't really fancy travelling back on my own. Buses at night were not the safest of places for a young girl to be. Not to mention the fact that Ash would have been getting on a different one, and this way I got to spend just that extra bit of time with her.

Thankfully, Tracy was nowhere to be seen. I couldn't deal with her glaring looks. No one mentioned her absence, which gave the indication she was still in their bad books.

I felt like gloating.

Ash insisted sitting in the back with me, even though the passenger seat was empty.

Now that was the straw that broke the camel's back. The smile I sported could definitely have been defined as a gloating one.

Chapter Ten

The next few weeks were a seesaw of emotions. On one end of the seesaw was my growing relationship with Sarah, whilst at the other was my definite attraction for Ash.

Don't get me wrong; I didn't just see Ash when we went bowling. No. We saw each other quite often at college, had lunch, or a coffee, and we did see each other at least one evening over the weekend, most weekends anyway.

Every time I saw her, this innate need to be more than what we were would fill me up, and I found it more and more difficult not to blurt out how I felt. This led to a rising sexual frustration that would rival any teenage boy's...*that* I can guarantee.

These hormones, these wild wonderings of my sexually befuddled brain, were tantamount to agony, and the only recourse I had was Sarah.

Poor Sarah. Poor sweet Sarah. I really liked her...honestly I did. But she wasn't...well, she wasn't...Ash.

But being filled with these raging hormones, hormones that needed assuaging, what else could I do but to try and get some satisfaction from the only person I could. And that wasn't me...as I had nearly formed calluses on my right hand...my left hand...my fingers... You get the drift.

So Sarah it was. And I did feel bad, but I also felt incredibly horny, too.

Evenings with Sarah had developed into something more carnal than I had anticipated from the first night at the cinema. I was still wary about who knew — and nobody did — but I was finding the deceit difficult to conceal, especially as I would flush beetroot every time somebody mentioned either of their names, even though I wasn't involved with Ash.

Sarah and I hadn't had sex as of yet, but it wasn't for the want of me trying. Our explorations had escalated, but not below the waistband. The upper halves of our bodies were explored thoroughly, with hands, fingers, mouth, lips, and teeth, but the achingly wet part went without.

Sarah was cautious...a little too cautious. I think she was still wary of frightening me off, although me trying to shove my hands down her pants should have convinced her otherwise, not to mention my begging her to let me touch her...for her to touch me.

It was just before Christmas that I got my wish.

After a very sexually frustrating afternoon drooling over my unobtainable friend, I met Sarah, nearly panting. She had to physically drag my hands from her groin at one point. As I sat there breathless, willing my throbbing need to behave, she asked me a very simple, but extremely promising question.

'What are your plans for Saturday night?'

Not much of a question, I hear you say. But I haven't finished yet.

'Would you like to stay over at my house? My parents are away for the weekend.'

Now…I imagine you are thinking I whooped for joy, or jumped her bones, or screamed out, 'Yes!' into the darkness. But no. I sat there and stared at her — mute…stupid…silent…stunned.

It was here. At last. My chance to relieve this tension, and I couldn't respond. Inside my head I was screaming, 'Tell her, you idiot…say yes!' But on the outside I looked like a statue, completely rigid, emotionless.

Only with Sarah's movement…her nervous movement…the slight shaking of her hand…did I break free from the spell that had befallen me. My eyes moved first, as I watched her gingerly take the steering wheel in both her hands and slowly increase the pressure. She was facing forward, her eyes digesting the night sky, trying to appear nonchalant but coming out pensive instead.

I lifted my hand slowly to her cheek and brushed my fingers down her face, past her jaw, down her throat, until they rested on her collarbone.

Blue eyes dipped to take in her hands before turning their gaze into my own waiting green eyes. It was not until I knew I had her full attention that I uttered those three little words, softly and tinged with promise: 'I'd love to.'

The smile that rained over her face could have melted the ice caps in the Antarctic.

We had a date. And my aching need couldn't wait, although my heart wasn't too sure.

Saturday night came around. Eventually. My shattered nerves said, 'About bloody time,' as seven-thirty arrived, and so did Sarah. And I had only left her two hours before.

My parents didn't say a word about me staying out all night at a friend's house. I hadn't told Jo, as I had only seen her briefly. I had walked in from work, and she had been on her way out to meet her boyfriend at the ice skating rink in Altrincham.

Not that I could have told her anyway. I couldn't lie to her about what I was up to and why I had to stay over at Sarah's house when there was a perfectly good bus service running from her house to mine. And she might have gotten her boyfriend to pick me up, as they would have to pass Sarah's to get home.

I'm procrastinating, aren't I?

Okay…I'll skip the journey…the offer of a drink…the desperate need to use the bathroom every two minutes…the polite conversation…everything up until the part I know you want to hear.

The consummation.

The deed.

The act.

The bountiful display of the beast with two backs.

The event that changed my views on life, love, and sex. The event I believed kicked out the last clinging vestiges of heterosexuality. The event that sliced open the bare longings of a sixteen-year-old girl in lust.

I knew it was on the cards...I knew tonight was going to be the night...I knew I was shitting my pants. But I still didn't expect it, if you know what I mean.

We were sitting on the sofa listening to an album Sarah's dad had brought back from his trip to the States. Bruce Springsteen's gravelly voice had just growled, *Hey, little girl, is your daddy home,* when she made her move. Her hand came out and caressed my thigh, and I nearly dropped the glass of wine I was nursing.

I got a bad desire...

Tell me about it, Bruce.

Sarah leaned over and gently released the glass from my death-like grip, placing it on the table at the side of the couch.

I can take you higher...

Her face came closer to mine, and her lips brushed against my mouth in a butterfly kiss.

I tasted her lipstick and leaned forward to capture those lips again, a little harder this time. I could feel her pushing back into me, and I slipped backwards onto the sofa, taking Sarah with me.

The kissing was getting more heated, and my heart was fighting to saw through my chest and scream into the night.

At night I wake with the sheets soaking wet...

Like my underwear. Definitely soaked.

My hands were on a mission and were definitely going under cover. As her tongue slipped into my mouth, the last thing I heard was...

Only you can cool my desire.

I'm on fire.

Oh, yeah...bring it on.

The kissing was passionate. All my inhibitions had packed their bags and headed for the airport. I was on a one-way trip to Satisfactionville, and Sarah was the driver. And God, could she drive!

Drive me to the brink of want...of need...of desire. Drive me to the insanity of a yearning to be touched that resisted rhyme or reason.

God, she was hot...and I was dying...she was so fucking hot...and I was squirming underneath her, my hands scrabbling for purchase on her bare flesh. Her fingers fumbled with the buttons of my shirt, nervous fingers struggling with the smallness of the shiny adornments, trying to force them out of their slits, her lips digging deeper into my own.

Cool fingers slipped underneath my cotton shirt and tentatively stroked below my nipple, which was ready and waiting for contact. Her thumb pushed the material down and rubbed the nipple, flesh on flesh. Like an impatient child, I pushed my breast into her hand, wanting her to take it all...move things along.

My hips were pushing upwards, striving to introduce one wet need into something firmer. And then back down. And back up...down and...up...constant...rhy...thm...up...staying...and...pull...ling back.

The contact of her thigh felt wonderful, the feel of her hand on my breast, divine. The pressure of her mouth on mine...bliss.

It wasn't enough; I needed more. God, how I needed more. I gripped her backside, such a firm, rounded backside, and pulled her into me.

Still not enough.

One of my hands snaked underneath the base of her bra, cupped her soft breast, and squeezed. Tracing my thumb across the erect bud, almost expert in this field by now.

Her moan filled my mouth, so I squeezed harder. Another groan...well, more like a moan. I tore my lips from hers and rained tiny kisses over her chin and throat. She raised her head to allow me access, which I took gladly, sucking and teasing the skin between my lips, silently begging for her to strip me naked and ravish me.

'Jesus...Lou...God...' I kept on kissing her throat, 'I need...we need...' I know. Tell me about it. 'We need to go upstairs.'

My lips pulled away, realisation dawning on me. I was just about to go upstairs and have sex. With a woman. First time...with a woman...or anyone, for that matter.

I didn't know what to do.

Don't get me wrong — I knew what I wanted to do, I just didn't know how to do it.

My face must have said it all. I actually felt my jaw drop and my face slacken. Sarah pulled away from me and ducked her head down to capture my gaze. 'What's up, love?'

I couldn't answer her, but I did close my mouth. Nothing more of a sexual turnoff than a gobsmacked expression.

Sarah looked at me intently, concern radiating from her. She thought I was backing out, that I didn't want this. 'It's not you.' More concerned looks, and I hastily added, 'I just...well...I...'

Confusion scrambled onto her features, suddenly to be replaced by a growing understanding, then a smile...a reassuring smile that warmed my belly and made me feel a little more in control. 'Don't worry, honey. You can leave that up to me.' I didn't know if I liked the sound of that, and my expression said so. 'I mean...well...I'll show you...guide you. It's a matter of doing what feels right.'

That was better. I planted a soft kiss on her lips and nodded in acceptance of what was to come. Without a word, she took my hand and kissed the palm as I curled my fingers around her chin.

And from a distance, I could hear my voice saying, 'Let's go.'

Nervous? You bet. Scared? Granted. Excited? I think that's a given.

Sarah led me upstairs to her room, her thumb brushing the back of my hand reassuringly, taking shy looks over her shoulder as we neared the place where I would soon lose my innocence and hopefully — the aching in my gut, chest, and groin.

Her room was like any other student's room, but I could tell she had tidied it up for my visit; the smell of polish still hung in the air. The lamp next to her double bed was on already, and the corner at the top of the duvet was folded back in invitation.

I heard the door close behind me and then felt Sarah come up behind. I closed my eyes and waited for her touch. I didn't have to wait long.

Her hands slipped onto my shoulders, and she gently caressed them. My eyes fluttered; it felt good. Her body came closer to mine, and I could feel her breath hitting my neck in short gasps. Then her lips...tentative in their quest...hovered over the nape of my neck, making all the short hairs at its base quiver.

I could feel her push herself into me, her breasts against my back, her hands slipping down my arms in one long stroke only to snake around my waist and up the front, to cup my breasts.

Nipples strained...I pushed into her hands...the butterflies in my stomach transforming into something more carnal...more wanting...more...*just* more.

Before I knew what was happening, I was naked. Sarah had slipped my clothes from my body...and I let her, completely unresisting under her hands...her lips...her mouth...her tongue. My knees were beginning to weaken, all my energy concentrating on the building sensations that were crawling over me like a rash...a very...nice...rash...a very...demanding rash...an erotic rash...a consuming rash.

I turned in her arms and cupped her face to stare in her eyes. I don't know what I was looking for, but for a split second I felt the rush of disappointment, as what I had been searching for wasn't there. I carried on anyway. She turned her face and planted a delicate kiss on my palm, reassuring me with her eyes.

Her lips were moist and inviting; her flesh was pliant and warm. My hands were nervous...shaking...trying to fulfil a need that I knew would kill me or drive me mad.

I undressed her, marvelling at her body, the body of a woman, the body of the woman I was going to sleep with. Well, not exactly sleep.

The bed was soft yet firm as I sat on the edge. Sarah sat opposite. Touching, stroking, caressing the fears and anxieties from me.

Desire was building and forcing the fear below...and down...and away. Mouths sought mouths, tongues sought tongues. Nipples were licked and nipped. Stomachs were treated to tentative fingers searching southward, southward to the pooling wetness of want that had collected around my dominant need.

Fingers parted lips and pushed down to the core of the moisture...the rising flood...the pit of delight. And like a good student, I followed her actions, to be greeted with a short gasp from her parted mouth, the air rushing against my face.

I could feel myself falling backwards...in slow motion, the movements sure and steady...a complete juxtaposition to how I was feeling.

A hot body covered my own — smooth and supple and ripe for the taking. Skin brushed against skin, the sweat mingling in a growing sense of neediness, the rhythm becoming erratic.

I pushed my thigh between Sarah's legs, and she clamped her own around it, capturing our foraging fingers inside. Her hips picked up the tempo, her breathing hoarse and fast...my breathing keeping pace...my hand rubbing her clit with growing confidence. I was mimicking her actions...nothing was truly me...nothing was what I had thought of myself...just a copy. But that didn't stop it from feeling good...from feeling incredibly good.

I looked into her face...grimacing with promise...her teeth biting her bottom lip as she thrust herself into me...onto me...her hand becoming more confused. I knew she was close.

'Fuck me, Lou! For God's sake, fuck me!' But...I thought I was. I was doing everything she was doing. 'Fingers...God...fingers...inside...now...'

Ah!

I lowered my hand to her entrance and waited outside, revelling in the feel of her juices dripping down before pushing myself into her...just one finger...slipping effortlessly...'More!' Just the one word, which was gasped out into my neck, her own hand raging on my craving desire.

A second followed, then a third. I could feel her pushing down and swallowing them inside, the tightening of her walls crushing my fingers as a low keening moan broke free from her. I knew she was cumming...and I forgot my own want and watched her...watched her...mesmerised by the agonisingly rapturous expression distorting her beautiful face as she came...falling forwards...her mouth open on my throat...the wail of her orgasm bouncing off my skin just before she sucked on my flesh.

Then I felt her smile, her lips twisting in the post-coital smile of the satisfied. Teeth nipped my neck and travelled upwards, along my jaw line, until they reached my mouth, where they covered my lips in a wet, contented kiss...soft and consuming.

Her hand came up to my breast and teased around the edge, slowly, until expert fingers rolled the nipple around, gently pinching at the same time. A spark of adrenaline rushed from all parts of my body, dissected itself and charged either to my breast or a more southerly region. Both were ready. Both were willing. Both were stoking a fire of expectation.

'Your turn, love.'

With that, Sarah began her descent...kissing and nibbling all my exposed skin along the way, building and prepping the fire burning below decks. The once smouldering heat was turning into something a little out of control. And it felt good. So fucking good.

Fingers reached their destination before her head and began to slip through the waiting wetness before moving to one side as her mouth lowered and...a tongue...licked...

'Jesus!' The sensation was mind blowing. Tender yet perfectly pressured along my clit. Just the tip of her tongue slipping with practiced ease along the top. My backside pushed upwards, forcing my want into her face. She pulled back, keeping the same amount of pressure.

I felt a flicker at my wetness, then moaned as she dipped at my opening. I wanted to spear myself onto that thick, wet muscle, allow her to sample the juices she had conjured. The flat of her tongue rested at the base until it began its ascent, coating my clit in an unbearably slow movement that was...just...right.

And then she went down again...then up...then down...up and down...slow and sure...then a little quicker...and harder...and my hips joined in the dance of the mouth and the tongue...making a threesome of rhythm...a glorious rhythm...a tempo leading to the upcoming crescendo.

Her hands grasped my hips and pulled me into her face, making exquisite contact. Lips covered my clit and sucked, and I could feel the orgasm raging...racing...ravaging through me like a stampede — unstoppable...dangerous. I watched her head bobbing up and down, saw the whitening of her knuckles as she gripped my pelvis stopping me from meting out my desire in panicked thrusts.

Then it all changed, the image I mean. The dark brown hair seemed black in the light; the rounded cheekbones looked chiselled...the eyelashes darker...the arms more toned and longer. She flicked her eyes to meet mine, and I saw them lighter...I saw them twinkle...

'FFFFFuuuuuuuccccccccckkkkk yeeeeeeeeeeeeeesssssssss!' I was over, my hands tangled in her hair, fingers twisting the thick locks into a frenzy of knots...hips grinding into her with a need for satisfaction. My eyes were tightly closed, and they were begging my brain to keep the image of those cheekbones...those eyelashes...those eyes, as I rode out my cumming on someone else's face.

God, I felt alive. I felt every nerve ending stand up and scream, 'YES!' as I dragged out all the sputtering sparks that had helped me reach my goal. Blood pumped to the key spot and collected, swelling the bud that was captured in Sarah's mouth. My breathing was erratic, and my chest heaved laboriously, but my heart was empty. I felt as if I had sold myself for a quick fix...sold out my heart for an orgasm. I felt shallow.

Sarah lifted her eyes to meet mine, and a stupid grin covered her face. My heart ached with guilt. I had used her. Used her. Used her to forget my attraction to Ash. I felt awful.

My smile was weak to say the least, but I don't think Sarah noticed...just thought I was weak from my climax. She clambered up my body, placing soft, wet kisses along the way until she reached my mouth. I could taste myself on her lips — musky...a little sweet...different. And evidence of what I had just done. But it didn't stop me licking around her lips trying to capture the taste of my traitorous body.

By all the soft stroking, kissing, and nuzzling she was doing, I think Sarah wanted to go at it again but I just couldn't...not then. My kisses became more chaste, intermixed with shy smiles and tentative strokes, until she finally accepted there wasn't going to be a round two, at least not right away.

She slipped to my side and pulled me over to her, my face pressing into the dip of her throat. It felt comfortable, lying on my side being held by her. Not fantastic, or something that filled me with peace or completeness...just comfortable.

Deft fingers stroked my arm, calming me for some reason, lulling my eyes closed...chasing away the demons of doubt...allowing me to doze off.

And that's how the evening ended — me in Sarah's arms, sleeping the sleep of the exhausted.

The exhaustion came courtesy of the depletion of emotions that had ravaged my body — the guilt, the yearning...the longing for something else...something different...*someone*...different. And the knowledge that *that* someone could never be mine.

Dawn found me lying on my side with my back to Sarah. She was spooned up behind me with her arm draped over my stomach; I could feel her breath on my skin. It was pleasant, but not the all-consuming emotion I had been expecting after making love for the first time.

I liked Sarah. A lot. She had introduced me to the part of me that was so well hidden I would have needed an archaeologist to uncover it. I liked kissing her, touching her...making love to her. I liked the sensations her mouth, tongue, and fingers brought out in me. I enjoyed the orgasm...the first one I'd experienced *with* someone else other rather than by myself.

But I didn't like the fact it wasn't Ash.

And I didn't like the fact I had used Sarah to fulfil the constant craving I had for my friend.

What to do?

Did I tell Sarah? Tell Ash? Go without sex? Rely solely on my right hand for comfort and contentment?

Or did I play the game — accept what I had with Sarah and just carry on?

Thoughts whirled around in my head, thoughts of Ash versus Sarah...and although I really wanted Ash to win, reason made me go with Sarah. The old adage 'better the Devil you know'.

A sigh escaped, and I felt Sarah's arm tighten around me.

Here goes nothing...or everything, depending on how you looked at it.

I turned in her embrace and began to kiss her throat. A contented whimper broke from her, and her fingers trailed along my spine, down to my arse, covering the flesh with goosebumps.

The fire began again...at first a flicker...then a flame...and then control was given over as I fell into her and her desire for me. Hungry kisses, touches, and whispered words fed the fire. I just had to be careful I didn't get burned...or burn Sarah along the way.

Chapter Eleven

Later that day, I left Sarah and made my way home. My heart was heavy, but I was definitely sore in certain places...a nice kind of sore, if you get my drift.

Jo was waiting for me as I entered the bedroom and hardly gave me a moment to catch my bearings before she bombarded me with questions. Mainly, where had I spent the night.

It was too much. The heaviness in my chest split open and seeped through the rest of my body, seeking release. I stumbled towards the bed, bag dropping to the floor, and fell into a heap, barely catching myself.

The sob wracked through my body and broke out into the stunned silence of the room — a distinct wail...a howl of agony...a definite realisation of what I had done. I had had sex with someone for the wrong reasons...used someone to satiate my own longings. And I was ashamed.

Ashamed.

Ashamed of my own inability to say no. Ashamed because I used that sweet girl. Ashamed because I enjoyed it. But mainly I was ashamed because I was gay...and I had held it inside, bottling it all away to fester and become something sordid and freakish. I knew it wasn't. How can two people loving each other be wrong, whatever sex they are?

The thought of telling anyone made me nauseous, collected in my throat, and physically choked me. Tears rained down my face, and I could feel the heaving sobs rattle and spill onto the covers of my bed. Jo was behind me, her smooth comforting hand on my shoulder, softly rubbing along the heaving muscles as she tried to soothe me.

Which only made things worse. My sobbing increased. I could hear her trying to shush me...calm me...comfort me...words jumbling over each other in an attempt to redeem themselves...to redeem me, in some unknown way.

I felt her lift me, turn me, capture me in her comforting embrace, and I buried my face into the safety of her, believing this would be the last time it would happen.

I cried...and cried...and cried some more. Jo stroked my face, removing the tears with loving fingers, planting soft sisterly kisses on my head, gently rocking me into a disturbing sense of oblivion.

'Come on, Lou...it can't be all that bad.' And I was off again, turning my face into her and burrowing deep, trying to hide my shame. 'If you are crying for what I think you're crying for, then don't. It doesn't bother me who you sleep with.'

I stopped mid sob. It kind of jammed in my throat in surprise, until it trickled out, all the power from it evaporating.

I lay there and...waited.

All I could hear was our breathing (mine, definitely more ragged) and the sound of my heart chasing the blood back into the shocked veins in a valiant attempt to bring all my senses back on line.

'What do you mean?' It came out small, distant, defensive.

Jo sucked in a breath, deep and full. 'I mean...I don't care who you sleep with, I'll still love you no matter what.'

I lifted myself up and stared into her face. She couldn't mean what I thought she meant. How on earth would she know who I slept with, or who I wanted to sleep with, for that matter?

Hiccupping sobs broke free, sobs of a child who has cried too long and too hard, and I met her eyes full on. They were clear and focused. Truthful. Caring. Open. Just Jo. My Jo. My sister, Jo.

I felt exposed. All the experiences of the night before played themselves out in my head. I felt my head shake itself from side to side, trying to dispel the image of Sarah between my legs...my hand on her wet...

'Lou?'

Reality snapped back, and I stared at her in awe. Once again Jo had shown she loved me...whatever. And at that moment I needed all the love I could get. But did she really know what, or should I say who, I was crying about? How would she feel when she realised I had used Sarah? Would she be as forgiving then?

'Tell me. Whatever it is, I will still love you. I'm your sister; you should know me by now.'

Images of Jo comforting me when my life crashed ten years ago. Sounds of her voice comforting me after bad dreams...words of advice...caring messages over the years. The feel of her hugs when I felt low...the pat on the back when I had done anything good...the ear I moaned to when I felt like a moan. Her laughter when I told her a funny story...the tears when I explained why animal testing was cruel...the jokes...the friendship...the always knowing she would be there... No matter what.

And she had been. Always there...always there...for me. In every way, shape and form, she had always been there.

Why would now be any different? She loved me. And I loved her.

The breath I sucked in seemed ice cold in my throat...like the winds of change. This was it. I had to tell her what had happened. I had to let her know who I was...what I had done.

I sat up, leaned over to my bedside cabinet, and snatched a tissue from the box. Jo watched intently as I wiped my eyes and then blew my nose vigorously. I was shaking inside, quaking with fear, but I knew this was the right thing to do. I had to come clean, had to share this secret with someone before it burst from me.

I fiddled about with my top, smoothing the wrinkles to no avail...wasting time. Jo sat there, silent, waiting, while I pratted about...nervous, swallowing rapidly.

I could tell she was just about to say something, but I beat her to it. 'I'm gay.' Short and to the point.

Jo's face didn't change at all. She just stared at me and allowed the simple sentence to be fully digested. As images of her slapping me ran through my head, I thought I had done the wrong thing.

She made her move, and I physically shrank away as her hand stretched out towards me. Her eyes clouded with dismay as she realised what I thought she was going to do, and she stilled her movement before pushing a stray lock of hair behind my ear, cocking her head to the side to stare into my eyes. Such green eyes...a little lighter than my own, but filled with...understanding.

'I know.'

Huh? How did she know? I only found out a few months back that I had feelings for women.

'How?'

'Just call it sisterly intuition. Sometimes I know you better than you know yourself.'

Relief formed and swirled inside me, but I didn't feel I had control over my feelings yet. Jo knew. Jo didn't care. Jo still loved me.

It all seemed too much to accept, and I had to quickly swallow the tears down again as she took my hand and gave it a squeeze. 'It's not the end of the world, you know.' I looked up at her, and she smiled at me, a soft sweet smile that seemed intended to reassure me. Tentatively, she sucked in a breath, bit her lip, and asked the million-dollar question.

'Did you stay at Ash's last night?'

'Why would I do that?' At least I think that's what I said.

'Well...erm...' She coughed. 'I thought you...her...erm...well...you know.'

'Me and Ash! Together!'

Jo leaned backwards, probably to escape the loudness of my voice. Her face showed surprise at my shrill tone and look of total disbelief. I drew in a sharp breath and tried to mentally fiddle with the volume settings of my voice box before repeating my previous statements, but now as questions. 'Me and Ash? Together?'

'I thought...well...there has always been... Oh never mind.' She looked nervous, to say the least, but not as nervous as I felt. I was sitting there, in my bedroom, telling my sister I was gay, and her response was to think I was shagging my childhood friend. If only.

Yes...if only.

Sadness welled up inside and began to squirm its way upwards and outwards. I wanted to be with Ash. God, did I! And what would Jo make of me sleeping with Sarah, knowing she wasn't the one I wanted to be sleeping with?

'It's Sarah.'

I could tell Jo didn't know who I was talking about. Sarah had never come into the house; she had always met me outside. The closest she had been was the front door.

'Sarah...who I work with.' A spark of recognition struck, and then she smiled the smile of someone who is completely without a clue. 'We started seeing each other about three months ago, but...' Could I actually say it? 'We only...erm...slept...together...*forthefirsttimelastnight.*' The last bit was a bit rushed, but at least I got it out, although my face was near incandescent by this stage.

So was Jo's. But there was something else underlying the red glow. Confusion. And this confused me...even more than I already was.

Seconds turned into minutes, and minutes felt like hours. The air in the room was becoming smothering, and I could feel the heat travelling up my body in waves, achingly aware I should say something...anything. Observations such as 'What about United, then?' didn't seem the right way to go for some reason. A bit more time elapsed before I put my blonde brain into gear and came out with a well-thought-through question. 'What's the matter?'

Pure genius, if I say so myself. Short. To the point. Succinct, yet oddly full of possibility. I watched her squirm on the bed, looking at Cliff on the walls for some kind of support. 'For God's sake, Jo, ask me...or tell me...just say something.'

Her lips pursed, readying themselves for action, and then...nothing. I stared at her. The nerves rustling around in my stomach had mogged off, fed up with the wait to flutter and be all dramatic. I poked her in the ribs, which brought a much-desired smile to her face, and I felt her physically relax. 'What is it, Jo? Have I disappointed you?'

'Why on earth would you say that?'

'By not being what you wanted me to be, you know — straight.'

The next bit surprised even me, and I had known this girl as long as I could remember.

She laughed...head back laughing...laughed...yep...laughed. I know...I'm repeating myself, but she...l-a-u-g-h-e-d.

Not happy. Not in the slightest. There I was, pouring out my innermost secret to the one person who I respected and loved, and she sat there laughing *AFTER* telling me she already knew. I wasn't a happy camper, by any stretch of the imagination.

Ire niggled inside me, and I wanted to stand up and stamp my foot, in the most adult way possible, obviously. But I didn't. I just sat there and glowered, waiting for her to stop, which she eventually did when she noticed my straight thin lips and firm jaw.

'Sorry...I'm sorry, Lou. It's just...just...'

'What? Just what?' I glared, and she tried to stop the spluttering laughter escaping from her mouth. So, like the injured party, I glared some more.

'You.' Well, that made me feel better, that's for sure. 'How on earth could you feel I could ever be disappointed in you, whatever you did?' She put her arm around my shoulder and pulled my stiff body into her arms. 'Maybe we don't always agree on things, or I don't like the things that you do...' I opened my mouth to interrupt. 'No, hear me out.' With that she shoved my head firmly underneath her arm, holding it in place.

'As I was saying,' I could feel the words rattling around her chest, echoey, thudding, 'I could never be disappointed in you...ever. It is all about acceptance...accepting we are not infallible. Accepting there are times in our life when we say and do things we are not proud of, but accepting we made a mistake and moving on.'

Her grip loosened around me, and I took the opportunity to look into her face. A weird angle, though, as I could see her face from the chin up, but she was still perfect in my eyes. She was staring straight ahead, totally focused on what she was saying.

'So, Lou, accept yourself, accept who and what you are...what you have done, and what you will do...faults and all. And if people love you,' a soft kiss on my forehead, 'whatever it is, they will eventually accept you. Disappointment is a brief emotion, something we look back and learn from, not something we build our lives upon.'

Wow. What a speech. Now, you already know how much I love my sister, but this took the biscuit. I felt my chest swell with pride at even knowing someone like this.

It was so true. We spend our lives in fear of disappointing others, but we fail to think that within this time we are disappointing ourselves. Something to chew over...definitely.

We sat there, snuggled up on my bed, and just listened to the sounds of each other's breathing. I felt so calm, so at peace, so...well...serene in a way, although I knew the feeling wouldn't last.

Jo broke the serenity.

'I honestly thought you were shagging Ash. You go on enough about how bloody fantastic she is.'

I shot up, peace...tranquillity...calmness shot to pieces, and my response came out so quickly, I think I nearly gave the game away. 'You're joking, right? Me and Ash...*as if*.' Maybe not the best response, but the speed and the fake tone of incredulity made up for my feeling of guilt.

She laughed again, a knowing laugh, a cocky laugh that made me wriggle with teenage anger. 'Right. I believe you, but thousands wouldn't.' And she laughed again.

Bugger.

Chapter Twelve

Christmas was just a week away, and college was coming to the end of term. Flyers announced a 'Chrimbo Get Together' at the Students' Union and promises of cheap drinks, music, and 'Lots Lots More', whatever that entailed. It was to be hosted on the same night as Sarah's Christmas get-together at Uni, and she had asked me to go.

But...Ash had asked me to go to the one at college.

Decisions, decisions. No contest. Ash won out.

Sarah was gutted I wouldn't be going with her, as she had planned something 'special' for afterwards. The worst part was I didn't even feel guilty, well...I did a little...erm...okay...I did feel guilty. She looked so lost when I told her I had already made arrangements, and she even offered to skip her own shindig and come to mine.

My heart stopped in my chest. No. She couldn't come to my do — Ash would be there, and...and...and...

And what? It's not as if you two are sleeping together, is it? Well, I am sleeping with Sarah, but not Ash...so where's the harm?

What if Sarah suspected I like Ash?

What if Ash suspected my relationship with Sarah? And was disgusted?

No. I couldn't let that happen. The more distance I could keep between those two the better.

Don't get me wrong, they both knew the other existed, but they didn't know what I thought about the other or what I did with one that I wanted to do with the other.

Yes...definitely confusing. Imagine how I felt.

Friday night came, and I was a bag of nerves for some reason or another. I was to meet Ash, and the rest of them, at seven-thirty, and my stomach actually got there before I did.

Wizard's *I Wish it Could be Christmas Every Day* greeted me as I entered the smoky bar. Students packed the place to the rafters, and all I could see was a sea of red Santa hats. Santa hats be damned. I couldn't concentrate on anything but looking for Ash.

It took me fifteen minutes to actually find her, well...for her to find me.

Having nearly given up hope, I had just gone to the bar to grab a drink, when I felt her behind me. When I say felt her, I mean *felt* her...*felt* her presence. It was like an electric charge scooting up from the base of my spine and into my hairline...shuddering shocks.

It was then I nearly swooned. The charges, or sparks, intensified exponentially, and raced through me looking for appeasement. She placed her hands on my hips and pulled me backwards towards her. Nothing sexual, but God, it felt it to me. Especially when I felt breasts against my back. Stranger still, I didn't even know for certain that it was her at this stage.

My body was reacting in a way that was beyond my control, and I tensed in her embrace. Ash felt this, and instead of releasing me to fall to my knees, she did the worst thing possible. She put those beautiful lips close to my ear and whispered, 'It's okay, Lou. It's only me.'

Her breath brushed against my skin and made every single hormone in my body sit up and beg. I don't know what got into me. I still can't believe the next thing I did. It was like I had no control at all left in me to stop myself...to stop my hands, that covered her own...to stop my head turning to face her...to stop my eyes fluttering closed...lips parting in expectation...to stop me reaching upwards to meet her divine lips...to...

'There you two are.' Stephen. Bugger. Or should I say lifesaver?

My eyes shot open to meet the intense blue stare of Ash, who I think looked even more startled than I did. Funny thing was, I know I had leaned upwards to kiss her, but I don't think I could have actually got that close to her. She was so close I could feel the tip of my nose touch her cheek. And although our faces were on an angle, it would have been a matter of an inch and a half before my lips would have covered hers.

A paltry inch and a half...an inch and a half and I could have tasted heaven. An inch and a half and I could have experienced the sensation I had only dreamed about.

An inch and a half and I would have had a lot of explaining to do.

Moving away from her seemed like I was moving in slow motion. Our heads moved apart, but the gazes stayed locked, albeit confused. I lifted my hands from hers to release her, but hers lingered on my hips for a few moments more, as if they were stunned into immobility and had to have time to recover.

Or was that wishful thinking?

All this time, Stephen stood next to us, waiting. He looked mildly self-conscious, and I think if he could have escaped, he would have...willingly.

I swallowed rapidly, although the dryness in my throat made this simple reflex seem like one of the twelve labours of Hercules. But I was trying to kick-start my mouth into action before the situation became even tenser than it already was.

'Hi, Stephen. There you are. I was looking for you.' No, I wasn't. But what did you expect me to say: I was looking for your gorgeous sister? Or, why did you interrupt me whilst I was trying to lay one on Ash? What about...Thank you for stopping me from making a total dickhead out of myself? Now that's a good one.

'We're over here.' And with that, he turned and nearly tripped over himself getting away.

Both Ash and I stared after him, fully expecting to see Cerberus chasing him.

'Come on, I'll take you back to the table and then get the drinks in.' Her voice didn't sound as self-assured as usual, and a seed of worry planted itself in my gut. What if she had realised what I was going to do?

Buggeration.

Double buggeration.

I nearly made my excuses and left...nearly. But how could I go home and know I could have spent the evening with Ash? There was no way I could have done that...no way. I just had to be more careful with what I let show, tighten the reins on my feelings, even more tightly than I already was holding them.

Up to five minutes ago, I had held them pretty tightly. As you have seen, I wasn't very good at reining these emotions in.

I would have to learn. And quickly.

The evening was fun. It was loud and garish, in a Christmas party kind of way.

You can imagine what it was like — a room full of teenagers, alcohol, and the freedom to act in the way they had not allowed themselves to act for the first few months of term.

We were all relaxed...well, to a degree. I was still reeling from the near social faux pas from earlier and didn't allow myself the freedom of going anywhere near the object of my desire. It would have been too tempting to just make a lunge at her, but...I couldn't do that. She was my friend, and however much I longed for her...yearned for her...craved for her touch...her mouth...her lips...however much I needed to feel her in my arms, I couldn't, no...*wouldn't* do anything that would jeopardise our friendship.

All evening I kept on stealing sly looks at her, devouring her with my eyes. She was beautiful...absolutely beautiful. I loved the way she really looked at people when she talked, the way her hands moved when she was chatting, the way she held a finger up to people when she wanted their attention, the way she tilted her head to the side...or threw it back in laughter.

One of the things I found breathtaking was the way she licked her lips, soft caresses from the wet muscle around lips that had been carved from rose petals. And the way she would bite her bottom lip when she was acting coy or thinking.

I could have sat there all night and listed everything I loved about her. Could have spent eternity spouting her beauty, like Shakespeare's sonnet:

And yet by heav'n I think my love as rare

As any she belied with false compare...

Nothing compared to her. Nothing could match the blueness of her eyes, the rose hue of her lips and cheek, the sound of her voice...*her* voice...her voice. I don't believe I actually listened to the words, I just got lost in it...allowed it to swirl over me and consume me.

All this from a few surreptitious looks. Imagine what I could say if I were allowed to fully digest her.

It was strange, though. Many of the times I stole a look, she would be looking in my direction. One time, her face was completely lost in thought, her eyes fixed firmly on my face. The previous times I had looked at her and caught her looking at me, she had quickly turned away. But not this time.

This time she just...stared. Her eyes seemed preoccupied, with what I don't know. They seemed to be looking at my mouth, but I think it was just wishful thinking on my part. Funny how self-conscious you become when someone is looking at your mouth. It is nearly impossible not to lick your lips. So I did. And so did she.

As if she was mimicking my action, those perfect lips were stroked by that perfect tongue, then the bottom lip, once again, was caught between her perfect teeth. I felt the groan leave my mouth before I had chance to stop it.

I don't know if it was that that made her jump back, as if she had been slapped, the confusion evident on her face. Or maybe it was the reality of the situation.

But I know for definite — for that split second she kept my gaze when she was focused, she must have seen everything I had tried so hard to keep hidden. There is no way she could have missed it. It was there for the taking. All the love that I had so carefully hidden had drifted to the surface for that brief moment...the brief moment she had looked straight into my face.

I felt exposed, betrayed by my own inability to dissemble. And in addition to feeling exposed, I felt ashamed.

After a few minutes, I made my excuses and went to the Ladies...or pretended to. Within ten minutes, I was in the back of a taxi on my way home. How could I stay when I knew she knew? How could I face her? How could I?

Exactly. How could I?

I arrived home a little after eleven. Both my parents were surprised to see me back so early, but I deflected their questions with a mumbled excuse about having to get up early for work the next day.

As if I cared about work. Or anything for that matter, except the look on Ash's face when she had seen all there was inside me.

I felt dirty. Unnatural. I felt like I should be kept away from anyone half-decent. I should have known being gay wasn't as easy as I thought it would be. I had accepted the fact I was different and foolishly thought the rest of the world didn't matter...mainly because they didn't have to know. Really, I thought I could keep this huge, dark secret tucked up inside myself and never tell a soul. The innocence, or should I say, the stupidity of youth, eh?

A blackness enveloped me as I trudged up the stairs, into the bathroom, into the shower to scrub this 'filth' from me. But the water didn't cleanse me like I'd hoped it would. The despair I had been feeling turned into anger...anger at myself for being who I was...for being different.

How could I have been so stupid? So fucking stupid? So ignorantly fucking ass-wiping dick-scraping stupid?

My bedroom was dark when I entered and I couldn't be arsed to turn the light on, just threw myself onto the bed and screamed into the pillow.

'What's up with you, lezza?'

Jo's new nickname for me rang through the air like a punch waiting to be thrown. I stiffened on top of the bed, the pillow half in my open mouth...and waited.

The reason I waited is because I knew if I had said anything at that precise moment, I would regret it. 'Oi, Lou! What's the matter?' The jesting had left her voice, and I could hear her concern. I could also hear her getting up from her bed and shuffling over to mine. I could barely see the outline of her as she leaned over me, silhouetted by the light coming through the crack in the curtain. I wanted to tell her to fuck off and let me rot in peace, but I couldn't...just couldn't.

A warm hand landed in the centre of my back and waited...no movement, except for my breathing, which was becoming laboured because of the pillow half suffocating me.

Time elapsed. I don't know how much, but it seemed an age. I could feel myself drifting off into a fog-filled haze, my long wet hair sticking to my face, arms, and neck. Her voice sifted in through the mist and seemed like a dream of some description, a fantasy...

'Tell me, Lou. Tell me.'

I was open to telling her, mainly because I didn't have the capability to stop myself. The words fell from my lips like a confession, maybe because they were.

'I'm in love with Ash.'

There was total silence. It actually felt like I had just spoken into the empty air, and I was beginning to believe the sensation of Jo's hand was just that, a sensation, until she spoke.

'Does she know how you feel?'

'I think so. I think she's guessed.' A calmness was in my voice I didn't expect; dreamlike once again. It is funny how you can experience one emotion and then juxtapose it with its opposite in the matter of an instant.

'What does she think about it?'

'How the *fuck* should I know? I didn't stick around to get my face slapped, did I?' I turned sharply, releasing the pillow...releasing the anger that had been welling up unbeknownst to me in the last five minutes...releasing the frustration and hurt and agony and despair that come with being in love with someone you just...can't...have.

'How do you know she would slap your face? You may have been surprised.'

That was it. I was boiling now. How dare she surmise how and what Ash would be feeling? How dare she try to make...try to make...try...to... make...make me feel better. I sat upright, my body invading her space, the stance threatening, but she didn't flinch, just stared me in the eyes.

'I said, how can you possibly know how Ash would have reacted if you didn't stay around long enough to find out.' I didn't move: I was stock still, staring. 'I never took you for a coward, Lou.'

Could I possibly answer that? Could I be angry at what she had said, considering it was the truth? I was a coward, plain and simple; a girl without a spine. And I felt even more ashamed of myself than I already had been. I felt the life seep from me once again, and I sat back against the headboard and closed my eyes.

'You have to tell her...let her know how you feel.'

A whispered 'I can't' wisped itself from my half-closed lips.

'What have you got to lose? You can't go on like this, Lou. I've noticed for a while you weren't happy.' I made a half-hearted move to interrupt, but she shushed me. 'No. This is not about you and Sarah. Even after you told me about the two of you, you still seemed sad.'

I shrugged and muttered, 'I'll get over it.'

'But why should you have to get over anything? Why can't you just put your cards on the table and level with the girl? You might be surprised.'

That was the second time she had said that — that I'd be surprised. I looked at her, the question evident.

'I don't know. It's just you two...well...even when we were kids, there was something I couldn't put my finger on.' She looked sheepish at her admission. I looked intrigued.

'Go on.'

'Erm...you two just...erm...well, seemed to fit, if you know what I mean.' I shook my head and waited for her to go on. She released a deep breath, shook herself, and then looked at me. I knew she felt uncomfortable, but I needed her to say it...say what my heart wanted to hear.

She coughed and then coughed again. 'I always felt like a spare part when I was with you two...always felt like I wasn't needed. Shush, Lou, let me speak. I felt you had a connection, something none of us could understand at the time. Didn't you wonder why I didn't hang about with you two?' I nodded. 'It wasn't because I disliked Ash, although I know you thought I did. I just felt...erm...out of place somehow.'

The proverbial penny clunked into my head like a two-ton weight. No wonder Jo always said for Ash and me to do our own thing but always gave the option to join her if I wanted to. Not Ash...just me. I kind of drifted off for a minute in an attempt to recollect anything that could have given Jo the impression she wasn't wanted...well...needed was more the word.

I have to admit I could see her point of view. Even as a kid I had always felt complete with Ash — like we fitted together in some strange way, like we were meant to be friends.

Friends.

Friends.

Not lovers...but friends.

That word stuck in my throat and choked my future. Friends. How could I expect her to want anything more than we had already? I had waited ten years for her to come back into my life, and there was no way I was going to bugger it up by making a pass at her.

If all I ever got from her was her friendship, then I would be happy with that, as I couldn't bear not having her in my life again.

But I loved her so much...so much...so much. How could I be around her all of the time and not lean forward to capture that perfect mouth with my own? How could I sit close to her and not drown in her eyes?

How could I face her again after tonight?

'Lou?' Jo's voice broke through my reverie. I faced her with a sad smile, and tears threatened at the back of my eyes. 'You are going to tell her, aren't you?' Slowly and carefully, I shook my head in the negative. She frowned at me, pushing her bottom lip out like a child in an attempt to make me laugh. That was the last emotion I felt like having.

She sighed, shaking her head whilst expelling a stream of breath. 'You are a fool, Lou. Tell her. For fuck's sake, what have you got to lose?'

I didn't miss a beat with my answer. What was there to consider? 'Everything, Jo. Everything.'

With that I turned onto my side, dismissing her with my back. There was no way I could tell Ash how I felt. In her eyes we were just friends, friends who barely knew each other after ten years. Imagine what she would do...say...if I was to proclaim my undying love for her? She would think I was an idiot...or a pervert...or both.

Pain was clawing at the inside of my rib cage, the heart was attempting to rip out of its nest and scream its agony into the air. But to anyone watching, I was still...rigid.

'Just think about it, okay? Life's too bloody short to hide behind fear. We'll speak tomorrow, right?' I didn't answer, couldn't. 'I said...we'll speak tomorrow, all right?' Her voice was firm and brooked no argument. I nodded, as I didn't trust my voice to be in charge of what I was feeling. 'Okay. Now get some sleep.'

A light kiss landed on my head, and I pushed my face in the pillow once again. A very effective way to muffle the sobs that were breaking out. And it saved me wiping the tears that were sliding freely down my cheeks.

Life is a bitch, isn't it?

Saturday found me trying to hold down the contents of my stomach, as the smells of the indoor market nearly strangled me. That was a mean smell. Jesus! Everything smelled off. It wasn't just the market, but also the lack of sleep I'd had the night before.

Jo's words had danced around my head and made me re-evaluate my situation — both with Sarah and with Ash. I had cried on and off all night, especially when I kept envisioning Ash's face the last time I had seen her. The blue eyes...the startled expression...her lips wet after she licked them.

Funny thing was, Sarah looked ten times worse than I did.

I could see she was fighting the smell of the cheeses...a definite sign of a mega hangover. Her eyes looked dull and lifeless, and her skin had a pallor most frequently associated with the dead.

Even when I said hello, all she could muster was a watery smile, but she gripped my hand as she passed behind the extremely small counter and whispered, 'Missed you last night.'

And of course I felt bad, because I had barely given her a thought. I conjured a smile from deep inside, and she gazed into my face before saying, 'Jesus, Lou, you look like I feel. Did you drink too much?'

I just nodded. What was I supposed to say: 'Well actually, Sarah, no; I didn't touch a drop. I just spent all night crying about how I love Ashley Richards.' The words 'lead balloon' and 'going over like one' sprang to mind.

The morning passed in its usual blur of activity. Customers queued and queued and queued for what seemed like eternity. I couldn't wait for lunchtime. The quicker it arrived, the better.

Five minutes before I was to go off duty, I felt a sensation creep up my spine and travel through my body like a shock of electricity. I had my back to the counter, but I knew if I turned around I would see the reason why my legs had lost their ability to hold up my weight. I gripped the side of the counter, my knuckles going white, and Sarah sidled next to me her face full of concern.

'Are you all right, Lou? You look like shit.'

I didn't feel all right, not by a long stretch of the imagination. A couple of deep breaths...a couple more...then a couple more for good measure. I turned, the action nearly my undoing. And there she was...like a vision.

She was leaning back on the end of the counter opposite ours, her arms crossed over her chest, her eyes fixed on me, although she couldn't quite see my face. There was no smile...just *the* look — stern and commanding. I was trapped in her gaze like a rabbit in the headlights of a car.

'Who's that?'

Sarah's voice sounded distant, and I had difficulty answering her. 'That's Ash.'

'Ash! As in *your* Ash?'

I wish. 'Yes. My Ash.' My voice sounded dead, lifeless...defenceless. I watched Ash rearrange herself, pushing her hips forward and trying to achieve some amount of comfort against the glass cabinet.

'What's she doing here, then?'

I wanted to snap, 'How the fuck should I know?' But I didn't. For two reasons. One — it wouldn't have been fair to take out my frustration on Sarah. Two — I knew what Ash was doing there.

I knew she had come to have a go about last night...and I was hoping it was just for deserting her and not saying goodnight, not for catching me drooling over her. Please. If there is a God...please don't let her know how I feel...please.

'Right, you two. Are you going to lunch now or what?'

Crap. Double crap. Crap times infinity.

I always had lunch with Sarah...always. And there was no way I could face having them both together, not after last night...not with feeling as rough as I did. I couldn't cope with Ash having a go at me, especially if she came right out and said — you know, about what I had showed her so clearly last night. What would Sarah do? Would she 'out' me, say that we were sleeping together?

Fuck.

I felt sick to my stomach. My stomach felt sick to my teeth. My teeth had gone numb...so had my brain, which had broken all ties with my mouth, leaving me mute and stupid.

'Come on, Lou. It's our turn.'

I followed Sarah down the counter, and from the corner of my eye, I saw Ash push herself away from the counter and start to follow us. Not good.

'Lou! Lou! Wait up!' I could hear Ash behind me, and it took all the gumption I had to turn and face her, plastering a smile there for the initial contact, pretending nothing was the matter. She was racing up to me, pushing people out of the way in an attempt to get there quickly.

'Hey, Ash. I was going to call you later.'

That stopped her in her tracks...for about two seconds. 'Didn't you see me? I was waiting opposite your stall.'

I could feel Sarah next to me, waiting to be introduced. Ash's eyes flicked to her in acknowledgement and then came back to rest on mine. 'No, I didn't see you; we've been busy.'

Sarah was nearly pushing into the back of me now, and I could feel my nerves shredding. I could tell Ash didn't believe me, but what else could I do? I couldn't tell her what had been going through my mind; I just did the 'running away' thing that I did so well.

'We need to talk.' She looked over my shoulder at Sarah. 'Alone.'

What to do? What to do? It all seems so small and harmless now when I look back, but at the time I was terrified.

I nervously looked at Sarah, my eyes adopting a beseeching look. She looked pissed off, which I didn't blame her for. So I gave her the puppy dog eyes once more, tossing a smile into the kitty. I saw the resolve leave her and she nodded her head in assent, albeit begrudgingly. 'I'll see you later, Sarah, okay?'

She just nodded, turned, and walked downstairs to the locker room. I turned back to Ash. 'I have to get out of this apron. I'll meet you at St. Mary's, at the back of the churchyard, okay?' I didn't even wait for a reply, just scooted down the steps and into the changing room.

Sarah was brushing her hair and glaring at me in the mirror. I smiled at her reflection, but she just lowered her eyes.

Saying I felt like a prize shit would be redundant at this stage. I think it is obvious. I walked up behind her and put my hands around her waist, lowering my lips to her tied-up hair. 'Sorry, honey. I...well...Ash and I had a bit of an argument last night.' Why was I lying...again? But I couldn't stop myself. 'I think she wants to talk about it.'

Sarah was still tense, so I went one step further and started to kiss the back of her neck. Soft, tender kisses, breathy kisses, kisses filled with promise, kisses that said, 'I want you.' Her body visibly relaxed, and I could hear her breathing becoming heavy and expectant. She turned in my arms and covered my mouth with her own — a hot kiss...a wet kiss...a tongue begging entrance to my mouth, which I allowed. I could feel myself getting lost in her and in the sensations her lips...her hands...her fingers were creating in me.

I could feel a pooling between my legs...an ache building, but they weren't for Sarah. They were for a certain woman who was now waiting for me in the churchyard. If things went badly, at least I would be in the right place; they could just bury me.

I pulled away from Sarah, a little too quickly, I guess, because she gave me a dazed look. 'Got to go. See you when I get back, yeah?' She nodded and tried to summon a smile.

I took off my apron and washed my hands, surreptitiously watching her in the mirror. Her gaze never left mine. I don't think she even blinked.

'Laters, then.'

'Can I see you tonight? My parents are out, if you want to come 'round.'

I was going to say no...honestly. But her face...she looked like she would crumble if I turned her down. I couldn't...

'Okay, great. We'll sort it out when I get back, yeah?' Her smile swallowed me, and she grabbed me by the hips and planted a kiss on my mouth.

It pained me that I couldn't return the affection.

With a weak smile, I turned and left her there.

Alone.

Ash was pacing in the churchyard, and I had only twenty minutes of my lunchtime left. I had tried to think of a plausible explanation about what she thought she had seen written on my face last night, but they all came out lame or an obvious lie.

I had convinced myself that whatever she said, I would just deny it. There was no point admitting it. I needed a spine to do that, and I didn't have one. So I would go for the denial or 'no comment'.

She had her back to me, but as I got nearer she turned abruptly...startled, her face showing confusion for some reason.

I smiled at her, hoping to stop the accusations before they got started. Another lie popped out of my mouth. And I didn't even expect it.

'I'm sorry I didn't say goodnight last night. I felt really ill...and I just had to get home.' Well...it could have been the truth. I did feel ill, but not in a 'poorly sick and can't eat custard' kind of way. The sickness was how I felt about myself, about what I had done, the fact I had shown the one person whom I didn't want to know exactly how I felt about her.

Ash looked at me with the same startled expression on her face, her poise was slightly askew as her shoulders twisted 'round. She didn't move toward me, just stood there and waited until I was right up close to her.

I stood and waited for her to answer or even remark on the explanation I had just tendered, and I finally realised I didn't think she had heard me so I repeated it.

'Did you feel it?' Huh? 'Did you feel that...that something?' My face informed her that I didn't have a clue what she was talking about. 'That tingling sensation...'

I stared at her. I knew exactly was she was talking about; I had felt it when she had been watching me at work. It was a weird feeling, almost electric.

Me being me, I just shook my head, and I still believe I saw disappointment flash across her face. She lifted her hand and brushed it through her long raven locks, completing its journey with a waggle of her fingers. 'What did you say?'

I had to swallow before I could answer her. 'Erm...just that I was sorry about last night. I didn't feel well, so I just went home.'

Concern flooded her face. 'Are you okay now? Should you be at work?' She came towards me and put her hands on my shoulders, her body close to mine, her face closer. 'You look all pale and blotchy all of a sudden. Come, sit down.'

I did feel pale and blotchy, but it wasn't because I felt ill...more like the sensation she evoked in me. I think all of the blood raced from my face to a more demanding region, but it had left some stragglers behind.

I let her lead me over to the bench and lower me down to the seat, her arm completely around me. I was in guilty heaven. I could smell her perfume — so light, so addictive...so her. I was entranced. So entranced I realised I had shut off the listening part of my brain. I tuned in to hear the last part of what she was saying.

'...and then I came looking for you. It was the doorman who told us you had left in a taxi ten minutes earlier.' She was rubbing my hands between hers, to get the blood back, I think, but take it from me...the blood was staying exactly where it had shot to minutes before. The hand rubbing guaranteed that.

It was her eyes that captivated me. Those deep pools looked into my face with absolute concern about my welfare; I was so lost in them I didn't even feel bad about staring. All I wanted to do was to lean forward and just...catch...those...perfect lips in mine and drown in her. I knew beyond a shadow of a doubt, I loved this woman who was half kneeling, half sitting before me. The woman who was holding my hands in hers...holding my heart in her hands.

I wanted to take those hands and place them on either side of my face, just to show her...to show her...I was hers...always hers. To show her I would be forever lost in her...my heart was forever lost.

'...and then I remembered you worked the market today. So here I am.'

Yes. Here you are.

'Sorry about leaving and not telling anyone.' My voice sounded like my head was under water — muffled and distorted — but Ash didn't seem to notice. She just flashed me one of those brilliant smiles that lit up the world — slightly crooked and filled with promise.

'Forget about it. We were just worried about you.' She patted my knee. 'Anyway...what are your plans for tonight? Fancy you — me — the pictures? There's a good film on. *The Terminator* with Arnold Schwarzenegger.'

I felt my face light up, and my heart screamed out 'YES!' but then I remembered. Sarah. I had promised Sarah I would see her tonight. Fuck. And then...fuck...again.

'I can't.' Ash's face fell. I saw the expression literally go from ecstatic to depressed in the blink of an eye. 'I've already made plans with...erm...Sarah.' She tilted her face to the side, the expression questioning. 'The girl I work with. We...erm...we...are going to...erm...' I couldn't say go to the pictures, as Ash would ask to come along. 'Erm...going to her friend's eighteenth in Stalybridge.'

All the time I was deliberating with my tale, she watched me. It felt as if she knew I was lying but didn't like to say anything. That made me feel more like the giant shit I had felt earlier. 'But I am free tomorrow...or Monday...Tuesday.' Was I throwing myself at her? Most certainly. All the ideas of avoiding her crumbled into dust and flew into the wind that was swirling its way around the stone structure of St. Mary's Church, taking my inhibitions with it.

The smile I so loved trickled its way back onto her chiselled face, spreading like sunshine and making me feel giddy just to be in its presence.

'How about all three?' She cocked her head to the side and waited for my response, which was to allow my jaw to drop and for me to sit there catching flies. A laugh came from deep within her, making me snap my mouth closed. 'Look...I miss you. Is that a crime now? Just thought we should see more of each other.' She grinned. 'And by seeing you for three nights on the trot...well...let's just say...it would be my pleasure.'

And mine. God, and mine.

'And...next time I ask you out on a Saturday night, maybe you won't have already made arrangements with someone else. You'd be all mine.'

God...I wish...I wish...I *so* wish I was all yours, Ashley Richards. From the bottom of my *ba booming* heart.

Chapter Thirteen

Saturday night saw me with Sarah, but not *with* her, if you know what I mean. Physically I was there, but my head and my heart were definitely somewhere else.

Even when she had her head between my legs, fucking me with her mouth, I was elsewhere. All I could do was think of Ash and wish it was her there — sucking and licking and kissing my most intimate place, wish it was her fingers that were playing with my nipple, her hand that was holding my hip down, her head bobbing up and down.

I didn't even try to stop my thoughts from straying. I just accepted the fact I was head over heels in love with Ash and wanted her more than I wanted to breathe. No guilt this time...nothing...except a fantastic orgasm that ripped through me and made me scream into the air, whilst thrusting myself onto Sarah's face over and over again...savouring the jolts spluttering from me...sweat coating my skin...cum coating my thighs, her face and mouth.

So, as I said, having illicit thoughts about Ash didn't stop me having an orgasm. In fact...it definitely helped.

Christmas came and went, and the majority of my time was spent with Ash. Sarah, quite rightly, was becoming more and more jealous. Even though I wasn't technically cheating on her, I was. Well, in my head — and definitely in my heart — and I knew I had to stop what I was doing to her.

I did like Sarah...really like her. She had been my first and would always hold that special place in my heart. She had shown me exactly who I was...and still am. I did feel bad, I knew her feelings for me ran deep; I could tell every time she looked at me.

And I knew I was actually doing more harm than good being with her, and I had to find the courage from somewhere to do something about it. Deep down, I just wished she would get fed up with me cancelling on her and go and find someone else.

I know...the true coward's way out. And I agree with you — I didn't deserve anyone, especially if that was how I was going to treat them.

New Year's Eve arrived resplendent and ready for action. I'd made arrangements to spend the evening with Sarah...out of guilt, I think. Ash had been disappointed when I told her. She accepted it with little fuss, but her eyes gave her away...and I felt torn.

Bloody hell. Why on earth should I be in this situation? Why couldn't I just be happy with Sarah? Why did I have to always go after the unobtainable?

Life, I suppose...the little things that are here to slowly drive us mad with longing. Ah well.

Anyway. I digress. Per usual.

Ash told me where she would be going and told me and my 'friends' to pop in if we were passing. Yeah, I could see that happening — me and Sarah popping in to see Ash, her brothers, the wonderful Tracy (who was back on the scene again after worming her way back in to Stephen's affections. Twat. Or twatette), and all our mates from college meeting in The Plough in Heaton Moor.

Manchester was heaving with people, and Sarah and I had tickets to New York New York, a gay bar, which had a live act on and a disco. At least we could be natural, as natural as I could be being underage and with the wrong woman.

All evening I sat with Sarah, refusing most of the drinks thrust in front of me by everyone and their mother (not really their mother — an expression if you will). As time dragged by, I became increasingly depressed and was constantly clock watching. And like all clock-watchers, I found time fucking about with my sense of reality. What seemed like an hour had been five minutes. I'm not even going to go into what an hour felt like, but believe me...it was agony.

Eventually, it was Sarah who couldn't stand it anymore and broke the silence between us. I heard it smash into smithereens as it hit the wall with force.

'I know you are not happy, Lou. Have I done something to upset you?' Her face was pained, the anguish clearly standing out, making her features appear gaunt and deathlike. Her eyes seemed haunted as she waited for my response, and I knew she wanted me to say something that would make this better...make us better.

What could I do? I could lie and just accept this relationship, or...I could tell her the truth.

'Of course you haven't, Sarah. I...am happy...' But just not with you, just not like this. 'You know I think a lot of you, don't you?' She nodded, her long hair flying around her head, her expression waiting for me to end the pain I could see written on her face.

Why was I just about to tell her another lie? Why was I treating her like this? This wasn't fair to her. She deserved so much more than my half-hearted attempts at a relationship. I knew I would never have a relationship with Ash, but that didn't give me the right to treat Sarah like second best. I had to learn to be on my own for the right reasons, not with someone because it was convenient.

She was still waiting for me to carry on, still waiting for me to burst her bubble. Still waiting. I could feel her breaking inside, and I knew exactly what she was going through, because I went through the same thing every time I was with Ash. I also knew that one day that would be me — sitting there, waiting to get my heart broken.

'I'm in love with someone else.'

I still remember her face when those words came out — stunned, lost, and broken all at the same time. The colour drained from her face, the whiteness stark in the club's lighting. Slowly, the face began to fold, crumble, fracture, splinter...rupture. Her hands flew outwards to mine in a vain attempt to capture my hands. A keening sound emanating from the pit of her stung my ears, and my chest ached: I knew it was my fault.

'Please...no. Lou, don't leave me...*don't...leave me*. I...I...love you...*love you*.' The first time she had ever said those words to me and the last. Tears rained down her face, and she lunged across the table trying to grab me, but I pulled away, tears rolling from my eyes, too. I can't tell you how I felt, can't tell you what emotions were running through me. All I knew was that I had killed something in that girl. She was devastated, and it was all my fault for wanting something, or should I say someone, else.

People were looking over at us, but I didn't care. I knew I should comfort her in some way, but how?

She leaned back in her chair, her hands over her face, trying to stop herself crying, trying to regain some composure.

'Sarah, I...I...never meant to hurt you, you must know that.' No answer, just muffled sobs. 'I didn't even know myself until after you and I had started seeing each other...didn't even know I could have feelings for another woman.'

Her face peeked over the tips of her hands, her mascara smeared all over her cheeks...and it was all my fault...all my fault. I watched her swallow rapidly, before she looked me straight in the eyes and said, 'I understand.' Such a soft sweet voice. 'Truly, Lou.' She stopped again, swallowed again, looked at me squarely in the eyes...again. 'Just remember...I...love you, always will.' And she was gone.

I was left searching the whole place from top to bottom for thirty minutes, but it was as if she had vanished off the face of the earth. Finally, I resigned myself to the fact she had left the place, collected my coat, and headed towards the exit. Eleven-fifteen on New Year's Eve, and I was going home. Good place for me, as I felt awful. I'd broken that girl, not just her heart...but her. And I doubt even to this day I have ever forgiven myself for it.

If I was heading home, can you please tell me why, at eleven-forty, I was pushing open the door to The Plough?

Beats me. But that's where my homing device had taken me. It had taken me home...home to Ash.

She was standing with her back to me, deep in conversation with some guys from college. I just stood there and watched her. She was so beautiful...so natural...such a catch for any guy in here. And that was the problem...it was the guys she was interested in...not girls. Like me.

As I watched, I saw her stop in mid-sentence and rub the back of her head, the side of her face quizzical, like something had just hit her. I looked around but couldn't see anyone laughing, and more to the point, I hadn't seen anything hit her either.

In slow motion, she turned...and looked straight at me, her face stunned for a split second, before she released the smile that was always ready and waiting. Then she screamed out, 'Lou! You made it!' and hurtled towards me, throwing her arms around my body and crushing me into her.

I was lost and found in her...the feel of her...the scent of her...just...her...all of her. My lips were so close to her neck — the special place on your neck where the throat meets the shoulder...the little dip. It was so tempting to just kiss her...suck in her skin...taste her. And to tell you the truth, I did have a little brush against it. It was bliss.

She thrust me back, and I thought she had caught me, but her expression said otherwise. 'I am so happy you could make it, with just over fifteen minutes to spare, too.'

Then, dear reader, you know what she did? Do you? Have a guess. Oh, I can't wait around for you; I'll just tell you.

She kissed me. On the mouth. Her mouth on mine. Bam. There...flesh on flesh...lips on lips...her arms around me, kissing me.

About bloody time, I hear you all say. But hold your horses, it wasn't a kissing kind of kiss. It was a 'Hey, I'm so excited to see my friend' kind of kiss. But who cares? She kissed me...on the mouth! And I nearly died...not of embarrassment — no way — of lust. The kiss was perfect, and I even got to sample a little bit of her spit, which I savoured after she pulled away and turned to shout the rest of them over. I pushed my lips into my mouth and sucked, just in case there was a little bit left lurking outside that I could have missed.

I know — I'm a sad fucker, but I bet nearly all of you have done the same thing at one time or another. Go on...have a think.

See. I told you so.

I was bustled forward into the group, where I was met by everyone. I could see Tracy hanging back, trying to calm herself. And I wanted to laugh. I must have really pissed her off. Ash left me for a few minutes, but I didn't really get the chance to miss her as everyone was asking me questions about what I had been doing earlier and why I had finally come to my senses and come.

I tried to answer them all, but Ash was back carrying a glass of something bubbly, a cheeky grin splitting her face.

As I looked at her, I felt a jolt of guilt for what I had done to Sarah, fleeting, but there nevertheless. Ash saw it. Would you believe it? She saw the expression flit across my face, and her own reacted to it, roughly mirroring my own. So I smiled at her, and she smiled back, slightly at first, and then a full-out beaming smile.

'Come on, Lou. Let's get ready for the countdown.' She grabbed my hand and pulled me away from the crowd and closer to the DJ, her fingers cool and long in my own sweaty, stumpy ones. I allowed myself to be dragged by her, couldn't resist really.

'You're not allowed a sip yet; you have to wait until midnight, okay?' I nodded and then placed my glass on top of the speaker before leaning back and looking at my friend. She followed suit. Her long frame stretched out as she leaned back, her hips pushing out, her arms flat against the speaker.

When she turned to face me she was nearly on my level, and I felt the breath catch in my throat. How on earth was I going to get through the night without telling her, without touching her, without losing complete control and kissing those faultless lips?

Restraint. And lots of it.

'What are you thinking about?' She was so close, I could just...

'Not much.' What else could I have said? The truth? I think I'd had enough of being truthful for one evening, don't you? 'Why?'

'You looked so serious.' I play slapped her in the belly, and she pretended I had winded her, and we both laughed before leaning back onto the speakers, totally comfortable with each other.

When the DJ announced there was only a minute before midnight, I fully expected her to drag me off again to find the others, but she just leaned forward and pulled me into standing position in front of her.

I stood there, like a piece of clay waiting to be moulded into any shape she wanted, totally at her mercy. She placed both her hands on my shoulders and stared at me — so deeply...so fully, I actually began to have difficulty swallowing. Then she lifted one hand and grabbed one of mine and placed it on her hip, before she did the same with the other one.

And there we stood. Her hands on my shoulders, mine on her hips...waiting for the countdown, although my heart was definitely waiting for something else.

'Ten.' She just gazed into my eyes, no expression readable. I stared back...transfixed. I actually missed the next few seconds, as I couldn't concentrate.

'Four.' People were chanting the numbers now, but I couldn't speak — I was lost in her eyes...in her touch.

'Three.' I licked my lips, nerves or expectation, I don't know.

'Two.' She licked hers, just a mirroring reaction.

'One.' I couldn't breathe. The thought of what I wanted to happen was eating me alive.

'Happy New Year!' I didn't hear the cheers around me, the people going wild and beginning to sing *Auld Lang Syne*. I wasn't aware of anything but the most tender kiss I had ever experienced in my life brushing against my lips, once...twice...three times. Then she pulled me against her again, leaving me stunned and my blood racing. Her breath was in my hair, her voice muffled, but my nerves made it seem as if she had shouted it. 'Thank you, Lou, for coming back to me...for coming back to me.'

Did she mean tonight? Or generally?

To tell the truth, I didn't care. I folded into her and just accepted what she was willing to give, losing the last vestiges of control along the way, her presence consuming me, ingesting me — mind, body, and soul.

And there we stood, wrapped in each other's arms for what seemed like a glorious lifetime, and all the while I knew this would probably be the last time I would experience this bliss, this heaven on earth. The first and last time...as I knew this was only a reaction to seeing me again after all those years apart.

Stephen interrupted us...again, shouting his New Year's greeting and expecting hugs and kisses from the both of us. I pulled away first, and I watched her eyes slowly open and focus on mine. They looked dreamy, for some reason.

'Come on, you two; you haven't even toasted the New Year yet.' With that, he thrust my glass into my hand, grabbing me around the waist and planting a sloppy kiss on my mouth, before grabbing his sister and picking her up to jiggle her around.

She threw her head back and laughed that really deep, sexy laugh of hers, and I felt a smile creep along my face. I lifted the glass in toast and silently mouthed, 'Happy New Year, Ash. And thank *you* for coming back to me.'

It was nearly a week before I saw Sarah again. She looked like crap. I had tried to call her the day after New Year's, but she wasn't taking my calls. Although it wasn't actually said, I could sense it in her father's tone of voice when he said she was out. It was not very welcoming, to say the least.

The next time I saw her was at work, but not really at work, if you know what I mean. She popped by to hand in her apron first thing on the Saturday morning, and it took her a long time to look at me, even after I kept on calling her name.

What did I expect? Hugs and kisses?

I tried to get her on her own but she wouldn't have any of it, kept edging away. Although she looked generally ravaged, it was her eyes that disturbed me the most. They were sunken and haunted. The sparkle she used to have had completely gone, and I knew it was all my fault. I had broken this girl, shattered her belief in me...her belief in life. That was what it seemed to me.

She only said two words to me — two words that stopped me in my tracks, two words that made me step back and away from her. 'Lou, don't.'

It wasn't what she said, it was her face...her tone, that made leave her alone. It was all too fresh — too open a wound for my inexperienced mumblings to slightly compensate anything she was going through. And although I had caused all this pain, I did actually know when to back off.

That was the day she quit the stall and left my life. I never saw her again, not even in passing, although I did hear she met someone else.

The reason for me never seeing her again will become obvious soon enough.

Ash and I were with each other constantly, and I was in heaven. She was everything one person looked for in a friend — truthful, trusting, honest, witty. I could go on and talk about her intelligence, beauty, and her wicked sense of humour, but I think you will guess I can wax lyrical about this girl.

In a nutshell...she became my world.

Ben was completely out of the picture (I bet you had wondered about the blond-haired wanker, hadn't you...he had moved on to another victim), so she was all mine...

...all mine...

...all mine...

...in a platonic way of course.

Unfortunately.

We spent nearly every night either at her house or at mine. We still kept up with the bowling, and I was getting better — although not by much. Why would I bother improving if that would mean I wouldn't get the guidance from her? And that amounted to lots of touching and full body contact. My favourite was when she came up behind me and wrapped her arms around my waist to turn me into position. She laughed every time and called me a fruit fly, because I couldn't remember which of the little 'arrowy things' to stand near and then which position to place my body.

Which, of course, I did remember. Perfectly, actually. But there was no way on this earth I was going to let her know that, was there? Not a chance.

The weeks flew by, and I was totally smitten with her — everything about her. But I should have known this piece of heaven couldn't last, and its ending came totally out of the blue. And not what you are expecting either. I didn't balls things up — profess my undying love for her, make a pass, let anything slip. I was completely innocent in the breaking apart of my world.

It was my parents actually. They told me we were moving away, far away, as soon as my one-year course had finished. Far away from Manchester, from Stockport...from Ash.

I could tell you how I reacted, but that wouldn't change a thing. I could tell you how I screamed at them, ranted...threw things...ignored them... refused to eat, but that would be superfluous, wouldn't it? You should know me well enough by now to realise my whole life had been tipped over and stamped on. Everything I had would be snatched away from me.

And my 'everything' rested with only one thing, one person actually. But you know that, don't you?

I didn't tell Ash about the move for nearly a week, and it wasn't even me who actually told her. Once again it was my parents, my mum in fact. I still remember her reaction, Ash's reaction that is. Such a simple sentence spewed forth from my mum's mouth...simple words, all ordered together perfectly, but simple nevertheless.

'Didn't Lou tell you we were moving to Norfolk?'

The smile Ash had been sporting froze, and I witnessed her physical struggle to keep it there...lips twitching, the surrounding area spasming...until finally it gave up and slipped slowly from her face, leaving her face blank — wiped clean, vacant.

Slowly, she turned to me, the question in her eyes but as yet silent. I watched her lips struggle to collect themselves into some kind of action, fight with the incredulity of the situation, until finally she said, 'Lou?' A cry of sorts. The word hovered in the air expectantly, waiting for me to revoke what had been said. But how could I?

I remember leaning forward, my hand outstretched, forgetting that it couldn't just reach out and touch her, in case it became carried away and couldn't stop...couldn't stop...touching her. I stopped. Drew back the rogue hand and clenched it into a ball, holding the traitor back with its twin.

'I...I...was...erm...'

'Lou?' Her voice held so much hurt, almost like I had betrayed her by not telling her.

'I was...erm...going to tell you.'

'When? As you were driving off?' Her tone sounded bitter, or should I say, hurt. I know I would have been hurt if she hadn't told me about something as life changing as that.

'No...I...well...' My mum watched the exchange with interest: watched me struggle to get the words out, watched Ash, pale, watched me grip my hands tighter. Watched as my world came tumbling down, like Jack and Jill. But this time it was Lou and Ash.

'Why don't you go up to your room and talk?'

I nodded at Mum's suggestion, words left me there to fend for myself. I gestured to Ash that she should follow me, and she did.

I walked up the stairs like Orpheus — valiantly hoping Eurydice was following, but terrified that if he looked back she would be gone. I fully expected to hear the sound of the front door closing, but all I heard was the creaking of the stairs. Eventually, I stood in the room with my back to the door, and I heard the sound of it closing behind me, then nothing. Complete silence. Well, except for the booming of my heart, which had decided that moment was as good as any to start performing a drum solo. I knew I had to get it over...knew I had to act as natural as possible...knew it would half kill me.

I turned around and forced myself to look at her face, adding a weak smile into the mix for good measure, hoping I wouldn't just curl up at her feet and beg her to love me...beg her to save me...beg her to tell me I would be with her, or she would wait until I moved back, like I promised myself I would as soon as I reached eighteen.

Her face was completely devoid of colour apart from blue eyes and the blood red lips...lips I coveted...lips I wanted to take and smother and never ever relinquish.

'Come sit on the bed with me.' I turned away again and plonked onto my bed, turning myself onto my side.

She just stood there and stared at me, then I saw her leg push down and propel her forward, as if she had been shoved. It seemed as if it took her forever to get to me, and I watched her every move, albeit surreptitiously. She seemed sluggish...reticent. I wanted it all to be over as soon as possible, to get it out in the open so my aching heart could start to mend.

Sounds dramatic, doesn't it? But if you have ever been in love, you will know exactly what I mean. The constant longing I felt inside hurt like buggery (to borrow another expression from my mum's vast list of expressions). No...I can't say that now, as it doesn't come close to conveying the agony I was going through. I was, dear reader, trying to save you from how I was feeling, but I think you deserve to know.

As I was saying, if you have ever been in love, you know how it feels. Even if the feeling is reciprocated, there is a longing...a yearning deep inside...a fear that at any one moment it could all be taken from you and you would be left gasping like a fish out of water.

And that is how I felt at that exact moment — like a fish out of water, gasping. Mouth smacking open and closed...fins flaying...everything becoming dim...distant...detached. All I needed was for Ash to untangle the line and throw me back in, save me in some way, but I doubted that was going to happen.

It was Ash who finally spoke, thus loosening the hook. 'When are you going?' Although the barb was gone, I was still out of the water.

I just shook my head and lifted my face to hers, which was now inches away from mine. I opened my mouth to speak, but nothing came out. I took a deep breath and tried again. 'I'm not sure. About six to eight weeks.'

'Six weeks! Six...weeks!' She shot off the bed so quickly it made me fall back, then she marched over to the other side of the room and stood facing the wall, her shoulders rising and falling rapidly.

Cliff was watching. It reminded me of Donny all those years ago. The feeling inside was exactly the same, but now I knew why I was totally devastated. It was because now I knew why I didn't want to leave her, and this time it wasn't just because she was my best friend.

'When were you going to tell me?'

Her voice was quiet, defeated. I just shrugged. She couldn't see me, obviously, so she asked me again, but this time she turned her head to look at me over her shoulder. And this time her voice was sterner...more forceful...insistent.

'I only found out last week.'

'You've known for a week, and you didn't say anything?' The tone of incredulity again, but there was a hint of bitterness harboured there, too. She turned to face me, hands on her hips, nostrils flaring. 'So when did you think you might get around to telling me, hmm? The night before? On the day?'

I couldn't understand why she was so angry. It was so unlike her. If either of us was going to be angry, it was usually me.

I was stunned, to say the least, which didn't help with the situation. She wanted answers and she wanted them immediately.

Me being me, I tried to answer, but it didn't come out the way I thought it would. I opened my mouth to speak and kind of choked around the enormous lump that had formed in my throat. I felt my face crease up and fold into a wrinkled mess, and tears plopped from behind my lids in a bid to escape the inner torment. Shuddering sobs tore from within and eased themselves through my teeth.

She was in front of me in a flash, bending before me on one knee... Oh, I wish! Her eyes had lost the coolness from minutes earlier and now held the warm tenderness of the girl I loved.

'Hey, sweetheart, come on, don't cry.' What a beautiful voice, rich yet soft. And this of course made me cry harder. 'Hey...hey, come here.'

Two strong arms folded around me and pulled me against a very warm, very full chest. I tried to breathe her in, but my crying got in the way. Every time I tried to inhale the scent of her, I shuddered with sobs. It was a perfect opportunity to be close to her...to feel her next to me...to be in her arms, and I wasn't able to enjoy it.

That thought made me cry even harder, making her more comforting...more loving...more enchanting, and it also made her hold me tighter, pulling me towards her and into her. I could feel my body responding to her touch...feel my face turning towards her throat...feel my lips opening up to kiss her neck...taste her neck...

'Lou?'

Reality came crashing back. I tried to pull myself away from her, but she held on tighter, her face pressing against the top of my head. I mumbled a response into her skin, illicitly enjoying the way my lips felt on her neck, until I felt her body tense around me...and then it went quiet for a minute — a bloody long minute at that.

A cough, which I could feel moving up her chest, and then she was rapidly swallowing and saying, 'It won't be the end of us, will it? We'll still see each other, won't we?' More rapid swallowing, but this time it was from the both of us.

'Of course, we will. I'll be starting Uni next year in Manchester.' I hoped. 'And then we can be just as we are now.' Or closer. 'And you can come and visit any time.' All of the time. 'Or I could come and stay with you.' Please.

She gripped me harder, and I returned the grasp. To anybody watching we would have looked like a pair of star-crossed lovers, but the only audience we had was Cliff and Madonna, and they didn't really count.

Ash pulled back and stared into my eyes...long and hard...like she was exacting a promise of sorts from me. It took all the control I could muster to not just capture her mouth with mine...to not tell her how I was feeling...to not look away in absolute terror that I would do the previous two.

'Promise?'

'I promise, Ash. This isn't the end, just a blip. We've survived being separated once before; I'm sure to God we can do it again.' I swallowed before I lied. 'And best friends will always be together, right?' I didn't just want her as my best friend, but I was still in my 'living in her shadow' phase. And as I folded myself back into her arms, inhaled her scent, gloried in the feel of her, I actually believed what I had said.

The innocence of youth, eh? More like the idiocy.

Chapter Fourteen

My parents went on countless trips to Norfolk to view properties and decided on one in Great Yarmouth, of all places. It was okay if you liked fun fairs and the seaside. Remember, this is what I thought as a teenager. Now I can see the beauty of the sea, but at the time, everything about Yarmouth seemed hateful, as you can imagine. Yarmouth would take me away.

Time seemed to race ahead, leaving me gasping and clutching at the metaphorical stitch in my side, but that sensation paled in comparison with how I was feeling when I thought of leaving Ash. Every minute I spent with her seemed like a gift. I devoured moments, savoured seconds, took snapshots in my head of her to keep in my memory after I was gone, for after I left her. It was a bittersweet time. Half of me was enjoying being with her more than ever, whilst the other half was screaming in agony knowing it would all too soon come to an end. The dates had come through for the move, and it was to happen three days after my seventeenth birthday. What a present.

When I told her what day we were moving, I watched her contain her sadness, almost in the same way I had to contain mine. But then it seemed like an idea had spread itself all over her, and her face beamed, which initially I was quite pissed off about. The selfish part of me wanted her to wallow in misery, pretty much the same way I was. Until she told me why she was smiling. She wanted to make sure I would have a birthday I would always remember. And I can tell you this...it most definitely was.

Was that a good thing or a bad thing?

Read on and find out.

All my belongings were packed up, except for a few personal things and clothes, and the house had the echoing quality houses have when they are no longer a home.

Jo and I had stuffed most of our things willy-nilly into black bin bags, as we couldn't be arsed to sort through things, and we both wanted to go out that night.

It was strange, really. I knew Jo absolutely idolised her boyfriend, but she didn't seem bothered about the fact we would be moving two hundred miles away. I mean...she had been seeing him for nearly a year, and she wasn't even a patch as upset as I was to be leaving Ash. And Ash was supposedly just a friend.

I actually caught her singing while she was packing. Cliff Richard songs. Her singing was bad enough, but to Cliff? Don't get me started...I guess her singing wasn't *that* bad. I could be critical, but I still remember *Waterloo*.

Before I knew it, my birthday arrived, but I couldn't get excited about it, as it meant I would be leaving in three days. Ash had called and told me to dress special, as she had booked a table for us for seven-thirty but wouldn't tell me where.

I was surprised no one at home commented about me going out with only Ash on my birthday, and I think it was because they had too much else on their minds to wonder what I was getting up to. And if they had seen me in the bathroom...well, let's just say I was relieving the tension, so to speak.

God. I needed to. All the upset of moving and my obsessive addiction to my best friend would have driven anyone half mad with desire, and I was no exception.

The shower had become my haven, the hot water an extra sensation for my body to adjust to. All I could think about was the blueness of her eyes, the plumpness of those oh so kissable lips; it wasn't just the water that made me wet.

I was flooding...in special places...hot places...secret places. And it wasn't long before I felt my hand sneaking between those folds and collecting that silky wetness on my fingers and smearing it into me.

One solitary gasp ached from my mouth. My fingers were trying to relieve the tension in my core, but I knew, beyond the shadow of a doubt, it would take more than my fumblings to quench the thirst.

I lifted one leg onto the side of the tub and pushed my shoulders against the slippery cold tile for some kind of support. Two fingers were either side of my clit, pushing and pulling the swollen nub upwards and downwards...upwards and downwards. I kept on dipping into the pooling wetness and coating the side of my lips, the sensation agonisingly beautiful. I wanted to push my fingers inside myself...fuck myself...feel the walls closing in to clasp around the solitary finger, but as yet that prize was still intact. I wanted someone more special than me to take it.

I wanted Ash to take it...and take it...and take it.

I had visions of being underneath a waterfall in a different place and time, visions of experiencing the same need and fire. Water swept down me in a swirling mass circulating around my one foot, rivulets contorting in the whirlpool, becoming lost in the flow of movement until escape was found in the sucking hole of the bath plug.

That's how I was feeling, like I was being sucked in. The want inside me was sucking me in...making my hand jerk and thrust, pump and thrash against the engorged crux of my longing. My head was tilted back, and wet hair spread on the wall, sticking to the tile, forgetting to fall backwards, forgetting to stick to my face.

I could feel the orgasm building as I pushed and rocked my hips in an increasing tempo of desire. I knew I was going to cum...I knew I was going to cum...I knew...I was...going...to...cum...cum...cum...cum...cum...

Teeth bit down onto my bottom lip to stop the almost whistled name from tearing from my throat in a plea for her to fuck me...and fuck me...and fuck...me...as I was cumming...thinking she was doing exactly that...pretending it was her fingers pressing into me, onto me, rubbing and eliciting the blazing burst of an orgasm that blinded me and made me lose all sense of time and reality.

Droplets of water gathered on my breasts, and I envisioned a perfect mouth opening around an erect nipple. Straight white teeth opened to allow a wet full tongue to snake out and hover over the aching bud. I felt myself arch up, lost in the delicious sense of fantasy, believing she was there with me. I knew if I leaned forward she would capture me inside her perfect mouth, knew those hooded blue eyes told me she loved me. And I knew I was going to cum again.

And I did. A wet back slapped against the wall; a wet backside pushed itself up and away, up and away, meeting and greeting frantic fingers. The other hand was busy rolling and flicking a stimulated nipple, alternating between tweaking and pumping the breast.

Until the cumming had passed. And my legs believed they couldn't hold me up anymore. My fingers were slick with my juices, and I circled the over-sensitive wetness, savouring the delight of a second cumming.

I slipped effortlessly down the wall and slumped into a heap, whilst water cascaded off the top of my head, shoulders, and back. My breath was short and ragged, my throat was dry, and I had difficulty swallowing. My eyes were closed, as I initially savoured the moment, until I made way for the feeling of despair that joined with the water in washing over me.

Tears spilled over and trickled down my cheeks, blending with the spray. I felt so alone. So alone. I had experienced something wonderful and consuming. It was hard to comprehend the consuming feeling was really connected with the realisation I would soon be leaving the woman I loved in a matter of days.

I wanted to tell her, wanted her to know the truth about how I was feeling. But how could I tell her this secret? Being a lesbian is one thing, but being a coward made up who I really was. Being a coward was the only thing stopping me telling her I was a lesbian, if you see what I mean.

I was scared of how she would react. I was scared she would never speak to me again. The truth was, I was scared she wouldn't want me as much as I wanted her...or just *want* me. Full stop.

And there I sat. In the bottom of the bath. Water splashing off me. Curled in a heap, with water splashing off me.

And cried.
And cried.
And cried.

Ash was a vision of beauty and raw sexuality, and I had difficulty tearing my eyes from her. Images of me in the shower filtered into my mind, and I could feel the heat travel up into my face, flooding it with an incandescent glow.

'Are you okay?'

I couldn't even answer, just nodded like a prat. She looked at me a little longer before shaking her head and pushing her way through the door and into the darkened room that promised sumptuous delights. The choice of restaurant was perfect — Italian, my favourite.

As the evening progressed, I was very much aware of two lads from another table desperately trying to get our attention, and I ignored them as best as I could. Ash just grinned at them and mouthed, 'Not interested', which obviously made them more eager to snare us. It took a firm 'fuck off' from me to let them know we weren't interested, which I delivered as Ash went to the bathroom.

The usual 'You must be lezzas' left their mouths, as lads tend to do when they are given the knock back. This time they were right, well, half right, and by the time Ash returned they had left. And no...I didn't tell them to fuck off again. I wasn't going to let two pimply gits try to intimidate me; it was after a chat with the waiter they left like puppies.

Totally satiated, food wise, we left the restaurant and caught a taxi to the Little Jack Horner, a haunt for underage drinkers. Ash was okay, as she was eighteen, but I was a year short.

The place was full of minors, and I felt quite at home. Ash told me to find a seat and trundled off to the bar to shortly return with a drink named 'The Blob', mainly because after too many of them, that's how you felt — like a big fat blob who was good for nothing. It had pretty much everything in it and tasted vile...but I drank it because Ash had picked it for me. I even drank the second one.

Ash didn't show any effects of even having had a sip of a drink, never mind two of the buggers. I could feel myself beginning to squint when she was talking to me and swore the next drink would definitely be a soft one. Then I nearly lost all my bearings as she got up and sauntered over to the jukebox, and it wasn't long before I heard the dulcet tones of Alison Moyet ringing through the pub singing *Only You* — just for me...just for Ash...just for the both of us.

The evening was becoming blurry, especially the line between reality and fantasy. I was beginning to believe I was actually on a date with the dark-haired object of all my desires. I was beginning to find it difficult to not touch her knee or her arm when we were talking. She even started to do that to me, especially when she really wanted my attention. I was transfixed and couldn't tear my eyes from any part of her anatomy that happened to land in my view.

Everything felt so right...so special. I actually forgot I was leaving in three days. I truly believed that if heaven did exist, it was here, with her, lurking in the pools of her blue eyes.

Before I knew it, the bartender was ringing his bell and shouting for last orders. A stab of disappointment raced through me, as I knew the fantasy had to come to an end. Unhurriedly, I put on my coat and then said I had to use the Ladies.

Inside the bathroom, I rinsed my face with cold water, just to get back a feeling of normalcy. Tired green eyes stared back at me from the mirror. Well, not tired exactly, more like disappointed.

'What did you expect?' My voice sounded rough and despondent. 'Flowers and a profession of undying love?' A snort left my nose, and I felt my body slump in the realisation that, to Ash, this was only a birthday night out. It meant a hell of a lot more to me.

I reapplied my lipstick and headed towards the door. I had to somehow snap out of my obsession and accept that Ash and I were friends and nothing more.

It's not easy, you know. Having the love of your life waiting on the other side of the door and knowing you are leaving in three, well, two, days and not be able to tell her how you feel.

A sigh escaped as I drew the door back, and there she was...resplendent in all her gorgeous glory, leaning with her back against the wall, totally casual and relaxed, her smile splitting her face in two.

I think I fell in love with her all over again.

I'm sure you can recollect walking down the street when you were worse for wear because of the demon drink. So, I don't have to tell you about the fiasco we had trying to get back to the taxi rank in town. We thought it would be easier to go to the depot instead of waiting for one to turn up. Erm...wrong.

It was fun, though, to give it its due. Fun trying to not stagger about. We weren't blotto, but we definitely knew we had had our fill. As pissed people tend to do, we linked arms just to try and steady each other. That made me far from steady.

The feeling of her next to me...the firmness of her body next to mine made my head swim with absolute longing to increase the contact. So I did. I leaned into her, languishing at the nearness of my heart's deepest wish. I was so caught up in the moment, I didn't realise I was holding her hand. Yep, I had looped my arm across her middle and pulled those slender digits into my own. The sensation of tangling my fingers with hers was an invitation to insanity. I was going crazy for her.

When I realised, instead of drawing my hand away like I should have — you know, like I had been burned. I did the opposite; I froze. And stared at her fingers laced in mine.

She stopped talking, and I could feel her breath tapping on the side on my face — short, sharp breaths that warmed much more than the skin on my cheek. As if in slow motion, I lifted my eyes to meet her gaze and was caught in a blueness that turned nearly violet in the darkness. I was transfixed. Couldn't blink, just stared. And she stared back — unblinking, too.

I wasn't aware of moving in closer. It must have been the alcohol, although to this day I still believe I was under the influence of Ash and Ash alone. The alcohol had dissipated to a distant memory.

We were inches apart. Our breaths mingled in the cold night air, twisting and turning into some unfocused fog, joining...connecting like they needed to melt into one to survive.

I could say what I did was a last ditch effort to claim what my heart yearned for. I could say I did it just to experience all that was Ash. I even could say I did it to quench the thirst I had for her — just the once, to touch those lips, to kiss those lips. To claim them for my own...just the once.

I can't say any of these things. Because I didn't know, still don't know why I did it, why I closed that gap between us and brushed my needy lips against hers.

If it had been just that — a kiss, however brief, then it all would be okay, and maybe I wouldn't be sitting here today writing this. If she hadn't returned the oh-so-brief brush of the lips with a kiss that was slightly longer, again, I wouldn't be sitting here. But she did.

I was lost. Control was a thing of the past...and I was lost.

My hand lifted to her face and cupped her cheek, revelling in the texture. Soft. Supple. Perfect. I pulled her head down closer to mine and captured her lips, holding them beneath mine...holding them still. And waited. I was surprised she couldn't feel my heart beating wildly in my mouth, as I waited...with my lips locked on hers.

Then...slowly...I felt her lips move, conveying what I was feeling in her tender kiss. Expectation soared as I moved my lips against hers, my hand pushing back into long thick hair to clutch at the nape and bring her face down into mine.

Pressure building, the kiss became stronger, finding the will to continue...finding the hope that she would collect what was rightfully hers. Then becoming more ardent. Wetness escaped my mouth and blended with hers. The taste was all I had ever dreamed it would be...but better.

Lips parted at a silent demand, and I could feel a soft wet tongue escape her mouth and beg entrance to mine.

Permission granted.

Her hands were on my hips, and she pulled me into her, increasing the pressure. I slipped my free hand around her waist to assist with the connection.

Wetness poured from between my legs as my heart continued to perform cartwheels in my chest, having left the confines of my mouth. Hips began a methodical rocking against each other.

Ash staggered back slightly, taking me with her. Before I knew it, she was up against the wall with me between her legs — pushing into her, kissing her, claiming her. All my inhibitions were gone.

I nearly came when her hand gripped my backside and pulled me into her, her groan entering my mouth as the kiss deepened into something carnal...sexually primitive.

It was shit or bust...shit or bust.

My hand left her waist and snaked inside her coat, inside her shirt, and hovered for a split second at the base of her breast. I could feel the heat of it taunting me, begging me to clutch and clasp and pump.

Who was I to refuse?

'Fuck...Lou...*God*...'

Her words sounded inside my mouth, as I continued to grind and push and kiss her. I was truly lost...totally immersed in all that was her.

If this was a dream, then I wanted to sleep forever.

But this wasn't a dream; this was me acting out all my fantasies. All my fantasies about my best friend...the friend I loved...was *in* love with. The friend I never thought would look at me twice.

I needed to taste her, lick her throat, suck her skin, sample the little crevice where her neck met her shoulder.

I craved to nurse her nipple in my mouth, rolling it around my tongue. I yearned to slip my hand between her legs and sample the wetness I hoped would be seeping from her.

I was like a child in a sweet shop. Everything was on display, everything for purchase, but I didn't know what to sample first. And like a child I wanted it all...needed it all. My hands were trying to touch all of her while savouring each caress. A gargantuan task. I was drowning...seeping...dissolving into her... Her lips were on fire; my libido was out of control. I was losing all sense of reality.

Her hands slipped their way tentatively underneath my jacket...the shirt...the bra...

God. The feel of those fingers caressing my breast, pinching the erect nipple which was becoming firmer and firmer and then... They stopped. And. Froze. Pulled away. To be shortly followed by her mouth.

Blue eyes were wide with shock; her lips glistened with my saliva, my hand still on her breast.

'I can't...*can't*...Lou. *I can't do this.*' She shoved me away, leaving me staggering backwards with disbelief pouring from me. And she ran...leaving me gasping. She ran...leaving me stunned. She ran...leaving me there...standing...with my broken heart in my hands.

Didn't see Ash. Didn't expect to.

Through the last three days, I had gone through all the phases, stages, and rites of passage nobody should ever experience.

Guilt. Anger. Frustration. Apathy. Then all of them again.

I couldn't tell you how many times I picked up the phone to call her, but chickened out at the last minute. Nor could I tell you how long I stood outside her house, trying to pluck up the courage to just knock. What would I say? What *could* I say? So, I just stood there...watching closed curtains.

I felt raw. Exposed. Tumultuous. Depressed. Manic. I felt everything but wanted. The feelings churning through me never stayed constant. Loneliness prevailed. Who could I tell? No one...not even Jo. What good would it do?

On the Saturday morning, after all our things had been loaded in the removal van, I felt the end of an era descending on me. The iron doors clanked shut and echoed the sound of the shutters falling into place in my heart. I felt it. Slam. Shutters down. *Finito.* It was a feeble attempt to block out everything and everyone, almost like a brick wall. As my dad laid his hand on my shoulders in a signal of our departure, I felt the key lock in my chest...like a knife twisting.

'Time to go, Lou.' His face showed concern as he gently rubbed my shoulder in an attempt to comfort me. 'You'll love it there, you'll see. It'll be a new start for all of us.'

Words stuck in my throat so I just nodded. Tears collected in my eyes but stayed unshed. Although I had my belongings jammed into black bin bags in the back of that van, I left everything behind in Stockport that day. Everything. My innocence. My hope. My heart — broken and wretched. But most of all I left behind the only person I knew I would ever love.

Now. That is no way to start a new life, is it?

I left Stockport feeling like a shell — empty, devoid of a future, bereft of my soul.

Chapter Fifteen

2004

You can tell by the year on this section that time had passed — too many years to go into detail about, too many years and events to dissect and analyse. One thing is certain through it all: I had spent the passing nineteen years growing embittered. Relationship after relationship grew and died, and the time in between was spent reflecting on how shit life truly was.

Stop.

Hold your horses. More to the point...I should hold my literary horses and just try and put you in the picture about a few things. You know — clarify a few things and put these things into some kind of perspective, box them, undo the files, and spill the proverbial beans. How else can you understand me or my life?

The first few months in Great Yarmouth (whomever thought of Great must have been tripping) were no picnic. They were, in a word, bollocks. And if you want more than one word, they were big, fat, hairy, camel bollocks.

As I said earlier, Jo didn't seem bothered about the move, and after two months in Norfolk, she told me why. She was leaving. Leaving me there...on my own.

Logic and reasoning told me this was okay; it was the pain in my chest that argued otherwise. Jo's counter argument was that she had only agreed to move to make sure I settled in okay. Very noble and sisterly.

Bollocks to that.

She went on to tell me her life was with Craig, her boyfriend, who had been setting up a flat for the both of them whilst she was babysitting me.

I know...I know. Years have told me that this is what people do when they love each other. They step aside from family, not 'fucking desert' them, as had I screamed at her. I also know that I was unreasonable.

To say I blew my stack would be putting it mildly, almost euphemistically. My exact words were along the lines of 'I don't need you to fucking babysit me!' and I'm too much of a lady to tell you the rest.

After my tirade, I watched her, really watched her. Watched her face crumple and the tears well up behind her eyes. Watched her nod her head, sharply. Watched her rapidly swallow and sit back on the bed and wait.

The comments I made were cruel, and like an injured animal after an attack, I withdrew into the corner to lick my wounds, wounds that for the most part I had inflicted on myself.

Emotionally, I was a mess. The two people I loved most in the world had deserted me, left me there to rot and wallow in self-pity. I couldn't see past it, couldn't see past that point in my life. It was too black.

The day she went I just gave her a hug, secretly inhaling her scent, believing it would be the last time I would ever see her. How dramatic! I gave a quick wave to her and Craig and then went inside the house, leaving my parents outside to wave the van off. The van that took Jo away from me.

I cried so hard I had a nosebleed. A cracker, too. My dad found me curled up on my bedroom floor covered in blood and went into panic mode, thinking I had tried to top myself.

Death by nosebleed. Just my luck.

After the initial discovery and the realisation I hadn't sliced open my nasal veins with a penknife, my dad put something cold behind my neck and told me to sit up straight, all the while I was performing those little hiccupping noises that people get when they have cried too long and too hard. Like kids, really.

I fumbled around the back of my head and fingered the ice pack, shuddering sobs escaping, bits of dribble from my mouth. I was confused. It didn't feel like ice, crushed or otherwise.

I pulled the pack around and stared at the tea towel that held the cold mystery parcel. He wouldn't, would he?

He had.

He'd used a medium-sized bag of frozen peas, its obnoxious green packaging now lying limply after having performed its duty.

That was the icebreaker, literally. I threw back my head and laughed, loud and long. Laughed until I felt the dribble of blood trickle down my face again.

Aw fuck.

Peas to the ready, and I was in position again, little spurts of laughter slipping out.

What a sight! Face smeared with blood and tears, sitting like I had a pole up my arse, clasping a bag of frozen peas to the nape of my neck like my life depended on it.

Maybe in a way, it did.

Weeks blurred. Months flew. Years screamed by. Obviously, I still saw Jo. She ended up moving to Norwich with Craig and their little boy, Simon...or as his Aunty Lou called him — Simple Simon.

I went to Manchester Uni, and I think I shagged half the girls on my course. Don't get me wrong, there weren't that many. Grin. Just enough. As I said before, well...nearly said...I could not commit to one person. Not would not...*could not*.

There was only one person for me, and I hadn't heard a dickie bird from her in years. But I still had her red jumper and books.

Bugger. If anyone actually went in the box in the spare room, they would think I had a tendency toward paedophilia.

How many people do you know that have a tattered red jumper that hasn't been washed for nearly thirty years hidden away and with that, a couple of tattered children's books? Not many, I guess, unless... Nope. Not going to mention Michael Jackson.

And you should also know, that on the days it rained — you know, really rained — I still got that jumper out and held it close to me.

Images of blue eyes, concerned blue eyes...Ash's twinkling blue eyes...filled me and left my heart breaking all over again. Echoes of *'Here. Put it on...you'll catch your death...'* would resonate in my head, making me believe she was actually standing before me.

And if I tried hard enough...believed hard enough...I could still smell her. Smell her scent enfolded in the fibres of that old red jumper.

Chapter Sixteen

You need a very brief description of what I do now. I'm what you call an Educational Psychologist...or Ed Psych. My job is to help troubled teens, and, for the most part, try to bring some order to the havoc that troublesome teens bring to school.

I work mainly for Norfolk County Council, and my job is to go into schools where and when needed. I enjoy my job most of the time, but like all jobs, there is also a shit side to it.

I like talking to teenagers, more so than to people of my own age group. I don't have to pretend to be something I'm not. I am just Ms. Turner, or Lou, the person that is there to help them through a sticky part of their lives. I am not just the person who is gay and single...the person who is cold and detached...the person who never speaks about her private life.

These kids are not bad, on the whole that is, as there is always one bad apple, yadda yadda yadda. What they have to go through at home is enough to make anybody weep. Abusive parents...physically, emotionally, and sexually. And not just their parents, either. Siblings, 'friends' of the family, other family members. But there are also other factors to consider — alcohol and drug abuse for starters, then illness. I've seen kids wail and rant about how unfair life is when they find out someone they love is terminally ill. One girl actually got home from school and found her mother dead on the stairs. Another witnessed his father OD in front of him.

Whatever people tell you, kids are not as resilient as you may believe. Their problems do not stop at the school gates, however much the teachers would like the lessons to carry on as usual. No. Kids try, for the most part. They have to, insomuch as other kids will smell their weakness and attack.

True. Have you ever heard a kid taunt another one because his mother is dying of cancer? I have.

So, as I was saying, kids, however much we love them, can be little shits. Vulnerable little shits, but little shits, all the same.

Consequently, when everything uproots itself, there I am, and although for the most part my hands are tied, I try.

My ambition is to help kids adapt and accept. I think it stemmed from my own upbringing. You know — the broken home thing, the feeling of displacement, the not fitting in. That made me want to do this job. Divorce and separation are becoming all too common, and as I said before, kids can only take so much before the dam bursts and their world goes down the pan.

So what do they do? Loads of things, actually. They can withdraw, react, or attack. Eating disorders are rife, along with social phobia, school refusing, sexual promiscuity, drug and alcohol abuse, self-harm, aggression, depression. Some even become elective mutes. I could go on...but then I would detract from what I want to tell you next.

Some of them become evil little fuckers who terrorise, vandalise, steal, antagonise, joyride, drink to excess, take drugs whilst stealing to feed their habit, and intimidate and assault people. One of these gems was Sam Read.

God, did I hate that boy. Hated him with a vengeance unprecedented...hated him and his cocksure grin...wanted to slap the little git senseless. In my opinion, he didn't have the sense of an earthworm, and at least earthworms are good for something.

He had a string of antisocial behaviour writs against him starting from the tender age of nine and had a curfew, which he was forever breaking, a curfew that entailed an ankle bracelet that alerted the authorities if he was out of his house after eight o'clock.

Do you think that stopped him? No way. It just egged him on. There wasn't a damned thing the police could do except take him down to the station and give him a warning. He wasn't old enough, and he played this to his advantage.

I didn't get involved until he took his behaviour through the school gates. And then that's where I stepped in.

As I said before, he wasn't a nice boy. Trouble was that he thought the world owed him a living; it was my job to show him that it didn't.

He stole, destroyed, and terrorised at any given opportunity. Ted Lawrence, his previous Ed Psych, had washed his hands of him, mainly because of the reign of terror Sam had inflicted. Obscene words had been sprayed along Ted's car, vulgar messages had been left on his answer phone, and Sam was stalking him whenever the chance came to pass. All this resulted in Ted's gradual wearing down. Fourteen years old and Sam knew every trick in the book when it came to the systematic breakdown of a human being. Sam was an out and out bastard, an evil bastard at that.

So, after Ted said, 'No more,' Sam was passed along to me. Whoopee doo. I was not a happy bunny, to say the least.

Sam broke into the school and vandalised everything and anything that got in his way. It was a mess...the Science labs were complete devastation, the computer room suffered broken monitors and smashed hard drives. To put you in the picture, it was thousands of pounds worth of damage. This time the police were involved on a bigger scale. They suspected that there were others involved; there was too much damage for just one little pipsqueak.

Sam had been caught leaving the school premises at 12:36 AM on the Sunday morning with a monitor under his arm. The question was — who were Sam's accomplices? It was the unknown faces they wanted, mainly because they had suspects in the pipeline and needed hard-core evidence to get them.

I was called down to the station at 1:45. Pissed off. Big time. It wasn't the usual thing for me to do. I had only ever been called down to the station on one previous occasion, and that was for possession of a class B drug. Not mine, obviously. A young girl who was in my care had given my number as a point of contact.

So here I was again and definitely looking worse for wear. I hadn't even met the little...I'll leave out that word or replace it with twat. I didn't understand why I'd been called out in the first place. Although I knew him by reputation, I had only been assigned to his growing case at the beginning of the week and met his social worker on Wednesday. There was no love lost between those two. Or with me, for that matter.

The desk sergeant was a man in his early fifties who had the face of someone who was sick and tired of filling in forms for delinquent teenagers. When I introduced myself, I saw his eyebrows raise to signify he thought I was one of those 'do gooders' who would try and get the kid dismissed.

Now, I had been woken up when I was in the middle of a dream with Jodie Foster...and we weren't reliving a scene from *Panic Room*, if you get my drift. It was more like *Contact*, but without the aliens and without the interest in talking to someone out of this world. It was out of this world, though. At least, it could've been if that bloody phone hadn't started ringing.

'Someone will be along to take you down to the cells in a few minutes, Miss Turner.'

At the gruff voice of the receptionist, Jodie disappeared, and reality came roaring back.

A few minutes my arse. More like twenty-five minutes. I was just in mid-rant about being kept hanging on by people who couldn't find their arse with both hands when I heard my name being called behind me.

Mmmm. I said 'called', didn't I? It was more like a question. Mmmm...again. Question? Or statement?

'Louise Turner?'

I froze, my finger still pointing accusatorily at the bloke behind the counter.

'Louise Turner. It's you, isn't it?'

My stomach...my poor stomach didn't know what to do. Mainly because it had been flooded with adrenaline fired by my heart. Every single hair on my body stood up to attention, and I could feel a sheen of sweat coat my upper lip. I knew I should have turned 'round and looked into those blue eyes, but I couldn't. I was paralysed, struck by Statues Disease...almost a caricature of Lord Kitchener.

'Miss Turner?' The desk sergeant looked at me with concern, and I probably did look weird, but I couldn't have cared less what anybody thought. 'Detective Inspector Richards is here to see you.'

I know! Well, I knew it was Ash. My Ash. My Ash was standing right behind me. But what I didn't know, or expect, was for Ash...my Ash to *be* standing right behind me — a Detective Inspector or otherwise.

I pivoted on the spot like my left foot had been nailed to the floor, my heart now sitting uncomfortably in my throat, waiting for a peek at the person who had abandoned it for so long.

It was like a dream sequence. Everything moved painfully slowly, like when you keep pressing the skip frame button on a DVD player. All movements were jerky and mechanical to point of torture.

And then she was there. Standing in front of me like a vision. So beautiful...so goddamn agonisingly beautiful. And still unobtainably Ash.

Her hair danced just below her shoulders, raven and shining. It draped the shoulders of a black suit jacket that hugged her slender body and contrasted with the snowy white of her shirt. Legs were encased in tailor-cut black trousers, which were complemented by flat, slip-on leather shoes.

Serviceable. Good for running, I bet. And that's where my focus stayed until I heard that rich voice once again.

'It is you. I *knew* it.'

My head snapped up so quickly I felt the muscles in the back of my neck ping into place. Blue eyes stared intently into my face, and I saw her customary crooked smile twitch around her lips. Beauty personified. She was a vision...a vision.

'What's the matter with you? Cat got your tongue?'

My mouth began to open and close in a fair imitation of a poor little fish hanging at the end of a line.

As words failed me, the smile slipped from her face, and she looked concerned. Or was it disappointed?

I watched her head shake, she was probably trying to clear it, and then there was an elaborate clearing of her throat. A hand shot out and stopped in front of me...extended in greeting. I just stared at it like a moron.

'Ashley Richards. Detective Inspector Ashley Richards.' The tone was curt and unfamiliar. It had lost the friendly quality it had held moments before. I lifted my hand and slipped my fingers into hers. I can actually remember closing my eyes ever so briefly as I savoured the contact before raising my gaze to meet hers.

She was staring at me in expectation, and for a brief moment I felt anger and pain come bubbling up from a well that had been filled when she rejected me nearly twenty years earlier. I told myself to get a grip; it was two decades ago, although it felt like yesterday.

But it wasn't yesterday. Shit. From somewhere deep inside I dragged up a smile and gripped her hand tighter.

'Hello, Ash. Long time, no see.'

The journey down to the cellblock was completed in pained silence. We had performed the obligatory 'hello and doesn't time fly', and then we had just stopped. That's when things started to feel uncomfortable. We silently communicated, mainly with nodding of heads in the direction of the door, that now would be as good a time as any to go and see Sam.

As we made our way to Sam's cell, Ash decided to put me in the picture about a few things. She'd been in Norfolk since the beginning of the previous week, a big wig 'imported' from Manchester Metropolitan Police because the man suspected of leading the thugs at the school with Sam was a Mancunian. She was in charge of the team that was investigating the group, which they thought was responsible for a new local crime wave.

Sam was a git, she said, but he hadn't done even a fraction of the things the rest of the gang had. He didn't realise they were using him, making him feel like part of them before they showed their true colours. Which included dealing, extortion, and fraud. And those were the crimes the police knew about. They'd never been able to prove anything on anyone in the group, though...until they had arrested its newest member. Nabbing Sam gave them the opportunity to step in and try and get someone to name names.

DI Richards was raring to make an arrest — and she wanted me to get Sam to talk. She wasn't too happy when I reminded her that everything Sam told me would be confidential and couldn't be used in a court of law. In truth, it could be, but we didn't really like to go down that avenue if we could help it. Puts the kids off when they want to confide. Not many of us would bare our soul if we thought the person we were telling would run off shouting it into the wind.

Then I reminded her that, by law, he had to have an Advocate with him.

'Bollocks.'

I couldn't believe she hadn't thought of it before. 'Excuse me?'

Ash leaned closer to me, and I could feel her breath on my face. Her eyes were steely blue, the twinkle absent. 'I said, bol...locks.'

I could feel myself cowering as her body imposed itself over mine. No wonder she was a DI; she could frighten the shit out of anyone. I mean...she was six feet tall and solid. Her face brooked no argument.

In my job, however, this kind of intimidation was par for the course. Somewhere deep inside me I grabbed hold of an iota of courage and straightened my back, pushing my face close to hers, close enough to feel her breath skitter along my skin and send tremors down my spine. Fuck. She was so beautiful. All I wanted to do was lean forward just another inch...and capture her soft lips...

'I said bollocks.'

That was it.

'And *I* said that I cannot divulge a client's personal information. It is confidential...all about trust. And you...' I took a step back and casually scanned her from head to toe, '...should know it wouldn't stand up in a court of law. An Advocate is required; he's a minor.'

My smug smile made her grit her teeth. I didn't just see her grit them, I *heard* it. And it made me smile even wider. 'So you see, *Detective*, I can't help you. This is a waste of both our time.' I turned to go. Her hand gripped the top of my arm and held me in place like a vice.

'Not so fast, *Miss Turner*.'

'Get your hand off me.' I attempted to prise her hand away, but she was holding on tight. I was tempted to kick her in the shin and make a run for it, but then I remembered I wasn't thirteen. I relaxed my body and just gave her a bored expression.

Her face showed she had been expecting the kick, and my relaxing and looking at her like she was pond life completely threw her. The beautiful face creased into thought, and I could tell she didn't exactly know what to do next.

Blue eyes shot to her hand, and her face creased even more before she slowly relaxed her grip on me, watching her fingers with fascinated intent as they reluctantly lifted.

'Thank you.' Short and to the point.

'Sorry. I—'

'Apology accepted. Now if you'll excuse me, I have a bed calling my name.' I didn't want to waste my time talking to Sam; I could do that in the morning. I turned to go, but my heart stayed facing her, shouting, 'Do you remember me? Do you remember how you left me to curl up and die?'

I felt the tears sneak up behind my eyes and threaten to expose me, and I quickly walked away, hoping that I wouldn't embarrass myself.

'Lou.' Spoken so softly, my name on her lips trickled in through my ears and down deep inside me. 'Please, Lou, I'm sorry. I...'

I stopped and turned to face her. I wanted to ask her what she was sorry for — trying to force me to find out information for her case or for breaking my heart. Sorry for fucking up my evening or for fucking up my life and making it impossible for me to forget her.

She stepped towards me, and I instinctively stepped back. I could see the hurt on her face, which she quickly masked with a cough and the straightening of her shoulders. Coldness slipped into place, and she once again became the professional.

'Look, I'll be straight with you.' Weren't you always? That was the problem. 'We need to get the ringleader behind bars and keep him there. I don't know how long I can stay in Norfolk, so we need information fast. This bloke is a nasty piece of work, very nasty.'

'Sam?'

'No. Danny Spencer. He's the new gang leader. The old one, Mike Adams, found himself slumped over the steering wheel of his car in Manchester as he was waiting for the traffic lights to change.' My eyebrows lifted in surprise. 'And Danny decided a nice getaway to Norfolk was exactly what he needed until the hue and cry calmed down. Thought he'd start a new gang here.'

'Bugger.'

'Exactly. We *know* it was him, but we can't prove it. Not that we miss the bloke he disposed of, it's just our best chance to get this little bastard locked up for a long time.'

'And where exactly do I fit into all of this?' I stepped closer to her, feeling the aura of her body envelop me, and my eyes fluttered closed as the vestiges of the love I felt for her tried to surface. I coughed, composed myself, and adopted the countenance of someone who is paying rapt attention.

'You could be the link we need.'

'Link? How can I be the link? I don't even know Sam...and he doesn't know me. I was only assigned to his case last week.'

'All the better. Look...' She reached out to take my arm, then stopped and pulled it back, securing it in place at her side. 'Look, Sam is the key. Danny is a bigheaded little fucker and loves to brag about what he's done, but he's not stupid. We have to find out anything Sam might know. If he's trying to impress or intimidate you, then maybe he will try to brag himself up.'

'I doubt that. He'll close up more likely than anything.'

'Maybe, but I'd like you to try.'

Her look was softening, and a smile played around her lips. I know, I know — I should have told her to shove it and walked away. But that smile, those eyes...God! I was a goner.

And that was the start of something I can only describe as a love/hate relationship. I'm not going to explain that comment. You'll have to read on if you want to find out why I loved to hate Detective Inspector Richards.

Being in the cell with that little shit was torture. After the initial 'Fuck you, bitch' and other similar poetic declarations, he settled on a moronic grin interspersed with lascivious leering at my chest.

I honestly don't know how I kept from slapping him senseless. Thirty minutes in his company made me feel nauseous, and I could understand why he was disliked by everyone. I try to see some spark of good in everybody, but however hard I tried...nothing. He was a bad 'un, through and through.

You could tell he was trouble just by looking at him. A shaved head that left a twattish fringe at the front screamed 'Jailbait!' — a definite contender for the clink — as did everything else about him. He must have weighed eight stone wet through and needed high heels to reach the skirting boards, but he had a wiry strength which was ten times worse than facing some six-foot body builder. Now his eyes — I still shiver when I think of them — his eyes were cold. Dead. Totally and utterly without a shred of compassion. Cold grey, but quick and sly. I knew he took in everything that was going on. This boy missed nothing and used everything to his advantage, like a predator. As I said, trouble, with a capital T.

Trying to be civil to him was agonising. I used all the textbook approaches, but they didn't have any effect on him. He was street smart, demanding he should have someone there to protect his rights. The station had tried to contact his parents, but there was no answer, either to knocking or phoning. Whether they were purposefully ignoring the attempts at contact, I don't know. They were probably used to getting calls, especially since Sam didn't give two shits about his court curfew or the ankle bracelet he had to wear to alert the authorities when he stepped out of his boundaries.

After thirty minutes, I'd had enough. I knew if I didn't get out of there, I would pull his grinning, waste-of-space carcass off the bunk and give him a good old-fashioned hiding. Don't get me wrong, I don't condone violence in any way, shape, or form...but come on! He would try the patience of a saint.

Ash was waiting for me as I stepped out; she nearly knocked me back inside the cell. I heard Sam shout, 'Evening, Inspector,' from behind me and grimaced as Ash gave him the look — cold and hard. Fuck. Even I was scared, and it wasn't directed at me.

'You might as well get comfortable, Read. You're going to be seeing a lot of this place.' The self-assured smirk on his face wavered slightly as Ash stepped forward. 'Get *real* comfortable, mate.' The 'real' came out as a growl rather than a word, her teeth chewing around it.

She made a big deal out of slamming the door closed, the echo ringing around the basement of the police station. 'Well? What did he tell you?'

'Look...erm...you really didn't expect him to spill his guts on a first meeting?' I didn't know why I was trying to soften the blow, and, in effect, sign myself up for more of the same. She raised her brow, her lips curving at the edges. I could see her mind working double time, and I knew I was going to regret answering the phone earlier that night.

'Well, tha—' She didn't get chance to finish the sentence, as the heavy door at the end of the corridor was thrown back and a woman came tearing through it, hair ruffled and, if I'm not mistaken, her blouse buttoned up wrong.

'Who's in charge here?' Stern, to the point, full of authority. I liked her.

Ash wasted no time in letting the woman know she was not taking any shit. 'Who the fuck are you?'

The woman stopped inches away from us and slowly appraised Ash from head to foot. The sneer grew wider as she progressed down the long frame, and when she reached the bottom, she started the journey all the way up to the face again.

Honestly, I could have cut the air with a knife. They just stood there and glared at each other like a couple of kids who were arguing over a toy. To be perfectly truthful, I was just as bad. Gormless is the word. I just stood looking from one to the other, kind of comparing them in a weird kind of way.

The woman was only an inch or so shorter than Ash and her hair was a shade lighter, and even though she looked like she had literally been hoisted out of bed, she was a stunner. I could feel my mouth beginning to water. Then I looked at Ash and realised that even though I was attracted to Miss No Name... Aw, you know — heart and all that.

'Erm...Louise Turner...Lou...Turner.' I didn't even realise I had stepped forward between the pair and turned my back on Ash to hold out my hand to the stranger. 'Ed Psych.'

Initially I saw a flash of anger sweep over her face, but then it turned into something softer, more...let me think...more appreciative. That's the word...appreciative, but not as in, 'Oh, I'm so glad you introduced yourself' appreciative. More like 'What do we have here?' whilst licking lips appreciative.

I heard a distinct cough behind me, and I could feel Ash becoming restless. The woman's eyes flicked over my shoulder and briefly landed on Ash before she gave me all of her attention, her hand slipping effortlessly into my own. 'Gemma. Gemma Jackson.' She closed her hand more firmly around mine, almost like a caress.

'Sorry to break up the party, girls...' The sound of Ash's voice sliced through our introductions. She wasn't happy about being left out. 'Detective Inspector Richards.' She paused for effect. 'I'm in charge of the investigation.'

'Really?' Gemma's voice came out cold and full of sarcasm. 'Well, then, *Detective*, you won't mind telling me why I only found out Sam Read is here thirty-five minutes ago.' That explained the hair and the shirt. 'Don't you know what you have done is illegal?' Ash didn't answer. 'Under the Child Protection Act, any minor must have an Advocate present at all times during questioning.' Her hand was on her hip, and she leaned back to glare into Ash's face.

'Really?' Ash's response was more sarcastic in delivery, and I was beginning to see the telltale signs of one hell of an impending bitch fight.

'Yes...*really*. I am within my rights to demand that Sam be released and—'

'Fuck that. That little shi—'

'Ladies, ladies, please.' My tone was coaxing, trying to forestall the inevitable blow up. 'This is not helping anyone.' I felt Ash stiffen, even though I didn't see her. Gemma's face looked as if it was etched from stone. So, I tried the oldest trick in the book.

I flirted.

I know. I wasn't even sure if Gemma was gay, but it was worth a shot. A smile was on my lips, and my hand was smoothing her arm before anyone could say Jack Robinson. 'Look, Gemma,' another smile, 'can't we just grab a coffee and talk about this. I mean...' I looked over my shoulder at a fuming Ash, directing Gemma's gaze there, and then looked at her squarely in the face before contorting my features into the expression that said we should pity the detective, as she knew not what she did. 'We could just...you know...' I stepped forward as if I was bringing her into my confidence, but in the process I eliminated personal body space.

Gemma didn't back away, and I could see a smile play along her lips. Just a little more, Turner.

'We could talk about Sam...and get to know each other a little better,' I paused, then added a hurried, 'in case we will be working together.' The look I gave her said I was interested in anything but work at that moment.

I could see her conscience fighting with her libido. Her fingers came up and played with stray locks of hair and then moved with deliberate agitation to the buttons on her shirt...the ones in all the wrong holes. I could feel a laugh bubbling up inside me, and I had the urge to tell her the buttons were all wrong, but that would have defeated my objective. There would be no way she would agree to anything I wanted if she felt like a prat.

'We could all grab a coffee.' Ash had decided to join the conversation at last. To be truthful, I felt relieved. I didn't fancy going for a coffee with Gemma alone...and to use an old adage, I had bitten off more than I could chew.

One look at Ash's face told me she wasn't happy about playing along with this woman, but the alternative was Sam Read walking out the door tonight. And after having spent just thirty minutes with him, there was no way I wanted him loose on the streets, that night or for a long time to come. Especially because it would fall under my jurisdiction to take care of him. That was the last thing I needed.

Gemma didn't answer, just looked at me and raised an eyebrow.

'Sounds like a plan.' I looked Gemma straight in the face, obscuring Ash's view of me whilst I grimaced and shrugged my shoulders in forced resignation. Even though inside I felt completely different.

Ash sighed behind me, a deep dramatic sigh that said she knew what face I had pulled, and I felt the colour in my face begin to darken to a pinkish hue.

'Shall I lead the way?' With that, she pushed past the both of us and marched to the door, leaving the two of us to stare at each other.

'Is she jealous? Are you two—'

'No way!' Quite forceful. Methinks the lady doth protest too much.

I shot a worried look in Ash's direction. She had the door partly open and was just standing there. I could only see part of her face, and I couldn't read anything. It was closed off.

Shit.

I don't even know why I wrote shit there. It's just a feeling I had at the time. Whether it's because I felt exposed, or maybe it's the fact I thought it reminded her of the night she kissed me and ran.

'Come on, then.' As I walked towards the exit, I felt a little less cocky than I had five minutes earlier.

Chapter Seventeen

Coffee was fine. Gemma wasn't as hard nosed as I had first thought. The only down side was that Ash seemed off. Put out might be the more apt expression. All the time we were discussing Sam Read, she answered briefly and could barely make eye contact with me or Gemma. She kept looking towards the door of the canteen, her mug of coffee gripped tightly in her hand.

Come to think of it, I don't think she actually took a sip.

After twenty minutes, we were all caught up with events. By all accounts, Gemma was no fan of Mr. Read, and this was definitely not her first visit to the cells on his behalf. Eleven times she had been called out to represent him, twelve including the current one. She gave us a brief history of his crimes and misdemeanours, nothing that was a surprise to us. Over the last four and a half years, he had been brought to book twenty-one times. Twenty-one times!

The only time Ash livened up was when Gemma said she should really go and speak to him. I saw her eyes become animated again, and she tried to hide the fact she was pleased to see the back of her by asking a question.

'Have you noticed any change in Sam and his behaviour in the last couple of months?'

A simple enough question, but Gemma chewed her lip, her brows furrowing. 'Well...erm...actually...now I come to think of it...' She leaned forward almost conspiratorially. Both Ash and I followed her lead, and we gathered across the table as if we were planning world domination. 'This last month, Sam's actions have been a little more bizarre...and his behaviour, too.'

'Any chance he could be on drugs?' Both Gemma and Ash looked at me and then looked away. 'No...not like drugged bizarre. More like he seems as if he is even more cocky than he already was. You know.' No, I didn't. And neither did Ash, by the look on her face. Gemma sighed the sigh of someone who is talking to an idiot, a pair of idiots, actually. 'I mean he acts like he doesn't care, like he is above the law.'

'He's always thought he was above the law, being caught twenty-one times should tell you that.' I couldn't hide the note of sarcasm in my voice. From the corner of my eye I saw Ash grin, you know — the crooked one that makes her seem so self-assured.

Gemma didn't notice, or if she did she ignored it. 'Above the law as in — he isn't afraid of being caught. Either he is trying to impress someone or he thinks he will get away with it for some reason.'

That knocked the grin off Ash's face. 'Has he mentioned anybody, anyone he is working for or with?'

'Not that I can remember. Erm...wait a minute.' And we did, literally, whilst she was wracking her brains trying to remember if King Shit had mentioned anyone else. 'There was one person he kept on about — someone called Danny.' We bolted upright on the chairs. Danny Spencer...it had to be him.

'I'm sure he said Danny.' There was another pause. 'A northerner who has come to Norfolk for a break.'

'*Think.*' Ash's voice was stern and controlled. 'Are you sure he said Danny? A northerner?'

'I think so, but I wouldn't stake my life on it.'

The conversation went on pretty much the same until Ash had convinced Gemma to try and find out a bit more about Sam's new friend. Funny thing was, she didn't really go into detail...not like she had for me, anyway.

After Gemma left, the silence between us was deafening. I fiddled about with my coffee cup, taking sips of the cold liquid, grimacing behind the cup. Now and again, I stole glances at Ash. She just sat staring ahead of her, her face unreadable and those blue eyes half closed as if she was contemplating something.

'If you've finished with me...' I let the sentence drift off, and drift off it did...and hung about in the air for a bit. I sat and waited a little longer.

It was weird, sitting with Ashley Richards after all of this time and not talking non-stop. We had never had difficulty talking, and even if we did stop for breath, it was never uncomfortable. Although, strangely enough, it wasn't uncomfortable now...just bloody weird.

Twenty years had passed and I was there with the person I had certified as the love of my life...obviously it was going to be weird. It couldn't be anything else. Too much had happened in my life since the last time I'd spoken to her. Too much water had flowed under that proverbial bridge for it to be any other way. I was not the naïve seventeen-year-old I was then. Thankfully.

'So, will you help us?'

Huh? Crap. I had done it again. I had missed the beginning of a conversation...again. I hadn't done that for years, and it was one thing I'd not missed. 'Help you do what, exactly?'

She leaned closer. 'Help us put those little fuckers behind bars where they belong.'

Her face was mere inches from mine, and my heart was hammering against my rib cage. I was certain she could hear it.

'Sure.' Good start, Turner. 'But I'm telling you up front, I'm not doing anything that's illegal.'

Ash leaned back in her chair and let out a loud guffaw. Yes, some people still use the word guffaw. I just sat and stared at her, the anger inside beginning to bubble. What the fuck was she laughing at? Me? She's better not be or else I...

'Sorry about that.' She didn't look sorry. 'It's just...just...we're the police and...' and off she went again. I thought this would make me angrier, but I felt a laugh building up in my chest and snaking its way into my throat.

It was good hearing her laugh. It made me feel good to see, and hear, her laugh. I loved the way she looked so relaxed and happy, like the old Ash, you know, instead of the Detective Inspector Richards who had a stick up her arse.

So I joined in, and the more I laughed, the more she did too. A weight seemed to lift from my shoulders for the time we were in a state of uncontrollable hysterics.

Sometimes we forget, as we grow older, that laughter is good for the soul.

It was nearly five-thirty in the morning by the time I turned my key in the lock of my front door. I should have been tired, but I was wide awake. Too much had happened in the space of the last four hours for me to just strip and climb back into bed in search of Jodie Foster.

Holding a steaming cuppa, I strolled into the spare room that doubled as an office cum storeroom and sat at my desk. Piles of crap surrounded me, and I shuffled through it half-heartedly, holding the beverage in one hand whilst using the other to sift and separate unruly papers. I couldn't concentrate on the job at hand, even burnt my lips twice on the tea. My mind was definitely elsewhere.

Placing the cup down on the desk, I turned my attention to the stack of boxes piled haphazardly in the far corner of the room. I stared at them for a while, just stared, before I tentatively moved across the room.

My inner voice was telling me to just leave it, go to bed…now was not the time. But I was on a mission. In for a penny, in for a pound.

I quickly moved the top three boxes, as I knew where the object of my desire lay. The top of the next box was the only one not sealed, and I pulled back the edges to reveal a tattered children's book, one of the two I had saved from that day. Reverent fingers stroked the rippled and browned surface, across the faces of some badly illustrated characters, before they tentatively grasped the edges as if it would suddenly crumble into dust.

I lifted it gently, placed a soft kiss on the cover, and laid it to the side. Underneath the book lay Yazoo's *Upstairs at Eric's*, the corners bent out of shape from being thrust into the box on countless occasions. It joined the book. Next came the ultimate: red, woollen, Ash's.

I lifted the jumper up to my face and brushed it over my lips, planting soft kisses along the front. Then I let the material hang limply in my arms before hugging it closely to my chest, like I was hugging a baby, protecting it…seeking comfort from it.

My heart felt fit to burst, to rip through my shirt and claim the owner of this jumper. But that was never to be. The red jumper was the only thing I would ever have of hers.

It was nearly lunchtime when I woke. The record was stuck and repeating Alison Moyet's voice over and over again, '*You…you…you…you…you…*', and one crumpled and slightly wet red jumper was nearly morphed into my face.

Chapter Eighteen

By three o clock Sunday afternoon, I was showered, fed, and back at the station. The police could hold Sam for twenty-four hours, but then they had to let him go. They could charge him, which Ash had said they weren't going to do, as it would ruin their chances of getting Spencer. My meeting with him was an effort to get on the right side of Sam. And if we were lucky, maybe we'd get a bit of information from him before he was released back into the community.

A different desk sergeant escorted me down to the cells, and I felt a little disappointed to find Ash was not present. I was even a little hurt. Stupid, I know.

As the desk sergeant was turning to leave, the question popped out of my mouth before I had time to stop it. 'Are you expecting Detective Inspector Richards back anytime soon?'

He stopped and turned to face me fully. 'She didn't say what time she'd be back, just that she was going to freshen up and eat.' His face said, 'Is that all?' and I just nodded and pushed the door open. It didn't even enter my head that the sergeant should have stayed with me, I was too concerned about other things...and because of that I wasn't paying attention. Big mistake.

I was just inside the room when I felt someone grab my hair. The pain was excruciating. I was pulled backwards and slammed into the wall, and Sam was on me like a dog in heat, his face pressed up to mine. The whites of his eyes gave him a manic air, and spittle was collecting around his mouth, spittle that flew into my face as he spat out, 'Bitch.'

I was momentarily paralysed. Momentarily. My knee came up to meet his jewels, and I felt them crunch into his groin. I would have preferred them to be introducing themselves to his nostrils.

A puff of air escaped him, and I saw the tears well up in his eyes, the only time I had ever seen any emotion in them. My right arm came up and caught him under the chin, pushing him backwards and around so he was pinned against the wall by his windpipe. My left hand went between his legs and grabbed his testicles, which were slowly descending to their rightful position.

I knew he wouldn't be able to move, as both my arm and my hand were pushing and squeezing him into submission. I leaned in closer, my face showing him I was not best pleased by his greeting, my eyes flaring anger and resentment, not just at him, but at myself, too.

The sermon I was going to deliver was cut off as the door to the cell was slammed back, and Ash came rushing in. Her hair was flying, and the panic in her eyes gave her the appearance of someone who had lost all sense of control.

'You okay?'

I nodded. I was too angry to talk, and I knew I would burst into tears if I opened my mouth. Sam was sliding down underneath my hand, and I looked at his face. Sweat poured from him, and his cocky stance had been well and truly eliminated.

Fuck. What was I doing? I could lose my job.

It was as if I had been burned. My hands shot from him, and he slumped to the floor, rubbing his neck and his crotch at the same time. For a brief moment he looked defeated, and then he looked me in the face. His eyes were full of hatred. If they could have spoken, they would have told me to watch my back.

'Get up!' Ash was standing in front of him, the tone of her voice warning that she was on the verge of doing something worse than I already had. I felt the fight leave me, all the energy seeping from my body.

Sam didn't move, just sat there glaring and rubbing. Ash didn't ask him again, she just leaned down and grabbed the shoulder of his shirt and yanked him off the ground in one swift movement. His legs dangled like a puppet's as she nearly threw him across the room where he stumbled onto the bed. 'Sort yourself out, Read. I'll be back in ten.'

With that, she turned to face me, her face softening instantly. 'Come on, Lou. Let's wait outside.' I saw her begin to offer her hand to me, stop, look at what she was doing, then pull back. 'Come on. We'll talk to him later, okay?'

I nodded. The last thing I wanted was to come back into that cell and face Read again, but a brief respite was good for a start.

Outside the cell, Ash turned to me, her face full of apology. 'I'm sorry you had to experience that. When the desk sergeant told me you were here and on your own…I panicked.' Panicked? Why panicked? 'I ran into the sergeant as I was going down. I'd told them I was okay to see Read on my own, and they took that to mean that he isn't a threat.' She snorted at the sergeant's density.

I could feel the emotion building up inside me, and the tears from earlier were begging for release. I tried swallowing rapidly to ease the pressure, but it just incensed them. One lone tear struggled free and trickled its way down my cheek.

'Hey, come on. You're safe now.'

Another tear chased the previous one. Bugger.

'Oh, Lou, come here.'

I found myself in the arms of the woman I had loved all those years ago, my face buried in her chest, the smell of her exactly the same, her arms around me and hands stroking up and down my back. That made me cry even harder, not because of what had just happened, but because I knew this was the place I belonged…and I knew it was a place I could never hope to stay.

This made me cry harder still, made Ash hold me tighter, made this all one big vicious circle.

I knew I should have drawn away and pulled myself together. Instead I guiltily stayed in her arms and pulled myself to pieces.

In this life, you have to learn to take every crumb. However much it hurts.

One very hot and shaky cup of tea later, I had explained to Ash that I had taken martial arts when I moved to Norfolk, as the class seemed like a good place to meet people of my own age. She was quiet the whole time I was telling her about how difficult I had found settling in. She looked surprised when I told her that Jo had moved back to Manchester soon after we had moved, and it seemed as if she was about to say something.

I paused, considering whether I should ask her to share what was on her mind, then realised she had settled back into her chair and her face had closed off. This was a definite sign she wasn't open for any major discussion. It would've turned into one; what else could it have done? The conversation would have moved to that night...the night...the night I had kissed her and she had kissed me.

No way. How could I even consider talking about something I knew she felt uncomfortable with? The past was best left there...in the past. There was no point dragging it up to analyse and decipher when all it would do was open up old wounds. *My* old wounds, at that. Wounds that had never healed in the first place.

'I spoke to Gemma after you had gone. After you left, I found her sitting in the canteen waiting to talk to me.'

Her voice sounded eerily distant, and I looked at her, which was more than she was doing to me. She was staring at the far side of the canteen watching two uniformed police officers playing cards and laughing. I didn't respond, just looked down at the empty mug I was holding fiercely in my hands.

'She seems quite taken with you.'

My eyes shot up and were captured in blue. 'Really?'

'Yes, really. She was disappointed you didn't wait for her to finish talking to Read. Said it would have been good to *compare notes*.' The last part of the sentence was spoken sarcastically and quite cutting. 'She asked me to give you this.' A piece of paper was thrust into my face. I had to pull back to try and focus on it before I could take it. 'Her phone number. She said, and I quote, "Tell her to call me *anytime*."'

If I hadn't known better, I would've bet money that Ash was...even if it was a teeny bit...jealous.

Nah. She couldn't be jealous of Gemma...could she? Why would she be jealous? Was it because I could get inside information and she couldn't?

'Well, are you going to take it or what?'

The piece of paper was dangling in front of me like the proverbial carrot, and Ash's focus was on my face, which by this time had gone scarlet. Slowly, my hand raised itself of its own volition to snag the paper between rigid fingers. For a split second, I could feel Ash resist the pull, and I looked at her. One eyebrow raised itself in mock challenge before the grin appeared.

'Oi, give it up, Richards.'

'Give it up! Give *what* up?' Her grip became firmer as I tugged again. She pulled it out of my grasp and then held it above her head. 'Don't know what you're talking about.'

Such a cocky grin. I squinted my eyes at her and feigned a scowl. 'Give it to me now.'

'Feisty little bit, aren't you?'

Her eyes were twinkling and I could see an inkling of the Ash I had known all those years ago. Beautiful. Happy. Off limits. Definitely that — off limits. My heart sank a little further in my chest, and I could feel it nudging my stomach into action, which had been snoozing peacefully for a while.

'Was that your stomach?' I blushed. 'Jesus, woman. Have you hidden a monster in there or what?' Could I go any redder? 'Let me feed you, and then you can call Miss Jackson.' She stood up and rummaged through her pocket to look for cash. 'Here.'

She threw the piece of paper in front of me and then sauntered off to the Servery, where she leaned on the counter, her gaze fixed on the dishes displayed in front of her.

I picked up the paper and unfolded it. Neat, small writing greeted me and two phone numbers — one was her mobile. *'Lovely to meet you. Fancy a coffee or something one day? Call me. Gemma.'*

Shit. I didn't think it would go as far as exchanging numbers. I only wanted to charm her a little bit so I could ease the tension of the situation. Double shit. Now what would Ash think of me? I looked up from the paper to see Ash staring back at me. Her expression seemed odd for a split second, like she was studying me studying the paper. Then, as quickly as it was there it was gone, and she turned around to pay the woman behind the counter before lifting a tray with a plate of something on it.

I felt guilty. Don't ask me why, but I did. Stupid, I know. For one thing, I was only looking at the piece of paper. And for another, why should it matter to Ash who I wanted to see? Although it kind of gave the game away about my sexuality. Then again, having me shove my tongue down her throat years earlier probably kind of gave her the idea I was gay in the first place.

Once. Twice. Three times. I folded the paper in my hands before I slipped it into my jacket pocket. Slam. The tray hit the table with such a force the salt and pepper pots fell backwards in complete submission.

'What the fuck—'

'Lasagne. You like Italian, right?'

Then she was gone. The lasagne was half off the plate and leaning nonchalantly on the tray. What on earth had gotten into her?

I shook my head. One minute she was playful, and the next she was throwing food at me. I couldn't work it out. I looked over to the Servery to see if she'd had an altercation with someone there, but there was only one rotund elderly woman wiping down the glass. She seemed perfectly happy...although slightly demented, if her grinning at her reflection gave any indication.

'Y'all right, dear?'

I nodded and looked back at the tray, then around the room. Empty. Even the card sharks had pissed off and left me to my slopped-out dinner and my own company.

But, as they say, the beast must be fed. I don't know who said it...maybe it was just me and my stomach, who decided now was as good a time as any to start whimpering again.

Fork in hand, intention clear. Dinner...gone.

Chapter Nineteen

'Fuck it!'

Ash let rip with the same two words. This time the two words were accompanied by her picking up a stack of papers and violently throwing them across the room. When I say throwing, what I actually mean is 'attempted throwing', as they didn't fall more than a foot away from her. Air resistance shortened their journey and swirled them into chaos, then spewed them back down.

The same two words came out again, but this time more vehemently than before and accompanied by, 'Oh, for fuck's sake!'

I couldn't help it, I swear. The laugh just popped out, honestly. I would've told Ash that if I hadn't been pinned by her stare. Jesus! That woman could stare. I think I even felt a little trickle of pee escape into my panties. And like all idiots, I laughed again, but this time it was from nerves. Again I had no time to explain.

'You think this is funny, do you? In two hours Read is walking if we don't do something.'

'I thought you were letting him walk anyway.' I took a tissue from my pocket and pretended to wipe my face, but I was in fact using it to stop myself from laughing again. I knew I should avoid making that mistake again.

'It would have been nice if we could've gotten some information from him before he was released.'

I had tried again to talk to Read, but he wasn't haven't any of it. His main focus was trying to intimidate me. Like I was going to be intimidated by that wankstain, but the gig was up as far as my getting him to squeal. I doubted he would give me the dirt from under his fingernails, and believe me, there was quite a bit there.

'Do you want me to call Gemma?' By this stage, Ash was on the floor gathering up the papers she had scattered in her rage. She gripped the papers tightly in her hand. Her knuckles grew white.

'Do whatever you like; it's your life.' Each word was cut out of stone.

'I know it's my life, but I was thinking about getting her to talk to Read again. He quite likes her...kept on saying how he'd like to give her one when he got out.'

'Must be contagious, then.'

I was getting pissed off with her snide comments about everything and everyone, especially when they were connected to me or something I had said.

'Look, Lady Muck, I don't have to be here you know. I'm—'

'Why don't you go then? You can always see Read when he gets back to school. That is your job after all, isn't it?'

The anger I had felt bubbling inside me for the last few minutes was aching to be released. My hands gripped the table edge, and I raised myself up out of the chair. 'You are an ungrateful bitch, do you know that?' She just stared up at me from her crouched position on the floor, one eyebrow rising into her hairline, her lips curling slightly. No answer, which got my dander up even more. 'I have spent all fucking day trying to help you out and all you can do is find fault...' Still she didn't answer.

I leaned over the table, my hands taking my weight. When I knew I had her full attention, I was off again. 'What is your problem? What the *fuck* have I done to warrant you being a pain in the arse?'

Ash pushed herself back onto her haunches and then stood up, the papers firmly in her grip. It seemed as if she had grown since she had been down there. The trickle of wee was back. The shadow from her tall frame hit the table and landed across my chest.

'You want to know what the problem is?' She threw the papers onto the table, and I followed their trail across the veneer and onto the floor again. 'The problem...' I looked into her eyes, such cold eyes, eyes that showed nothing but contempt. 'The problem is *you*.'

The last word was spat out. Honestly. I felt the metaphorical wetness hit my face like a slap. Most people would have shrunk back and crawled into a corner. I wasn't one of those people. I have wished I was, though, on many occasions, not just this one.

'*Me*? You weren't saying that at two-thirty this morning when you were nearly begging me to help solve your little problem.' I kicked the chair away from me. 'Link, my arse.' I snatched my bag up from the floor. 'And *you* can kiss it.' I accompanied the last sentence with a loud slapping of the aforementioned body part.

Within two minutes my feet were hitting concrete, and I was storming away from the station. I could hear her calling after me, but I just lifted my hand and gave her the two-fingered salute — the old British wave of insolence — and kept walking without even looking back. If I had, she would have seen the tears glistening on my face. She would have known that she had broken my heart all over again.

Never again. Never ever again. This I would make sure of. I couldn't handle going through it all again.

Two days later I was snug and cosy in my front room with Gemma Jackson. Honestly, I invited her over to talk about Read, who had not been to school since his release. I should have guessed that talking about the case would have been the last thing on her mind. I should have known that from the minute she realised it was me on the phone. It was amazing how the professional 'I take no shit from anybody' voice changed and wrapped itself around her mouth to fall like velvet-covered love letters from silken lips.

Yeah...corny crap. But that's what it sounded like or would sound like if you were into all that mushy stuff. In retrospect, I should have worn a chastity belt and swallowed the key. But we are not all gifted with the art of prophecy, are we?

It wasn't too bad to start off with. Or should I say *she* wasn't too bad to start off with? She was quite the lady, even sat on the far end of the settee. She was slick, though, I'll give her that. Every gesture or piece of information she thought I should look at was handed to me in such a way that she was steadily getting closer and closer.

Me, being me, and thick as custard, didn't even notice until she was just about to make her move. And even then I had to have it nearly spelled out to me. I know I give the impression I am a bit of a Lady Thriller. I'm not. My motto is 'If it falls on your lap and is willing, then go for it.'

I flirt. I am a flirt. But an innocent kind of one, the kind that is shocked when it actually works. The kind that when a woman smiles at me in an empty room, I still look over my shoulder just to make sure she's smiling at me. Then look over it again.

So, the move, Gemma's plan of attack.

As I said before, she edged her way slowly but surely, very much like a snail on tranquillisers, until she was right next to me. I was reading the court minutes of Read's last hearing, skimming through it really, when I felt her eyes on me. Eyes that two minutes earlier had seemed a bit further away.

Have you ever noticed that when you feel someone staring at you, you can't help but look at them? It works in kind of the same way as a tractor beam: you're pinned...and then you get sucked in. That's what happened. I didn't intend it to, it just sort of happened – in a weird, Star Trek way.

It felt as if I was slowly falling forwards and into her. It was millimetres...honestly...millimetres until touch down and then...

Brrrrrrrriiiiiiiiiiiiiiinnnng! Brrrrinnnng! Brrrrinnnng! Brrrrrrrriiiiiiiiiiiiiiinnnng! Saved by the doorbell. My eyes, which had been slowly closing, shot open to reveal Gemma's face up close and personal.

'Ignore it,' slipped softly from her parted lips.

Brrrrinnnng! Brrrrinnnng! Brrrrinnnng! Whoever it was, definitely wanted to be let in. And for that I was thankful.

'Just let me...' I nearly sprinted away. Fuck. What was I doing? Two thoughts raged in my head. The first: 'She's offering herself on a plate! She's hot and willing. Why are you answering the door?' The second: 'Ash.'

There she stood, or slouched, against the wall. One arm languished against the brickwork, whilst the other dangled behind her back. If I hadn't heard her insistent doorbell ringing, I would have thought she was as laid back as she pretended to be.

'What are you doing here?'

'Can we talk?' She pushed herself away from the wall in one fluid movement and stood erect, straightening her jacket as she did so. 'Inside.'

I just stood there, paralysed for a moment. She was on my doorstep. Waiting for me to let her in. Wanting to talk...not shout or hurl abuse...to talk.

I was unable to answer her so I stepped aside to let her in. The biggest and boldest lump in my throat had taken root, a bit as if I had swallowed an apple whole. It wasn't until she had put her foot inside the door that I remembered Gemma sitting in the front room.

Shit.

Once again, why shit?

I don't know...but it's a good a word as any. To say I knew Ash didn't like Gemma would be saying I knew England's weather is a bit crap. It's redundant. But why get in a tizzy about it? Why resort to toilet language to express this knowledge, the knowledge that Ash didn't like Gemma and that Gemma knew it.

'Erm...I'm not alone.' Ash's body stiffened, then forced itself to relax. The eyebrow raised itself, and she looked at me as if to say, 'go on.' 'Gemma's here.'

The first raised eyebrow was joined by its twin, leaving her eyes wide and her expression open. Obviously shock.

Wait a minute. Why shock? Didn't she think I would call Gemma because I knew she didn't like her? Stuff that. I know, I know — irrational. But you must remember that every time I saw this woman, rationality flew out if the window.

'If I'm interrupting...' She turned to go.

The voice was cold and reminded me of a slap I had received from a girl at school, who, by the way, had very cold hands. She had her back to me by this point and was stepping back outside. 'Wait! I thought you wanted to talk.' Blue eyes scrutinised me from over her shoulder, her body rigid, her hands clenched. God. I knew she didn't like Gemma, but this was a little on the extreme side. This wasn't the Ash I had known. That Ash had been happy and sociable, even when I knew she didn't like someone. Like Tracy, for example — the Goth queen.

'It can wait; it's no biggie.'

Before I knew it, I was outside, my hand clenching her arm, holding her back. I know I didn't pull her around, I know she only half-heartedly wanted to walk away, but the relief in my chest when she turned to face me was immeasurable. 'Look, come inside. Have a coffee.' I saw doubt flit across her face. 'Tea, even.' Was I begging? 'Orange juice?' The last came out more like a squeak. But it worked. I saw the smile glimmer around her lips, felt the muscles relax in her arm, throughout her body.

'Okay. Just a cuppa, then.' I released the breath I didn't realise I had been holding captive in my lungs until it hit the air outside with an audible oof.

When I led a grinning Ash back into the lounge, Gemma's face was a Kodak moment if ever I had seen one. She had made herself comfortable on the settee — shoes off, hands behind her head — the perfect example of, as my mum always says, 'Getting your feet under the table.'

When she spotted Ash, Gemma nearly broke her neck sitting upright, but then stopped and lounged back again, almost like she was announcing we had been doing something a little risqué.

'Do you mind?' Ash slapped her foot, indicating she wanted to sit down next to her. Another Kodak moment. I would have loved to have filmed it, sent it off to one of those TV shows where they pay money for people fuck ups. Couple of hundred quid in the bank.

Gemma made a song and dance out of getting herself straight, huffing and puffing her way into a seating position. Ash stared at her for a while before asking, 'Do you work out?' They glared at each other. 'Or is it asthma?'

I saw Gemma open her mouth to respond and inserted an offer into the temporary silence. 'Coffee? Tea? Anything?' They both looked in my direction, back at each other, and then back at me. They spoke at the same time.

'Coffee.'

'Tea.'

I didn't get it. Why did they dislike each other so much? I mean, they both had a job to do, and if they were civil to each other, they could scratch each other's backs, if you know what I mean. But no. It was like having two hateful teenagers sitting there sulking. And we all know how teenagers can sulk. Big time.

I took my time in the kitchen. My chief thought was to leave them to it. I couldn't be bothered with getting involved with petty squabbles and tiffs. For Christ sake, we were all in our thirties. We should have grown out of it by now.

Initially, the next room was quiet. I believe I could even hear the clock ticking. Come to think of it, I should have known, and I definitely shouldn't have left them alone together.

Raised voices seeped into the room. I couldn't quite make out what was being said, just knew they weren't talking about the price of bacon. Then Ash's voice came thundering in, blanketing out all other sounds.

'I'm just saying — don't fuck us about!'

Bollocks. At this rate, they would never be able to come to a compromise concerning Read's case. The shit was definitely hitting the proverbial fan, and the only person who might stop it was making the scrappers a cuppa.

I lifted the mugs, took a deep breath, stepped through the doorway and into the hall, just in time to hear Ash's 'Fuck you' farewell and then see her storm out of the door.

Steaming beverages tightly gripped in each hand, I stood there looking all the world like a learning driver gripping the steering wheel. I felt the colour drain from my face, but I knew that this situation must be resolved. I would have to work with Gemma again, and Ash... Well, it was Ash, wasn't it?

Cups thrown to the wayside...or in actuality, placed carefully on the sideboard, making sure to balance on coasters...and I was off, tearing down the hallway, out of the front door and down the road.

Her car door was open, and she was just lowering herself into the driver's seat when I finally caught up with her. It sounds like quite a ways, but it was only a matter of about thirty metres.

'Where are you going?' I was breathless. Yeah, I know — thirty metres and breathless. It was more from nerves than anything else.

The look she gave me just before she slammed the door in my face could have melted concrete. Not one to be deterred, I banged on the window and motioned for her to lower it. I could see her lips moving but couldn't make out the words. I motioned again. This time she grudgingly slapped her hand on the button, eliminating the barrier between us, turning her head in my direction in one sharp movement.

'Why are you going? I've made you a cuppa.' Good call, Turner. Any more persuasive gems like that one hiding up your sleeve?

I saw her bite her lip before she answered, saw her try to contain something from bubbling out, and I knew that for that small mercy, I should be grateful.

After a couple of swallows, she managed, 'Look, you're busy with...with...what's-her-face. We can chat later without Big Ears listening.'

I should have said okay and walked away. Should have, but no. Miss High and Mighty came out to play. 'Her name's Gemma.' Ash glared. 'And I don't think it's right, you slagging her off behind her back.'

She tried to deny it, saying she wasn't slagging her off, that she was telling the truth. Gemma did have big ears. But I was on a roll. I suspect that it was out of panic or something very much like it. You must have been in the situation where you feel one way and act in the complete opposite. You know — like when your child nearly gets hit by a car and you grab him and give him a good telling off, but inside you're thinking, 'My baby...my angel...I was so scared.' The words coming out of your mouth make it seem like you're someone who has problems stringing a sentence together: 'Why you little...' and 'When I get you home, you...' Disjointed because of the deletion of nouns that should never be spoken to a child.

Obviously, my attitude antagonised Ash. Obviously. And when I got to the part where I shouted, 'What's your problem?' I should have known what was coming next.

Next thing I knew I was halfway back to my house, the anger pouring from me with every footstep, the hand gestures not fit for the faint hearted. All I could hear were two things: the blood rushing past my ears and the roaring of her car engine as she sped away.

Gemma was waiting for me at the door, coffee cup in her hand, the look of 'Oh, poor you' fixed firmly in place. Do you know the first thing I thought when I looked at her? Nope, not about the kiss...or where it could lead, not about how she could help me with my case, not even what she and Ash had argued about. None of the above.

The one thing that sprinted into my head and jumped up and down was — fuck, she did have big ears.

Chapter Twenty

What was it with her? Why did she have to be such a — I don't know — such a pain in the arse? You would think we would be all over each other, in a friendship kind of way, considering we hadn't seen each other in twenty years. But no. The only thing that was getting any action was my ability to go off on one at any given opportunity. What had happened to the Ash I had known back then? The present Ash seemed so cynical and angry all of the time. Where had that happy-go-lucky girl gone?

Metaphorical head-scratching moment, methinks.

I hadn't heard from her since that day two weeks earlier. Funny thing was...I missed her. I know. Twenty years without a word and then poof, there she was, back in my life again. In the flesh. Looking more beautiful than my heart remembered...and acting completely different.

Ah well...

Work was taking up most of my time, especially since I had taken over Read's case. I spent my time reading through his files, speaking to teachers at the school — who all thought he was a wanker, too. I even interviewed his mother. Would have liked to speak to his father, too, but he was serving four years in Wandsworth for breaking and entering. Nice to see the family genetics didn't stop with good old dad.

His mother was neither use nor ornament. The typical council estate haircut and the skin-tight Lycra leggings found on the extremely rotund, to use a tired old euphemism, were firmly in place, along with the continuous chain smoking. Maybe her fringe wasn't peroxide after all.

I spent, or more to the point, wasted, over an hour with her. She was trying to hold a conversation with me, watch some crappy daytime show, and smoke herself stupid. Now, if I believed she could walk and chew gum at the same time, this wouldn't have been a problem, but she couldn't. End of story.

Eventually I decided to call it a day and made arrangements to return later in the week. Her acknowledgment to my statement was a brief look in my direction, a nod of the head, and then back to gawp at the talking box in the corner.

It was on my second visit that I saw Ash again. Bugger.

A younger version of Sam let me into the house, and I could hear voices being raised in the front room. My stomach forgot all about the smell as my head and my heart both recognised Ash's voice above the din of the TV. At least it put a stop to the gagging and retching I had to endure because of the smell of stale chip fat and cigarettes. But then again, there were the butterflies to contend with — a whole battalion of them inside my gut.

'Can we turn off the TV, madam?'

I didn't hear a response but thought I'd gone deaf when the house took on an air of eerie stillness.

The scene that greeted me was something you would probably see on a crime prevention poster. Ash stood there in all her six-foot glory, hands on hips, two uniformed policemen flanking her. She was looking down at Mrs. Read with nothing but contempt on her face.

'I said I don't know where 'e is. 'E doesn't tell me where 'e's going.'

Ash just stared, the eyebrow twitching, using it to lift and help pin the woman even more firmly in her chair. She moved a step forward and lowered herself to Sam's mother. 'If you know what's good for you, you'd better start—' She stopped, froze suddenly, and then raised her eyes to mine. Her mouth dropped just a little, then snapped back into place.

'Detective Inspector, good to see you again.' I couldn't believe how normal my voice sounded, a little too self-confident, in complete opposition to how I was feeling.

Ash stood up sharply, straightening her jacket with the palm of her hand. The look of shock had completely vanished, and she looked in control once again, the cocky grin appearing on command. '*Miss* Turner. What a pleasant surprise.'

The two police officers looked at each other, then me, then Ash. Neither of them said a word. Mrs. Read was reaching for her cigs, apparently believing she was off the hook for the moment. Ash's hand shot out and trapped hers on top of the gold packet. 'I have already asked you nicely, don't smoke in front of me. I don't want to breathe in your smoke.'

Mrs. Read nodded, her hand slipping from underneath Ash's to release the cigarette packet, although her eyes never left it and I could see her lips twitching with the need to hold the cylindrical cancer stick in her mouth and puff away a few more years of her life.

'I do have an appointment. Four-thirty, remember, Mrs. Read?' Of course, she didn't remember. I could see it written all over her face. Not a spark of recognition...not...a...spark. Not surprising, really, considering she had been watching a re-run of Sally Jesse Raphael the last time I was there.

'If you're after Sam, he's not here.' Ash's tone was brusque, matter of fact and definitely to the point. If she had just said, 'Fuck off,' it couldn't have been clearer. 'And we don't know where he currently is, do we?' She shot a glare at Mrs. Read, who graced both Ash and me with a brief look before shaking her head and surreptitiously looking back at her cig packet.

'I haven't come to speak to Sam, just his mother.'

'Do you mind if we sit in?'

It should have been taken as a reasonable request, but...I don't know...it just got my back up for some reason.

'Erm...actually...I'd like to cover some sensitive areas with Mrs. Read today. Mainly to do with Sam's absences from school and...' I caught the expression on the mother's face. She was trying to play it cool, but she knew her ticket was up. If a child continually played truant, then the parents were fined. It was the first time I had her full attention.

Ash spotted the change in her, too, and I knew she badly wanted to stay and ask questions that she felt, as I did, the mother would be more receptive about answering.

'No can do, Detective. This is a private case. If you want to find out more, you'll have to make an appointment with me.' I smiled to soften the blow. Bollocks, did I. I grinned, full out — teeth, the works. Ash's teeth were grinding together, so I grinned wider. Both officers and Mrs. Read were watching me with avid interest, so I coughed...coughed again...and composed myself.

'So, if you don't mind...'

'I think it would be wise if we stuck around for a while.'

'Okay.' I saw the smug smile light on her mouth. 'Just make sure you close the door on your way out.' The smile slipped. 'We can make arrangements for your appointment when I've finished.' Her smile...completely gone.

It wasn't until I saw her back disappearing through the door that I allowed myself to breathe again. I'd fully expected her to go off on me, as I had been up close and personal to the temper tantrums the new Ash threw when things weren't going her way.

The fact that my heart was begging her to stay was another matter completely. Funny things, hearts — they still recognise their desire even if somewhere deep inside they actually know they didn't have a chance in hell. Unfortunately.

I turned in time to see Mrs. Read lighting a cigarette, the obvious relief on her face making me want to hurl. I wanted to tell her to put it out, be more assertive, but instead I just placed my briefcase on the floor and bent over to retrieve Sam's file.

To the naked eye, I probably looked completely on task, but my head was far from the point at hand. It was with my heart, and that was on the other side of the door.

As expected, Ash was waiting outside for me. What I didn't expect was for her to act sheepish. The uniformed officers were nowhere in sight; it was just her.

'Hey, you okay?' That tone, it was like a blast from the past — soft, caring. The Ash I remembered. I felt my insides do a jig, and I felt a sense of home pervade me.

'Fine. Does the term "sing like a canary" mean anything to you?'

'I didn't mean with Fag Ash Lil in there. I meant, are you okay?'

Once again I was surprised. Her tone was softer, and she actually seemed to want to know how I was feeling. As a woman of few words, I shrugged and mumbled, 'Yeah.'

She came towards me, and the swagger that had been prevalent the other times I had seen her was well and truly gone. Worry radiated from her face, and I couldn't understand why. I had only been in the room with Mrs. Read for just over an hour, and I wondered what had happened to make such a change in Ash. Did I have a face full of spots? Or look flushed?

I knew I felt fine, but you know how it is — when someone asks you if you're okay and looks at you like you are at death's door, you feel a little queasy. This time was no exception. My stomach gurgled and churned, and I had the distinct impression my blood was surging up into my ears. Damned overactive imagination. To add insult to injury, I felt my paperwork slip out of my hands and flutter all over the front garden. Not good.

Ash moved quickly, chasing after errant sheets, slamming her foot down on top of the little buggers, snatching them up until she had them all safe in her hands. Obviously I was dying, so I couldn't help.

'Here you go.'

And there she was — standing directly in front of me, offering the papers like a sacrifice. My fingers reached out and clasped the corners of the sheets, as if I would be burned if I touched the places where her hands had been. I couldn't even say thank you lest I hurled up over her; I just raised my eyes to her chin and smiled weakly.

'Look, Lou, I...erm... Look, I'm sorry for being a twat.' I looked up. 'You know...earlier.' I faced her fully, her blue eyes were intense. 'I don't know why I acted like that. I'm just under a lot of pressure to catch Spencer.'

Her voice trailed off, and my stomach and nausea calmed down a little, but the butterflies were back...jigging again. Little tykes. 'No problem. I understand there must be a lot of pressure to pin something on him. By the sounds of it, he thinks he's covered his tracks pretty well.'

'Can we go and grab a coffee or something to eat and talk about everything? I think there are a few things you should know.'

I was intrigued, but I just nodded. It wouldn't hurt, would it? Just a coffee, or a coffee with a bun...or two?

I didn't even think about the near-death experience I had undergone minutes before. My stomach was on the case, more so than my head was.

We went to a café bar called The Lounge. Tables scattered around the room were populated by couples in deep discussion, mainly couples of the same sex. I'd been there before, numerous times, actually, and it was at my suggestion we were there again. Ash didn't seem bothered by the fact that this place was a rendezvous for gay people. In fact, she looked very much at home there. Actually knew where the restrooms were without me pointing them out.

'Coffee?'

I nodded at her and claimed a table snuggled up in the corner. Within two minutes she was back, slipping her jacket from her shoulders and draping it over the back of the spare chair.

'Why didn't you pick the sofas? They would have been so much more comfortable.'

I looked over into the corner where two sofas were nestled together and noted that one was already occupied by two women in deep discussion. 'This is more private.' Her eyebrow twitched, and she sat down in the chair opposite, shuffling it around a little so it was closer to me.

I was at a loss for words, you know. She was too close to me, in my space a little, if you know what I mean. I began to look at the paintings that were for sale on the walls, anything but looking into her eyes. Stupid, I know. I couldn't spend the whole time looking away from her, but I didn't feel capable of controlling the surging in my gut. I think it was her smell...the smell of her...the all-consuming smell that tantalised my nostrils and virtually obliterated my reason.

'Firstly, I'd like to apologise.' That got my attention, and I turned and faced her. She looked so serious, so intent on making me understand what she was going to tell me. 'Not just for today...for, erm...the other two times, too.'

I could see the rapid swallowing that indicated she was dying of embarrassment, and I knew it had taken a lot for her to apologise. Anyone with an ounce of compassion would have said not to worry, it was okay. I just stared at her, silent, expectant, wanting her to squirm.

Our eyes were totally connected, and it was such a weird sensation, almost as if I was being absorbed. Then she blinked...and blinked again...and then blinked again, accompanied by a shake of the head, like reality had just hit her, like she had just realised where she was and with whom.

'I...erm...well, I honestly don't know what got into me.'

If I had been able, I would have put her out of her misery, but I was a little gobsmacked — not over what she had just said, but what she hadn't said...what I felt coming from her. I felt a clamouring of something in her...something clamouring to me...something wanting to be there with me — mute, content — and I couldn't quite grasp the implications or the motivations.

'Just been under so much pressure and I took it out on you.' Her eyes left my face, and my skin felt cold. A strong hand reached out, started to play with the sugar sachets on the table, and that made my focus drift to those capable digits. 'I was out of order, but...' One of the sachets burst between her fingers, and the sugar fell onto the table. The grimace on her face was instant, but she tried to cover it up.

'Two coffees and a Chelsea bun?'

The waiter's voice broke through, and I saw Ash's eyes flick around to take note of the waiter and the tray he was carrying. Her movements were jerky, and she looked on edge. The time from the announcement until the waiter had gone seemed interminable. Sounds of the café took centre stage, and I felt uncomfortable being there, almost felt alone in a room full of people.

Ash had her face turned slightly from mine, and I studied her unnoticed...until her expression changed and I knew she would be turning back to face me. It seemed like it took forever for her head to swivel 'round, but by the time it did I was already engaged in the contents of my cup, pulling it towards me like a barrier.

In my head I kept seeing the open look on her face, the 'something' that had been there. I felt a seed plant itself inside my gut and stick. Deep down inside I wanted what I had seen to be there, to actually have been there — that want, the same want I had, only not as far down.

'Here you go.' Soft. Her voice was so soft.

My eyes lifted slightly and scanned the table. Her hand was holding out the plate with the Chelsea bun perched on it like an offering. The feeling washing through me promised agony. And all over a fucking bun, at that. It wasn't the fact I had a bun or that I had actually wanted a bun; it was the fact she had thought I wanted a bun and got me one. It's stupid. The feeling was unreasonable and stupid, and the deep ache ripping through my chest was testament to this stupidity. I must have been due on my period. I always turned into a mard arse just before it. You know — cry if someone wins a holiday on some crappy daytime show, the works.

'Thought you might be hungry.'

And I was off — straight to the Ladies, gripping my belly to indicate I needed the restroom for a call of nature rather than to release the emotion welling up inside.

Inside the stall, I leaned my head against the wall and allowed the feeling to consume me. I couldn't grasp the cause of it. It was only a bun, for Christ's sake. But then again, it wasn't. It was the feeling of connection, the feeling that she and I had connected, for however brief a time. My reaction came from fear; I know that now. Fear of allowing this feeling of connection to take hold of me, take hold and open up to hurt all over again.

Back at the table, Ash looked up from a small book she was holding in her hands. Her eyes sought mine, and I could see the lines of worry etched on her face. A smile I didn't know I could conjure planted itself on my face, and I slipped back into my seat with a mumbled, 'That's better,' before reaching out and grabbing the cooling coffee.

'You okay?'

I flicked my eyes to hers and back to my coffee again before nodding vigorously. 'Much better, thanks.'

We sat there in silence for a while, the bun sitting untouched, the coffee becoming cooler and cooler. Ash kept shuffling around in her seat, crossing and uncrossing her legs. I knew she wanted to say something and had the distinct feeling I wasn't going to like it. It was only after we had ordered a second coffee that Ash plucked up the courage to speak. I honestly wished she hadn't bothered. I wished she had kept her mouth shut and just let me live out the rest of my life in ignorance.

'Lou?'

It was something about the tone, I think. Something in that one word, that one syllable that forewarned me.

'I've a confession to make.'

'Confession?' She did look uncomfortable. My staring at her seemed to make her even more ill at ease, and she semi-stretched her arms out in front of her, almost like preparing herself for battle.

'You know you were called to the station to see Read?' I nodded. 'And I...erm...acted surprised to see you?' I nodded again, but this time she just stopped and looked down at her hands whilst I dwelled on the two words 'acted' and 'surprised'.

'Go on.'

'I told them to call you.'

Huh? Told them to call me? But how did she—

'I know you're wondering how I knew about you...well...erm...well...this is the tricky part.' I leaned forward; my interest totally piqued. 'Remember Danny Spencer?'

'What has he to do with anything?' I leaned back, emitting a deep breath as I did so.

'There is no easy way to tell you this, but...I think you have a right to know.'

'Know what?' A tinge of anger was coating my tone, maybe because my initial response to her acting surprised was slowly drifting away. And secondly, I had a gut feeling I wasn't going to like what she was going to tell me.

'Well, erm, Lou, please don't get mad at me.'

'Just tell me, Ash.'

'Danny Spencer is...erm...he's your brother.'

I actually felt my mouth gape, actually felt the lips part and the slackness take root. I had a white screen inside my head, and there was nothing coming onto it. I felt blank, emotionless. I just sat there, half leaning towards her with my mouth open.

'Well, your half-brother.'

That seemed to generate some kind of reaction anyway. A jolt of feeling hit me in the gut and made me sit back in the chair, my eyes focused on her face.

'He's—'

'Fuck it, Ash! There's no fucking way I'm related to that twat!' The words were out, and they didn't come out quietly. Heads turned in the café, and I lowered my voice before continuing through clenched teeth, 'How on earth could he be related to me?'

'Calm down, Lou. I'm just—'

'How on earth—'

'Well, if you—'

I was half leaning over the table by then, the adrenaline pumping through me. I felt angry and cheated. My head was totally in a spin; nothing made sense. It wasn't the fact that I was related to him, as I really didn't know him. It was the feeling of being used. Ash had only contacted me because I was related to Danny Spencer. That was the only reason. That was the reason, the reason she had called me the link...not Sam's link, but Danny's. Now I was angry, fucking angry. Of all the—

'Lou, let me explain.'

'What? What can you explain? That you fucking used me again.'

I saw her lips move around the word 'again', and she seemed to chew over it, but her expression stayed blank...well, more like confused. The shaking of her head seemed slow and out of focus. My eyes were burning, and I could feel coolness enveloping me, a telltale sign of my rising temper. I felt slow and sluggish but wired and primitive at the same time. My forearms tingled as my muscles spasmed.

At that point, her eyes looked away…only for a split second, but they looked away. It was then I knew for sure. Ash had wanted to use me to get to Danny Spencer, whoever the fuck he was. My fingers curled around the edge of the cup that held my now cold coffee and I couldn't stop the action — lift, tip, and hurl.

She sat there with the cold coffee all over her face and shirt, her eyelashes flinging off the excess and the once separate hairs collecting into tiny groups. Her mouth opened and stretched, pushing the liquid away. I stood, leaning over the table, the empty cup clenched between my fingers, knuckles whitening.

'Fuck you, Ashley Richards! Get the fuck out of my life. Got it?'

Then I was gone. I didn't care how she felt; I had to go and see my mother, had to find out some things. Deep down I knew Ash was telling the truth, but on the surface I just couldn't accept that such a bastard was any relative of mine. As I said, I didn't know anything about him, not even his age or the colour of his eyes. The only thing I knew was that he was a nasty piece of work and that Ash claimed he was my half-brother.

I was not happy. For more reasons than one.

Chapter Twenty-One

In less than forty-five minutes I was banging on my parents' door. Yarmouth was only twenty-five miles from Norwich, and I floored it to get there in that time. Anger flooding through me, I couldn't distinguish whom I was the angriest with: Ash, my parents, or myself.

My anger with Ash blended into the anger I held for myself. I'd trusted her. Again. I had let my guard down with her, again. I had been kicked in the teeth and told to keep my perverted feelings to myself, *again*. Well, not as much told about my feelings the second time, but there was the feeling of being used. I felt she had used me as a way to help her crack the case. That was something I doubted I would ever forgive.

My parents were another matter entirely. They must have known this guy existed, even if they didn't know I was working with a student who was linked with him. I should've at least heard his name mentioned before now.

I knew he wasn't my mother's son. That left only one connection. The bastard. The dirty, teenage fucking pregnant getting twat of a bastard. The same bastard I hadn't heard from for over thirty years and even then it was too soon. Even when my brothers and sister Angie had gotten married, he hadn't turned up...or couldn't be contacted. He had shown in more ways than one that he wasn't dad material. Oh sure, he could get a woman pregnant, but it takes more than a feisty spot of sperm to make a dad. A hell of a lot more.

'Lou?' The surprise in my dad's voice stopped me in my tracks for a split second. He sounded so happy and pleased to see me, and this was supported by a huge grin as he leaned forward and pulled me into a hug. 'What have we done to be receiving a treat like this?'

Now that was a loaded question. A mere five minutes later, I think he was sorry he'd answered the door.

It is never good to hear how heartless a member of your own family can be. My father was an out and out bastard. However angry I had been when I had stormed out of The Lounge, it paled in comparison to how angry I was when my mum told me what he'd done.

If you cast your memory back, you may remember I overheard that he got a girl pregnant or something to that effect. I had been eavesdropping on a conversation between my mother and her sister. The letter...in his workbag... Remember?

She was seventeen, as it turned out, and pregnant by a man who was in his forties. Turns your stomach to think he slept with a girl who was only a year older than his eldest daughter. Shows you what kind of man he was.

Nine months later (five and a half after my mother walked out on him), a baby boy was born. Daniel Lee Spencer.

Danny Spencer. *The* Danny Spencer; the one who was at that moment in Norfolk trying to assemble a bunch of cronies to do his bidding.

It took a few minutes for me to collect myself. It was his age that had knocked me for a loop. I had automatically assumed he was in his early twenties — at the very most. Don't ask me why, probably because he had a kid like Sam Read on his books.

Why would a man who was in his thirties want to have teenage kids running around him? No mention of Michael Jackson here, please. I mean — in his thirties and using bits of kids to do his dirty work...getting them on his side, pretending he was their friend.

Just the thought of that makes my skin crawl. That's not normal, is it? Then again, it was the perfect age to catch the unsavoury elements of society; you can sculpt them to be what you want them to be, the younger the better. And Sam Read would love the fact that someone — an adult at that — was taking him seriously.

Thinking of it in that light, it made perfect sense. They were his protégés — dispensable, gullible, cheap. They could cop the rap if the shit hit the fan, and Spencer would just flit off back to Manchester or whatever rock he had crawled out from under.

But why Norfolk? Why near me? Did he know I was there? Ash had said she knew where to find me because of him, but what did that mean? Was he after me, my family, my mum...for some reason?

I sat on the dining room chair, slumped really, my head resting in my hands, completely resigned to the fact my neck couldn't support it at the moment. I could hear my mum's voice trying to get through to me, telling me she hadn't wanted to hurt me even more than I had already had been, saying I would always be her baby. It was as if she was there with me — some kind of subliminal support stemming from all the years she had said exactly the same things.

Tears trickled through my fingers and plopped onto my trousers, the wetness making patches that appeared darker than the rest. I was fascinated, in a comatose kind of way. I felt like I had been lied to on so many different levels. I understood why my mum hadn't told me, and I honestly didn't care if my father had twenty kids by different mothers. So what made this hurt so much? What made the ache inside my chest, the ache that gripped and pulled and wrenched something inside until I felt like screaming for it to stop?

My parents hadn't lied, they'd avoided the truth, conveniently forgotten to mention something they thought would hurt me. But someone had lied, someone I had thought I could trust with my life, trust with my all. Ash.

She hadn't just lied: she had used me. Used me. Used me to get what she wanted: an arrest, another glowing recommendation of a job well done, another pat on the back or maybe even a promotion. Maybe a bigger and better office with less paperwork and a bigger and better pay packet. But in the using, she had crippled me, the one person who had trusted her implicitly.

And for that I could never forgive her. Never.

I could smell coffee, could feel the heat of it. My dad was pushing a cup in front of my face, and he was bending so low he was almost kneeling on the floor. Concern etched his tired face, and I felt my heart fill with love for him, that sad kind of love. The kind of love that makes you so very aware of what you have and also what you don't.

'Thanks, Dad.' My voice revealed the rejection I was feeling, the hurt of unrequited love, the agony of betrayal. All in those two words. My parents were unaware of why I was feeling as I was and part of me wanted to tell them it wasn't them, but I just didn't have the energy.

The room was deathly quiet; all that could be heard was the clinking of the cups as they hit the saucers and the intermittent sound of liquid being sipped from china.

As uncomfortable moments slipped by, the feeling of rejection ebbed, slowly replaced by anger. Boiling anger, blood red anger, and it was aimed directly at the woman who had been the cause of so much of the self-pity inside me — the self-pity that I no longer wanted to carry. Ash had used me, and there was no way I was going to get used again.

I wasn't a victim, no way. I was allowing myself to feel like this. I was allowing my feelings to override my reason and make me close up inside, metaphorically antagonising the old wound that had been sliced open by a new injury. Lemon juice in the ever open gash, you might say.

Fuck this. There was no way I was going to let this get to me.

It felt as if I was progressively dismissing the side of me that had felt the hurt and replacing it with a new strength that I dragged up from deep within me. I had to focus on the present. Had to form some kind of rationale from what had happened.

Okay, however much I hated the fact, Danny Spencer was my stepbrother. There was nothing I could do about it, so why stress myself out?

The next fact to face: Ash had used me. Get used to it.

I sat up straighter in the chair and inhaled deeply, held it in, then blew it out in one long breath. My parents were watching me intently, probably expecting me to crack off again, but I just smiled. I think that freaked them out more than if I had lost my rag and danced a temper tantrum around the house. 'Thanks. I'd best be off.'

My mum opened her mouth to say something but stopped after the initial goldfish manoeuvre.

I stood and swiped a hand down the front of my trousers, catching the wet patch where my tears had fallen. Handbag in hand and destination clear, I bade my farewells and left.

I was on a mission, out for revenge. I was going to make sure Ashley Richards knew she couldn't mess with me anymore.

The only drawback was that I didn't know where to find her. But find her, I would. Fucking too right.

Chapter Twenty-Two

Though anger enveloped me, I behaved normally, that I can guarantee. Everyone I spoke to, I did so to coolly; not once did I raise my voice. Even when the sergeant at the station refused to tell me where Ash was staying whilst she was in Norwich. It was nearly ten-thirty by the time I got home, none the wiser but determined. As I was unlocking the front door, I promised myself that tomorrow would bring me the address of one tall and very cocksure detective inspector. And I would settle the score.

The key was firmly in the lock by the time my body alerted me I was not alone. Someone was watching me. I turned in the *Hammer House Horror* kind of way — the hairs on the back of my neck standing to full attention, very much in empathy with the ones on my arms.

Streetlights made shadows on the pavement, and they appeared to move. And my hands started to wiggle the reluctant key in the lock a little more frantically. I knew how to handle myself, but I wasn't going to walk into trouble. I heard a movement come from just behind the hedge, and my stomach clawed at my throat. The door fell inwards, and I stumbled through, clumsily grabbing at the handle in a last pitch to save me hitting the floor. I would have done it, too, if my handbag hadn't slipped off my shoulder and landed heavily on my forearm, making me miss the handle.

Well and truly spooked, I landed awkwardly and tried to scramble further into the house. I heard someone approaching, heard a voice saying my name, but panic consumed me and I was trying to kick the door shut. A hand grabbed my ankle, and I let out a yelp, or more accurately, a scream of terror, and kicked wildly at the grasping hand.

'Lou, Lou! It's only me.'

I recognised the voice as being Ash's and instinctively kicked out again, wanting to hurt her. Her hand had my foot in a grip I can only describe as vice-like, and the only result of my kicking was that I was scooted backwards along the floor a little further.

Her frame loomed above me, and she looked huge. A memory from over thirty years ago flitted into my mind...the memory of the first time I'd met her.

'Are you okay?'

Almost an echo of the first words she ever spoke to me, and again I felt the tears well up in my throat, leading me to think I wasn't okay but I would be damned if I was going to admit it to her.

Ash offered her hand to help me up, but I slapped her hand away. 'Fuck you!' I struggled to my feet. Not taking my no for an answer, she grabbed my clammy hand in her cool one. Some things never change. At least mine were a lot cleaner this time.

Just like all those years ago, she towered above me, dwarfing me with her size and her presence. One deft movement later, I was in her embrace. No chance of staggering forward, just vroom...into her chest, head first. A little voice inside my chest whispered, 'Stay here', but the gob on display said, 'Get your hands off me!' and shoved her away.

Her arms were outstretched in a mime's welcome, and I slapped at her again. 'What're you doing here, Ash?' I snapped, my hands trying to smooth down my clothes.

'Came to see if you were all right.'

'What the fuck do you think?' My head poked out, birdlike; my hands were on my hips. 'You fracture my world and then come to see if I'm *all right*?' I blew out a sarcastic breath. 'You're more fucked up than I thought.'

I turned to go; she grabbed my arm and tried to spin me around. I froze in place, and so did she. 'Get off me. I've nothing left to say.'

'Please, Lou, just hear me out.'

There was pleading in her voice, and I wanted to back down and let her speak, but I was too hurt, too fragile, and she would only screw me up again. 'I think you've said all you need to say.' I yanked my arm free, but she was not to be deterred. She grabbed my arm insistently. 'I said, get your hands off me!'

My name was falling from her lips, but I didn't want to see her, let alone hear her ever again. As I tried to shrug her away, she pulled me and I half turned towards her. Then things got a little hazy. I can't exactly remember what happened; all I remember is that I tried to slap her. My arm pulled back, my hand was flat and ready for connection. But it never happened.

I remember the speed of it, the power lacing it, the anger swelling behind it, but my palm never reached its destination. Ash caught my hand and pulled me towards her. She had me pinned. One hand was caught, my other arm held fast, so I kicked her. Nothing from her in response, not even a wince of pain. I struggled, but she held me tighter. So I did the only thing I knew how to do — I screamed in her face, loudly. Words of hatred, words of betrayal, words I could never repeat. She flinched, and I felt her grip loosen slightly but not enough to release me. Her lips tightened into a thin line, and I knew she was thinking. Then she pounced.

Those lips were now on mine, hard and tight, muffling the screams still pouring from me. Her hand released mine and pulled me closer to her, and I took this opportunity to thump on her arm, pull her hair, slap her and slap her and slap...her.

The kiss stayed firm and unwavering, except for a tiny movement from her lips...a tiny movement that was building to a little more movement, then a little more...then I felt my own move against hers. I hated myself for it, but I couldn't help it. Rationally, I reasoned that if I could distract her, pretend to be playing along, then I could lead her into a false sense of security...make my escape.

But our lips were against each other's...more movement...less pressure...more intense...sucking me in...blurring my reality. Her mouth opened a little, so did mine. My hand stopped hitting her and was just holding the top of her arm. I could feel myself falling into her, falling bodily, lips and mouths and tongues falling. Fingers began tracing along arms and backs. The kiss deepened, wetness passing from one mouth to another stoking a need...stoking a fire I thought was dead.

Before I knew it, my fingers were tangling in her hair, pulling her closer and into me. Her thigh pushed its way between my legs and rubbed against the want gathered there. A gasp mingled with the spit and tongues and teeth — mine or hers, I don't know — but it felt wonderful.

Her hand left my arm, swung behind her to push the door closed, and then she turned me and walked me backwards...never breaking the contact, her thigh tantalisingly chafing my groin.

Against the wall. She pinned me against the wall. Her lips deserted my mouth and began to devour my neck. Hands searched out the hem of my top, and cool fingers slipped beneath. Strong and sure of purpose, they cupped the underside of my breasts and caressed them. In contrast to the primitive suckling on my neck, her fingers were gentle, almost reverent.

God, I wanted her! Wanted her touch. Wanted her mouth. Wanted her to take me and take me and take me forever. My upper body pushed into her, pushed my breasts more firmly into her hands. A thumb broke from the pack and rubbed across my hardening nipple. Fuck, it felt good.

I lifted my leg and wrapped it around her to establish a firmer contact between my legs. My hips began to grind into her, rhythmically in tune with hers...and her mouth and her fingers and...God...I needed more. Needed her.

Thoughts of revenge flitted to the surface, only to be drowned by the growing desire coursing through me. I slipped my hands down her back and pushed them below the waistband of her trousers, craving the feel of her skin, pushing her into me. I could feel the building of release...cleaving...gnawing...begging.

In unison, our hands were 'round the front and fighting with the buttons of trousers. Pop, pop, then the zip. Then the hands inside. The first touch of fingers on desire. The wetness more than a gathering...more than reason...more than I had ever hoped it would be. She was wet for me. So fucking wet...for me.

And I was wet for her.

Slick fingers slipped and tugged and pushed and held. God! It felt like I'd died and was living out my fantasy in heaven. Oblivion was beckoning me, but I fought it. I wanted to remember this moment, the first moment I touched her.

'No.'

Her voice struck my skin, and I froze on the spot, my hand down her pants. A surge of anger erupted from my gut and stuck in my throat. I had fallen for her charms again. How could I have been so stupid? How could I have allowed myself to get into this position?

'Not here. Upstairs...properly.' Her staggered words broke out and trickled over me, and I was surprised how the anger dissipated to bliss in just a short space of time.

Lifting me away from the wall was effortless. Turning me in the direction of the stairs was performed in a dance-like way. Her hands and fingers were still inside my underwear, as were mine in hers. Lips were capturing and clashing as I waltzed staggeringly towards the stairs with my partner fully attached to me.

At the base of the stairs, we began again, kissing fervently and trying to continue the coupling started minutes before. I could feel her pulling back, but this time I knew it was because she wanted this to be more than a quickie in the hallway. I didn't know what she wanted it to be, but by that stage, I didn't care.

My room was dark. Only the light from the streetlights enabled me to see her. But I didn't have to use my eyes to know her; all my other senses were wrapping themselves around what was ultimately her. I could smell her scent; you know...*her* scent. It was compelling.

Her arms were around my waist, and she was rubbing slow circles at the base of my back, her lips taking and possessing my mouth as if they were taking and possessing me. Trousers slipped effortlessly from skin, down ready thighs to expose dampness on underwear. Fingers slipped inside, whilst another hand battled with buttons on tops. Shoes were discarded.

The air on my skin promised me something it never thought it would get. Ash.

Flesh tingled in expectation. Breasts were discovered with searching fingers, nipples erecting under thumbs.

Her mouth delivered pure pleasure as it traced paths up and down my face, throat, and shoulders. Her tongue was inquisitive, as was mine, and wanted to taste everything...wanted to taste all of her.

I pulled her backwards toward the bed, needing her to take me...needing those fingers in places that ached for her. The constant throbbing drumming between my legs was becoming unbearable. I needed just a touch...a stroke...a caress.

Her movements were swift and sure, and before I knew it, I was on my back, sprawled on the bed with my legs parted in invitation. Ash crawled up my body, the feel of her skin against mine pure bliss...no other word could describe it. It was as if we began to morph into each other on contact, melting into one another.

Lips met lips in quest of fulfilment. Hands sought places to worship; tender strokes grew more insistent. The rhythm was steadily increasing, and the wetness from me was smearing itself over her leg, making me glide effortlessly over her. Each and every meeting of flesh was exquisite. I couldn't get close enough to her.

She was moving downward...lips leaving a fiery trail as they danced along my throat and neck, suckled my breasts, flicked my nipples; her hands were slipping along my sides.

Hair tangled in my fingers, soft silky strands I had only ever dreamed of touching. I could feel the heat of her scalp, feel the movement of her head as it moved along — around and up and down.

Leaving the silk of her hair, my fingernails etched a path down her spine, either side, until they reached her arse. Firm and round...and grinding. It was perfect, just how I had always dreamed it would be.

I could hear my name on her lips, feel my name on her lips...the same lips that were now on my skin and moving towards destiny...towards hope and expectation.

Hot breath tantalised my need, and I pushed my hips upward, closer to her face. Her hands were holding onto my hips, and she pushed me back onto the bed.

The first touch of her tongue as it parted my folds made me gasp aloud. I have never felt anything more exquisite in all my life. It was slow and searching...moving upwards to my clit in one stroke, the warmth of her breath exciting it more fully and heightening my primal need.

Hips jerked. Vulnerable to her touch, I just wanted more. Blood thundered in my ears, making it nearly impossible to concentrate on anything but her mouth...her fingers on my hips...her tongue.

God, her tongue. It was moving with agonising precision — up...and down, up...and down. Groans rose from between my legs, groans of desire. My fingers were back in her hair trying to guide her to my ache, trying to make her slip her tongue inside...taste me from the inside out, just as I wanted to taste her...just as I wanted to love her.

'Take me. Just...*take me.*' The words came out stunted and breathless, but their urgency was unmistakable. I wanted this woman to own me and possess me and love me in any way she wanted. Any way. I was hers, always had been. And whatever happened after this, at least I would have experienced being loved by someone I had spent my whole life craving and spent half my life trying to forget.

A solitary finger circled my entrance, swirling and teasing. I pushed my hips down trying to capture it inside me, but she just moved it away. I was frustrated. I needed her inside...I needed her inside... In. Deep. Full. Captured.

An involuntary jerk of my hips pulled it in, and I groaned out her name. The finger stayed put, throbbing inside me — or was I throbbing around it? Whichever it was, it felt like I'd come home again.

It slipped out and then in and then out and then in, slow and sure, brushing along my walls as it curved and pushed. Another finger joined the first and waited inside me. I pushed again and tried to raise myself to look at her. Blue eyes stared intently at me from between my legs, and I felt a spurt of juice shoot from deep inside.

'Kiss me; please...kiss me.' I had to have those lips on mine, had to know this wasn't an illusion, a figment of the fantasy I had harboured for years.

Without removing her fingers, she crawled up me and laid her frame over mine. Her hand was between my legs, and an errant thumb began to brush against my clit. I spread my legs wider, wanting to suck her inside, and wrapped my leg around her waist, opening myself up for her even more.

Her mouth covered mine, and her breathing was ragged. I was so consumed by her, so enthralled by her, I wanted this to last forever, but knew I wouldn't take long to climax. Kisses feathered across my throat and neck, and then she nipped the flesh.

'God, Lou. God! I want you want you want you...' The words tumbled from her mouth and tattooed themselves onto my skin. With every word she pushed inside me, like she was possessing me.

Her movements were becoming more frantic, more animal. She was fucking me...fucking me, fucking me, and it was deliriously brazen. My breast was nearly inside her mouth; she suckled it like she was starving. I pulled her head closer, and she groaned into me. One of my hands glided around her arse and pulled in sync with her thrusting, jamming her fingers home.

I could feel it coming. I could feel myself cumming. I wanted to cum with her, for us to cum together. I needed us to cum together...*needed* it.

My hand stopped gripping her arse and slipped between us to halt the pounding of her fingers inside me. 'Ash, let me touch you; let me...touch *you.*' She pulled her fingers free, and I slipped my leg between her legs and rubbed my thigh along a soaking want.

'Oh God...Lou. *Fuck!*' She half bent over me as the sensation ripped through her, my other leg slipping down her calf and stroking the back of hers. Her arm supported her as she leaned back and pounded against my thigh, smearing it with her essence. I sneaked my hand between the gap and through soft pubic hair to her swollen clit. She stopped in mid-thrust to allow my fingers access.

Two fingers parted her folds, and a gasp left her mouth. I watched her eyes flicker closed then reopen with desire raging in them. A soft snort indicated that there was no turning back for her; she was close, as close as I was.

She knelt in front of me and leaned back slightly, allowing me to circle her core. Her hand was back and tantalising my opening in rhythm with my attentions to her. I raised my leg and supported her whilst I slipped two fingers inside, just as she slipped two inside me.

We both growled with hunger as our hips began a dance — thrusting and pushing in the need to capture and take and own. The need to cum was agonising, and our movements became more forceful, more intense. I could feel her walls clasping around my pulsating fingers as surely as I could feel my own walls spasming.

'Cum for me...cum for me...' Her voice was deep, growling. The words weren't a request, they were imperative to her survival.

White and bright and clear and so fucking intense, I was over. Fighting...clawing...gasping out my cumming, my cries mingling and merging with her sob of release. Uncoordinated coupling, jerky and euphoric, we thrashed and plunged out the last vestiges of delirium before she collapsed on top of me, my fingers sliding from within her. Her mouth was wet and soft as she kissed me. It was deep yet gentle, and I felt so much more giving and taking between us in that one kiss than I had from everything that had preceded it.

Her body moved against me, trying to elicit the aftershocks, trying to slake the need to begin again. Trying to quell the raging inside us both.

But I had waited too long for her, too long for this. I needed to take her again, fuck her again, own her again. I needed to love her until I couldn't move and couldn't think of her anymore.

I knew I would never have enough of her, never love her enough, but I would die trying.

As I rolled her onto her back, I thought, 'This is going to be a long night.' And an enjoyable one at that.

By the morning light, we were dazed with exhaustion. The whole night had been spent discovering each other, over and over again. It was only due to dehydration that we finally stopped, and I lay my head on her chest and nuzzled my face underneath her chin. Soft kisses lingered in my hair, and I wished I had the strength to lift my head and claim her mouth again.

'I need water. Want some?'

The vibrations of her voice rippled through her chest, and I snuggled deeper into her. I didn't want to move, didn't want to break our connection, but I knew I needed liquid. I nodded slowly, the movement of my face bringing me closer to her chest, and I couldn't resist a sly flick of my tongue against a sleeping nipple, a nipple that shot to attention immediately, giving the impression it was searching for its assailant.

Ash slithered from underneath me and slipped her shirt on. 'Won't be a tick.' And she was gone, leaving the room decidedly empty.

I lay back on the pillows, closed my eyes, and sighed. I felt completely contented, at peace at last. This was what should have happened twenty years ago.

My eyelids shot open. 'Fuck!' I sat up. *'Fuck!* What have I done?' My hands covered my face, and I scrambled for some sort of rationalisation of what had taken place. I had just had unbridled sex with Ashley Richards. Ashley Richards.

The Ashley Richards who had dropped me like a stone twenty years ago.

The Ashley Richards who had used me to get closer to Danny Spencer.

The Ashley Richards who now knew I knew about Danny Spencer...and still needed my help to get him.

A fleeting bolt of self-pity shot through me, only to be replaced by anger at what I had allowed to happen. I had been such a fool. Again. I had fallen for her charms. Again. It was amazing how many 'agains' there seemed to be when I was with her.

I swung my legs over the side of the bed, slipped on my sleeping shirt, and readied myself for her return. Two minutes later, the door opened and she came trotting in, barefoot and naked from the waist down. Two glasses of water in her hands, she grinned at me as she leaned back on the door to push it closed. Glaring at her, I sat stoic.

The smile froze momentarily, before slipping completely from her face. 'Lou?'

She had the decency to look concerned, but at that time I didn't think of what she would be feeling. She had gotten what she wanted or *thought* she had gotten it.

'What's up?' Silent footsteps brought her closer to the bed.

'You think you're so clever, don't you?'

'Huh?'

'You heard.'

'Lou...I don't know... What's up?'

She moved closer, but the expression on my face warned her to stop. I had the sheet clutched in my hands, the same sheet we had shared minutes before, that reeked of our lovemaking. 'Don't play games, Ash. I know.'

'I haven't a clue what you're talking about.' She moved towards me again. 'Can we just—'

'Don't come any closer.' I didn't recognise my voice, just buried my head in my hands, trying to stave off the onslaught of emotion welling up inside me. I didn't want the fire to dissipate; I needed the anger to get me through this. My nails dug into my scalp, and I grimaced at the pain of it, although it wasn't a patch on what I was feeling inside.

A sob broke the stillness of the room, and that sob didn't come from me. 'Lou?'

Her voice was pleading with me, saying so much in just that one word. I could feel the ropes around my heart tug and pull, trying to dislodge the bitterness which was trying to embed itself there. My hands left my face, and I looked in her direction, though not at her face; I couldn't handle looking at her face. I looked at her hands, two hands holding water, water in glasses that was moving and jittering around inside the vessel as if it was on board a ship.

Splosh. It hit the stripped wood floor like a brick. Splosh. Another thudding in such a quiet room. The tears that had begun to seep out of my eyes and down my face stopped...took stock...waited. Splosh.

I looked at her hands. They were trembling, and so were her arms. I could see her stomach quivering too, retching and rolling. But I couldn't listen to anything now. Eyes. I had to see her eyes. I knew her eyes, knew them.

Her head was bent, and I could only see the top of it and the bottom half of her face. I waited, waited for her to look at me.

If I had blinked, I would have missed it — that solitary tear that fell from her chin and against her shirt with a muted plop. I watched the dark patch spread into the size of a penny piece, and then another...plop. Her shoulders began to move, ever so slightly, then her tongue came out and flicked itself over her lips.

'What have I done?' The tone sounded like how I felt — rejected.

The answer I wanted to spew out lodged somewhere between my throat and the roof of my mouth. I opened my lips to speak but couldn't, just chewed around the words, mouth pursing and relaxing as if I were chewing an elastic band.

'Tell me, what have I done?' A little bolder, but still fraught with the same something that was inside me.

'You used me, Ash.'

'Used you? How?'

Her eyes met mine, and my chest tightened. Two words clambered around inside my head, 'Be strong. Be strong.' But I felt anything but strong at that moment, sitting on my bed with my heart in tatters. I should have been feeling elated, but I was far from it.

'You fucked me to get what you wanted.' The accusation hit the air and hovered over her stunned face.

'Yes, I did.'

The pain ripped through me. She admitted it so readily.

'I wanted you. Always have.' Huh? 'For twenty years I've wanted you. It's always been you.'

Blue eyes met mine and pleaded with me, but I was angrier now. How dare she lie about it? How dare she stand in front of me and treat me like an idiot.

'You liar...you fucking *liar*!' The last bit screamed from deep within, and I was on my feet and over to her, thumping the tops of her arms in temper. Water splashed everywhere, all over the both of us, but it didn't cool me down. 'How *dare* you!' She just stood there and took it, her fingers gripping the glasses more firmly. 'You ran away. Told me you couldn't. You weren't like that—'

'I never said I wasn't like that...like you...like us.' Her eyes flashed as they looked straight into mine. 'I ran because I thought I'd taken advantage of you.'

'How on ear—'

'You were drunk. I kissed you when you were drunk, and I felt so ashamed.'

I felt the symbolic punch to my gut. My jaw dropped open and snapped shut again. I felt like a twat. But I just stood there in front of her, completely at a loss for words. For some reason I was finding it hard to digest what she had said. Especially the bit where she said she felt ashamed. Why on earth would she feel ashamed? It was me, my fault.

Ash moved past me and placed the half-empty water glasses on my bedside cabinet before sitting on the bed. I turned to look at her, and my heart clenched. That once vibrant face was devoid of all colour; her eyes looked dull and lifeless. They were staring ahead like she was looking through time to that fateful night twenty years ago.

I didn't move straight away; I just let her collect her thoughts. One part of me didn't want to know what she was going to divulge, but the other half...well the other half thought it would die if she didn't tell me.

She lifted her glass from the table and downed the whole lot, although there was hardly any left to drink. I felt my own thirst come raging back, but before I could move she was holding my glass up in front of me, inviting me to take it. I sensed that the invitation was for more than that, though.

I walked forward as if through treacle — lifting my feet seemed an impossible task — and slipped my hand around the cool glass, brushing my fingers against hers in the process. A jolt blasted through me, and I tried to contain my shudder with the deft movement of glass to mouth, followed by rapid swallowing.

After placing the empty glass back on the side table, I tentatively joined her on the bed. We sat there in silence until I decided enough was enough. I needed to know. 'What did you mean? About being ashamed?'

Looking at her profile, I could see the swallowing bobbing in her throat, so I lowered my gaze to her clasped hands on her lap. The fingers were tangling and untangling, fighting the urge to break apart and do something physical.

'I'd...erm...liked you for so long.' She swallowed. I knew she was feeling pain; I could feel it. I didn't say anything. 'Long before that night. But I never thought you thought of me that way...thought I was a freak to fancy my best friend.' She rubbed her eyes. 'I honestly thought it was a phase, something I would grow out of. But it never happened. It seemed as if every day I wanted you more.'

She stopped to collect herself; I continued to wait.

'It's more than that though...much more. I think it started when we were kids.'

'What?' Now this was freakish.

'I don't mean I started wanting you when we were kids; I mean the connection I always had with you. Then when you fell back into my life,' 'fell' being the operative word, 'I thought I had found you again and there was no way I was going to let you go.' She turned and looked at me. 'It started so innocently. I was just so happy to have you back. And then I began to look forward to seeing you...then miss you when you weren't there.'

Her hands tried to clasp again, but I claimed one and began rubbing my thumb along the back of it. This emboldened her; I could see by the way she took a deep breath before continuing. 'It wasn't long before I began to crave you...you...everything about you. Your smile...your smell...your laugh. The way you wrinkle your nose when you are just about to grin.'

A small smile graced my lips at that, and she smiled back. 'Like that.' A little laugh came out of my mouth; I felt embarrassed.

She sighed and turned away, her face wistful. 'It was agony being with you, but even worse when I wasn't. I was so frightened of you finding out, thought you'd be disgusted and tell me to get lost.'

I gripped her hand more firmly, just a quick squeeze to make sure I knew this wasn't happening in my head. Yes. This was real. She was real.

'When I found out you were moving to Norfolk, I thought my world was coming to an end. It seemed like the other side of the world.' She lifted her head and turned to face me. 'I thought I was going to lose you without ever telling you how I felt.'

'But why didn't you tell me. You must have known I had feelings for you.' I nestled my hand on the side of her face, cupping her cheek. 'I more than adored you. I...loved you, Ash.'

The smile spread over her face like a blush, and like blushes, the grin was totally contagious. Then her eyebrows dipped at the centre as a frown took its place. 'Loved?'

Shit. Had I gone too far, said too much?

'You mean you don't now? Love me, that is.'

I wanted to lie and say no, thinking that maybe it was too soon to admit what was clambering up my throat in true confession. Emotion won out.

'Never stopped.'

There it was, out in the open, not taking any notice of rational thought or reasoning. And by the look on Ash's face, I believed my heart had made a better decision than my head ever could have.

Her arms were around me, and I was engulfed by her body, her scent tantalising and teasing, her chest heaving...breathing ragged. A muffled 'Thank you, God' was chanted into my hair like a catechism. Arms tightened and I could feel her shaking. I knew she was crying; I had never seen her cry before, apart from the solitary tear from earlier, and it unnerved me.

'Hey...hey...what's up?' I tried to pull away, wanting to look into her face and reassure her everything was all right, but she just clung to me tighter, and I could feel the moisture seeping into my hair. I held her in my arms, brushing long languid strokes up and down her spine as I waited for her to stop. Arms loosened eventually, and she pulled back to reach for a tissue.

After wiping her eyes and blowing her nose, she looked at me and gave me one of the most endearing smiles I had ever seen. She was Ash...my Ash...Ash, the girl I knew...Ash, the woman she was now.

'Better?'

'Much thanks.'

'You still haven't told me.' One of her eyebrows lifted in question. 'Why?'

'Why what?'

'Why you actually kissed me the night of my birthday? And why you ran?'

'I told you why — I felt ashamed.' I tilted my head and looked at her straight in the eyes. 'I need a drink.' I raised both my eyebrows. 'I do...I spilled most of that.' She pointed to the bedroom floor.

'Okay. You get settled, and I'll go and get us both some juice. But you'd better reveal all when I get back.'

The trip to the kitchen was made on extremely wobbly legs. I was surprised they had the capability to work at all, what with all the angst and emotional upheaval I'd been through. In less than five minutes, I was pushing the bedroom door closed and padding towards the bed.

Ash was sprawled back, her head and shoulders propped up with a pile of pillows, and she shifted to make room for me, her hand reaching up for the glass. Two gulps later, it was empty. She slammed the glass on the table. 'See? I told you I was thirsty.'

I climbed onto the bed and snuggled next to her, one arm around her waist and my head on her chest. It felt so right to be there with her, so peaceful. I think she thought she was off the hook for the explanation. 'Tell, Richards.' I felt her chest push out as she drew in a deep breath.

'Well...I erm...it...was...'

'Oh for God's sake, Ash, we've slept together. I've told you I love you... Just tell me!'

The story she came out with filled me with a myriad of emotions, but mainly melancholy. I so wanted to turn the clock back and change the events leading up to her flight that night. I wished I had just told her; I wished I hadn't had so much to drink that it made her feel she had taken advantage of the situation.

After she admitted she'd run because she was scared about the consequences of her actions, she stopped; I just stared at her.

'What?'

'You still haven't told me.'

'I have, too. I bottled out because I thought you were drunk and would regret it the next day,' she said adamantly.

'That's not what I meant, Ash. Why didn't you bother explaining why you ran? You could've said you were drunk, too.' I looked up at her. 'How could you have left it twenty years to tell me? I thought you felt something for me.'

'I didn't leave it twenty years.'

I propped myself up onto my elbow and looked down at her. 'It's been twenty years, Ash. From that night to the night you showed up...nearly twenty years.' I looked down at her mouth and then back to her eyes. 'You could have at least said goodbye.'

'I tried. I came to your house and stood outside, I don't know how many times. But I just couldn't face you. I thought if I called you and spoke over the phone, it would be easier.'

'So why didn't you?'

'You were cut off.'

It was true. My dad had disconnected the phone the day before we were to move to make sure he'd done it. But then something new dawned on me. 'You had my new number. Why didn't you call me in Norfolk?'

'I did.'

'You could have— *What?* No, you didn't. I think I'd remember, Ash.'

'Spoke to Jo.'

'You spoke to...*Jo?*' Shit. 'What did she say? She didn't tell me you'd called.' I looked up at her; she looked uncomfortable, chewing her lip, probably thinking how she could get out of the conversation that was starting to appear more like a confrontation. One of those little 'oh, what the hell' sighs came out, and I saw the resolve kick in and her mouth purse.

'After we'd had a little chat, I told her I thought it would be best if you didn't know that I'd called.'

I sat up straight on the bed, removing myself completely from the warmth of her body. 'You called and then said not to tell me?' I couldn't believe it; it must've been soon after we'd moved because Jo moved in with Craig not long after.

Then a thought struck me. 'What did she say to you?' Ash shook her head, as if to say it didn't matter, but I needed to know. You would, too, wouldn't you? You'd want to know why the sister you thought the absolute world of would betray you like that. She knew how I felt...she knew I loved Ash...she knew that I'd kissed her... Shit. She didn't know. I hadn't told her.

'What did she say to you, Ash? Please. I need to know.'

Ash looked uncomfortable. 'Jo loves you, Lou.' I just stared; it seemed that my world had suddenly gone tits up, you know...when you can't really grasp something...think it must be wrong...think the rest of the world has gone crazy and imagined something that you couldn't possibly perceive. 'She was only thinking of you.'

I pulled back further, as if to try and see the bigger picture, but my brain was fucked. Ash held her hand out, palm upwards as if in offering, fingers extended. I just sat there like a laughing Buddha ornament, frozen to the spot. My eyes said, 'Tell me...tell me...tell me...'

She sighed, knowing I wouldn't give in until I knew. 'Come here, baby, and I'll tell you.'

I resisted for a few seconds and then laid down on top of her, my hand sneaking around her waist and pulling her into me.

And then she told me, word for word, what had passed between the two women I loved so much. There had been no tears...no tantrums...no shouting, just an agreement. It was for the best. For whom, I didn't know. The best for Jo? Ash? Because all that crap about making a fresh start and leaving me to get over her and get on with my life certainly hadn't been the best for me.

A maelstrom of emotions swirled through me. I didn't know whether to laugh or cry...scream or sob...rage...spit...thump...demand...become complacent...sullen. Too many emotions, too many.

Eventually my screwed up insides came to a decision. Not consciously. It was only the feeling of wetness on Ash's skin that alerted me that I had been crying. The tears had seeped unknowingly. Surprise released the pent-up emotion bubbling underneath the surface, and the floodgates opened. I felt cheated. Cheated. *Fucking* cheated! How dare they decide for me? How dare they think they knew what was best?

'How dare you! How fucking dare you!' It was out, and there was no going back. I was up and off the bed in a flash, the room almost spinning. It was totally unfocused, a little like the conversation, a little like my brain. 'How could you presume to decide what was the best for me? You didn't even ask me, didn't even get my side of the story.'

'Lou—'

'Don't "Lou" me!' Spit flew. I was seething. Wait until I got hold of Jo. Wait until...

The next thing I remember was being in her arms again, and she was holding me against her, gripping me, shushing into my hair. I was fiercely angry, but her presence was soothing me...soothing the ire away...soothing it all away.

'Please, Lou, don't be mad.' I attempted a half-hearted wriggle. 'Don't blame Jo. She was just looking out for you...like she always has.' I thought of Jo, thought about how she had always had something against Ash. Do you remember me saying about distrusting Jo, distrusting her after the lemonade incident? Well, this certainly wasn't lemonade; it was something that couldn't be mopped away.

Soft kisses were in my hair, and the anger was seeping away...flowing away...drifting away. I was hurt by what they had done, but I needed to speak to Jo about it, needed to hear her tell me why she had done what she had. Funny thing was, I could understand why Ash had stepped away from it all. She was still reeling from the acknowledgment that she had a crush on her best friend and felt like a circus freak. Obviously she would back down from the situation, believing that I would be better off without her.

But Jo had known the truth. She knew I had feelings for Ash. She knew I was in love with Ash, yet she told her to leave me alone. The only person I wanted to tell me the reason for that was Jo herself, and I would get to that as soon as I could call and make arrangements to see her. That was the kind of thing that had to be done face to face.

It could wait until the morning, because I had better things to do...like concentrate on my future instead of my past.

It was about ten o'clock in the morning when Ash's mobile shrilly brought us both back into consciousness. She slung her naked body half off the bed and rummaged around on the floor to retrieve her trousers, which held the warbling beast. All I could do was stare at her. She was absolutely stunning sprawling there in all her magnificent glory, her backside tantalisingly close...close enough for me to trail an illicit finger over the curve. But I stopped myself just in time.

Ash randomly pressed the keys to accept the call, and when she turned to face me she looked totally exhausted. We had spent a while earlier trying to come to terms to what had happened and eventually had agreed it was something that, with time, could find a place where it belonged – in the past.

I watched Ash talking into the phone, her eyes hidden behind heavy lids, and I knew she was harried. Work was calling, and I could see the tension in her mouth. I ran a finger, the same one that had been so tempted seconds before to touch her, along the underside of her bottom lip, and remembered where those lips had been last night.

Her smile changed the path of my finger, and I looked into the bluest eyes I had ever seen. And they were twinkling...for me...at me.

I mouthed, 'I want you' and she grinned and held up a digit as if to say, 'one minute'. But I couldn't wait that long.

My fingers slid across her chest and along her collarbone. Ash bit her lip and tried to keep her voice steady as my fingers crept lower and circled her breast. She shook her head, but it was only a half-hearted gesture, so the fingers ventured lower as I lifted myself up and over her. Circles on her belly, brushing fingertips that were determinedly going lower and lower and...

'Haaah!'

The air escaped her mouth as my fingertips reached her nub; it felt wonderful. She pinned her eyes on mine, her conversation becoming more staccato, the person on the other end of the phone becoming more confused as the answers were less and less focused.

I decided to let my mouth join in, and lips began to skip along her belly whilst my hand was between her legs. Her voice was becoming curter with the caller, telling whomever it was that she would be there as soon as possible.

Guilt sneaked in as I thought it unfair to lick her belly and stroke her whilst she was trying to take in information, so I pulled back, only to have her hand rest on my head and urge me back down.

Peeking up at her, I saw the glint flashing in her eyes and knew she was horny. Fingers tangled in my hair, and I could feel the pressure on my scalp increasing. My lips brushed against her pubic bone, and I nuzzled in deeper, glorying in her scent. Two fingers separated and guarded her clit, opening her wider, opening her up to my watering mouth.

One flick of my tongue, and she gasped, the slamming shut of her mobile echoing around the room. Her hands gripped my hair and pushed me down and into her, her hips rising off the bed to allow me full access.

With the flat of my tongue, I eased from her opening and upwards in an agonisingly slow movement, my fingers slipping to the side, up, and over her thigh. I pushed her legs apart, and she scooted backwards to spread herself wider. Inside me, muscles clenched and spasmed; I wanted to take her roughly…take her fully…take her and own her and make her mine.

But I didn't.

I drew my tongue back downwards, using just the tip along her swollen clit until it reached her core again. Ash's stomach sucked in, and I could hear and feel the air being held and released, emitting a groan in its wake. I gripped her thighs, one under and one over, and pulled her towards me as I buried my face into her, breathing her in deeply.

'Jesus, Lou…God, yes! Take me…take me.' I rubbed my face into her like I was giving her an open-mouthed kiss, my lips moving, miming the words, 'I love you', hoping they would be swallowed up inside her, just like I wanted to be.

Another stroke with my tongue upwards…then down…up…then down…up…then…

'I need…to taste…you…need to…taste you…too.' Her words undulated into the air, but I knew what she wanted. I slipped my hand back between her legs and eased my fingers into the place my tongue had just left.

Effortlessly, I swung my leg over her middle and scooted backwards until I straddled her face, my fingers never missing a beat. Her hands gripped my hips and eased me downward until I felt the sensation of her tongue flicking against my clit. I jerked forward as a spasm shot along every nerve in me.

A couple more flicks and then a suck and then…oh God…it was ecstasy. My eyes closed, and I rocked on her tongue, my fingers still pushing and pulling along slick folds. One minute I was rocking, the next, my face was once again between those precious thighs, and I was delighting in the taste and texture of this woman…*my* woman…underneath me.

Without warning, we entered each other with tongues ready to be lost inside, tongues ready to caress walls that begged to be loved. The intense feeling of my approaching climax was mushrooming, filling me with a sense of union, of two people melding into one and becoming complete again.

Actions were becoming frantic. Mouths were eating, consuming, devouring, sucking; tongues were dancing and flicking. I could barely breathe, and Ash's breaths were ragged coming from underneath me. Neither of us wanted to stop; both of us needed to cum...

I could taste the change in her — salty yet still as sweet as honey, and I knew she was close...as close as I was. I delved deeper into her as she delved deeper into me. Harder and faster. Harder and faster. Hard and fast...hard and fast.

We both cried out, and the wetness shot from inside me and coated her face. My nails were digging into her thighs, and I was riding her unabashedly. Her hips lifted and floundered in the air as her climax robbed her of all coordination.

My name was inside me, being chanted through parted lips, lips that were soft and moist and pliable in their weakness.

It was blinding, but I knew at that moment I had never seen so clearly in all my life. The absolute knowledge of what it was like to be totally and utterly immersed in someone else raged through me, making the world seem to disappear until only she remained.

And there I was, wrapped tightly in the arms of the woman who, even after twenty years, held my heart so easily. The woman who held my everything so easily.

And there we lay. Content to just be.

Chapter Twenty-Three

She left thirty minutes later, freshly showered and looking like perfection. The pang of loneliness hit as soon as I shut the front door behind her.

I had so many things I needed to sort through and reflect on, mainly about what was going to happen next and what I was going to do about Jo and the phone call. Events of the past seemed too much to even contemplate at the moment. I had to concentrate on moving forward. And the way to do that was to put the past behind me — deal with unfinished business.

I called Jo's number and fiddled with a pen as I waited for her to pick up. Her voice echoed through the phone as I distinctly heard her shouting at her youngest son to, '*Leave the bloody gerbil alone!*'

'I need to meet with you and have a chat.'

'Lou? What's wrong?'

'I've been talking to an old friend of ours...or should I say an old friend of mine.'

It went quiet for a few seconds, and then her voice came back, distinctly softer. 'Who?'

'Ashley Richards.' I let the two words hang in the air, and I waited for a response. I knew she was trying to think of something to say, but there was nothing she could say to me that would avoid the fireworks she knew were going to erupt.

'When do you want to meet?'

She hadn't asked why or how I'd met Ash again, didn't question the fact I'd asked to see her...or the way I'd asked her. She must have known I knew what she'd done, what they had both done. I told her that Ash was down on business and I had met her at the police station. I didn't mention why, just that we had met again.

It was a strange call, distant. Usually our calls to each other were full of fun and ribbing, but given the circumstances, that was the last thing this exchange could ever be.

I didn't invite her around to meet at my place, which was a sure-fire way of telling her I was angry. We made arrangements to meet later that day in town after she had got rid of the kids. After we disconnected, it occurred to me that it was a bit strange that my parents hadn't called her and warned her about my visit yesterday — which made me wonder if she was in the dark about our stepbrother, too.

I showered, dressed, and ate some lunch, knowing I wouldn't feel like eating after our confrontation later. The thought of Jo doing anything to hurt me stuck in my throat. How *could* she? She loved me, didn't she? She always said she wanted me to be happy, but look how that turned out.

I was thirty-seven years of age, and I hadn't been in a serious relationship in my life, not since Sarah, that is. And while I was thinking about her, was I really serious about Sarah or was she just an aside until I could get what

I craved — Ash? Had I been holding out for Ash all of these years, not allowing myself to move on with my life?

But was that Jo's fault, or mine? Training told me that I was in charge of my own happiness: no one could dictate to me how I should feel; only I could make the decision how others affected me, at least to a degree. After all was said and done, it had been me who had pulled back from any commitment, preferring to keep relationships casual. If the other woman wanted something more, I just made my excuses and left.

Time passed so quickly, I found myself rushing to get myself in order before I had to meet Jo. I was rummaging through my bag looking for my mobile when the doorbell sounded. Fuck. I decided the best thing to do was to answer it on my way out and call Jo to tell her I was going to be late.

A bloody double-glazing bloke stood there, grinning inanely and trying to sell me windows. They are so insistent...and smarmy. He tried to use his charm on me, but I gave him the look that he had a cat in hell's chance of getting me to buy anything from him. I grimaced and tried to tell him I was running late, and like all salesmen, he didn't listen to a word I said.

Keys. Bag. Phone. The only thing I could do was push past him, throw an excuse over my shoulder, and make a run for it. Before I could, I heard a smashing sound coming from the back of the house.

'What the fuck?' I turned in the doorway, trying to listen to the noises of the house.

'It seems like one of your windows needs replacing.' I looked over my shoulder at the salesman, whose face was full of concern now. 'Do you need a hand, love?'

I frowned at him, but before I could say anything else I heard movement coming from near the kitchen area. What made me step inside the house, I will never know. Whatever it was that made me so open and vulnerable like that will never be repeated. I was inside, the salesman behind me, and then someone came out through my kitchen door. Sam Read. Shit.

I turned to tell the bloke behind me, but he was smiling — not at me, but past me.

'I'm in, Danny.'

'I know, son. Well done.'

Danny? Danny Spencer and Sam Read? I heard the door slam and felt my stomach hit my knees. There I was, in my house with two people I would never want to be alone with. It was amazing. The smarmy bugger I had spoken to minutes before was completely gone, and in front of me stood a man who looked like trouble. With a capital T. The smiling charmer was laid to rest, and someone sinister had taken his place. In short, I was shitting myself.

'What do you want?' My fear was evident in my voice. I heard Read laugh behind me, and it was closer than before. I turned my head and looked into those cold grey eyes, turned back and was greeted by green, familiar green. Green like mine, like Jo's.

'You, sis. I want you.' His lip curled upward, showing the left side of his teeth, almost doglike, and I felt like a small animal that was cornered.

I gripped my keys more tightly, the metal poking into my hand. The other hand held my mobile, which I slipped into my jacket pocket. My brain was fucked, and I was fucked if I couldn't get my brain to stop being fucked. Aw shit...I know — I'm swearing too much. But I had also lost the capability to string a sentence together without the aid of the anti-euphemism.

All I knew was that I needed to be on the other side of that door. Images of a bloke slumped over a steering wheel in Manchester came skipping into my head. I didn't want a repeat performance; I didn't want to be the star of the show. I didn't want to have my identity confirmed through dental records. There was only one thing I could think of doing, and that was to make a run for it. Problem was — Spencer was in front and Read was behind, thereby blocking the front and back exits.

Read was snug up behind me now; I could feel his rancid breath burning my neck. Spencer was grinning a wolfish grin, the grin of a bloke who was about to get what he wanted. Not on my shift he wasn't.

'Okay, what do you want with me?' He was just about to speak when I kicked him in the shin, hard. Then with the keys half hanging from my hand, I thumped him squarely on the bridge of his nose, hearing the satisfying crack as his nose broke under the blow. Read grabbed my hair, and I elbowed him, an 'oof' bursting out of him before I followed through with a backward punch in the face.

I knew I had seconds. Spencer was smearing the blood and tears on his face, so I punched him again before stamping on his foot. 'Fucking bitch!' spewed from his mouth as he bent over. I pushed him and ran.

The door was just ahead, but my legs felt like they belonged to someone else. Frantic hands grappled with the lock, and panic was another enemy. The cool afternoon air brushed against my face, and I was close to escaping when a strong hand grabbed the back of my jacket and yanked. As we struggled, my keys flying outside, the door was pulled open, exposing the scene to the outside world.

'Help me!' Two words, that's all I had time to scream before the door slammed shut again and I was face to face with a very angry, bloodied Danny Spencer.

He came right up to my face and yelled words I couldn't decipher. I felt my body cringe backwards as the spit splattered over my face and neck. An arm raised, a hand loomed, and then it was goodnight Vienna.

I felt like crap. My head felt like crap. My lip and cheek felt like shit. Unfocused images played tiggy it with reality, and my stomach was playing right alongside. But where?

It was my front room. I was stuffed into the corner of my front room — on the floor, out of sight. I didn't know how long I had been out, didn't remember getting there. Bollocks.

Spencer was on the sofa staring at me, a bag of ice pressed to the side of his nose, waiting for me to fully focus on him before he moved. Read was rooting through the drawers of my cabinet and systematically pocketing whatever took his fancy.

'Sit down, Sam.' Spencer's voice was low, and that made matters worse. It had the tone of the controlled, yet uncontrolled, if you know what I mean. He leaned forward, set the ice pack to the side of him, and stared intently into my face, waiting for me to be fully alert.

'So, there's a family trait lurking there after all.' He gently touched his nose and looked at his fingers to check for blood. Read slouched against the wall and tried on his most sinister leer for size. 'Seems we're more alike than I realised.'

Cheeky fucker. As if. 'I'm nothing like you,' I spat out.

'I wouldn't say that. You have a mean left hook.' He smiled, or tried to smile, but the swelling made him look deformed. 'Bet you're wondering why I decided to pay you a special visit, aren't you?'

The glare I gave him told him I didn't give two fucks why he was there. I had nothing to do with him. We might be related by the wankstain of a father, but that was where the connection ended.

'You're right. It all stems back to dear old dad.'

'I haven't heard a word from him in thirty years. Why do you think I want to know about him now?'

Spencer sat back on the sofa and eyed me warily, whilst Read looked at his grubby fingernails, methodically cleaning them with his teeth. The room was quiet, too quiet. If I concentrated hard enough, I had the distinct impression I could hear the air move.

After a few minutes, Spencer leaned forward again, cleared his throat, and spoke clearly and slowly. 'Funny you should say that. I haven't seen the old man for well over twenty years myself.'

'And?'

The look he gave me told me to shut up, he was speaking, and however much I wanted to tell him what I thought of his criminal leanings, I knew now was not the right time.

'As I was saying...' Read snorted behind him, and Spencer threw him a look over his shoulder that made the young boy's face pale. 'Dear old absent dad.' He stood up and came closer to me, and I felt all the hairs on my neck stand to attention. 'I could say that I missed him, but it'd be a lie. All he ever talked about was his little girls, his little angels who were taken away from him.'

Now that was a surprise. I had never thought he'd given us a minute's thought; he treated us all as if we were either dead or non-existent.

'Imagine, all your life being compared to someone else. How clever they were, how they were a credit to him...how he missed them.'

Spencer was close, not overly so, but his presence was oppressive. I didn't feel safe. He didn't seem quite with it. He began to walk away, and I felt the fear lift from me. A tingling sensation vibrated at my side; I initially thought it was nerves until realisation dawned on me. It was my phone vibrating in my pocket. Thank fuck.

After making sure Spencer and Read were looking away, I slipped my hand inside and pressed a key. Whoever had called would now be expecting me to answer, but instead they would be greeted by either the sound of nothing or the muffled conversation I could make happen in the room.

'For ten years I was told how I wasn't good enough, or bright enough, or *anything* enough. He blamed me for him losing his family.'

He said this with a mixture of pain and anger, and I could hear the anger winning out. He was slowly losing it, and I didn't want to be there when he did.

'But if you wanted to introduce yourself as my brother, why didn't you just knock on my door instead of imprisoning me in my own home?' I just hoped the person on the other end hadn't hung up the phone but stuck around and heard the last part.

'Did I say you could speak?' Again I prayed that whoever had called could hear. This was not the joyous family reunion you saw on daytime TV, unless of course it was Jerry Springer. This could get ugly. No. There was no 'could' here. This *would* get ugly if someone didn't stop it, stop him.

He started muttering under his breath, and I couldn't hear what he was saying. I wasn't sure he was speaking to anybody apart from himself, and that's what unnerved me. I looked at Read, and he even had the sense to look concerned.

'You know, I've not been a good boy.' His attention was back to me. 'Even killed someone once.' A smile flitted over his face and supported his fucked-up sense of pride about what he had said. 'Now he was a bad 'un. Poor old Mike.'

A confession. In front of me…in front of Read…in front of the person I hoped was listening in. Mike Adams was the gang leader who had been killed in his car at the traffic lights. It must be the same Mike, mustn't it?

'Then I thought I would pay my other family a visit. See if they were all he cracked them up to be.' By this time, Spencer was on the other side of the room, standing next to Read. 'It's nice in Norfolk, isn't it?' I didn't answer him, just glared. 'I said…it's nice here, isn't it?' Still I didn't answer. And that was a big mistake.

'Come on now, you're not giving your little brother the silent treatment, are you?' Spencer started walking towards me, his eyes turning into slits. But that didn't stop me, even though I knew I was pushing my luck.

When he got right in front of me, I looked at him with disdain before saying, 'What do you expect? You force entry into my house, hit me, and throw me in the corner. What do you want, the red carpet?'

The words were no sooner out of my mouth than I felt the sting of a backhander slamming into my face. The blow would have hurt anyway, but my cheek and lip were already swollen from the previous hit. My hands were up and trying to protect the already sensitive area, but he wasn't having any of it.

He grabbed my wrist and yanked me to my feet, giving me a violent shake on the way. 'A little fucking respect would be a start!' Another hand grabbed the top of my arm, fingers digging in to help Daniel grip me tighter. 'You think you're so fucking perfect with your flashy job and flashy life. You're no fucking better than I am!'

The punch to the gut winded me; the one to the side of my head made everything go black again.

When I came around, Spencer was sitting on the sofa, flicking through a magazine and looking bored. I couldn't see the clock from where I was sitting but the room looked darker, so I gathered the afternoon was ending.

'Ah...Sleeping Beauty awakens. Enjoy your nap, sis?' His tone was light-hearted, on the verge of jovial. To tell you the truth, that unnerved me more. How could he just sit there and not acknowledge he was the one who put me to sleep?

'Thought you were going to sleep the day away.' He set the magazine down on the coffee table and sat back into the cushions, really making himself at home.

The last time I had come around I had felt like crap; now I couldn't even begin to tell you what part of me hurt the most. All I can say is that my toes were okay, although I think that was on account of I couldn't feel them. I was cramping up, and my head and stomach were killing me. Breathing was beginning to become a chore.

I heard a noise from upstairs, a thumping on the floor. Read was up there, probably seeing what he could pinch from my bedroom.

'Where are my manners? Would you like a cuppa?' I tried to reply to his question, but my mouth refused to work. I had an idea that if he left the room maybe I could make a run for it, although by the feeling — or lack of feeling — in my legs, I doubted I'd pull it off. Still, it was worth the risk. So I nodded and then grimaced as pains shot through my scalp.

'Sam!' Spencer looked toward the ceiling. 'Sam! Get your arse down here and get the kettle on!'

Aw fuck. Plan A was out the window. The problem was — I didn't have a Plan B.

Read came down the stairs like a baby elephant in ballet shoes, holding something in his hands. Something red.

'Guess what I've found.' He came into the room, totally animated. 'This weirdo has kids' clothes in her room.'

The red item was thrust into Spencer's face, and he shied away from the lad's hands like they were going to hurt him in some way. Trying to play down his obvious weakness, the definite flinch, he laughed and rubbed his eyes as if to say he couldn't see it because it was too close. Read handed him the object, but I knew what it was...knew before he had mentioned the fact it was kids' clothing. It was Ash's jumper, from three boxes down in the office. Read had been busy, must've really gone to town in the rummaging department.

Now I know it's just a bit of wool, just a colourful bit of wool woven into some kind of shape with needles, but it was all I had of her...of our life as kids...of that indescribable innocence that was childhood. I could feel the anger building up inside but didn't have the strength to do anything about it.

It was the way they were both handling the jumper, as if it was nothing, as if it was contaminated, when they were the ones contaminating it.

'What do we have here then? A little kid's jumper in the house of someone who works with kids.' Spencer laughed. 'This is priceless.' I knew it was but for different reasons than he was thinking. 'I wonder what your boss would think about this...a woman to boot.' He threw his head back and laughed.

I collected all the saliva I could into my mouth, just to be able to form a few words. 'It's mine. From when I was a kid.'

'Yeah, right. Why on earth would you keep a jumper from all those years ago?' Spencer sat forward, the smile splitting his face and his body language saying, 'Go on, entertain me.'

I swallowed, the tightness in my throat becoming uncomfortable. 'It was the last thing my dad ever gave me...*our* dad.' I watched the smile slip down his face, watched it disappear and be replaced by a longing so painful, I actually felt sorry for him.

'Go make a brew, Sam.' Read tried to interject something. 'Now! Make a brew. Tea for two.' The smile was back, not as cocky, but he was trying to gain some of the credibility he thought he had lost by showing something other than anger. It's a pity he didn't realise he would have gained more respect if he showed he was human more often.

Read hovered a little longer, wanting to keep on about the red jumper, but I knew he was a little wary of Spencer. He had good cause to be. The mood swings Danny displayed were unnerving. One minute anger, the next cheerfulness. And the mutterings under his breath were a cause for concern. He was truly fucked up, and it didn't take my psych training to tell me that. Anyone, even Read, could see Spencer was struggling to stick to the plan, but he was losing the battle. And I was crapping myself.

There was no guessing what he was capable of. By his own admission, he had killed before and seemed proud of it. But with the mention of *our* father, his unpredictability had been unleashed.

'Erm...Sam? Tea. Now.' This drew the attention back to me. We were alone, unfortunately. For once I would have welcomed Read's presence. Better the devil you know...

'So, a present from Daddy. More than I ever got.' The atmosphere changed again, and then he was on his feet and walking over to the fireplace, the jumper firmly in his hand. He was stroking it in an almost loving way, like it was connected to the man himself. I was mesmerised, watching his shoulders slump as he leaned over and brought the jumper to his nose and mouth. A smashing sound came from the kitchen; it sounded like Read was having good time breaking up my house. Spencer didn't bat an eyelid; he was absorbed.

Beeeeeeeeeeeeep! Fuck. My phone. Low battery. Spencer shot 'round and glared at me. My hand was already in my pocket, trying to finger the off button but not managing it. Beeeeeeeeeeeeep! He was over to me like a shot, his breath on my face, his eyes emitting a spark of madness.

'That had better not be what I think it is.' He was that close, I could see the spit collecting around his lips. 'Give.' I shied away from him, expecting a fist to come up at any moment and knock me into kingdom come again. 'I said *give!*' His hands were trying to get in my pocket, and the more he tried, the more I resisted.

The struggle was becoming quite violent. Scrap that. It was violent, no question about it. The mobile was clenched in my hand, and Spencer was prising my fingers back one by one to try and get to it. I could see by the LCD the message 'Low Battery' interspersed with the credit amount that always displayed itself after a call. If he got the phone off me, he would know I had used it. And where would that leave me? Probably under the patio in a bin bag or at the bottom of the Norfolk Broads sporting concrete slippers.

There was only one thing for it — not let him get it. Simple to say, but painful to carry through. He was nearly breaking my fingers, so I did the only thing I knew how to do — I bit him, hard. On the side of his hand.

His yelp lured me into a split second of a false sense of security before the yelp was followed by a crunching backhander that threw me backwards and the phone forwards.

My eyes were glazing; focusing was becoming an issue again. I could just make him out scrambling on all fours, hunting for the phone, when the room seemed to shrink and become fantastical once again. I thought I saw a person looming in the doorway, but it didn't seem like Read; the image seemed taller, more threatening.

Then the image seemed to fly into the air, as if it was falling off a precipice. It lurched, held, and fell — right on the scuttling figure of Spencer, who had just found my phone. The noises I could hear were vicious: thumping and smashing, fists hitting flesh, air being expelled from lungs in a painful rush.

I tried to bring my focus to bear, but it was too hard to even open my eyes and process what was going on. My hearing was perfect, but everything seemed surreal. Voices blended into the other sounds, and nothing made sense. I distinctly heard Spencer tell the other person to get the fuck off him, but I didn't hear the newcomer answer. Then there were other sounds. Footsteps, lots of footsteps. Shadows and shapes began piling into the room. Voices...concern...anger.

As I felt a hand on my face, I knew I could finally let go. I knew it was her, knew it was the one who would always love me.

I knew it was Jo. And I allowed the blackness to take me.

I drifted in and out of consciousness, unaware of the passing of time. I knew I had been moved from my house; I'd felt the open air on my face and neck, was vaguely aware of the slamming of a door and people around me mumbling. But nothing made sense. It was as if I was wrapped in bubble wrap, insulated from the outside world.

I wish I could have said the same for my head. The pain lancing through it was agony and made my stomach retch. I just wanted to fall into the darkness, let it envelop me for good, let this pain go away, but they wouldn't let me rest. They kept trying to get me to open my eyes, to wake up, to listen to their voices. It seemed too much like hard work, painfully hard.

At one time I opened my eyes and concentrated on green eyes so like my own and I felt fear race through me...honestly believed it was Spencer, but then the reassuring voice of Jo filtered down to me. These eyes, they were softer, showed emotion — compassion and love. They weren't the deranged eyes of my stepbrother. I think the memory of those eyes will haunt me for the rest of my life. I always look at people's eyes...have to look...it's the only way I can trust them.

'Don't worry, Lou; it's only me.' Then her voice drifted over her shoulder, and I could hear her talking to someone else whose voice I didn't recognise.

I was in a bed — white, Spartan, clean, and clinical. Beeps and clicks and the smell of disinfectant. Lights in my eyes, blinding...retracting...detracting from reality as sleep once again took me away from the pain, took me away from the noises and pressure.

Finally, they let me go.

The first twenty-four hours in hospital were filled with examinations, especially of my eyes, to check if I had a concussion. Which I had. It was no surprise really, with the number of blows I'd received to my head. I also had one broken rib and two cracked ones and five butterfly stitches in my eyebrow where Spencer's ring had caught. My mouth was a mess — swollen, bruised, and split open on the inside. Other than that, I was fine. Back to fighting form...ish. I knew I would heal; almost all of the wounds were superficial, except for the concussion, which would sort itself out eventually. I hated the cracking sounds inside my head, which, the doctor informed me, were the sound and sensation of my brain realigning itself.

Yuck, I know, but I thought you'd want to know, considering you've gotten this far.

I wasn't allowed any visitors for this first twenty-four hours, which was good in a way, because I was too out of it to actually talk to them. But you can guess who was the first through the door on the second day. Yes. Surrogate mum, Jo.

I know you're thinking, 'What about Ash? Where's she?' She came in later, and I had the distinct impression she had let Jo have time alone with me before she made her entrance.

Jo. My Jo. My big sister who loved me and looked out for me. Had always had my best interests at heart, at least, to her way of thinking. The way she came bustling in, taking control of the situation — telling people I needed more pillows, more water, less light. I smiled at her and waited for her to stop fussing before I demanded to be hugged. Hospitals always make me feel like I needed to be mollycoddled and made a fuss of.

And then there she was — hugging me, crying into my hair about how worried she'd been...how she'd heard me on the phone when she'd called... heard me trapped with a man, a man who had hurt me. She told me of the helplessness she'd felt, how she'd always wanted to protect me and how she could hear him...hear me...and could do nothing about it, except take the phone to the police. Then she lost the ability to speak; she just sobbed and shook. I held her, trying to be the comforter...take her role for a change.

It wasn't long before her words came tumbling out once again. 'I thought I'd lost you, Lou. Thought...thought he'd...kill you before I co...could get there.' More shaking and crying, and I could feel my shoulder becoming wetter. 'I co...couldn't hang up and call the police. Couldn't turn it off, had to listen... Ran to...to...the police station.'

'Shush shush shush. Come on, Jo. This can wait.'

'Need you to know...need you to know.'

'I know, Jo. Come on, sit down.' My words were muffled against her hair, but she loosened her grip and sat on the edge of the bed, one arm still about my neck. Her eyes were swollen and red. There was a look of absolute devastation painted on her face, and I needed to make her see I was okay, that she could stop worrying. 'Come on, love. I'm okay. Look.' I dipped my head below hers and smiled. I should have realised that would make her feel worse, if the feeling I had in my face gave me any indication.

'Look at your face...your beautiful face.'

'Hey, I'll heal. It's just a little swelling and bruising.'

She was off again, head in her hands and sobbing. I tried to calm her by rubbing her back, tried to cajole her into realising I was okay.

The door to the room opened a crack, and then a little more, and then enough to allow a dark-haired head through. A dark-haired head attached to a very worried face. A worried face that contained two beautiful blue eyes. Two beautiful blue eyes that were looking at me, flicked to Jo, and then to me again.

'Come in, Ash.' The smile she sported was a mixture of relief and 'I don't want to intrude.' I just flicked my head in silent beckoning. The next minute she was in, closing the door carefully and quietly behind her.

'Hey, how are you?' Ash stood alongside the bed, opposite where Jo was trying to sort herself out. 'How's the head?' Her hand tentatively touched the side of my face, and I willingly laid my cheek against her palm, my eyes fluttering closed. A thumb brushed along my bottom lip, taking care not to touch the bruising.

I opened my eyes and looked straight into blue. They were so gentle, so full of love, and totally absorbed in my own. There was a feeling of total connection.

There was the sound of a cough, and for a split second the connection between Ash and me was broken. But it was enough to make me aware that Jo was staring at us with astonishment, and the cough was a means to get our attention, rather than the onset of a cold.

'You two are...erm...are...' She couldn't say it, couldn't ask whether we were an item. Good job, too, because I didn't know if we were. I knew what had happened between us, what I wanted to keep happening between us, but I didn't know if that was possible. We were so different, lived in different places.

Ash looked me in the eyes again and then leaned forward and brushed her lips against mine in answer to Jo's unfinished question and as an affirmation of what had happened between us a couple of days ago...the day my world began to spin again.

I tried to increase the pressure of the kiss, but my mouth was having none of it; I winced in pain.

'You okay, baby?' I nodded and touched my mouth, expecting to see blood on my fingers. 'And hello, Jo. Sorry I didn't get time to chat the last time I saw you.' I looked from one to the other, my expression demanding clarification. 'Jo came to the station just as we were going to raid Spencer's place. She had your phone and was trying to get the desk sergeant to listen to it. He wasn't very helpful.'

'He was a total wanker...treated me as if I had lost my mind.'

'Well, in his defence, you weren't making much sense. Every time he tried to take the phone from you, you wouldn't let it go.' Ash smiled at Jo, taking the sting out of the statement. 'It's a good job we were there. I thought I recognised your voice — a little older, but it stood out against the Norfolk accents. Then I heard the name Lou.'

At that Jo laughed, and Ash followed suit. I looked from one to the other and wondered why they were laughing. 'Sorry about that, Jo. I just needed to get the phone off you.'

'Sorry for slapping you. I didn't realise what was going on. Thought someone was trying to nick it from me.'

'Are you two going to tell me what you're talking about? I feel a bit left out here.' I leaned back against the pillows and pouted, at least, I tried to, but I cringed at the sharp pain that ripped through my face as I puffed out a lip.

Ash sat down on the bed and gestured to Jo to tell me her side of events. I was 'all ears', to use another of my mum's many nonsense phrases. Not literally 'all ears', but you know what I mean.

It was Jo who had called me, although I guess you gathered that already. She was worried when I hadn't turned up...thought I was teaching her a lesson or some such. She'd had a good idea why I had wanted to meet and thought I was too pissed off with her to bother turning up. So, when the phone was answered and she didn't hear my voice, she hadn't thought much about it, just went into defence mode, telling me her side of the earlier events with Ash. Then there was still no recognition from me, but she could hear me talking in the background. Heard the words 'imprisoning me in my own home'. Heard a man she didn't recognise bragging about killing someone called Mike.

I saw a glimmer of a smile flicker along Ash's face, and I knew why. She had the evidence she needed to put Spencer behind bars for a more serious crime than just breaking into my house. 'Will that stand up in court?'

Ash shrugged but still looked contented with the fact Spencer had slipped up. 'We checked his place out last night.'

'And?'

'He's a very sick man. The things he had stored there... Well, I can't really divulge any of that at the moment. We're still collecting evidence.' She grabbed my hand and brought my fingers up to her mouth, then turned it over and kissed my palm. I stroked her cheek, needing to be sure this was really happening and not just a figment of the concussion.

'I would tell you two to get a room, but you already have.' We both looked at Jo. 'I feel like a gooseberry. I'll be outside.' And she was off at a near run, the door slamming her on the arse as she left. As I was just about to slip my hand around Ash's neck, Jo poked her head back around the door. 'By the way, Mum and Dad are waiting.'

'Tell them to hang on a few more minutes.' She nodded and disappeared. I slipped my hand around Ash's neck and pulled her to me, planted a soft kiss on her lips, and then guided her head to my chest. She sighed in contentment as she relaxed into me, and I wrapped my arms about her, as she did to me.

And there we lay. In each other's arms. Oblivious to the world and everyone in it.

Chapter Twenty-Four

The next few days flew by. Jo finished telling me everything that had happened. She had called me and gotten the scenario with Spencer, but it was the events after she had the attention of one dark-haired woman that made my heart swell.

Ash had eventually gotten the details from Jo about what she had heard and what was happening. Jo told me she had never seen such a mixture of emotions lash through a person, and she should've guessed then it wasn't just a working relationship we had going on. But she did say how impressed she'd been watching Ash organise everyone in the station in such a short amount of time.

They had found my keys outside, but they couldn't just walk in; they didn't know what they were dealing with. Good job, too; I was in there, and even I didn't know what was going on. Eventually they had the house surrounded and Ash told them she was going in the back way. Everyone was against her doing it, said they had specialists lined up to get into the house. She insisted, said it was her case and she would do what she thought best for all parties.

By all accounts, she had been outside the back for less than five minutes, trying to gauge her best course of action. She noticed the smashed kitchen window and was just about to go in when Read entered, laughing to himself and rubbing his hands together. He was so totally absorbed in being a smug little fucker that he didn't even notice a six-foot woman climbing through a small window. No wonder he always got caught when he was up to something. He was thick.

She came at him from behind, tried to take him down swiftly and quietly, but she didn't allow for the fact he was holding a sugar canister in his hand. She whacked him on the side on the neck, and he went down like a sack of spuds — and so did the glass container.

There was no reaction from the other room, but she could hear Spencer shouting at me and demanding whatever I had in my hand. At the sound of me being slapped, all rationality went out the window. She didn't even consider whether there were more than the two people in the house; she just needed to get to me. When she got to the living room door, there was Spencer on all fours, scrabbling around looking for something. She went for him, just leapt over and got him.

The people on the outside, Jo being one of them, heard the commotion and decided to make their move. They used the keys, as that would be quieter than breaking in, but they could have used a bulldozer and still not have been noticed.

The scene was violent, but Jo said her primary concern was getting to me. I was out of it. My eyes kept fluttering open, as if I was trying to focus but it just too difficult. She said that when she placed her hand on my face, I just went...flaked out. She thought I'd snuffed it, and she went ballistic.

Ash had contained Spencer, and two police officers fixed handcuffs on him. Then it was Ash who calmed Jo down, took her hand, and squeezed her fingers. It was Ash who gently pulled me forward and into her arms. It was Ash who stroked the side of my head, tenderly checking the cuts and swelling. It was Ash who laid me down and smoothed my hair.

The ambulance crew came and took me away just as the coppers were dragging out a raging Spencer. Read went like a lamb, handcuffs behind his back, his eyes downcast in submission. He knew this time he wouldn't get away with anything.

After Jo stopped talking, she just looked at her lap, her fingers refusing to lie still. Her eyes flicked up to meet mine, and I knew she wanted to say something else. 'What?' She looked back at her lap. 'Jo? Tell me.' I leaned forward and grabbed her fingers, pulling her hand and arm over to me. 'Whatever it is, we need to get it out into the open.'

A swallow. A look. A decision. 'I'm sorry, Lou...so sorry.'

I knew what she was apologising for but couldn't say anything, so I nodded. 'I thought it was for the best. I thought if you made a fresh start, a clean break...then...you could get on with your life.'

'But you knew how I felt about her, Jo. You knew how much I loved her.'

She gripped my hand. 'I knew how you felt; I watched you agonise over Ash for so long. But I never knew she felt the same...never knew she loved you.' Loved me. Jo said Ash had loved me. 'How do you know that now, but not then?'

'Cos she told me yesterday. She said I had been wrong to make a decision that involved you without telling you.' Jo leaned closer to me, fully capturing my attention. 'And then she said she understood why I had done it, why we had both done it – because we both loved you...in different ways.'

'She said that? She said she loved me?'

'And, Lou, I think she still does.'

I didn't hear anything else that she said; I was too absorbed with the words, 'I think she still does.'

My heart was leaping about inside my chest, but my head was saying, 'Please let her still love me...please.' I know it seems unreasonable. I know I should have just accepted that deep down I knew she loved me, but I couldn't. I felt too insecure. Maybe because I wanted it so much.

The next thing I knew, I was buried in my sister's arms, and she was crying into my hair. 'I love you, Lou. I'm so sorry...so sorry.'

I wanted to tell her it was okay, it was in the past, but I couldn't. Not because I didn't forgive her, nope, but because I couldn't breathe. So, like all good sisters, I gave her a hug that knocked the wind out of her.

Ash came every day to see me, but nothing was mentioned about...erm...anything really. She chatted about the case and how Jo could stand as a witness to what had happened. They had found quite a bit of evidence in that raid on

Spencer's place, and that was another nail in his coffin. He had pictures of me and Jo...of Jo's kids coming out of school...of my mum and dad. Fucking freaky, it all pointed to one thing: when he'd finished with me, he'd intended going after the rest of them.

I can't, in all honesty — hand on heart and all that jazz — swear that he would have killed me. His main focus was to let me know how angry he was at being second best, never once understanding that when it came to our father we were all second best.

Enough about him, enough about how fucked up he had made Spencer, how he had destroyed more than one person's life, and how his actions had nearly cost us our lives. And if I never saw him again for as long as I lived, it would be too soon.

I could justify everything by saying that without him I would never have seen Ash again, but in essence, it was his fault that I was dragged out of bed in the middle of the night, loaded into a taxi with bin bags as a suitcase, and lost Ash in the first place.

I know. I said 'enough about him', but sometimes we have to go over things in our minds just to try and make some sense of it all. I came to the conclusion that no matter how many times I went through any event that involved him, it would never make sense.

Back to Ash. Yes — you, like me, want to know what was going to happen next. At least you don't have to wait for the ultimate knock back, sitting with bated breath waiting for the yay or nay. You don't even have the agony of loving her so much you thought if she walked out of your life you would just curl up and die.

Now. I'm not saying you have never experienced this...or never will, just not with Ash...not my Ash.

I wasn't as fortunate.

Having her come in to the hospital every day, feeling the tenderest of kisses on my lips. Looking into those eyes that consumed me, having her so close to me yet so distant. I wanted to just ask her, ask her to tell me what would happen next...or maybe the cliché 'Where do we go from here?' But I was too afraid of what the answer might be.

I know you may have no patience with my cowardice, but I was no fool. I knew her life was in Manchester, knew that her job, her home, her family — everything was nearly two hundred miles away. And the same for me. Everything I had was in Norwich; everything I wanted was likely to be leaving me, going back to her life without me in it. And that made my stomach churn, which didn't have a patch on the feelings surging in my chest. To say I was in agony would be putting it mildly. I can't put into words how I was feeling, how the situation made me ache.

Six days after being admitted, I was discharged to my home, escorted by the woman who occupied my every waking moment...and sleeping ones, too. The swelling on my face had disappeared, and there was just the ghost of bruising on my cheek and inside my mouth. It was the bloody butterfly stitches that were the bastard, itched like buggery...if buggery itched, that is.

Standing outside my house, panic swept through me. I know — completely irrational. The man who had held me prisoner and made me fear for my life was being held in the cells at Bethel Street Police Station. He couldn't hurt me now. But the mind is a funny bugger — plays tricks and reruns scenarios again and again, usually the ones you don't want to relive.

'Here. Let me.'

Ash took the key from my hand and swiftly unlocked the door. I hesitated momentarily, then stepped inside.

Total recall: me being dragged back inside by an irate Spencer; me being slammed against the door with his face thrust into mine; me waking up in the front room facing a stranger who was determined to hurt me.

I squinted, trying in vain to dispel the images, stiffening my back and shoulders as if that was going to help. Ash's hand was on my back, and she was gently brushing her palm up and down in soothing strokes. I felt the tension begin to dissipate...just from her touch.

'Come. Sit down.'

I was guided into the front room, and the blood began to pound as my glances raced around the room seeking evidence of the events from nearly a week ago. But it was clean...sorted...in order. All except for one thing that seemed out of place, one thing that was neatly folded over the arm of the settee.

Something red and small. Something that seemed so vulnerable and out of place. Something that originally belonged to the woman standing right behind me.

I don't have to tell you what it was. But as my eyes landed on it, a mixture of emotions whirled through me: pain, regret, longing, hurt, anger. I think you get the drift.

Then the feeling that surged up was a feeling of being exposed. What would Ash think if she saw the jumper? Would she think I was some kind of freak? I had to get rid of it — and quick. It was this thought that propelled me forward into the room.

Just as my hands slipped around the softness, her voice came clearly from behind.

'I was surprised you had kept that for this long.'

Fuck.

'I doubt I'll fit in that now.'

Double fuck and mashed potatoes. I mean, what do you say? I'd been caught — red jumper handed — and my face was approximately the same colour as the wool.

Her body was right behind me now and looking over my shoulder, if the feeling of her breath on my skin was any indication. It had a lovely cooling quality.

'Do you remember that day, Lou? God, we were so wet. The rain came from nowhere, didn't it?'

Strange, but this was the first time we'd ever discussed that day. We had talked about me leaving in the dead of night, but not that day...the day that was embedded into my memory like an oasis. It was, as I've said before, one of my favourite memories — the day we went to Concroft Park. It was the day I realised Ash was everything I would ever want or need in my life.

And that was still true even now.

I didn't even realise I had lifted the jumper to my face, didn't realise I was crying into it until I felt her arms around me, turning me, holding me. Being there, like she had always been. But unlike that day, now I knew I loved her — not in a friend loving a friend way, but *loved* her…was *in* love with her.

And it hurt even more this time. Because I knew she would be leaving me, instead of the other way 'round. And there was nothing I could do.

Was there? Was there anything I could do to stop history from repeating itself?

I could tell her, let her know I wanted this forever. Tell her she was my everything, my all, my reason.

But what if she didn't want that? What if the night we had spent together was enough for her? What if Jo had been wrong and Ash had loved me then but not now? Did I dare risk it all?

Christ! Any more questions? Fuck.

Why couldn't I just stop sniffling in her arms, look into her eyes, cup her face, and tell her…tell her…tell her? What could be so bad? The worst she could do was say no.

And that's what stopped me, her saying no. I honestly believed that hearing her utter that single syllable would be my undoing.

I didn't even realise I was gripping her like a man clutching a life raft cast out at sea. My face was so far into her neck I had trouble breathing anything other than her, but that's all I wanted to breathe — her, her scent — commit it to memory alongside the scent from the red jumper and the smell of the rain.

'Hey, Lou, you okay?' I nodded into her and held onto her even more than the aforementioned clichéd man on a life raft. 'Come on, love…take a seat. I'll make us a cuppa.'

It surprised me that she didn't to have prise my fingers from her as she pulled away. I think it was a subconscious decision on my part to let go and not only now, but…

The jumper dangling loosely from my hand, resignation apparent, I sat and waited for her to come back with two steaming mugs. I lifted my gaze to be captured by blue eyes, which surveyed me, their expression open and raw. She placed the drinks on the table and sat down next to me, turning her whole body to face me. I kept my eyes averted…couldn't bear the scrutiny…didn't think I could be strong enough.

'Lou?' I answered her with a weak, 'yes'. 'Look at me.' I flicked my eyes to her and then back to looking straight ahead. 'Look at me.' Her hand cupped my face, turning it toward her and holding it in place.

'Can I tell you something?' I nodded against her open palm. 'Are you sure you want to hear it?' I hesitated…and then nodded again. The butterflies in my stomach were going crazy. 'Sure?'

'Positive.' I fixed my eyes on hers, my breathing hitched, knowing that this 'something' would either make or break me. When I nodded, she swallowed, but her eyes never left mine.

'I love you.'

Three little words. That's all they were. Three little words...but they were the three little words I had longed to hear for nearly all of my life, but only if they were uttered by the woman who was not just holding my face in her hands, but my heart...my future...my reason for being.

'I love you.'

There they were again — assured and...waiting for a response from me beyond wide-eyed wonder.

'I...I...I...' The words jammed in my throat, not from nerves or fear, but from bloody excitement.

'You don't have to say it back just because I said it.' She tried to look nonchalant, but a shadow appeared behind her eyes.

'I...I...' I was sounding like a retard...and she was pulling away from me. I still couldn't get the words out, so I did what any self-respecting person who had swallowed her feet would do — I kissed her. Hard. With everything I had. If I couldn't say it, I had to show her.

Her lips were unresponsive at first, but I carried on. Needed her to know, needed her to understand I loved her, too. I cupped the back of her head and pulled her in, deepening the kiss, increasing the contact. Her mouth opened a little, and my tongue took the opportunity to slip inside.

She sucked at it, caressed it, loved it. She fell backwards onto the couch, taking me with her. I was sprawled over her body, my mouth devouring her, my hands eagerly stroking her face, her throat, and shoulders until I had one hand on either side of her. Then I pulled back, pulled away from the kiss, and just looked at her beneath me.

'I love you, Ash, so much...so much.'

The grin split her face, and she grabbed the back of my head and pulled me back down to recapture my mouth.

I was falling into her, headlong, unguarded. And I was so happy to finally let go.

Chapter Twenty-Five

How we made it upstairs is beyond me, but we did. I can't remember undressing, can't remember lying back; I only remember the feel of her skin on mine as she lowered herself down on top of me. The feeling was pure heaven. Skin slipped together like silk, caressing yet smooth. Hands coaxed and guided, worshipped and revered.

Kisses elicited guttural moans; breasts rubbed against each other, squirming together in their need for contact. Her hand slipped between our bodies and gently squeezed the mound of flesh, causing me to moan deeply into her mouth. Hips danced rhythmically as the pressure built.

She was between my legs, one leg around her waist pulling her deeper. I could feel her pubic bone chafing my need, but I needed to feel all of her, needed her to possess what belonged to her — claim it and own it — take it with her fingers, her mouth, her tongue, her all. My hand strayed to her arse and stroked it before pulling her in. It was firm and undulating blissfully beneath my fingertips.

The whole was an affirmation of the spoken 'I love yous'. Lips kissed, tongues wandered, and breathing became laboured. It was perfect, a perfect connection. I could almost hear the click of us slotting together.

As she kissed me, I stared at her face, willing her eyes to open and allow me to see inside her, and when she did I was lost...forever lost. The love and depth revealed there was breathtaking.

Her hand cupped my face, thumb gliding over my lip and chin, the rhythm never varying. I opened my mouth and snatched at her thumb, capturing it between my lips and sucking it in. Blue eyes flickered closed and then opened again to expose the unabashed yearning that had been hiding just below the surface. The same yearning that cascaded through me. I thought I was going to lose control.

Her thumb was replaced by her mouth, and I wanted to climb inside, crawl down deep inside her, and stay there. Hide up. Camp there inside her chest, claim squatter's rights. I just needed to be with her, needed to become a part of her.

Then the lips were gone, and my mouth felt robbed, felt cheated and exposed, until there they were on my neck, on my shoulders, my collarbone, and then on to my breasts. One hand threaded itself into her hair, as my other left her backside and stroked the small of her back. The movement of her mouth on my nipple was agonisingly wonderful — short flicks and rolls, followed by sucks and holds.

I just needed her. Needed her. Needed...her, any way she wanted, any way she desired me; I just craved contact, craved her.

Lips on my belly dipped into my belly button. I felt the dip and rise of her head before she moved further down until her nose nuzzled my pubic hair. Eventually she ventured lower, a firm tongue parting me and stroking along my folds, my legs widening even more to give her access. She was so gentle, so tender, so slow, as she moved downward toward the pool of wetness that was flooding from me.

She circled...and circled...and circled, driving me crazy with the need for her to fill me. Lap, lap, lap...then the circling again. I was trying to push down on her, trying to make her tongue slip inside. The pounding in my chest was becoming unbearable; my mouth was dry, and I kept on licking my lips, sucking in air in the process.

Inside. Just a little. Push. A little more. Push...and inside fully. The moan shot from my mouth, my fingers digging into her head and pushing her face into me. I could feel her breath hitting my skin and dispersing like ripples in water. Her fingers were digging in the tops of my thighs, trying to ground me, to stop me from forcing myself upward. She waited a little while before she drew her tongue out, leaving me wanting again.

'Please...Ash...*please*...' The begging was needy and unashamedly wanton; I couldn't stand the emptiness the absence of her tongue had created.

Then it was inside me again, and I felt the sensation rip all along my spine and travel to my fingers, which were pulling at the tangled locks of her hair. Slow pumping actions...her head was rhythmic, but my hips were frantically trying to increase the tempo. The feeling of her eating me was divine. She was consuming all I had to offer as it flooded freely from deep inside to coat and captivate her.

Nothing else mattered, just her and me...me and her. Connecting. Her inside me — that was the only thing, the only sensation I was aware of, and it was building and building, promising ecstasy.

Have you ever had the experience of having it all, but it still not being enough? Experiencing the ultimate connection, but needing more?

That's exactly how I was feeling. I was so close, but there was something missing, something that was stopping me from tipping over. I needed more from her. I needed her...needed to touch her, take her, make her feel what I was feeling. I needed her to share this with me, become one with me. I wanted her to know everything about me. I wanted to tattoo myself inside her, spoil her for anyone else.

It took all the self-control I could summon to pull her away from my wetness, pull her up towards my face, feeling her body glide over my sensitive flesh. But the feeling of her mouth covering mine, the taste of me on her lips and tongue...God!

When I slipped my hand between her legs to glide along her folds, to feel how soaked she was, I knew this was what was missing — our joining. The previous time we had made love paled in comparison to this.

Stoking and caressing. Slipping along and pinching the engorged nub between fingers. Movement of bodies polishing the sweat into each other, breath on skin, lips on mouths, thighs between thighs. We were getting to the place where reality was fading and all that mattered were the taste and touch and smell and sound and sight of each other.

The sheet beneath me was gathering and twisting: we were gathering and twisting. Breathing was becoming more laboured, but I still had to kiss her just as badly as she needed to kiss me. I could hear the catching in her throat, staccato gasping, and I knew she was on the verge, as I was.

We entered each other at the same time, fingers slipping effortlessly inside. Walls spasming and clasping the fingers deep inside; bodies thrusting together and names juggled into the air in long breaths expelled from deep inside, from a place I never knew existed.

Perfect. One word. This coupling...this joining...this connection of two people who had just become one. Perfect.

My mouth was dry, my tongue rough, my skin soaked. I was totally drained, with barely the strength to glide my tongue over parched lips. Totally contented. I felt totally contented and whole for the first time in my life. It felt like this was where I belonged, where we belonged.

Her free arm up and underneath my back, Ash placed a gentle kiss on my mouth before half lying on top of me, her fingers still inside gently pumping, eliciting mini shocks.

I had one arm over her shoulder and held her to me, as if she might vanish if I let go. The fingers of my other hand slipped out and rested on her mound, and there we lay...in each other's arms — content, connected, and finally at peace.

Sleep claimed us, and I dreamed of a beautiful blue-eyed woman who lay in my arms, a beautiful woman who I knew loved me.

Loved me. Loved...me.

And I loved her.

The next morning, we barely had time to talk about anything. All I knew was that she was leaving for Manchester that afternoon and taking Spencer with her.

First and foremost, he was wanted for the murder, and now that they had evidence on him in that crime, they were taking him back to be tried within that jurisdiction. That didn't lessen the charges I had against him, but that was a different case altogether, and he would be tried for that one separately, back in Norfolk. Read was in a detention centre, so I really didn't have any worries on that front. The other gang members from Norfolk had either fled or been picked up for some misdemeanour or another. That didn't stop me from worrying about Ash's safety, as she was going into the thick of things. She had to go back and sort through all the evidence to make sure Spencer would be going to prison for as long as possible, but she also wanted to pull in his cronies to make sure they got their share of the punishment. Not an easy feat.

The kiss she gave me as I stood at the door was perfect. It wasn't hard or passionate...just...just...everything, and I felt myself sinking into her. We held each other, neither of us saying anything, totally content in each other's arms.

As she pulled back and looked down at me, her eyes twinkled again, but I saw the difficultly she had in raising a smile. It came out slightly crooked and even more beautiful than usual. I wanted to beg her not to go, to stay there with me, hide up from the rest of the world and responsibilities...so I could keep her safe and warm and loved. But I didn't say anything, just nodded my head like I had accepted the situation and I was giving her permission to leave.

'I'll call you when I can, okay?' She placed her fingers under my chin and raised my face to hers, placing a soft kiss on my lips. 'Okay?' I croaked out something that resembled a yes. 'It won't be easy for a while, but remember,' she leaned down and brushed her lips across my ear, 'I love you.' Each word danced on my flesh, and again my voice failed to form a response, but my feelings were as clear as if I had spoken.

I grabbed her hands and did what I had always wanted to do. I lifted them and placed them on either side of my face, just to show her...to show her I was hers, always hers. To show her I would be forever lost in her, that my heart was forever lost.

The look in her eyes — God, if I could put that into words, I would be the most gifted writer in the world, past or present. I doubt there were the words to convey what I could see there. I don't think they have been created yet, but they were spoken just the same.

A kiss, then another, then another...then she was gone, leaving me gasping for the want of her, leaving me stunned and frozen to the spot. She left me standing there with her heart in my hands.

Two months. *Two*...months. Seven phones calls in two months.

I know, I know — it was because of the case. That was the rational thing to think. Ash said it would be dangerous to keep in contact whilst the case was still going on, said it was an 'I'll ring you when I can; it's too risky for you to call me' scenario. There were many of Spencer's angry associates to deal with, and she wanted me to be out of the picture for a while to make sure I didn't get any more unwelcome visitors. As if that would have stopped Spencer from getting put away for murder. But Ash said if they knew I was connected to her, they might try and use me to get to her, as she was the lead investigator and therefore chief witness for the prosecution.

Evidence they had collected in his Norwich apartment included a notebook with names of blackmail victims; a gun, which tests had shown was the one involved in the death of Spencer's predecessor, Mike Adams; and also evidence of drug pushing. Ash had said she doubted they would even need to call Jo to testify to what she had heard. The police wanted to keep the assault case separate for the time being. They would prosecute him for the murder, then attempt to get the second sentence to run consecutively to the first. If the murder case was muddled with evidence about what Spencer had done to me, the jury's focus might get confused.

It was on the fourth call that Ash admitted the reason she'd become involved in the first place. She began the case with another detective at the Met, helping him do some research before she passed the reins over to him. Then she found out who Spencer was, and her primary concern became keeping me safe.

And that's why she had come to Norfolk. And that's why I was called. And that's how in the precinct she had known me even before I had turned around.

All the things she said all made sense to me now — me being the link, her pretending she didn't know about the Child Protection Act. Any copper worth their salt would have known about that, never mind a detective inspector, but at the time I was too fucked up to notice those things. The reappearance of Ash in my life had completely thrown me for a loop. And then there was the way she treated me; she had been such a bitch.

She had done that to try and detach herself from me, she said, insisting she would have been good for nothing if she let her feelings for me cloud her judgement. And she needed to be on the ball; Spencer was no fool, with no feelings for anyone. Even his own mother pressed charges against him for assault when he was fifteen. She put up with his temper for years, but the final time he had beaten her she had said enough was enough.

If he would beat up his own mother, what would he be capable of doing to a sister he had never met, to a family he had never met? And Ash wasn't going to take any chances with my safety, even if it meant making me hate her.

I asked her why she just couldn't tell me who he was in the beginning and be done with it. When she laughed, I got offended, and then she laughed again. I went silent, and she started calling me lovey dovey names and making kissing noises into the phone. After each new endearment, I just said 'Tell me', until she sighed and told me that if I had known I would have acted completely differently to Read and it would've gotten back to Spencer; then he would have known...and yadda yadda yadda. And had I ever seen a cornered rat?

Yep. She was right. I was crap at acting, always had been.

God, I loved this woman.

And God, how I missed her.

Work was hectic at first, especially as I had loads to catch up with after my absence. I signed Sam Read off my books and passed him over to some other poor soul; it turned out to be Gemma Jackson.

She was a little off with me at first. Even though she had called a couple of times and left messages, I'd never gotten back to her after the dust up at my house between her and Ash. But I used the Turner charm on her, without being flirty this time, and before long we were actually speaking like two women who got along rather than just wanting to get into each other's underwear. Or, more precisely, Gemma trying to get into mine.

'I always knew you two had some kind of history. I could feel it.' Just like Gemma to get right to the point. 'But whenever I tried to get an honest answer out of either of you, nothing.'

'There was nothing going on.'

'I said "history". You can't tell me you two never got it on in the past.' I shrugged, a half-smile briefly flashing across my face. 'I knew it.'

'You know nothing.' And she didn't. You can't call one kiss a relationship, however much I'd wanted it to be.

'I know enough to tell there was definite friction between you two, although it didn't stop me from trying.' A grin spread over her face, lightening the mood.

All the time she had been talking, I kept giving her ears surreptitious looks. They seemed bigger, although I knew they weren't. It was the thought of Ash saying they were that made me think they were. Not a good way to get on the right side of someone if all I could do stare at was her ears. It was something kids usually do. And like a child, I wanted to laugh and point at them whilst chanting 'Big ears...big ears...' Very mature, especially because I have just said we were acting like two women, two grown women.

We chatted for a little while longer, mainly about the case, although she couldn't help ribbing me about my relationship with Ash. By the end of our meeting I had the distinct impression she was going to ask me out on a date again, but I watched her mull it over a little before she spoke.

'So are you with Ash now?' I smiled and nodded and watched her face fall, then rise again. 'Exclusive?' I nodded again. She gave me a quick hug and muttered, 'You know where I am,' then she was gone, and I felt relieved.

When work slowed down and I had the chance to dwell on Ash's limited communications with me, the feelings I had been suppressing rose to the surface. I tried to convince myself that she hadn't called for nearly two weeks because of the case...but why not? I knew the case was coming to an end, knew the jury was out, and things were extremely tense.

I had been following the proceedings through the news, well, online versions of the news, as it was classed as a local story and hadn't really made it to the Nationals. The Manchester Evening News Online followed the events methodically, painting a picture of a man who was caught up in greed and cruelty, him being the cruel one. In a snapshot of Spencer being led from court, I could just make out the striking figure of Ash hovering in the background. Her face was looking downwards, but her eyes were peeking up through the front of her hair, which had fallen forward. I knew she wasn't looking at the camera, knew that she was checking on Spencer, but I felt like she was looking at me, and it fascinated me. Time and time again I would go back to the My Pictures folder and seek her out.

I had edited it so it was just her, and I would stare at the screen, maybe just trail my finger along the curve of her face. Or I'd try and capture her gaze, force those blue eyes to meet mine.

God, I missed her. Missed her smile, her laugh, her voice. Missed the way her eyes twinkled when she looked at me. Missed the feel of her, the touch of her lips, her mouth, her tongue. And I wanted to pick up the phone and call her, just to hear her voice and know she was missing me, too. But I had promised — too risky and all that.

It was on the Tuesday morning that I couldn't stand it any longer. I had finished all my paperwork, and boredom had settled over me. The server had gone pear shaped, so I couldn't access any of my files or the Internet. There was only one thing for it — a visit to my sister, the dependable, nagging one, who had called me constantly for the last two months to tell me to get my lardy arse over to see her...or to come and stay with her, Craig, and the kids for a while. We had only seen each other a handful of times since everything had blown up. As I said, I had kept myself busy.

Poor Jo, she knew there was something wrong as soon as she opened the door. As usual, my sister knew me better than I knew myself. Craig made excuses about tidying the shed and left us alone. Bless him. He was the epitome of a brother-in-law — solid, yet scared shitless of hearing anything that involved me and my relationships. The kids were sent to their rooms and, as sulking teenagers do, they stomped up the stairs to attack their CD players and make the house vibrate. Two bollockings later, the volume decreased to a mere thrum and pulse in the living room where I was sat with Jo.

'What's going on, Lou?' Just like Jo — always to the point. 'Have you heard from Ash?'

It was bubbling away inside me, fermenting and threatening to spill over. All the emotions I had held down were clamouring at the back of my throat. I kept swallowing repeatedly, hoping that I could just tell her I missed Ash without all the amateur dramatics I was sure were going to follow.

I nearly managed it. Honestly. I sat silently, swallowing, clasping and unclasping my fingers around the handle of my handbag. I had just digested the last vestige of misery when she slipped her arm around my shoulders, and it all came pouring back. And out of my mouth in a wail.

She held me, shushing me, stroking my back in her tender way, and letting me know without the need for words that she loved me, that she was there, that she would always be there.

It was a while before I could even attempt to tell her what was the matter, but typically Jo, she sat there and held me and waited. A feeling of peace enveloped me, a calmness I hadn't felt for quite some time, and I let it wash all over me before I began.

'I miss her so much.' There was no need to say whom; Jo pulled me closer, making me feel like a teenager again. 'I can't even call her.' I started to cry and splutter about how unfair it was that I couldn't see her or speak to her whenever I wanted to...how it wouldn't hurt just to hear her voice now and again...like at bedtime, just to say goodnight.

Jo let me go on and on and on. She didn't interrupt, just held me and nodded in all the right places. But in the end, she asked, 'Why haven't you gone to find her?'

'Don't you think I want to do just that?' I sat back and away from her, wiping my face with the back of my hand. 'But I can't. The case...too risky.'

'What case?'

Huh? Had my sister finally lost the plot after all these years? 'What case? *What case?*' My tone was incredulous. '*The* case. The *Spencer* case—'

She interrupted my flow. 'But that's over. It finished early this morning.'

My mouth hung open, my tongue hovering near my bottom lip, forming the beginning of the word I had just been about to utter. The lips closed slowly, my face taking on a semi-pout.

When I concentrate, I frown. Can't help it. I couldn't grasp what she was saying, so I leaned forward and frowned harder. And Jo moved back, slightly but noticeably.

It seemed like ages before the 'What's up, Lou?' sounded.

I frowned more. I think I was stunned, you know, rabbit in the headlights syndrome...

Jo seemed a little uneasy, and I'm not surprised. If I had been in her position, I would have been, too.

'So...erm...why don't you call her?'

That kind of snapped me out of my trance, and I lifted my eyebrows, dispelling the frown once and for all. 'Call her? *Call her?*' It didn't sound like me; it was distant and very reserved. And that was definitely not how I was feeling. 'Oh, I can do better than that.' I stood up abruptly and snatched my handbag from the sofa. '*Much* better.'

'What're you going to do, Lou?' Jo stood up and placed her hand on my arm, and I just looked down at it and then back to her face. I don't know what my expression said, but she took her fingers off me like she had been burned. 'Lou? Tell me.'

'Are you sure the trial is over?' When she nodded, I didn't even ask for any more details, just turned and headed toward the door.

'What are you doing? Lou?' I just kept on walking. 'Lou! *Answer me!*'

I stopped at the front door, turned, and looked her squarely in the face. 'I want to find out why she couldn't be arsed to let me know the case was over.' I grabbed the door handle. 'And also find out what the fuck she's playing at.' I opened the door.

'You can call her from here if you want.'

'I said I'm not going to call her.' Jo's eyebrows raised into her hairline. 'I'm going to ask her in person. I'm going to Manchester.'

'When?'

I smiled at her, winked, and stepped through the open doorway. 'I'll call you when I get there.'

Chapter Twenty-Six

Back home, changed, bag packed, in the car...and then I was on my way.

The miles were eaten up with mutterings that became increasingly angry, and by the time I reached Chesterfield I was livid. I couldn't wallow in self-pity; screw that. I was fuming. How dare she? How fucking dare she lead me on and make me believe that we had a future?

It was all too much. After all the perfect time we had spent together, however short. Maybe it was just me: maybe I just couldn't believe that anyone would want me, especially her. But my self-doubt didn't override the anger I was feeling, the kind of anger that wished it could kick me up the arse for being so stupid. Again.

'Can't call you...too risky,' I mimicked in a sarcastic tone. 'I don't want you to be in danger.' Same sarcasm. I can't begin to tell you how many times I said that as the miles slipped away underneath my tyres.

Images of the last time I had seen her danced in my head. The phone calls we had shared replayed themselves, and instead of feeling the longing I had previously, the memories fuelled my anger even more.

It wasn't until I got to Stockport Road that I realised I didn't know her address. The dawning realisation hit me as I saw the sign for Levenshulme, and I closed my eyes and slammed my head on the headrest.

I pulled over into the car park of a local pub and just sat there wondering what I was going to do. I could have called her, but I didn't want to alert her and give her time to think of an excuse. It would have been so much simpler if she was listed in the telephone directory. The only thing I could do was go to her parents' house and ask.

Decision made, I pulled out of the car park and headed for Levenshulme — a place I hadn't visited in nearly twenty years.

It certainly wasn't hot and sticky, and promise had long since fled the area. These days my imagination conjured up images that could be pretty frightening, and a lot of them had actually happened. The once-packed streets were empty of people, just cars parked haphazardly, and I doubted children could play tiggy it and kerby, as avoiding cars would be impossible. Noise and pollution were the new black.

It was Levenshulme, once an affluent part of Manchester but now filled with students, ethnic minorities, and a budding professional sector. The roads leading to Ash's parents seemed small and winding, and it dawned on me that it wasn't because I was bigger now, because I hadn't grown; it was because I had never driven there before.

As I turned into their road, I felt sick. Nervous sick, I think, but sick nevertheless. It was weird how the road seemed exactly the same, especially after all the changes I had noted on the way. I felt sixteen again, like the very first time I had been to Ash's after the first time we had been separated.

I parked the car opposite their house and just sat there and collected myself. I had been driving for nearly four hours, but it felt as if I had just left Norfolk minutes before.

I was still angry, bloody fuming, actually. I didn't want to knock on their door and start ranting and raving at them for something they probably knew nothing about. So I sat and waited, waited for a miracle to make me rational. When that didn't happen, I decided that the only way I was going to find any peace was to knock. So I did.

I got out of the car, walked up to the door and knocked, then knocked again. Then rang the bell. I was just about to ring it again when the door opened.

It was Ash's mum — older, but still the beautiful woman I remembered...even though she looked pissed off.

'Why don't you take the bloody door off next time?' And then she stopped and looked me up and down, a growing realisation appearing on her face in the shape of a smile. 'Well, I never. It's little Lou Turner, isn't it? Well, not so little anymore.'

'In the flesh, Mrs. Richards.' It was out before I could stop it.

'Well, I never. How long has it been — twenty years?'

She was peering into my face, just to make sure. I should have known what was coming next, but I wasn't thinking straight.

And after all those years, it still hurt like buggery. She gripped my cheeks and gave my head a waggle, and I was transported back to a time when I'd had a little bit of chubbiness to keep me safe.

'Where are my manners? Come in, love.' I couldn't answer, so I just nodded, then sighed with relief as she let go of her death grip on my cheeks.

The house was still the same, and I fully expected to see Ash come bounding down the stairs and then remembered why I had turned up there in the first place.

'Mrs. Richards?' She stopped in front of me and turned. I tried to keep my voice light, you know, not let any emotion trickle through. 'Could you give me Ash's address?

'No.' I looked at her in surprise. 'Not until you have a cuppa with me and tell me what you've been up to.' She walked through into the kitchen, leaving me a little gobsmacked.

I waited patiently whilst she was pouring the tea, even laughed and nodded in all the right places, but all I wanted to do was to find Ash. I went through her quickfire round with no problems until she asked, 'Are you seeing anyone?'

The teacup seemed huge and clunky as I raised it to my lips to moisten my suddenly dry mouth. She leaned forward expectantly, so I just nodded as I was swallowing, then changed it to a shake of the head.

'Make up your mind — are you or not?'

I spied a slight smile at the corner of her mouth. The answer I wanted to give was 'yes', obviously, but things being what they were, how could I? Ash had not contacted me for two weeks, and then I found out the case was over.

'I always hoped you'd become a Richards.'

I looked up from my cup and smiled at her. I remember one of her sons having a bit of a crush on me when we were kids, but that was a long time ago.

'It would have been lovely to have you in the family, but I could tell you weren't interested in Anthony or Stephen...even though Stephen thought you were the bee's knees.' She sighed and picked up her cup, and I followed suit, taking a good long drink, hoping to finish it so I could get away. 'I really hoped you and Ash could've gotten together.'

The tea shot out of my mouth and nostrils, half choking me on the way out. I coughed and spluttered, wheezing a stuttered 'What?' as tears streamed down my face. Mrs. Richards came 'round the table and thumped me on the back...repeatedly, which did nothing for the coughing, just increased the tears. With a final intake of breath, the coughing subsided, my face the colour of beetroot from embarrassment and exertion.

'Are you okay now?' Her face was dangling in front of mine, and all I could muster was a half-hearted nod. 'Sorry about that. I always thought you two...ah...well...you know.' I looked at her, wiping my eyes but silently asking her to go on. 'I thought you two were a couple when you were teenagers. When you left, I thought Ash was going to pine away to nothing.' She lifted the teapot and gestured. I nodded; my throat was like sandpaper.

She didn't speak whilst she was pouring, just concentrated on the job at hand. It seemed like it took forever to fill two small cups.

'Everyone was really worried about her. And then one day she just walked into the front room, announced she was gay, and walked out the front door. We didn't see her for three days.' She slid the cup over to me and then concentrated on putting sugar in her own as if what she had just said was completely normal.

'And?'

'And what?'

'What happened? Where did she go?'

Mrs. Richards shrugged. 'She wouldn't say. We were so worried about her, that by the time she came back, her announcement didn't seem to matter.' The tea she was stirring was whizzing around the cup, the spoon making a grating noise.

I didn't know how to reply. Just sat there, cup in hand.

'It was just good to see Ash happy again.'

'Why? Did she come back happy?' I felt a little annoyed at that, although I have no idea why. It was twenty years ago, after all.

'Not then...she was still a miserable little bleeder. I mean when she came back from Norfolk a couple of months ago.' A greying eyebrow lifted into nearly grey hair, a smile playing around her lips. She took a tentative sip at her tea, and I sat and waited. Again. 'Ah, that's a lovely brew, if I do say so myself.' She took another sip, and I felt like shouting at her to put the bloody cup down and tell me.

But she still had that evil streak running through her, the one I'd found funny when she was tormenting her sons and husband, and Ash, of course.

She was waiting for me to ask her, and I wasn't backward in coming forward. I would play her game.

'What do you mean, "when she came back from Norfolk"? Was she happy about the case?' I leaned forward and gave her a crooked smile whilst inside I wanted her to just tell me what I wanted to hear.

'No. That's not what I meant.'

She leaned toward me with the same little smile. Then nothing. Bollocks. I was getting too old for this. 'Well, could you tell me what you *do* mean?'

'Yes.' But she didn't.

Patience flew out the window and was replaced by a need to know. 'Pack it in and tell me.'

Just like her daughter, she threw her head back and laughed, laughed until tears fell down her face. I laughed right along with her. I don't know why, just did. Emotions liberated, it wasn't long before I was sobbing into the tablecloth.

Her hand was comforting on my shoulder. Smooth strokes sandwiched between a gentle circling motion. A shushing sound was right next to my ear, and she was saying my name over and over, urging me to 'dry those tears'.

But it had all become too much — the anger, the frustration, the needing to know one way or the other — and the dam burst. I was sobbing my desolation into white linen. It didn't last for long, just a short burst to alleviate the emotions whirring around inside me. Lately, all I seemed to do was cry.

When I eventually pulled myself together enough to look up, she was sitting down in the chair next to me, her face the picture of motherly comfort.

'I'm sorry, Lou. I'm an evil old bugger sometimes...ask the kids.' I didn't trust my voice to tell her that it didn't matter, so I shook my head and gave her a watery smile. Her hand covered mine and squeezed it firmly before she just held it in her own. It was so warm and comforting to just sit there for a while without the burden of words. 'When she came back from Norfolk, she seemed like the Ash we all knew...the happy Ash. It was like she had laid the ghosts to rest.'

I kept quiet, just listened.

'She was busy with the case, you know — the Spencer one, so we didn't see her as much as we wanted.' Another squeeze on my hand. 'But when we did, she was full of what had happened in Norfolk, full of meeting you again.'

She got up and walked over to the kitchen counter where she rummaged about in the drawers looking for something, and then she was back. A piece of paper slipped over to me, her aged fingers half covering it. 'This is what you want. Go and ask her yourself; it's not up to me to tell you.'

I tentatively tugged at the corner until I felt the note within my hand. It was Ash's address. Heaton Chapel. If I left right away, I would be standing on her doorstep in just over ten minutes, less if I floored it. But I hesitated slightly, mesmerised by grasping my future in the palm of my hand. It took a nudge and a, 'Well...what are you waiting for?' to kick start me.

'Nothing. Nothing at all.' I leaned forward and pecked her on the cheek, was just about to leave when I turned and grabbed her in a fierce hug. 'Thank you...so much.'

She hugged me back and said a muffled, 'Whatever for?'

'Everything.' And then I was gone, door slamming behind me, car starting and crunching into gear and one thought in my mind: Heaton Chapel, here I come.

I didn't give myself time to think, just tear arsed it down the A6 towards Ash's house. It never occurred to me that she might not be there, and somehow, I seemed to have forgotten the fact she hadn't called me.

When I left Ash's mum's, it was drizzling with rain, and by the time I reached Heaton Chapel it was pouring down. The rain bounced off the bonnet and windscreen in kamikaze pellets. Naturally there was nowhere to park near her house, and I had to squeeze into a tiny gap two roads away. I didn't care.

I didn't care that the rain aimed itself straight at me and soaked me to the bone.

I didn't care that my hair was plastered all over my face, and water was trickling into my mouth.

And the only reason I was running was so I could see Ash again...because I didn't care about anything else.

It wasn't until I stood poised, hand over doorbell, that the realisation of what I was doing hit me. Why hadn't she called?

Then I grinned. I would ask her.

I had to ring the bell three times before the chain on the door clattered and clinked, and the lock shuddered as it was released. I sucked in a breath and waited to see those blue eyes once again.

But they were brown, dark brown, and pretty. And set in an even prettier face, a face surrounded by dark brown hair and attached to a slender neck and slim body.

And the brown eyes were looking at me in wonder, trying to figure out why a complete stranger was standing on their doorstep, pissed wet through, and with her mouth open. A stranger who also had her hand half poised to ring the bell again, finger frozen.

'Can I help you?' A musical voice, lilting and captivating.

A muffled, 'Who is it?' came from inside. The voice, although distant, was definitely Ash's.

'And you are?' The lilting voice was more quizzical, showing signs of confusion.

'Whoever it is, get rid of them. There's a bed in here with your name on it.' The brown-eyed woman looked over her shoulder; when she turned back, she was grinning.

'No one...I'm no one.'

That was pretty easy to write, but the actual labour of saying those few words was agony. I felt like a no one; I felt like a fool. Once again I had been misled by self-promise and hope. I hadn't even questioned what Ash's mother had said, I just thought...ah well, you know what thought did. As my mother would always say, 'Followed a muck cart and thought it was a wedding.' It doesn't make sense, I know, nothing did. Not now that I knew she didn't want me as much as I wanted her.

I could hear footsteps coming from upstairs and saw Ash's feet and shins appear at the top. It was my cue to leave, to go...to just fucking go and not come back. So I did. Turning, I heard her voice, disbelief evident.

'Lou?'

I ran, rain pelting me, cold, penetrating rain that tried to take my breath away.

'Lou, come back!'

Her voice seemed echoey, distant. I increased my pace, the chill from the rain making me shiver. The coat I had on was thin and flimsy against the downpour, but I didn't care.

Her hand grabbed my arm and pulled me to a stop, swinging me around to face her. She was soaked, too, wearing a cream t-shirt and holding a jacket in her hand. We were both shaking with cold, but mine was laced with anger.

'Lou?' She was smiling, an uncertain smile. 'Where are you going? Didn't you hear me calling you?'

'Get your fucking hands *off me*.' It was a stuttered growl rather than a command, and I reinforced it by trying to tear her fingers from my arm. 'Why...don't...you...go...back to your bird?'

'What bird? I don't understand. Lou.'

She grabbed my other arm and held me fast, so I couldn't even thump her. All I could do was try and wound her with words. 'Her! There! Standing in your doorway! Why didn't you just tell me you were with someone? Why lead me on?'

The image of her standing there with the rain pummelling down on her will forever be etched into my mind, joining all the other images I had. Her hair was a tangled mess of wetness, clinging to the side of her face, her fringe dripping water into her eyes. The pale cream t-shirt was like a second skin, transparent and heavy; her jacket was on the ground by our feet. Rivulets of water raced down her face and collected at the top of her lip. She just stood there, staring right back at me.

'Wendy?'

So that was her name — Wendy. The woman who had what I wanted. The woman I could never compete with. Ash's woman.

Her hands became limp on my arms, and her grip all but melted away. 'Wendy?'

'Yes, Wendy, for Christ's sake. *Let me go!*'

'But Wendy—'

She released me, but I didn't go; I was caught up by the look on her face — confusion and something else. I swallowed deeply, licked my lips, and began. 'You could have just told me, Ash.' I thought my voice was admirably controlled. 'I would have understood.' That was a big fat lie. 'You could have called me and told me and about the case, too.' True. She could have. Beginning to have doubts whether the calm in my voice was going to carry on, I said, 'Look. I'd better go.'

Her face was still showing shock, but her wrinkled lip and raised eyebrow indicated that she was recovering. It wasn't until I turned to go that she stopped me again. 'But Wendy is not my girlfriend. She's—'

'Your shag?' The bitterness was back and laced with anger.

'Don't be stupid.'

Like the adult I was, I gave the mature answer. 'Whatever.' I felt like sobbing. The rain was making matters worse, as it was steadily increasing in pace and rhythm, making words come out spluttered and deformed. '"There's a bed here with your name on it." Does that ring any bells?'

'But she's just—'

'No need to explain anything to me, Ash. I think I understand perfectly well what is going on.' The tears were overflowing, and the choking sobs were out and damned mad. But I couldn't be mad. Spent too much time being mad, spent too much time hankering after something unobtainable. Now it was time to let go.

'Come here.'

Her voice was quiet, barely a whisper. Her hands were trying to cup my face, trying to get me to look at her, but I shook her off in desolation.

'Lou, listen.' She pulled my hands from my ears where they were trying to stop the flow of her excuses filtering in and down to the aching in my chest. 'I love you...shush...listen.' The rain was becoming angrier. 'Wendy is not my girlfriend or ever likely to be.' My face was soaked and not just with rain. 'She's Stephen's wife.'

'You're shagging your brother's wife?'

The laugh came loudly, but when she saw my face, it stopped as suddenly as it had started. She was pissed wet through, hair clinging to her neck and cheeks, her clothes as soggy as if she had just stepped out from underneath a waterfall. Her eyebrows drew together. 'You are joking, right?'

'But you said you wanted her in bed.' Was that a whine?

Her head shook from side to side, the grin appearing until it developed into another bout of laughter. She stopped, tried to answer, then laughed more loudly. 'No! I'm packing. Bed and all.' My face said 'huh', so she continued. 'Wendy is helping me pack, and you knocked as we were halfway through dismantling the bed.'

'Packing?' Did I squeak?

'Packing.' She stepped closer to me, diminishing the space I had deliberately left between us. 'Upping sticks and moving.' Closer still. 'To be with my woman...my love...my everything.'

Her hands were on my face, and I didn't struggle. They felt at home there; they belonged there.

'To be with my reason.' Her thumb trailed across my lips. 'And that's you.' She gave me a gentle kiss. 'You.' Another kiss...featherlike. 'Always you.'

This kiss was deep, sucking me in and blinding me to everything and everyone apart from her. The rain melted away. When she pulled away and looked into my eyes, I was lost all over again. So much love. So much...

'Want to help me pack?' The ability to speak completely deserting me, I nodded. 'Here.' A jacket was shoved in my direction. My eyes looked into blue, clouded with concern. 'Put it on. You'll catch your death.'

'But—'

'But nothing. Put it on...no arguments.'

The scene from over thirty years earlier replayed itself in my mind. Ash — younger, but still the same; me — still an idiot when it came to the weather. I watched her as I pulled the jacket on, loving the sight of her as I pulled the thick red material into place. The jacket was barely settled on my shoulders when she grabbed my hand and began to pull me along, then her arm shifted to encircle my waist and she held me to her as we splattered through the rain.

The front door ahead of us, I could feel her slowing down. As we reached the gate, she stopped, turned to me, and pulled me towards her again. Impulsively, I threw my arms around her neck and planted a full kiss on her mouth.

The kiss was an affirmation, a promise of things to come. Lips, tongue, and teeth mingled and melted in a love that had grown from a seed of friendship.

We held each other...held each other...held...each other, and without words told each other that this was forever.

Ash actually had called to tell me that the case was over and she was making arrangements to move, but I hadn't checked the answer phone before I left for Manchester. Some things never change, eh?

Her family threw a farewell dinner at her parents' place, and people I hadn't seen for years turned up to say goodbye and good luck. Her parents treated me like I was one of the family, and Ash's mum kept winking and nodding at me all evening. I felt fully accepted. Ash's father's toast was, 'To the future...to new beginnings.'

And it was...for the both of us.

I chatted with everyone, even Wendy, although I felt like a dickhead. I mean — I had made a total twat out of myself in front of my girlfriend's sister-in-law.

My girlfriend. Mine. Sigh. Anyway, where was I? Oh, yeah...

I chatted with all of them, remembering things from when we were kids...remembering Tracy, the psycho bird who had been jealous of something that was non-existent. By all accounts she worked in Customer Complaints at the local supermarket, had three kids and a husband who spent most of his time trying to get away from her. Talk about sweet justice...

And that brings me to Spencer...

With a recommendation that he be given psychiatric help, Spencer had been convicted of premeditated murder and had been sentenced to fifteen years in Strangeways Prison. The British legal system being what it is, he would be unlucky if he served more than ten. That was why Ash had wanted to keep the assault against me separate: the evidence was leading to a case of attempted murder. It still makes me shiver to think of what could have happened if Jo hadn't called. However, that crime had been committed in Norfolk, and Ash had moved the case there, transferring from the Met to Norfolk police for the foreseeable future.

The trial was to start six weeks after she had moved, giving her time to organize the testimony and evidence. The only problem was, we could not be seen as having a relationship because that would jeopardise the case, as the jury might think she had coerced me into giving false evidence.

My ray of hope was Jo, of course. She was the key witness in the case, even though the assault had happened to me. I was useless, as I couldn't really remember all the facts, and Jo never forgot anything…apart from the reason why she pissed all over me when we were kids.

But…hey…new beginnings, right?

Finally.

In two days, Ash and I were back in Norwich. We discussed the possibility of moving in together but decided we would take one step at a time. Years had passed between us, and we had to get to know each other again.

Erm…and finally…

I know, I know, I said the last bit was the end, didn't I? Well, I couldn't really end this story with the last shot of my sister pissing all over my back…or could I?

Nah.

I should end it with a moral, but that's cliché. What about a summing up? Nope. I think you get the gist of it all.

I could give you some advice; how about that? You would probably tell me to bugger off, so that one is out the window.

I should really end where I started — you know, structure and all that. But why look back?

Why live in the past when your future is bright and beguiling? We learn from our mistakes…true, but sometimes we don't learn quickly enough. We end up repeating the same ones over and over again, like some fucked-up *Groundhog Day*.

I mean, some things you learn through age and experience, like — don't bother hiding under the bed when police pass your house, whatever your brother's girlfriend says. Or that rabbits don't hurt as much as broken bricks on the back of the head. Even — don't fight with your mum when she has Derbac and a lit cig.

But love? Do we ever learn not to love? Do we ever learn through being in love never to love again? I know to some people love is the ultimate four-letter word, but do we really ever stop wanting to love and be loved?

Yes. In some cases.

But throughout the heartache and the pain there's another four-letter word waiting in the wings. Hope.

And I think that through this four-letter word, however well hidden, we can attain the ultimate four-letter word. Battered and bruised...a little shy and resentful...sometimes angry and misplaced...but it's there all the same.

So...what else to say?

Me, well I went through the stage of wanting it all, to wanting it all to end...wanting the pain of being in love to stop. Love is an agony of want and desire and rejection, true. But what if it's the real deal? You know — what if she's *the one*? What if the person you love loves you back? Do you say, 'No, thanks. I had some earlier'?

Or do you take love in both your hands and pull it to you...cradle it...support and protect it? Do you nurture it, then watch it grow and grow and grow? Yes.

We should take what we can from life and should give back just as much, because if we don't...what's the point?

Ash and me, well, eventually we got there. Took us most of our lives to realise, but I wouldn't go back to when I was a teenager. Both of us are way past all that now. Life has seasoned us with experience, and it has made us stronger, made us aware of what we have, and that we should cherish every moment.

And we do.

She has been in Norwich for eight weeks, and I treasure every minute we share. It almost feels as if my life started again when she walked back into it. In a way, it did, but I had the foundations of my beginnings to build on. That's what makes me who I am today.

We are still living apart, as the case is underway, but we see each other as much as we can. And it is bliss.

I love her, you see. Love *her*. And she loves me right back. I know because we take the time not just to tell each other, but to show it, too. In little gestures and comments...looks...guiding hands and soft kisses.

I think you've heard enough about me and my life for one sitting, however comfortable you might have been to start off with, so...

I will love you and leave you, for now. Mainly because I have a gorgeous woman reading over my shoulder and she wants all of my attention.

You don't blame me, do you?

You got this far, I might as well tell you a little about myself. If you are interested, that is.

Born and raised in Manchester, I moved to Norfolk when I was seventeen, where I have dallied and dillied with gusto. I still live in Norfolk in good old Blighty, teach English to hormonally charged, or challenged, teenagers, and spend most of the day saying, 'Tuck your shirt in!' I have two Border Terriers that are either soft as butter or auditioning for 'Krays — The Musical'.

If you liked this story, then please feel free to contact me at: fingersmith@hotmail.co.uk

Of better still, you can let my publishers know. Maybe they will sign me up again. Insert a grin somewhere here.

Other works by LT Smith:

Hearts and Flowers Border

A visitor from her past jolts Laura Stewart into memories... some funny...some heart-wrenching...but she needs to deal with all of them before she can open the door to allow her past to shape her future.

A story narrated by a woman who needs to relive the past in order to learn from the uncertainty of youth. Can she move on to the future she desires and deserves? Join the delightful experience of the retelling of events, in which most of us will recognize the flush of first love.

ISBN: 978 - 1 - 933720 - 02 - 9
(1-933720-02-6)

Available at your favorite bookstore.